THE SYMPHONIES

RUSSIAN LIBRARY

R

The Russian Library at Columbia University Press publishes an expansive selection of Russian literature in English translation, concentrating on works previously unavailable in English and those ripe for new translations. Works of premodern, modern, and contemporary literature are featured, including recent writing. The series seeks to demonstrate the breadth, surprising variety, and global importance of the Russian literary tradition and includes not only novels but also short stories, plays, poetry, memoirs, creative nonfiction, and works of mixed or fluid genre.

■ □ ■

For a list of books in the series, see page 479

Translated by
Jonathan Stone

THE

ANDREI BELY

SYMPHONIES

Columbia University Press / New York

Published with the support of Read Russia, Inc., and the Institute of
    Literary Translation, Russia
Columbia University Press
Publishers Since 1893
New York   Chichester, West Sussex
cup.columbia.edu

Library of Congress Cataloging-in-Publication Data
Names: Bely, Andrey, 1880-1934, author. | Stone, Jonathan,
    1977- translator.
Title: The symphonies / Andrei Bely ; translated by Jonathan Stone.
Other titles: Simfonii. English
Description: New York : Columbia University Press, [2021] |
    Series: Russian library
Identifiers: LCCN 2021004538 (print) | LCCN 2021004539 (ebook) |
    ISBN 9780231199087 (hardback ; acid-free paper) |
    ISBN 9780231199094 (trade paperback ; acid-free paper) |
    ISBN 9780231552936 (ebook)
Subjects: LCSH: Bely, Andrey, 1880-1934—Translations into English. |
    LCGFT: Short stories.
Classification: LCC PG3453.B84 S513 2021 (print) |
    LCC PG3453.B84 (ebook) | DDC 891.73/3—dc23
LC record available at https://lccn.loc.gov/2021004538
LC ebook record available at https://lccn.loc.gov/2021004539

Cover design: Roberto de Vicq de Cumptich

For Melanie, Toby, and Rivi

CONTENTS

ACKNOWLEDGMENTS

T his book would not have been possible without the help of many colleagues and friends. I am deeply grateful for the support of Irina Paperno, Robert Hughes, Joan Delaney Grossman, Olga Matich, Stiliana Milkova, Giovanna Faleschini Lerner, Carrie Landfried, Rachel Anderson-Rabern, Scott Lerner, Katy Theumer, Veronika Ryjik, Curt Bentzel, and Jennifer Redmann. I am fortunate to have had the pleasure to work with Christine Dunbar and the Russian Library editorial staff of Columbia University Press.

Isabelle Roman was an invaluable assistant in the early stages of this project, and her research into these texts and the draft notes she prepared for the *Northern Symphony* contributed greatly to its final form.

I am also extremely appreciative of the support of Franklin & Marshall College's Office of the Provost through the Faculty Research and Professional Development Funds, the Office of College Grants Resource Funds, and the Research Scholars Program.

As always, my deepest gratitude and most profound debt are to Melanie, Toby, and Rivi. It is to you that this book is dedicated.

NOTE ON THE TEXT

T he text and notes for this translation are based (along with frequent cross-checking in the original editions) on the most scholarly edition of Bely's *Symphonies*: Andrei Belyi, *Simfonii*, ed. A. V. Lavrov (Leningrad: Khudozhestvennaia literatura, 1991). As do all Bely scholars, I owe Aleksandr Lavrov an immense debt of gratitude for his lifetime's work of editing, publishing, and explicating much of Bely's writing.

Names and Russian words are transliterated using the Russian Library style guide, except in the references, where the Library of Congress system is used.

INTRODUCTION

From the balcony of his family's second-floor apartment on the Arbat in Moscow, Andrei Bely would watch the hues of the sky change at sunset. As he described it in a poem from 1902,

> I looked into the distance—a spider web stretched
> into the blue
> with gold and radiant threads . . .[1]

These were instances of a world transformed—the everyday became magical, the ordinary became mythical. Peering out into the city, Bely saw its familiar reality altered into an aestheticized vision teeming with mystery and beauty. Decades later, in his memoirs, he would mark these moments as the beginning of his life as an artist. For Bely, the turn of the century was when his "life came into harmony with his worldview."[2] This was the period when Bely was embarking on his literary career by adopting a new, Symbolist, persona and composing the first of his "Symphonies." These significant early prose works reflected the core tenets of his literary worldview. Their centaurs and giants, princesses and knights, enchanters and beasts, philosophers and adventurers were not part of a distant realm, but could be found right there in Moscow. Bely saw them from that balcony, bathed in gold and azure, no less present than the seemingly unremarkable passersby below. His writings from the early years of the twentieth century are glimpses into his own personal mythology and artistic maturation. Yet they are also paradigms of modernist literature. They show the idealism and exuberance that greeted this new era and the awe and wonder that came when writers embraced such transformative powers. Published in relatively quick succession, Bely's four *Symphonies* (*Dramatic Symphony* [1902], *Northern Symphony* [1904], *The Return* [1905], and *A Goblet of Blizzards* [1908]) demonstrate a reformed vision of the world that reflected the combination of optimism and fear that accompanied the new century. They fused the banality of life, the intimacy of love, and the magic of the extraordinary. Bely's vision of the world was captured by the emerging literary and artistic movement of Russian Symbolism.

RUSSIAN SYMBOLISM

Symbolism resides at the initiating moment of literary and cultural modernism in Russia. Despite its relatively short life span of barely more than three productive decades, the modernist movement in Russian literature and culture effected a sea change in Russia's aesthetic output. Between the 1890s and the 1920s, the dominance of the realist novel subsided and Russia experienced a renewal of artistic experimentation that would come to be known as the Silver Age of literature.[3] While modernism had been percolating in the west since the 1850s, it arrived rather abruptly and belatedly in Russian at the very end of the century. By the late 1880s, a sense of stagnation regarding the state of Russian literature had set in and modernism appeared in part as a reaction to the aesthetic crisis of the decline of realism and the novel. The Russian modernists were aware of and in contact with their European counterparts, and Russian

Symbolism shared many of the key traits of its western manifestations: a tendency toward nonlinear or fragmented narratives; the impulse to shock the reading public through language and imagery; the prevalence of subjective perspectives intended to mirror modern psychological states. While the Russian movement's individual aesthetic components align with many of the theoretical and scholarly descriptions of European modernism, Russian modernism was marked by a pervasive preference for the ideal over the real. This often manifested itself in a mélange of literary, religious, philosophical, and metaphysical elements that revealed a distinctly eschatological undercurrent to nearly all aspects of modernist creation.[4] There is hardly a better example of these themes than Bely's *Symphonies*. Russian modernism was concerned with the transformative capacity of the word, and for a brief moment in Russia, it appeared that art's power to change and even save the world would triumph. This short-lived utopianism would leave an indelible impression on all of twentieth-century Russian literature and culture. It comes through in Bely's *Symphonies* in the tension between an imaginative restructuring of modern life and the utterly mundane people and events they describe.

Symbolism arrived in Russia in a bold moment of self-designation and proclamation. Three slim volumes of poetry titled simply *Russian Symbolists* were published in 1894–1895 and caught the attention of several prominent literary critics, who very publicly panned this new movement.[5] This cultural development was a formidable element of Bely's early life, one that would soon prompt the student Borya Bugaev to be reborn as the Symbolist poet Andrei Bely, "Andrew the White." The force behind these first collections was the poet and editor Valery Bryusov, who would serve as an early mentor for Bely. Six years Bryusov's junior, Bely inhabited the same geographical and cultural milieu: they both attended the prestigious Polivanov Gymnasium and Moscow University. The poetry that Bryusov wrote and published at this time resonated with the aesthetic and philosophical leanings of a growing coterie of Russian writers and established a niche that Bely could slip into several years later, with Bryusov's help and encouragement. Bryusov offered the Russian reader poems that elicited a musicality and ephemerality that marked a disjunction with the real, phenomenal world and showed modernism's fundamental differences in both form and content from the nineteenth-century Russian novel. By the end of the century, the loosely unified ranks of the Russian Symbolists had swelled to include such strong poets as Zinaida Gippius, whose powerful sense of otherworldliness would help guide the movement's epistemological considerations; Konstantin Balmont, who wrote mythically charged impressionistic verse; Fyodor Sologub, who added a sense of magic and decadence to Symbolist poetics; and Dmitri Merezhkovsky, a poet of keen theoretical and aesthetic sensibilities. All of these figures are present in Bely's *Symphonies* by name or allusion.

When the next generation of Symbolists (including Bely, Alexander Blok, and Vyacheslav Ivanov) appeared at the turn of the century, the movement had reached the apogee of its talent and would dominate the literary sphere for the rest of the decade. The essence of Symbolism can be gleaned from Ivanov's well-known formulation: moving from the real to the more real.[6] Nevertheless, it should be added that the Symbolist worldview did not entail abandoning the real, but rather the simultaneous experience of the phenomenal and the noumenal. Russian Symbolism strove to access knowledge and experience beyond the confines of the perceivable world and was thus drawn to mysticism and gnosticism (the theology and poetry of Vladimir Solovyov were extremely influential).[7] With their neo-Romantic tendencies, the Symbolists desired to reinvigorate a Russian poetic tradition and placed such nineteenth-century figures as Fyodor Tyutchev and Afanasy Fet, paragons of a subtle and complex Romanticism, at the center of their canon. By privileging the aesthetic, they sought to achieve a revaluation of Russian literature and to elevate the transformative power of poetic language into art's primary function. In addition to such a dramatic shift in the purview of Russian literature, the Symbolists set a significant precedent for the publication and dissemination of their work. They bypassed the traditional journals of the nineteenth century (in which most of the century's major novels had first appeared in print) and founded their own publishing houses and venues of print.[8] This move would be instrumental for subsequent generations of modernists, who would embrace the capacity to employ the materiality and typography of their publications in the creation of their aesthetic. All of Bely's *Symphonies* were published by Symbolist presses, giving him direct control over crafting their formal and stylistic hybridity. Symbolism—as an art form, a worldview, and an organized literary movement—was at the heart of Bely's life and career from the very moment he was born as a writer.

ANDREI BELY (1880–1834)

Andrei Bely, meaning "Andrew the White," came into being at the very turn of the century. Twenty-two-year old Boris Nikolaevich Bugaev adopted this pseudonym and alter ego in 1902 when preparing his first book, the *Dramatic Symphony*, for publication. This identity emphatically distinguished his persona as a Symbolist writer from that of the student of physics and mathematics—a middle-class Muscovite, son of a renowned mathematics professor. By choosing the path of the modernist artist, Bugaev would occupy a prime position in the creation of a new art and a new consciousness. Over the next three and a half decades, Andrei Bely proved himself a modernist to the core. He experimented with form; he experimented with sound; he experimented with genre. His 1916 novel *Petersburg* is a masterpiece of twentieth-century fiction, and his poetry and theoretical writings have earned him canonical status in Russian literature's Silver Age. Bely's complex understanding of the Symbolist project infused reality with otherworldliness and fueled his ability to merge the realistic and the fantastic. His works are immersed in the ideal while still offering stark reflections of turn-of-the-century life.

At the crux of Bely's writing is a clear expression of the modernist preference for highly subjective revaluations of the surrounding world. He coupled poetry and prose with voluminous theoretical works exploring the philosophical and epistemological roots of the new century's "new art." As a Symbolist, Bely could transform the phenomenal world through myth, magic, and language. The four *Symphonies*, along with his first book of poetry, *Gold in Azure* (1904), superimpose explorations of modern psychological, philosophical, and aesthetic states onto Bely's own intimate world and biography. For Bely, Symbolism was a way of life, a stance he maintained even as Symbolism's dominance in Russian culture waned and gave way to other expressions of the avant-garde in the 1910s. This was when he wrote two major novels—*The Silver Dove* (1909) and *Petersburg*—and consolidated his theoretical writings into three hefty (and, to some, barely readable) volumes. The combination of mysticism and realism, of a deep engagement with issues of language, epistemology, and society, that had originated in the *Symphonies* comes to a culmination in *Petersburg*, a novel first published serially in 1912–1913 but set in the chaos of the revolutionary year 1905, squarely in the middle of the period of the *Symphonies*. *Petersburg* is a strikingly modern work that interweaves elements of a family drama, a psychological thriller, a novel of detection, a political plot, and a love triangle in an unapologetically fragmented narrative.

Bely's career after the 1917 revolution reflected the peripatetic life of the Russian intellectual in the early Soviet years. He lived in Berlin from 1921 to 1923 but subsequently returned to Russia and spent his final years in the relative isolation of the village of Kuchino, outside Moscow. During this time he produced a number of significant retrospective works, from his *Recollections About Blok* (1922–1923) and his autobiographical narrative poem *The First Encounter* (1921) to a novel drawing on his childhood, *Kotik Letaev* (1922), and culminating with his unfinished memoirs, of which three volumes were published—*On The Border of Two Centuries* (1930), *The Turn of the Century* (1933), and *Between Two Revolutions* (1934)—which present a thorough picture of Russian intellectual life in the late nineteenth and early twentieth centuries. By the end of his long career, Bely had produced some of Russian modernism's most paradigmatic works as well as some of its most dense and esoteric writings (in the realm of both literature and theory). Despite the breadth and diversity of his literary output, Bely maintained a degree of coherence in his approach to literature and advocacy of a distinctly Symbolist worldview. The title of an essay from 1928 professes this lifelong aesthetic allegiance: "Why I Became a Symbolist and Why I Have Remained One Through All the Phases of My Intellectual and Artistic Development." In the period when he wrote the *Symphonies*, Bely's career and identity would come into focus. When he began the *Northern Symphony*, at the very end of 1899, Bely's Symbolist tendencies were suppressed beneath the uniform of a first-year student in the department of physics and mathematics. By the time he published *A Goblet of Blizzards*, in 1908, he was brazenly at the forefront of Symbolism, one of the most active participants in its literary and theoretical activities. The group that clustered around Bely in these early years, explicitly showcasing their affiliation with myth and fantasy by calling themselves Argonauts, "embodied with great consistency the primary and most characteristic feature of the Symbolist attitude toward reality: to perceive the world as a quasi-artistic phenomenon, to attribute to reality the qualities of a literary text."[9] That text was the *Symphonies*.

THE *SYMPHONIES*

The *Northern Symphony* is a novella-length work of prose (albeit with a distinctly modernist structure) that partakes in the style and imagery of a fairy tale.[10] Yet couched in this seemingly juvenile form is a sophisticated exploration of social interactions and the psychological and emotional aspects of love and loss. The playfulness of these children's characters is often undercut by a foreboding sense of doom, a reflection of the modernists' interest in the apocalyptic. Similar in length and structure, the *Dramatic Symphony* captures the combination of banality and meaning in everyday life. It engages with philosophical and existential questions while also reflecting the nuances of family life in the late Russian imperial period. *The Return (Third Symphony)* is a more straightforward novella that presents the interplay between the transcendental and the real. It skirts the boundary between literature and philosophy and taps into the instability of forms and genres that characterizes modernism. Bely's final *Symphony, A Goblet of Blizzards,* is a mystical love story that further complicates the conventions of realism and narrative cohesion with which the other *Symphonies* had been engaged. It encompasses the wealth of aesthetic, philosophical, and theological themes and texts that contribute to Bely's own worldview and his presentation of Symbolism.

The *Symphonies* showcase Bely's early mastery of a style of writing in Russian that is at times perplexing and evocative, yet always gripping. Bely's relationship to language, style, and form was marked by a desire to innovate and revolutionize Russian literature. The protean quality of his writing can be felt at every level—from book to chapter to paragraph to line to word. This fluidity gives Bely's works the appeal of something surprising, strange, and new. But his novelty also presents a unique set of challenges to the translator. The *Symphonies* are part of Bely's experimentation with genre and sound. They are fragmentary and yet have a cohesion achieved through a clear narrative progression. Their style varies from prosaic to poetic to musical. Their plot oscillates between the fantastical and the trivial, with a distinct infusion of irony and satire. To sustain these many divergent forces, Bely has imbued his stories with repeated words and phrases (often nonstandard or even neologistic) that function as leitmotifs threading its fragments together. I have preserved these echoes and replicated the odd turns of phrase Bely employs in their creation as much as possible. While treating these as works of prose (which they ultimately are), I have attempted to remain faithful to the visual and aural qualities that give his writing its musicality and structure in order for the English reader to appreciate how these "symphonies" looked and sounded to the readers they first enchanted in the opening decade of the twentieth century.

Readers of the *Symphonies* cannot help but be struck by their strangeness. Vladimir Alexandrov offers a pithy catalog of the myriad ways these works were unlike anything a reader had experienced before:

> Their most striking characteristic is fragmentariness: the texts consist of sequences of short paragraphs that are sometimes linked only metaphorically or by means of leitmotifs; narrative points of view change often; symbolic imagery expressing the frequently occult inner experiences of the narrator is intercalated with, and occupies nearly as much space as, the intermittent exposition of setting, plot, and character; and the organizing beliefs and hierarchies of values in the works are hidden, requiring the reader to become involved in deciphering the texts more actively than do most narratives from previous eras.[11]

In addition to being literary works, the *Symphonies* are musical, philosophical, autobiographical, visual, and theurgic compositions that continuously destabilize all notion of genre and bombard the reader with vaguely familiar allusions and echoes (both internal to the work and drawing on outside elements). Roger Keys has delved deeply into the philosophical and aesthetic contexts of the *Symphonies* and has shown that, even with their seemingly undirected and amorphous forms and plots, these works contain Bely's "perennial theme [of] the whole of his creative career [. . .] the split between the world of matter and the world of spirit, and how it might be overcome."[12] The vision of a world transformed is always lurking at the edges of even the most realistic and biographical moments in the *Symphonies,* and as readers we cannot escape the sensation that a centaur or serpent or mystical eagle may suddenly interrupt our evening walk home. The simultaneity of both this world and the other is the most constant feature of these stories because it was how Bely had come to see reality around him, a reflection of his view from the balcony on the Arbat. Aleksandr Lavrov captures the intimacy of the form that Bely has created: "Bely's arrival at the *Symphonies* was not so much the result of a conscious, teleological search for a new genre as an unpremeditated discovery of an adequate means of self-expression."[13] One of the most frequent words we encounter in the *Symphonies* is "passerby." Bely fixates on the anonymous Muscovites, a city whose population had surpassed one million around the time Bely began writing the *Symphonies,* because he sees in each of these ordinary and unremarkable characters the potential to be mystical, magical, mythical. By casting his transforming gaze over them, he pulls them into his vision, into the world of the *Symphonies.*

The *Northern Symphony* takes place in an exclusively magical and mystical realm. While it is the only one of the *Symphonies* not to be at least partially set in the "real" world, it resonates strongly with a distinctly modernist mood and outlook. It's a family drama, a child's fairy tale, a contemplation of love and loss, an exploration of faith and doubt, and a close examination of the sinister tendencies of human nature. In conjunction with the experimental structure and form Bely employs and his intentionally perplexing description of the work's genre as a "symphony," this story shows an impressive degree of complexity for its nineteen-year-old author (Bely would turn twenty two months before finishing it). It is here that the reader first encounters some of Bely's innovative literary techniques, most notably his use of line numbers throughout the work. This, along with a tendency for melodically repetitive words and phrases, signals the novelty of a *Symphony* and propels Bely's writing into a liminal space between prose and poetry. The work's simple plot about three generations of rulers—a frightful dead king, his fearful son, and his bold granddaughter—gives Bely license to depict the wild fanciful creatures (giants, centaurs, and fauns), satanic knights, and evil princes who populate the unnamed kingdom and its preternaturally gloomy woods. Its skeletal story of a king too scared to lead and his daughter who braves the unknown to return to her people and save a prince dallying with evil becomes a platform to show dark rituals and landscapes teeming with fairy-tale creatures. Bely excels at immersing the reader in this world and, as Keys puts it, his "deeper purpose was, as ever, a theurgic one. He wished to present a vision of the other world which would be as valid for the reader of this fiction as for the characters and the narrator within it."[14] The *Northern Symphony*'s details, its use of color and musical resonance, establish its ideas, emotions, and mood, which themselves serve as a short course in the transformed perspectives emerging at the turn of the century. Alexandrov notes the accumulation of symbols—words and images that vaguely hint at otherworldliness—in the *Northern Symphony* and sees in these Bely's interest in eschatological and Gnostic themes.[15] In this work, Bely introduces the key terms of his Symbolist aesthetic, threads that would run throughout the

Symphonies and continue to appear in his prose, poetry, and theo-retical writings for the rest of his career.

A year before he wrote the *Northern Symphony*, Bely finished a work that he destroyed (but of which an early draft has survived).[16] This "pre-Symphony" is more overtly celestial than the *Northern Symphony* but sheds light on Bely's intentions to infuse these works with a sense of their cosmic significance. Such ephemeral notions as timelessness, Eternity, and horror find ready representation in the *Symphonies*, in part a result of young Bely's obsession with Nietzsche. By putting these concepts at the forefront of his aesthet-ics and giving them a distinct place in the sphere of the literary, Bely affirms their presence in the lives of his readers. Before the age of twenty, Bely was able to tap into the prevailing currents of the day—its fascination with the Apocalyptic, its fixation on the mysti-cal and darkly spiritual, its search for other realities, and its belief in the transformative vision of the artist. No simple fairy tale, the *Northern Symphony* is a foray into another realm that has the same emotional resonance as our own.

The *Northern Symphony*'s lack of overt verisimilitude is more than compensated for by the inescapable familiarity of the *Dra-matic Symphony*. Yet its banality and simplicity belie its novelty and engagement with modernist innovation. It takes place in the streets and drawing rooms of Moscow and is comprised of the miscommu-nication and misunderstanding experienced by its young protago-nists. Emili Metner, who would come to collaborate closely with Bely later in the decade, summarized the story for readers of the Ekaterinoslavl newspaper *The Dneiper Regional*:

A romance (at least symbolic) between the "democrat" (Pavel Yakovlevich Kryuchkov, a young man who is a liberal critic and always elegantly dressed) and "the fairy tale" (a rich and beau-tiful young woman); a psychological tale about the fate of a young philosopher who went mad because he understood the infallibility of Kant's "Critique of Pure Reason" and who, when he recovered, turned to mysticism; a tragicomic history of the "gold-bearded ascetic"—the mystic Sergei Musatov (the main story line), in whom "certain mystical extremes are ridiculed." The material for the *Dramatic Symphony* is quite rich. It could be called a philosophical and even mystical work; it plays out on the backdrop of an everyday reality that is close at hand, even relevant such that it has popular and polemical notes.[17]

Written during the course of 1901, the *Dramatic Symphony* closely mirrors significant moments in Bely's life. As he embraced his identity as a writer, Bely immersed himself in discussions of Symbolism and Decadence, mysticism and religious philosophy. He turned his gaze to the world around him, and his unvarnished depiction of it dwells on dirty streets, criminals, unpleasant characters, and the overall repetitiveness and boredom of life. But the mundane becomes lofty through the musicality of the work's leitmotifs, the glimmer of the ideal that shows itself in all things. This is his work that most subtly and intimately considers the relationship of this world to the other: Eternity prowls around the rooms and streets; symbolic meaning lurks in every chance encounter and word; hypertrophied images and colors replace their more banal counterparts. In his interrogation of otherworldliness, Bely strikes a balance between irony and earnestness. He demonstrates the absurdity of inscribing meaning onto every word and encounter while also affirming the existence of higher planes of knowledge. Bely has fashioned a semantically dense work that references many of the people, places, and ideas circulating in Moscow in 1901. But the *Dramatic Symphony* transcends such a purely representational relationship to reality by adding a layer of "conceptual meaning," as he describes it in his opening discussion of the work. Consequently, the *Dramatic*

Symphony abounds in tension between its various levels of meaning, creating for both readers and characters the sense of a clash between its harmonious and disharmonious elements.[18]

The *Dramatic Symphony*'s philosophical framework is the most prominent of those points of connectivity among types of meaning. A few years after writing the *Dramatic Symphony*, Bely characterized Symbolism as a "worldview." For him, the works of Vladimir Solovyov and Friedrich Nietzsche (both of whom died in 1900) were at the heart of that worldview, and their voices and presence resonate throughout the *Dramatic Symphony*.[19] Solovyov in particular haunts the text. His poetry, philosophy, and theology resonate in practically every character: he rises from the grave and walks around Moscow; the ascetic Musatov takes his writings on the Antichrist overboard (as Solovyov himself observes); he is read and debated in the literary soirees Bely describes with mockery; his poetry is on the lips of characters experiencing joy, sorrow, and ecstasy; and his concept of the Divine Feminine, one of the most powerful ideas driving Bely and his fellow Symbolists' understanding of love, is at the heart of the work's central character—the fairy tale.

Among the many autobiographical elements of the *Dramatic Symphony*, the most striking are the ways Bely incorporated his mystical love for Margarita Morozova into the story. She is his fairy tale, and the letters he wrote to her in 1901–1902, signed only "your knight," are filled with words, images, and ideas that can be found in nearly the same form in the *Dramatic Symphony* (to the extent that she learned the identity of the letters' author only after reading the book). Morozova was a socialite and hostess, the wife of a wealthy merchant and prominent art collector, whose "decadent house" was the site of literary gatherings that Bely attended. Their friendship would last for decades, and they would partner on founding a publishing house in 1910, but these early letters are more than the vestiges of a youthful infatuation. They offer a clear look into the fluid relationship between life and art that fueled Bely's writing and the profundity with which Solovyov's notion of the Divine Feminine affected Bely. Solovyov postulated a female counterpart to Christ—Sophia—who was both of this world and of the other, and the Symbolists were quick to adopt this idea in their writing and attempt to incarnate it in their lives. In writing the *Dramatic Symphony*, Bely made no distinction between his real-life outpourings to Morozova on Eternity and mystical love and the fictionalized ideal of the fairy tale. They were "a single text, different generic variations on the theme of 'life creation' that would occupy the entirety of the author's inner life."[20] As a central tenet of Symbolism, "life creation" conveys a profound belief in the power of art to shape reality and reveal its higher truths. The *Dramatic Symphony* is a paradigmatic example of how exuberantly the Symbolists could assimilate life into their art while also seeing the contours of the more real in every crevice of the world they inhabited.

The concept of otherworldliness is on display at full force in the Third Symphony, *The Return*. Written in 1902, it was part of Bely's sustained engagement with the idea of a literary symphony as a genre-bending vehicle for expressing his aesthetic and philosophical views. *The Return* shows another plane of existence directly in its opening section and presents the reader with the undiluted language and imagery of a world beyond the border of reality. The first part is set in an overtly symbolic and allegorical space (possibly even another planet) populated by a mystical child and old man, sea creatures, the King of the Winds, a bird-man, and an evil sea serpent. It shows a cosmic battle between good and evil that takes place in the noumenal, the realm of signs. When the story switches to the realm of experiences, the phenomenal, we are returned to Bely's Moscow and follow the fairly unremarkable like of Evgeny Khandrikov. His story is tragic and psychologically realistic—he struggles in his profession, his wife dies, he suffers a mental breakdown, and he dies by suicide. Yet his existence is accompanied by a constant awareness of the looming presence of a higher plane of being, the Symbolist more real. Through dreams, visions, hallucinations, and imagined encounters, he sees glimpses of his other life. The child and other good and evil figures, escaped from that world into his, either help him or destroy him. Living with this awareness of the ephemerality of reality and its connection to the noumenal drives Khandrikov insane.

The Return is clearly linked to the first two *Symphonies*. It transports us to a highly aestheticized world, as did the *Northern Symphony*, while also showing how the minutiae of daily life, the essence of the *Dramatic Symphony*, are able to reveal otherworldly secrets and mysteries. It too abounds in myth, magic, love, and sadness and utilizes Nietzsche's philosophy to demonstrate the effects of modernity on everyday people. However, *The Return* structures these encounters rather differently than the other *Symphonies*. By first immersing the reader in a fully realized depiction of the symbolic realm, this work emphasizes the ubiquity of symbols in the "real" world. As we and Khandrikov navigate Moscow, elements of the first part of the story become recognizable in the people and events around him. Reinforced through the meanings attached to names and repeated leitmotifs in descriptions, the link between these planes of reality seems undeniable. The magical and mystical is seething beneath the surface of reality and, like a palimpsest, we need only scratch off one layer to reveal that the ordinary can be extraordinary. In his programmatic 1857 poem "Correspondences," Baudelaire invokes the notion of a "forest of symbols" in describing our journey through world.[21] Khandrikov is the epitome of one wandering through a space oversaturated with meaning. He is the ideal Symbolist protagonist, the essential inhabitant of the *Symphonies*— one who sees a transformed reality in the humdrum activities of daily life and recognizes the symbolic potential surrounding him.

While the first three *Symphonies* are somewhat of a piece in their overall aesthetic and stylistic qualities, *A Goblet of Blizzards* is either a monstrous aberration that runs amok with the themes and images of the previous works or the densely fruitful culmination of a decade in which Bely sought to integrate literature, philosophy, metaphysics, and aesthetic theory. This final *Symphony* is undeniably the most experimental and least accessible of the four (a point Bely conceded in his opening comments) and is often characterized as an artistic failure. While its intentional incomprehensibility and relative plotlessness alienate the reader, *A Goblet of Blizzards* does still reflect the autobiographical, philosophical, and aesthetic motivations that informed Bely's previous three *Symphonies*. Additionally, it anticipates the more radical structural and linguistic innovations of Futurism and high modernism and lays the foundation for Bely's most celebrated achievement—his novel *Petersburg*. It continues the pattern of the *Symphonies* functioning both as a record of Bely's own emotional and intellectual states and a more general commentary on Russia's literary and philosophical culture at the moment. In his attempt to balance theory and practice, Bely created a difficult and opaque text that mirrors the milieu of Russian Symbolism in the first decade of the twentieth century.

As is common in the *Symphonies*, the essence of *A Goblet of Blizzards* is a sad love story. The mystic Adam Petrovich falls erotically and spiritually in love with a beautiful woman, Svetlova (who is linked to the woman clothed in the sun from the Book of Revelation and Solovyov's Divine Feminine). Svetlova is unhappily married to a wealthy engineer on the brink of ruin and is pursued by the vile Colonel Svetozarov, who has the power to save or destroy them. Loosely based on Bely's attempt to run off with Lyubov Blok, the wife of his close friend Alexander Blok, the emotional turmoil of the story gives it a sense of grounding in real life and genuine psychology, complete with an allusion to the challenge to a duel that Bely had issued to Blok in August 1906 (unlike in the story, Bely's and Blok's duel did not take place). Bely finished writing and editing *A Goblet of Blizzards* in Europe, where he fled after the disastrous denouement of this courtship. Lyubov Blok occupied a significant place in Symbolist mythology as the perceived embodiment of Solovyov's Divine Feminine and the inspiration for Blok's famous first book of poetry, *Verses to the Beautiful Lady*. Bely would revisit this moment in his life in a major subplot of *Petersburg* in the form of Nikolai's infatuation with Sofia. Yet the cathartic retelling of this episode in *A Goblet of Blizzards* was accompanied by mundane and ironic depictions of the debates and polemics raging within Russian Symbolism as well as extended forays into mystical and religious spheres (in both the physical form of a monastic life and the symbolic form of the blizzard motif). The exemplar of a *Symphony* that Bely has developed here—a mixture of the intimate emotional states, realistic details, and lofty contemplation—links this genre to his developing theories of Symbolism.

A *Goblet of Blizzards* does not clearly distinguish between ideas and physical form (in this way it anticipates the reification of thoughts that Bely calls "cerebral play" in *Petersburg*). Metaphoric language takes on a life of its own by fluidly moving between the abstract and the concrete. Snowflakes become diamonds and white bees, and as readers we must accept those as both artistic comparisons and real transformations. In *A Goblet of Blizzards*, language vacillates between the literal and the figurative, between meaning and nonsense, often partaking of both modes at once. This fourth *Symphony* continues Bely's quest to bridge the phenomenal and noumenal and reveal the presence of the other world in the reality surrounding him. It particularly resonates with the onslaught of essays Bely wrote between 1902 and 1910 articulating his views on art, culture, and philosophy. Two articles from that period are especially relevant to *A Goblet of Blizzards*. Bely's "Symbolism as a World View," which was written in 1903, focuses on Nietzsche's role in the development of modern life. The article's discussions of Eternity and the contemplation of cosmic forces complements the imagery used in *A Goblet of Blizzards* and transports them to a theoretical essay. Bely's assertion that humans come "into the world and immediately begin knocking at the door of the nonworldly"[22] is an equally fitting description of a Symbolist writer and a character in a Symbolist work like *A Goblet of Blizzards*. In the aftermath of writing the *Symphonies*, Bely began writing about language from a linguistic and philosophical context, a critical approach he would maintain for the rest of his career.[23] His 1909 "The Magic of Words" delves into the notion of metaphoric language in ways that help us unravel his previous works. Bely addresses a tension that proliferates in *A Goblet of Blizzards*, the question of literal and figurative images, by acknowledging the impossibility of the reification of metaphors and then going on to admit his desire to believe in their reality: "in the deepest essence of my creative self-assertion, I cannot help believing in the existence of some reality whose symbol, or representation, is the metaphorical image I created."[24] For all of its complexity and abstruseness, *A Goblet of Blizzards* quite masterfully suspends readers in such a liminal state, strands them between the real and the more real. The ensuing blend of confusion, frustration, insight, and enchantment are fundamental to Symbolism's use of art to propel us into a higher plane of knowledge, a consistent goal of all four *Symphonies*.

Early in its appearance in Russia, Symbolism was called a poetry of hints.[25] It is an aesthetic that relies on implicit understandings, nuanced readings, and barely perceptible allusions and echoes. Bely's *Symphonies* embody the changes that literature was experiencing in the early twentieth century and are quintessential works of modernist experimentation and innovation. They fundamentally alter the relationship between reader and text and make the familiar strange and the strange familiar. They transport us to worlds that resemble our own but reveal the elements of artifice and magic that allow us to see the truth of our place in the universe. For the Symbolist, art is no less than the complete transfiguration of life, and the *Symphonies* are representations of the "new art" par excellence. In this first decade of his momentous career, Bely understood that the function of modern artists was to endow the seemingly small details of their lives with cosmic significance. That level of meaning allows the *Symphonies* to soar and pull us out of turn-of-the-century Moscow, out of our unremarkable lives and into the realm of the Infinite and Eternal.

NORTHERN SYMPHONY

(First, Heroic)

Dedicated to Edvard Grieg[1]

INTRODUCTION

1. A big moon floated past scattered clouds.

2. Here and there peaks rose up, overgrown with young birch trees.

3. Bald hills could be seen, spotted with stumps.

4. Sometimes pine trees appeared, clinging together in lonely clumps.

5. A strong wind blew, and the trees waved their long branches.

6. I sat by the stream and, in a rasping voice, said:

7. "What? . . . Still going? . . . Haven't dozed off yet?

8. Sleep, sleep . . . Oh, you broken heart."

9. I was answered with an amused laugh: "Sleep . . . Ha, ha . . . Sleep . . . ha, ha, ha . . ."

10. It was the rumbling of the giant. Above the stream I saw his humongous shadow . . .

11. And when I lifted my eyes in fright to the rustling, rebellious treetops, from the tops of the pines the giant's eye looked at me.

12. I sat by the stream and said in a rasping voice,

13. "Must you chop wood for such a long time, such a long time? . . . And mow the grass?"

14. I was answered with an amused laugh: "Ha, ha . . . Mow the grass . . . ha, ha, ha . . ."

15. It was the rumbling of the giant. Above the stream lay his humongous shadow . . .

16. And when I lifted my eyes in fright to the rustling treetops, from amid the tops of the pines the giant's face grimaced.

17. The giant flashed his white teeth and laughed, laughed until he fell . . .

18. Then I curled up and said in a rasping voice,

19. "Oh, I'm a young fool, a little owl, a smashed accordion . . .

20. Is a broken stick good for anything other than stoking the fire?

21. Oh you, cloudy timelessness!"

22. . . . But here my piney friend, the giant, jumped out of the grove. Bending over, he sneered at me . . .

23. He whistled into his hand and wagged his fingers in front of my dumb nose.

24. I quickly gathered my godforsaken belongings. I got out of there . . .

25. A big moon floated past scattered clouds . . .

26. It seems to me that the night lasted for ages and that millennia spread out in front of me . . .

27. I imagined many things. I discovered many things . . .

28. In front of me, on the misty horizon, a melancholy giant played with the blue clouds.

29. He picked up a blue clump of cloud, shimmering with silver thunder.

30. His muscles tensed, and he growled like a beast . . .

31. The silver lightning blinded his mad eyes.

32. His white stony face blazed and shimmered from the sudden bursts and pops ...

33. And so he picked up bunches of blue clouds that covered his legs ...

34. And so he tore the clouds and scattered them around himself, and my mouth formed frightening songs ...

35. And watching the titan's exertions, I roared senselessly.

36. But then he raised the whole blue cloud onto his powerful shoulders and walked with the blue cloud along the vast horizon ...

37. But then the melancholy titan fell and came crashing down, and his white stony face, blazing in the lightning, showed itself in the gap between clouds for the last time ...

38. I never learned more about the fallen giant ... The blue clouds suffocated him ...

39. And when I cried and wailed over the suffocated giant, wiping my tears with my fists, I heard whispers in the windy night: "These are dreams ..." "Just dreams ..." "Just dreams" ...

40. Disheartened, I sensed that the spirit of timelessness was about to start singing its vile songs as it buried the unruly giant.

41. About to, but didn't, and it froze with the weakness of an old man ...

42. And then I finally heard something like the gallop of a horse ...

43. Somebody was racing at me from a distant hill, hooves trampling the poor earth.

44. With astonishment, I realized that the centaur Bentaur[2] was flying toward me ... he held his hands over his head, spread apart ... he flashed a smile ... it was slightly terrifying.

45. His raven black body trampled the spent earth, swinging his tail.

46. In his deep melodious voice, the centaur shouted to me that from the hill he had seen the rosy heavens ...

47. That the sunrise can be seen from there . . .

48. And so the centaur Bentaur shouted to me in his melodious voice, as he rushed past me like a whirlwind.

49. And flying into the distance, the mad centaur was shouting that from the hill he had seen the rosy heaven . . .

50. That the sunrise can be seen from there . . .

PART ONE

1. One spring night the old king[3] lay dying. His young son bent over the old man.

2. The crown on his old curls shone with an ominous flame.

3. Lit by the red flame of the hearth, the king spoke into the dark night: "My son, open the window to the knocking. Let me breathe the springtime!

4. The springtime . . ."

5. The wind burst through the widow. And with the wind something else flew in, twirling the curtain.

6. A lonely passerby could hear death through the window of the old castle. And such were the words from the window: "One more gust and I'll fly off . . . You will be powerful and glorious, my son!

7. Build a tower and call my people to its summit . . . Lead them to summits and don't forsake them . . . Better to fall along with them, my son!"

8. The curtain stopped fluttering in the castle's gothic window: it drooped.

9. The passerby didn't know what had happened, but he understood one thing: night.

10. Pitch black night . . .

1. Flocks of northern knights gathered by the ancient throne, and on the throne a young man spoke new words, embracing the beautiful queen, his young wife.

2. The points of his crown and his red mantle glittered when he rustled his black curls, full of song.

3. He spoke of summits where there is eternal sunshine, where the eagle speaks to the thunder.

4. He invited them to stand over the abysses.

5. He said that the clouds must retreat, scorched by the sun, and that night is a delusion.

6. His royal clothes burned with fiery patches in front of the throne, amid the silence of the grave.

7. The warriors were gloomy because he spoke of twilight to the knights of the twilight, and only the young queen listened ecstatically to these songs.

1. The sun set. A blood-red ray of light burst through the gothic windows and fell on the king. The young king looked bloody.

2. In horror, the queen backed away from her spouse.

3. The gray-haired fanatics erupted in laughter, the glint of their armor on the walls, happy for the desired vision.

4. Evening shadows stretched through the open doors, and the flock of northern knights plunged into the shadow.

5. Through the shadow only the gloomy faces of the fanatics, encased in steel, appeared, twisted into ridiculous smiles.

6. All around was silence.

7. The king hung his head. Black curls fell onto his marble brow.

8. He listened to the silence.

9. He was afraid. He forgot the words of his late father. He and the queen fled from these lands.

1. They ran through northern fields. They were bathed in moonlight.

2. Beneath the moon was a clump of sickly northern birches. They breathed in the endless desolation.

3. The queen wept.

4. Her tears, like pearls, rolled down her pale cheeks.

5. Rolled down her pale cheeks.

1. And despair wrapped the sleeping city in its black cover. And the lonely heavens grew cold over the sleeping city.

2. A foggy melancholy uniformly tilted the trees. The trees were bent.

3. Only shadows wandered the streets, and even those just in the springtime.

4. Just in the springtime.

5. One who is worn out by long sleep will sometimes appear at the threshold and sadly listen to the arrival of the night.

6. And the courtyards and the gardens were all empty save the bent trees and green lakes where the waves washed over the marble of the staircases.

7. Sometimes someone sad would float to the surface of the water. He would swim steadily, cutting the watery dampness with his wet gray hair.

8. Sorrow, with its airy-black robes and unchanging pale face, was on the marble of the terrace.

9. A black swan, the swan of sadness, pressed itself affectionately to her legs while sadly crying into the silence.

10. The night's shadows fell from all over.

1. The late king lifted the marble lid of his tomb and walked out into the moonlight.

2. He sat on the tomb in a red cloak trimmed with gold and a pointed crown.

3. He saw the despair that coursed through the city, and his face darkened with chagrin.

4. He knew that his son had abandoned the land.

5. With his dead hand he threatened his fleeing son and continued to sit on the tomb, propping his ancient head in his tired hand.

1. But the young king and queen were running through lonely fields. They were doused in moonlight.

2. Beneath the moon was a clump of sickly northern birches. They breathed in the endless desolation.

3. The king wept.

4. His tears, like pearls, rolled down his pale cheeks.

5. Rolled down his pale cheeks.

1. They finally made it deep into the woods and for many days ran through the trees. The distance was dark and blue from the trunks. A goat-legged woodsman hobbled among the trunks, disappearing off to the side.

2. Goat-legged creatures could still be found in the woods.

3. They weren't ashamed, and when they found a forest field with a lonely marble tower, they began to make their way up to the top of the great marble tower.

1. In these lands many centuries stretched to a culmination, but the king and queen were just now climbing to the top of the marble tower.

2. The morning watched them with an overcast gaze as they ascended the winding white-marble staircase, occasionally stopping to glance out the turret windows.

3. The woods swayed, the woods rumbled. The woods rumbled.

4. Rumbled.

1. It wasn't yet sunrise, but the pale morning light shimmered. There was something refreshing in the roar of the trees, which, rumbling, shivered and chilled in the sadness.

2. The king and queen were already above the woods: an expanse of moaning pines and woody, hilly fields opened up to them through the fog.

3. Over there, on the hunchbacked field, a lonely pine tree noiselessly nodded into the distance, seized by the wind.

4. A free bird, flying off to the side, greeted them at the peak with a sharp cry.

1. The clouds woke up, warmed with affection. The tower jutted out from the pink mist. On its top was a terrace with an extraordinary marble bannister.

2. On its top the king in a red mantle extended his arms to the east.

3. The queen smiled.

4. Diamond tears dripped from a passing cloud. A low dark cloud moved toward the west.

5. And straight ahead was the azure—free and pale blue.

1. In that hour, the princess was born.

2. The red mantle fell onto the marble bannister. The king, dressed all in white silk with diamond flashes of the morning, prayed over his child.

3. A blue infinity, the blue purity of new life, glowed as it met the prayer.

4. The king sang over his child. With every chord he plucked a rose from the strings.

5. And so the day passed. A flock of swans stretched out into the north. The stars—golden studs—pierced the sapphire blueness.

1. The king fell asleep over his child with a song. The queen also fell asleep over her child.

2. They were alone, alone in the whole world.

3. Like a cruel bird, eternity was flying through the dark of night.

1. The princess grew up at the top of the tower.

2. Her mother, dressed all in silks, would speak wondrous words, and her father would pray to the dawn.

3. And in the distance white swans would fly, surrounded by blue, and she would follow them as they disappeared into a passing cloud, as they cried in the snow-white cloud.

4. And she rests her head on her mother's shoulder. Closing her blue eyes, she listens to her father's songs.

5. Her father plucks rose after rose from the strings . . . Scarlet and white—they fall to the ground, illuminated by the faint dawn.

6. Tears of pearls drip from a passing cloud, and the trees roar in the dawn clouds.

7. To the young princess, it seems she is receiving the impossible, and she sings to her father, the king.

8. In her voice there is the sigh of those forgiven after the storm, and in the curve of her mouth is the memory of distant grief: just as if someone were grieving her entire life, asking for the impossible, and at the dawn received the impossible, and, relieved, wept for the last time.

1. But then sadness crept into her father's songs, into the songs of the king. And just white flowers, white and deathly pale, fell from his strings.

2. The king bowed his head and sat, his face drained of blood.

3. He, the king, sensed the noiseless flight of the dark swan[4] from his native land. They called the dark swan the swan of sadness.

1. And so they lived on top of the tower, taking in the height in their lonely kingdom.

2. Silver sparkled in the king's curls. Wrinkles were etched into her mother's face.

1. Autumn followed summer. The dark clouds were reflected in the river, sparkling with leaden streaks.

2. A lonely pine tree floated past the deserted peak. A gray cloud obscured the tops of the trees.

3. They went to live in the heated room under the terrace. Only rarely did they stroll along the terrace.

4. The princess would step out in warm clothing, edged with ermine. The stately king shielded his hands from the cold with his sleeves.

5. He loved to stomp his feet in place to keep warm. His nose would turn red. Examining their surroundings, he would tell the princess, "Soon it will snow."

6. Ravens flew by and cawed.

1. The weather turned nasty. Her mother would sit by the window in the heated room. She didn't dare step into the chill of autumn— she was gray, she was stern, she was resigned to her fate.

2. Her father speaks of past grief. He bows his head. He stands there, sorrowful.

3. Then the dark swan flew up and sat on the railing of the terrace.

4. The princess was afraid of the dark swan. The called that swan the swan of sadness.

1. And then the downpours poured down. It was humid. The northern winter arrived. The polar lights glowed on the nighttime horizon.

2. The wind, called Howler, flew over the peaks of the forest and pressed the heart with dull foreboding.

3. It was warm and cozy in the heated room. The heated room had a hearth that burned quietly, furs covering the walls, and benches in brocaded velvet.

4. Here, huddling together, they spent the winter.

5. But above their heads, it seemed like someone was walking . . . Steps echoed on the terrace. As if one of the chilly drifters of the icy pole was resting there.

6. And then the drifter would tear away and continue its chaotic wandering.

7. In the heated room they listened to the snowstorm without complaint. But in the window there was the sound of weeping, because that was where the dim mist pounded and the pale winds flashed.

8. The young girl rested on her royal mother's knees and dreamed. Her father had taken off his red clothing and was left in white silk and a crown as he silently darned the holes of his red clothing and sewed them in gold.

1. Once a year the night blazed in flame: unseen forces set off the illumination. A strange color burst through the frost patterns on the window. Everywhere were reflections and fiery marks.

2. The king approached the princess in his patched clothing sewn in gold. He shook her shoulder. Holding back a smile, he said, "It's Christmas night . . ."

1. Occasionally the frosty patterns vanished from the windows. The pure night peeked through the window.

2. In the depths of the night—in the heavens—burned and shone other, distant worlds.

3. Pressed to the window, all three of them marveled at the heavens and spoke about a better world.

4. And then the springtime would begin to greet them.

1. And so passed year after year.

1. But a sleepy city protruded, all alone, from the distant northern fields, wrapped in sadness.

2. The late king was still sitting on his tomb, waiting for his son who had fled. Years passed, and his son had not returned.

3. Then the dead man gripped his staff and walked haughtily to the lonely castle; he came back, dragging the purple of his mantle behind him.

4. There—he's already walked up the marble stairs, above which a strange cloud was floating. There—he's already entered the throne room. Darkness had taken seat on the heavy throne, the ruler of this land.

5. The old man sat on the throne and summoned the black swan. In his mute, cold voice, he said to the swan, "Fly to my faithless son and bring him back here . . . Here people are dying in his absence.

6. Tell him that I have risen from the grave and sit on the throne myself, awaiting him . . ."

7. The swan flew out of the open window. It soared over the royal gardens. It brushed up against the bent tree . . . And the tree trembled and, having trembled, went back to sleep.

8. Day broke. A red ray of light fell through the gothic windows. The images of sullen knights indifferently gazed from the walls.

9. The dead ruler sat on the throne, hunched with the centuries, and turned scarlet with the sunrise.

1. On a spring night the king and queen sat at the top of the tower in their pointed crowns and red, patched mantles.

2. The princess stood by the railing, breathing in the springtime. She was a northern beauty with blue eyes and a sad smile that melted memories.

3. The king sang his songs with the voice of an old man, trying to strum the strings of the lute with his trembling hands.

4. Just one flower fell from the strings, and it was pale as death.

5. The king bowed his head.

1. Evening's glimmer fell onto the points of the crown. They blazed, like a wreath of fiery red poppies.

2. Wrapped in purple and crowned with poppies, he sensed the noiseless flight of the bird from his native lands.

3. And in the heavens the black swan was flying and beckoning the king to follow. It sang of an abandoned people and called him to his far away motherland . . . With this cry, the swaying trees floated away through the sleepy peaks.

4. The king sat with his lips pursed. His black shadow lay flat on the marble of the terrace. The moon, that pale melancholic, already gloomily yawned above.

1. And then he stood up. He spread his arms out towards his surroundings. He bid them farewell. He left for his motherland.

2. He told his wife and daughter, "My beloved ones, I am being called from the hazy distance . . .

3. My people are calling . . . My people are in darkness, destitute . . . They call.

4. I'll return soon . . . I'll see you again soon . . . I'll lead my people out of the hazy distance . . .

5. Don't grieve, my beloved ones."

1. And the king descended from the heights along the winding white marble staircase, and the princess stretched her thin white arms to him, parting with her father, but her mother held her back; tears flowed from her royal mother's eyes and froze in her wrinkles.

2. The king himself covered his wrinkled face with his red sleeve. He paused more than once on the winding staircase.

3. He glanced through the windows of the tower. He saw the black swan, spread out in the sky. He didn't dare turn back.

4. He descended farther. The distance was covered with moaning, bent pine trees.

5. Something gave off a fresh roar nearby. When it moved farther away, it was as if the trees were listening to departing gusts of wind.

6. Soon they saw the king down below, below among the woody fields. He seemed tiny.

7. He waved his arm and shouted something. The wind carried his words off to the side. He entered the deep woods.

1. The eastern cloud, which had been on the horizon all night, lit up with a morning flame. It consoled the princess.

2. The dark, low cloud moved off to the foggy west; it was no longer dripping diamond tears.

3. The consoled princess started singing and clapping her hands: "He'll be back . . . We'll see one another again . . ."

1. The distance was dark and blue from the trunks . . . The tired king got lost in the woods. His purple robes were all torn up and the points of his crown snapped.

2. He couldn't make his way to the distant northern fields, to return to his native city, nor could he go back.

3. He grieved for those he left behind.

4. The distance was dark and blue from the trunks.

1. The stooped colossus, alone in this world, rested by a silver stream.

2. Because really, he was just a fairy tale.

3. Hour flowed after hour. The cold current of the stream murmured, "Time-less-ness . . ."

4. The colossus stood up. He wandered nearby. Alone! Incomprehensible! . . .

1. The snows of the humped hills flashed with a lily flame.

2. At the dawn, the swans of this familiar row of hills stretched out to the far north.

3. The princess stepped out onto the terrace dressed in light, pink silks. Her elderly mother whispered and dreamed in the heated room.

4. And the young princess felt that she was—alone.

5. Alone.

1. The king wandered in the virgin woods—guided by a crown of aromatic roses.

2. The distance was dark and blue from the trunks.

3. A goat-legged woodsman hobbled among the trunks. He disappeared off to the side.

4. Goat-legged creatures could still be found in the woods.

5. From time to time, the ground shook with the heavy steps of a passing giant.

6. A stream flowed by. It murmured and shimmered. The exhausted king sank down next to the stream.

7. A dark cloud of sadness hovered over him.

8. An old face, furrowed with wrinkles, looked at him from the water: it was his reflection in the stream.

9. He understood that the old man was dying. He would never see them again.

10. He cried out, "My beloved ones . . ."

11. Dreamy spirits rippled over the stream. They grumbled and laughed at pointless old age.

12. Overcome with thirst, he bent down to the stream. His reflection rippled along the surface of the water.

13. The old face trembled in the waves . . .

1. The voice of the passing giant died away over the top of the woods.

2. Sadness, pacified, hovered invisibly over the king.

3. The king lowered his crowned head. He closed his eyes.

1. The century-old ruler sat on the throne, blood red with the sunrise. A black swan flew in through the palace window and spoke:

2. "Do not wait for your son. He's died from weakness. He wandered through the dense woods, returning to his motherland . . .

3. I saw the tower. Your granddaughter sits there, a beautiful princess—a lonely, northern flower . . .

4. Lonely, northern flower . . ."

5. And the deceased royal sighed deeply and said, "I will wait for the princess, my granddaughter—the lonely, northern flower . . .

6. Lonely, northern flower . . ."

7. He smiled a dead smile.

1. The trees grieved. The clouds, shocked and agitated, dragged themselves along the tops of the pine trees, like clumps of white cotton.

2. All night you could hear grieving and rumbling on the dawn . . .

3. In the morning, the princess stepped out onto the top of the tower. She learned that her father had died.

4. As she sat on the railing and quietly wept for her deceased parent, the swans stretched in a familiar row from distinct lands.

5. The spring was still young.

1. It was evening. In the sunset there was still a good deal of dull fire and even more gold. A bank of clouds stretched out there, calm and cold . . . and they blazed gold.

2. The wind chased off the fire and the gold a little: the dark blue evening was catching up.

3. A light steam rested over the fields and woods. A cold wind blew. She trembled from the passing cool air. She shut her bright eyes. She was lost in thought for a while.

4. She was tired from sorrow and rested in the quiet evening. The evening was becoming cloudy and sorrowfully blue.

1. That night the old queen in the heated room remembered something and opened the window. A sympathetic wind touched her gray hair, and it waved and shook in the sorrowful dusk.

2. The old woman inhaled the smell of violets and lilies of the valley with her sunken chest. She stepped onto the terrace to breathe the pale blue cool air.

3. She stood and was silent.

4. Bats were already scurrying here and there through the air in their uncertain flight.

1. Then the old queen, wrapped in the silk night, turned her gaze to her daughter. She bid her farewell, preparing for the journey.

2. A light wind rustled her curls, white like the snow. Her curls waved. The light wind brought the king's delayed greeting from distant dark woods.

3. The old woman gestured with her hand toward the distant dark woods, and they both wept. Then the old queen told her daughter, "I know what you hid from me."

4. And they both wept.

5. Then the old queen told her daughter, "I've been preparing for this for a long time: I've been listening to mysterious messages by night.

6. And now that this has happened in the dark woods, I have no reason to wait. Don't weep for me or for the king . . .

7. I am entrusting you to Eternity . . .

8. More than once It has already stood with us in times of sadness. From now on, It will be both mother and father to you."

9. The old woman trembled. Tears streamed from her eyes, and around her head—curls . . . She began to stream and melt like a cloud.

10. Night bent over the weeping orphan in the guise of a pale and somber woman in black.

11. The pale woman in black kissed her and called for her devotion.

1. The lonely princess grieved for a long time.

2. Grieved for a long time.

3. She couldn't look at the silky, blue night without tears.

4. Sometimes in the silky, blue night the king's delayed greeting flew over the treetops.

5. Delayed too long.

6. Sometimes a familiar misty cloud floated over the tower.

7. And the princess stretched her arms toward it.

8. But the indifferent cloud moved off into the distance.

1. Time, like a river, stretched forward without pause, and in the flow of time hazy Eternity was reflected.

2. It was the pale woman in black.

3. Dressed in a long cloak, she bent her dark silhouette over the lonely princess. With a droning whisper, she whispered strange words.

4. It was beyond joy and grief. Her smile reflected the stamp of Eternity.

1. A gray bird flew in. It sat on the railing. It looked around with a native's glance. It let out a worried cry.

2. The princess felt as if she were drifting off into eternal sleep.

3. She prayed that the dream of this life would pass so that we could awake from the dream.

4. The pacified woman looked into the princess's eyes with timelessness.

5. She dressed her in her own black airy robes. She called her to the faithful.

6. She pressed her own pale, peaceful face to the princess's cheek.

7. They whispered about the great unknown and that which was impending.

1. A year passed.

2. And another year . . . Time soothed the wounds of loss.

3. Only in the curve of her mouth did the traces of grief remain.

4. She devoted herself to Eternity.

1. It was springtime. Blue violets bloomed by the stream.

2. The transparent stream continued to complain about something, shaking the currents.

3. Sometimes the sounds of bagpipes wafted from the distant trunks.

4. The playing of the goat-legged fauns . . .

5. The violets bloomed. Tears fell.

1. And so passed year after year.

PART TWO

1. The woods were enormous and untouched. The flora rumbled strangely in the wild. There were no paths. They barely even knew about paths.

2. Still, the forest was not deserted: woodland creatures of all sorts lived here.

3. By the bonfire, they celebrated the miracles of the new moon and the red devilry.

4. Occasionally, in the darkness, you could glimpse the ruby-red eyes of an old gnome; he wasn't a woodsman, but he climbed out of his burrow to smoke a pipe with pick in his hand: underground, he fought with gravity.

5. During these hot August nights, forest dogs would run about, black and mad; they were like people, but for their loud barking.

6. On Saint Lawrence Night,[5] the hunchback would also come.

1. At the hour of the foggy sunrise, damp yellow tones spread in the distance. Blue blocks filled the horizon. Block piled upon block. They sketched out plans and built castles.

2. Fiery zigzags rumbled in the blue clouds.

3. In the pale morning, the colossus Riza would walk among the clouds.

4. Quietly, Riza would knock over the blue blocks, wading up to his knees in the clouds.

5. At the hour of the foggy sunrise, he sat on a cloud by the horizon, cupping his clean-shaven face.

6. Riza's stony face silently laughed, and he trained his glassy eyes on the distance . . . He sent his cloak flying toward the heavens and let it float off on the wind . . .

7. It disappeared, pierced by the sun.

1. These were the dark times of giants and violence.

2. Knights' castles were nestled amid the boundless woods. The knights would leave them in order to rob passing travelers.

3. Thieving and murdering.

1. At that time, you could encounter a gloomy horseman with a hooked nose and goatee.

2. The horseman rode through the forest and called for his goat-legged brother.

3. In response to this call, the goat looked out from the forest with dull eyes, filled with horror: it was no coincidence that goats accompanied people to the witches' sabbath.

4. The knight pressed his hands to his chest, glanced at the goat, and, in a coarse bass, sang, "O, my goat-legged brother! . . ."

5. For he was the knight with the goatee. For he had goatlike traits: he led the accursed choir and danced with the goat in the dark forest.

6. This dance was a *goat jig*, this sorcery—*goat summoning*.

1. There was a hill covered with spruce. A cloudy distance spread out from the hill. It was evening.

2. A giant red sphere crawled across the black enamel of the horizon. The passing knight sadly struck up a bandit's tune.

3. In the distance, on the mountain, silhouettes of towers broke through: it was the fortress. Behind it, heavy blue cupolas rose up, casting off bolts of lightning.

1. The knight's fortress was old and gloomy. Its windows were made of stained glass.

2. The lower portion was a labyrinth of dark corridors.

3. A boy lived there. He was pale and shy. His eyes already shone black like the grave. This was the knight's son.

4. The shy boy's childhood was swaddled in dull darkness.

5. Before, a silvery voice had resounded from the darkness. A kind, thin face had appeared from the twilight.

6. And then his mother's face drowned once and for all into the drowsy darkness. The silvery voice no longer resounded.

1. Through the fog, he remembered the knight with the hooked nose, black goatee, and sharp glance.

2. Even animals were wary of his swarthy father; dogs showed their teeth and howled at him.

3. He recalled his swarthy father's brief visits to the fortress.

4. They would hide the icons. They were afraid. Strange people stomped and made a raucous in the corridors.

5. The pale boy met an odd stranger in the illuminated corridors.

6. One autumn, lightning killed the swarthy knight.

1. The quiet boy had a marvelous tutor with a fiery mantle shrouded with the mythical twilight.

2. He led the boy to the fortress's balcony and showed him the hazy shadows. Red and filled with inspiration, he taught him how to see the fantastic.

3. And the fantastic would visit the boy: he became acquainted with the giant Riza . . . At night Riza would come to the fortress, open the window of the small, pale dreamer's room and tell him about the lives of giants in his rumbling velvety voice.

4. Sometimes on a sunny day, the giant knocked on the child's window with his finger.

5. Sometimes in the evening, old Riza would walk past and cast his long shadow onto the fortress.

1. But childhood ended. With it, these hazy fairy tales floated away.

1. He became a handsome young man. He had thick curls and wore a suit of armor. His face was pale with distinctive features: a big nose and a curly beard.

2. It seems that he too was distantly related to the goat.

3. He became the knight of these lands. He could often be found lost in thought on the bank of the great river.

4. Waves rolled on the river.

1. The former knight wore iron armor with a raven feather in his iron helmet. He had a hooked nose and was restrained.

2. One autumn they brought him to the fortress with a black-and-blue face, incinerated by a bolt of purple lightning.

3. After his death, they spoke about the St. Lawrence days madness. About how a blood-red meteor landed near the fortress and the steward spent the night pacing the corridors.

4. About how he carried the red orb on a silver platter. He served the hot orb to the old knight.

5. Seized by the horror of magic, the knight shook the hot orb and, in his coarse bass, sang, "Orb, my orb."

6. This was the rite of the orb horror.

7. The young knight knew that in the old places, the old fumes of the orb-induced ravings and horrible goat magic were exhaled: he abandoned his grandfather's fortress and built a new fortress on the bank of the great river.

8. And when he rode up to his new home, the angry woods rumbled in the distance, making threats.

1. The young knight wished to have hazy dreams, but in his soul the strength of his ancestors rose up.

2. Sometimes, he would walk up to the window and admire the fiery stars, lurking by the window . . .

3. They urged him toward familiar patterns . . . They nodded and smiled . . . They asked him to fulfill the familiar rituals of horror . . . They whispered the familiar, unfathomable words . . .

4. The young knight knew that it wasn't God calling him forth . . . Frightened by the arrival of the Unknown, summoning him into the night's stillness, he painstakingly bowed before the illuminated Crucifix.

5. Because in the old places, the old fumes of the orb-induced ravings and horrible goat magic were exhaled . . . And everything nodded, everything smiled . . . They asked him to fulfill familiar rituals of horror . . . They whispered unfathomably raving words.

6. So the knight mounted his horse. Like one on fire, he raced past the woods and ravines to drown out the words of the Unknown, who was calling into the night's stillness . . .

1. Occasionally, small golden daisies and little crimson crosses would sway in the woodland clearings and the fear would melt away, turning hazy and sadly contemplative.

2. Occasionally, the dawn would spread, and high up a white storm would form above the cold feathery clouds, and they would scatter into the pale blue.

3. The horror would flee, blazing with lightning from the distant west.

4. Then the young knight would stop his horse at sunrise and rest from the fear.

5. At his feet small golden daisies and little crimson crosses would sway on their long stems . . .

1. When the knight rode deep into the woods, a light breeze would blow from the deep woods.

2. As if the sound of a woodland harp were fading in the wooded distance. As if expressing sadness over the sunlight.

3. As if pleading that the dream of this life would pass and we could awake from sleep.

4. The evening was already turning a melancholy blue, but the knight still listened to the wafting breeze.

5. The wooded distance was already moving toward the blue, hazy gloom. In the gloomy, wooded blueness the crimson fires were already burning.

6. Somewhere in the distance a woodland hag was flying past on her pig. The whooping and stomping of the goat-legged creatures echoed.

7. The contemplative knight returned home.

1. Once, at sunset, the knight was riding in the woods toward the intriguing sounds. The mountain prayer echoed closer and closer, like a fiery whirlwind.

2. A green stream flowed. There was a flame on the emerald waters.

3. Two dreamy gnomes stood on a hill in the woods. Their gazes followed the passing knight, their bony faces resting on their short arms.

4. They were listening to the song of the dusk.

1. In front of the knight there was a clearing in the woods, and in the clearing a tower.

2. High up . . . as if in the fiery sky . . . the unseen young princess stretched her delicate, pale arms toward the setting sun.

3. A white lily in red velvet. She had dark blue eyes and a sad smile.

4. She pleaded that the dream of this life would pass and we could awake from sleep.

5. The dazed knight listened to this song with excitement, this song of blazing constellations and the fiery rings of Saturn.

6. The impossible seemed close at hand.

1. It was evening. The giants had come to the horizon. They pushed aside blue clumps of clouds. They stuck out their still faces.

2. The princess's prayers reached even them, like the sound of a silver horn . . .

3. The giants sat on the clouds, their clean-shaven faces drooping. They remembered . . . happiness . . .

1. Even more distant woodland peaks rustled with her twilight song, while the princess had already sat down on the railing with a sad smile.

2. She stopped singing, the princess—a white lily in red velvet! . . .

3. A white lily! . . .

4. A tender look flitted over the stranger in shining armor and an olive green mantle. He stepped into the clearing to bow to the princess, pressing a white flower to his breast.

5. The east went dark. The mist had already settled. He was handsome and pleasant, but still he seemed to be distantly related to the goat.

6. Even though he was noble.

1. From that moment, as soon as the evening bells had died down and the red light of dusk was extinguished, the pleasant stranger would come to bow.

2. He was pleasant, but still he seemed to be distantly related to the goat.

3. Even though he was noble.

4. From that moment, he would appear every evening as soon as it cooled off.

1. The distant snowy cones burned with an amethyst fire. Swans flew over the northern fields.

2. On foggy evenings, they perched at the top of the tower. Above them the peaceful northern star flickered.

3. He wore gray clothes. Silvery white lilies were sewn on them. A pale blue cross shone from her breast.

4. She bent over him like a tender sister, like a sweet evening friend.

5. She pointed to the constellation Ursa.[6] She had a melting smile, a little sad.

6. She sang turquoise fairy tales.

7. The young knight forgot about the hellish onslaughts. He gazed upon the passing clouds and his evening sister.

8. In the pale morning, he returned from the heights of the tower, calm in his sadness.

1. They chanted a prayer. The pines, wrapped in sleep, murmured about the ideal.

2. There was an awful drowsiness in the pine groves. Blue flowers bloomed by the stream, in the lonely wooded clearing.

3. The goatlike shepherd, Pavlushka, tended to the woodland flock.

4. With his long ears, he listened to the call of the glimmering stars. He snorted haughtily and strummed a scoundrel's song.

5. Pavlushka couldn't drown out the voice of truth and drove his flock into the wilds of the goat sorcery.

6. The pines, wrapped in sleep, murmured about the ideal.

7. Somewhere they chanted a prayer.

1. They said, "Where is your kingdom, you—the unknown princess?" "I had an earthly kingdom, but now I don't know where it is . . . My kingdom is the morning of resurrection and the sapphire skies. This kingdom of sapphire dreams can't be taken from me."

2. "Where is your crown, you—the unknown princess?" "I don't have a crown. There is only one crown—the crown of the heavens and that is open to all."

3. "Where is your fiery mantle, you—the unknown princess?"
"I don't have a fiery mantle. Even without a mantle, the Lord sees the fire of my heart . . .

4. It glows in the night like a red gem . . ."

5. The young knight was saddened and offended by the princess's incomprehensible magnitude.

6. A single bloody scythe rose in the black vault of the sky.

1. A hunchbacked steward lived in the knight's fortress. His pounding step resounded in the stone corridors day and knight.

2. His old, smooth face smirked in the darkness.

3. Behind his back, there were whispers that along with the late black knight he too partook in god-defiling horrors. And that even now he hadn't abandoned his old ways.

4. More than once he had been seen in the dark autumn night creeping like a spider and stealing glances at the young knight. He scattered green powder. He brought the mages who knew of goat sorcery in from the woods. More than once the goats had gazed at the young knight.

5. Such was the old steward.

1. The young knight prostrated himself before the Crucifix, lit by a lamp, and thought about his youthful sister. The red lamplight shone on the gray walls. It had the power of a prayer.

1. The vanquished gloom burst from the corners, retreating into the void.

2. And one wanted to embrace the whole world, to pray for all of its inhabitants.

3. The night of prayers forced its way through the narrow window, along with the calm north star.

4. But . . . somewhere within the walls . . . resounded the pounding step of the vile old man. The pure prayers fled. The old hunchback knelt by keyholes in dark corridors.

5. With a thief's gaze, he noted the young knight's doubts. With his mind, he conjured the idea to partake in the horrific dark rituals. He mumbled the raving incantations.

6. And then . . . he continued his lonely stroll, lighting the dark space with the flame of a hidden torch. His smooth yellow face smirked in the darkness.

7. Such was the old steward.

1. The dull footsteps died down on the stones, but the knight, intoxicated with the noxious ravings, laughed, devising horrors for the princess, his sister.

2. Foul streams of orb horrors and goat sorcery seeped through the keyhole, allowed in by the depraved steward.

1. The young knight was the princess's only brother. She loved him with a pure heart.

2. But now he rarely visited her tower. Sullen and contemplative, he concealed something from her . . . They no longer had an easygoing friendship. It was a complex game.

3. When she began speaking about Eternity, the knight's brow wrinkled and he said, "Quiet, I don't love you like that."

4. When she asked, "How, then, do you love me?" he left her, scowling.

5. It was a July night. All around grenades and bombs exploded. They filled the darkness with momentary flashes . . .

6. That was the lightning.

1. At that time, it was hot. The days of woodland madness trudged on . . . Often at night, bluish-white masses crossed the sky. Mass piled upon mass. They sketched out plans and built castles.

2. The blacksmith Anthony worked the bellows and stoked the flame in the bluish-white forge, and St. Anthony's Fire[7] embraced the heavens . . .

3. A raving struggle and clashes of lightning were afoot . . .

4. The princess, pale and suffering, prayed for her friend, who had begun to act strangely. The sky shone and lit the road in the woods by which her friend would come.

5. An unfamiliar figure limped along the familiar path.

1. That night the young knight shut himself in with the hunchbacked steward. He waved his arms and spoke burning words.

2. The steward was silent, focusing his bandit's eyes on the madman.

3. The previous night a stranger had come to the hunchback—he was wrapped in a black cloak and had chicken claws instead of feet. Today they sat there, leaning their elbows on the table, bowing their pale faces toward one another, speaking of horrors and building fortresses.

4. Then the stocky steward saddled his horse and rode to the clearing to tell them about his success. The signal blast echoed. The bridge was lowered.

5. The black horse carried the steward over a deep moat. Its iron shoes pounded.

6. Behind him, the midget on guard signaled. The bridge stretched over the deep moat.

7. Such was the old steward.

1. The princess still prayed for her friend, raising her eyes to the heavens.

2. A white lump sat in the sky, and by the horizon rested a smoky boar's head. Short bursts of thunder resounded from the boar's head.

3. They mutely cursed the prayers and mocked her sadness.

1. One sunny day there was a storm in the woods. It tore off green branches and showered two riders with them. This was the knight and his vile steward.

2. One sunny day there was a downpour with thunder.

3. Not far from there, giants walked by with hurried steps and then disappeared into the depths of the horizon.

4. The knight was morose and pale, and the old steward followed his young master's doubts with the gaze of a crow . . .

5. Again arose the image of his father, incinerated by purple lightning, and the old steward pointed toward the clearing where, through the thin beech branches, you could see a lonely chapel: that's where they reveled in Satan.

1. The day passed. Rays from the setting sun bathed the meadow and the woods in a thick yellow. Evening shadows stretched out from the edge of the woods.

2. The riders moved along the illuminated meadow by the edge of the woods. There were two of them. Their black horses in red blankets with gold embroidery neighed boldly, and riders' shadows seemed disproportionately long.

3. The riders were trotting. The older one was reassuring the younger one about something.

4. A breeze was blowing. The shadow of an unknown giant stretched over all the land. He stood blocking the sun, proudly and alone. His crowned head stood out, lit with a pink shine.

5. The giant looked over God's creation, spread out before him. He was alone in this world.

6. He wanted to forget, to doze off. He left the world ineffably.

7. There in the distance stood the lonely giant, wrapped in the evening twilight.

1. In the evening, the sky cleared up. Wandering flames appeared between the trees, among the gloomy damp. A delicate half-moon was in the dark blue sky.

2. In the field by the ravine, where the ferns grew, they sat—singed.

3. The red bonfire blazed.

4. The old woodland conjurer reached his long arms over the bonfire . . . Red from the fire and filled with inspiration, he taught him how to see the fantastic.

5. And then they all danced a jig of love, ringing their purple bells.

1. Amid the greenery of the woods, the jet-black horses in red blankets appeared. Two riders dismounted. One was the hunchback; he stayed with the horses.

2. A blood-red mantle enveloped the other's elegant features. Under the mantle was black steel. A plume of ostrich feathers swayed over his head.

3. With his right hand he grasped his grandfather's heavy sword, and with his left he drew up the edge of his mantle.

4. He walked up to the tower, his pointy spurs getting tangled in the tall grass. At the top of the tower, she stood all in white, as if in a mantle of air, her soft fingers barely touching the marble bannister.

5. Her tender profile stood out sharply against the bright blue starry night.

6. Flashes of revelation flickered in her half-open mouth and sad blue eyes.

7. From time to time, she bowed low, dutiful and white, and then raised her silhouette back to the pale blue evening world.

8. That was how she prayed. The silver half-moon shone over her.

1. The knight paused, but then in the nearby bushes the hunchback coughed, and the knight began to climb the marble staircase, his spurs clinking.

2. And when he reached the top, she focused her dark blue eyes on the distant void. A cloud was frowning there; it used to be the dawn.

3. But then he knocked twice with his sword. She smiled in fright. She didn't recognize her sweet brother. When she did, she smiled at him.

4. And so they stood, silently.

1. He said, "You asked me, and so I've come now to tell you something new. Like a flame, it's burning my soul.

2. You're wrong, praising otherworldliness . . . I am the son of a knight. There is the strength of iron in me.

3. Come with me to my fortress. I love you. I want to marry you, princess from an unknown kingdom."

4. Sparks flew from his eyes.

1. The woods were imposing.

2. During the days of madness, among the trees the ringing voice of the mage resounded and resounded, summoning the thin silver sorcerers to their sorcery.

3. During the days of madness:

4. "With a thirst for the day, by the flame among the mist the fauns, sorcerers, and goats revel.

5. All equal in our dance, a glorious dance in the mist! . . . The goats! . . .

6. The fauns!"

1. The young princess stood, pale from the moonlight; her delicate royal profile was downcast. Silver tears dripped from her eyelashes.

2. Her deep melancholy was hidden. She spoke slowly and calmly. Her voice was quiet, with a touch of sadness.

3. "Beloved, I do love you. And my love is invisible in this world. It's the sigh of the birch branches.

4. You didn't understand this. You wrecked our friendship, pure like the lily . . .

5. White . . .

6. It pains and saddens me . . ."

1. The old conjurer danced by the ravine, where the ferns grew, lifting the edge of his purple gown.

2. His beard shook . . . His gray curls snaked around his mesmerized face.

3. The flame snapped in front of him, and at times it looked like he was wrapped in translucent, red silk.

4. Occasionally, he jumped through the fire; at those moments, his purple clothing filled up like a sail above the transparent silk of the red flame.

5. And around him the sorcerers rejoiced, reassuring one another, "Look, the old man is celebrating!

6. He's celebrating, celebrating! . . ."

1. Listening to the songs of the woodland conjurer, the knight moved closer to the princess and said, "I will shower you with rubies and garnets . . . I will win a purple mantle for you with my iron sword.

2. For you are an uncrowned, kingdomless princess . . ."

3. "I've already explained that my kingdom is not of this world. There will come a time when you will see it.

4. I do have a purple mantle: it's the purple of the dawn which will soon blaze over the world.

5. There will come days when you will see me dressed in this purple . . .

6. But farewell! . . . It's time for us to part . . ."

7. The crazed knight approached the princess with a cry, "I'll get you down from these heights," and then he seized her by the waist and started to descend with his prize . . .

8. But over the crumpled princess's head arose the fierce image of a ghostly old man in a royal mantle and golden crown.

9. His bloodless lips moved. He threatened the knight with his misty hand.

10. Then the young knight understood that he had no crown or purple mantle and he had stumbled into the pitfalls of the past.

11. He descended, wrapped in his cloak. His whole body trembled. A bunch of black ostrich feathers swayed above his head.

1. The conjurer continued with his favorite songs and dances, "O my flowers, pure as crystal! Silver!

2. You are the morning of days . . .

3. Gold and fragrant, you are subtle—showering with gold, luminous, pure as crystal.

4. You are the morning of days."

5. And still celebrating, he cried, "More and more tenderly do I love you."

1. In the blue night she stood, alone, at the top of the tower. She was a pure beauty of the north.

2. Alone.

3. In the morning she was still standing there in a crown of forget-me-nots with the dawn behind her.

4. The lonely pink hazy tower melted into the east.

1. At dawn he was sitting with the hunchbacked steward in the clearing, weeping bitterly.

2. And the stout steward waved his hands and whispered to the knight, "Don't grieve, mighty lord, I know how to console you . . ."

3. The dawn was golden, and a red flame blazed on the horizon.

4. The lonely pink hazy tower melted into the east.

1. They sat by the dying fire, resting after the dance. They listened to the silence.

2. The sound of a horse's step seemed to resound in the distance.

3. They were soon startled to find that the centaur Bentaur was rushing toward them . . . He held his hands spread above him. From afar he flashed his lightning smile and shouted about the golden dawn.

4. The mad centaur flew past them like a whirlwind and rode into the distance . . . he was slightly terrifying.

5. They climbed the hill in order to greet the golden morning banquet, which shimmered over the woods, all in crowns of fern . . .

6. The conjurer stretched his arms toward the wine-tinged golden horizon, where the last patches of the hazy tower floated by, melting, and he sang to the sunrise, "Carefree and gold as Eternity, you laugh at this ancient world . . .

7. Don't be troubled by our tardy feast . . . With your bright red flame blaze over the trees . . ."

PART THREE

1. At those times, everything was enveloped in the fog of Satanism. Thousands of unfortunate souls had dealings with the dark kingdom. The sin of the witches' and goats' sabbath hovered over the land.

2. Even innocent children had dark dealings.

3. At that moment, the gloomy Catholic with chicken legs was still wandering in these parts.

4. On some foggy fall evenings he would walk by the edge of the woods, rustling the dead leaves, drawing up his long black robe. The poor villagers hid from him.

5. They mouthed incantations and made the sign of the cross over their windows.

6. The gloomy Catholic would surreptitiously and imploringly knock on the doors of their homes; he offered the villagers a thieves' bargain.

7. Sometimes the doors would unlock and the fools would allow in the stranger with chicken legs.

8. The mocking Catholic would often enact a black mass among the stones and heather, served by the demons Astrarot and Godipotomus.

9. He offered the faithful who had gathered around a scarlet beet: this was a parody of the liturgy.

1. In the cities, the pious wrestled with dark forces. They burned wood chips on the squares to ward off witches and sorcerers.

2. The pious peered into one another's windows. They accused each other of shameful sorcery.

3. The pious stood watch . . . In the clearings of old ruins more than once they came upon respected heads of households performing Satanic leaps and flights on a broom.

4. The monks devoutly chanted, "Pereat, Satan," and introduced the guilty parties to the Spanish boot. They grasped it firmly.

5. Drawing up their long robes, they clamped the bloody feet of the unfortunates with steel wedges and forced them to swallow glass and dance in the fire.

6. They made bonfires and placated an obscure hell with smoke and burnt offerings.

7. At those times, everything was enveloped in the fog of Satanism.

1. Toward evening, the heavens frowned. Clumps of cold blue flew over the autumn land.

2. The knight sat on the terrace of the castle, frightened and pale. He wore a black cloak of mourning, edged with silver.

3. The river rumbled before him. It flowed with the darkness of a black night. Only the crests of the waves shimmered white and metallic.

4. Everything was full of a mystical terror . . . In the distance someone's boat sailed by, leaving a steel streak in its wake . . .

5. The knight knew that this was a bad omen and that it wasn't a fisherman in that boat . . . It was completely dark.

6. Vague silhouettes were visible, and the murmur of the waves was audible.

7. The dwarf on guard sounded his horn, proclaiming the arrival of strangers.

8. They gestured and conferred.

1. The old steward came to the terrace to announce the appearance of the unfamiliar hunchback.

2. He stood there—an amazing silhouette in the dark of night! . . .

3. The old steward bowed his grey head onto his hunched chest and moved away, and the hunchback approached the young knight and uttered illicit words about familiar horrors.

4. The knight looked at the guest, painfully remembering something.

5. Finally, in a moment of insight, he recalled the goat's gaze and, in a magical amnesia, screamed, "O, my goat-legged brother!"

6. Then he remembered the whole abyss of long-gone goat-sorcery, and somewhere nearby, through the clouds, a red flame erupted and vanished.

7. This was St. Lawrence eve. The blood-red meteor fell. The steward's round eyes shone evocatively, and then his criminal head once again dropped onto his hunched chest.

8. All three were given back stallions. The night received them in her embrace.

9. It rained that night, and dull tears pounded the windows panes. The distant woods rioted. In that riotous noise, the wails of a blizzard were audible.

10. And it seemed that death moved with quiet, but confident, steps.

1. A chapel stood in the woodland clearing by the silver stream. During the day, many people came here to pray, even though the chapel was in an impure spot: goat-legged fauns gathered by the silver stream.

2. You could hear the thumping of their goat-legged hooves here.

3. The young goats congregated here even on sunny days; they twisted ridiculously in the shadow of the cross.

4. At night, crimson horrors were performed at the chapel by an old wastrel—the priest of these parts: this was an illicit chapel.

5. It was made by the inhabitants of the forest, and here they danced the goat jig.

6. The night before, a disgusting mass with goat's blood had been performed here. The old wastrel gave a communion of sorcery to the young knight.

7. The old steward and the hunchback congratulated the young knight on performing horrors.

1. The morning was pale. Autumn had begun. Dry crumpled leaves flew along the roads and fields. The sky hadn't been blue for some time—it was an autumn gray.

2. There had even been a frost, and the mud dried into pale clumps streaked with ice.

3. A prophetess appeared in these parts. She walked around the castles and villages, barefoot and wizened. She raised her prophesying finger to the autumn-gray sky.

4. In a low and weeping voice she spoke of the Lord's tolerance, that the horrors would not last for long, of how the Lord would send them a saint.

5. A dark blue shroud stretched out somewhere in the distance from her words, and over the shroud shone the cold autumn night, blue with moonlight.

6. In the heavens a song echoed about the rings of Saturn and eternally joyous Vega . . .[8]

1. The evergreen pine trees, blown by the storm, quietly moaned in the cold blue autumn night.

2. A dimly lit terrace was above the forest giants, and standing on it was she whose tender hands were stretched to the heavens.

3. So she stood with her hair down to her shoulders, praying to Eternity. Her gentle profile melted into the starry blue backdrop of the night.

4. The spark of revelation trembled in her half-open mouth and sad blue eyes. On each eyelash hung a piously silver tear.

5. She prayed for her brother, bowing and then again reaching out to Eternity, repeating the same words: "Can he not be saved? He is miserable."

6. In the morning she was still standing against the dawn. The parting cries of the cranes could be heard: there . . . they flew . . . an eternal triangle.

1. Time, like a river, flowed without stop, and misty Eternity was reflected in the passing of time.

2. It was a pale woman in black.

3. Wearing a long mantle, she bent her dark silhouette over the lonely princess and whispered odd words: "He grew tired . . . He won't perish . . . The horrors have horrified him . . . He is miserable . . .

4. He is fated to misty timelessness . . ."

5. The forest murmured.

6. The murmur grew, like a hushed conversation, like the lament of the scattered leaves.

1. The comforting woman looked into the princess's eyes with timelessness, brushed against her with her airy-black robes, pressed her pale and peaceful face to the princess's cheek.

2. She branded her with a kiss, the kiss of Eternity.

3. It was beyond joy or grief, and the princess's smile was special . . .

1. The cold autumn morning was marked in the sky's crystals with a pale green light.

2. The dour knight, wearing a mourning cloak, was lost in thought by the sandy ravine. He stood by the hill overgrown with heather, remembering the witches' sabbath, horrified by its horrors, by the ceaseless din in his ears.

3. Nearby, at the edge of the ravine, young birch trees spread out, grumbling with a lament for spring.

4. Under the birches sat someone mad and humongous, like a crumpled statue, drilling his glassy eyes into the young knight.

5. And when he turned his pale face to him, the one sitting flashed an impossible smile. He beckoned with his giant finger.

6. But the knight did not heed this terrible call.

7. It was nothing new. Many times already, the remains of the night could be imagined in the light of morning. The knight covered his delirious head with a black cloak.

8. The hulking mass leaped up. It screamed that it was no fairy tale, that it was a giant, but the knight covered his ears.

9. So the neglected giant left for other lands. His complaints could be heard far in the distance.

1. The steward gave orders. The castle stirred. They were preparing for an evening guest.

2. In the evening they awaited the gloomy Catholic himself and prepared for the horrors.

3. The ancient icons were removed.

4. The young knight was sickened by the approaching abyss of filth. He went into his refuge of solitude.

5. He was oppressed by its awful familiarity, but he dared not pray to the Lord for deliverance after his blasphemous acts at the witches' sabbath.

6. He whispered, "Who would pray for me?"

7. The sun was high in the heavens . . . Night was already nearing. The servants were stirring.

8. The ancient icons were removed.

1. A cold wind blew in the evening. Low bunches of clouds flew over the gray towers of the castle. The guard, wrapped in his cloak, flashed his halberd.

2. The moat bridge was lowered and the castle blazed with festive fires.

3. Along the roads and through the woods, a line on foot and horseback stretched toward the castle, from who knows where. There were goats and hunchbacks and black knights and witches.

4. The wild boar, a witch, rode a pig.

5. The old dwarf constantly stepped onto the bastion to sound his horn and announce a new arrival.

1. The accursed steward would step out to greet the guests.

2. Hunched, completely doubled over, he spread his arms and spoke with a smile . . .

3. The words echoed, "Greetings, my lords! . . . So you've gathered here for the goat jig, basically, for the goat jig?

4. We'll catch those of little faith in our nets, like spiders . . . Ha, ha, ha . . . in our nets! . . . Isn't that so, darlings?

5. Darlings of the gray horror . . ."

6. And with these words he followed the guests . . .

1. When the clock croaked ten, it announced the start of the horror.

2. They were already sitting at tables.

3. Then the wind moaned, and a dull autumn rain fell.

4. Drinking bowls clinked in the hall, dimly lit by torches. They feasted. They listened for the knocking of a late guest.

5. The place across from the host was still empty. The fateful hour was approaching.

6. Servants brought in the cauldron, and the hunchbacked steward took the lid off the steaming cauldron and made a joke.

1. They served the young goats. Their intoxicated mugs contorted with laughter. Piglike and sheeplike. These wolf people gnashed their teeth.

2. At the table, they performed the midnight treachery, lit by smoky torches.

3. An amusing fat man heaved himself onto the table, dirtying the brocaded tablecloth with his rough boots and the nails in their soles.

4. He held a golden goblet filled to the brim with hot blood.

5. At a pause in the festivities, the fat one sang a vile song.

6. The choir joined in with him.

1. The gloomy Catholic sat on a stone far away in a clearing in the pines, looking into the distance at the festive lights of the castle.

2. The Catholic was heading to the welcome feast, but misty Eternity had appeared.

3. She had howled and raged with the foul weather, and a baleful voice resounded from the stormy sighs.

4. She looked at the Catholic with glossy eyes. She said, "O you, melodious, outrageous, inviting darkness! . . . Stop, leave . . . He no longer desires horrors . . . He is miserable . . .

5. He loves misty timelessness . . ."

6. The gloomy Catholic was afraid and went off into the pine grove.

1. The clock struck midnight. The old steward entered the hall.

2. He motioned for silence and opened the outer doors wide.

3. He then stood by the doors, bowing his gray head onto his hunched chest.

4. The cloudy foul weather began to whip through the open doors. Those seated shivered from the autumn wind.

5. The torches smoked. The blood-red flame drooped, it shook in the wind—it was going out.

6. The pale, dour host stood up from his seat and lowered his eyes. He stood waiting for the terrible guest.

7. Everybody grew quiet and chanted enticing incantations.

1. But the hours passed and the night grew lighter, and no one came. Just before dawn, the outline of an imposing woman in black passed by the open doors.

2. This was misty Eternity, alone.

3. They then understood that their host was not worthy of a visitation. They left the feast empty-handed.

4. They eviscerated their host with spiteful glances.

1. The knight was saved. The horrors had passed. All that was left was deep sorrow.

2. In the gray morning he stood on the tall bastion and listened to the shrieks of the wind—of northern Revun.[9]

3. Somewhere lonely Revun was flying by, aching the heart with a dull foreboding.

4. And down below, the unknown prophetess approached the castle gates, shaking her arms and speaking of the Lord's tolerance.

5. She called on them to repent. She said that the Lord took pity on the northern lands. That he would send them a saint.

6. She said, "We are all tired . . . The horrors have horrified us . . . We are miserable . . .

7. O, if only we could have misty timelessness . . ."

8. The woods rumbled and whispered. This whisper grew like a fierce conversation, like the sad lament of the scattered leaves, dying from their sadness.

1. In the morning, the despondent steward ran into the woods, offering explanations. He cried tearfully and beat his chest.

2. But the goat-legged woodsmen chased him away.

3. All day the hunchback ran among the pines, chased by a herd of whooping and whistling woodsmen.

4. They stomped their goat hooves. They threw rotten branches at the hunched back of the deceiver.

1. Years past. The day came. The princess came down from the high tower, fulfilling the heavenly commandment. She came to chase away the darkness.

2. She took a long stick and attached her shimmering crucifix to its end. She walked along the edge of the woods, holding her crucifix over her head.

3. At times you could see the red cap of a hidden gnome popping up from a knoll with two ruby eyes intently following the princess.

4. The black knights trembled in their castles as she approached, and the unholy chapels collapsed and fell through the earth, consumed by flames.

5. The demon left the possessed, and he praised God.

1. Years past. The dead king sat on the throne, waiting for his faithless son. Then a breeze stole into the hall and whispered to the downcast king about an unexpected joy.

2. And a smile passed over his dark face. And he stepped off the throne. He took the horn, which hung on the wall, and stepped onto the terrace.

3. The old, deceased king, dressed in red and gold, blew into his long horn.

4. This was how he greeted his granddaughter. She came up the marble steps with her stick topped with a crucifix.

5. And her grandfather the king led her to the throne.

6. Then he quietly bid farewell to the returned princess and dutifully went back to his tomb.

1. Day and night, the saved knight remembered the sweet image of his sister, the princess, tortured by the past. The past could not be relived.

2. He donned his armor and, pike in hand, galloped into the distant woods and ravines, digging his spurs into the black stallion.

3. For solace, he would often call to battle a woodland beast, a bearded centaur, and run him through with his pike in the heat of the hunt . . . More than one bearded centaur fell, fists clenched and twitching, covered in blood.

4. Often he would stand over the corpse of a bearded woodsman with a horse's body, unable to forget it.

5. With crimson blood still dripping from the end of his pike, he would cry out in the woods by the stream, "If only I could see her and undo the past . . ."

6. From somewhere in the distance a murmur approached. The murmur of Eternity . . . Somewhere the treetops swayed and you could hear, "You will see her, but the past cannot be undone, not until death has arrived and you are covered by your shroud . . ."

7. The cold stream, running over a submerged stone, babbled, "Timelessness . . ."

1. The beckoning horn soon announced the newly appeared ruler of these lands, and knights lined the roads to pay tribute to the far northern city.

1. From the throne the young ruler spoke new words: "I have brought light from the peaks . . .

2. Let all be enlightened and none left in the darkness . . .

3. Before, you were called to the peaks for happiness, but now I will bestow it on you for free!

4. Go and take it . . ."

5. So she spoke in her snowy-shimmering robe and diamond crown, smiling a special smile . . . just slightly sad . . .

6. In her voice was the gasp of forgiveness that follows the storm, and in the curve of her mouth, memory of an extinguished sorrow . . .

1. Knights in armor came and kneeled before the throne, their plumed helmets in their hands.

2. To each she offered her hand, lily-white and aromatic, and they held it to their lips.

3. She smiled at each one.

4. But then a young swain kneeled, looking at the princess with eyes black as the grave.

5. He froze in fear.

6. Everyone noticed that she became ever so pale and the smile vanished from her crimson lips.

7. Then she coldly offered him her hand.

8. A fleeting cloud of sadness and inexpressible tenderness misted her gaze as he bowed his boisterous head before her.

9. When he looked at her, her gaze was once again covered in a veneer of indifference.

10. The knight left the throne room, stumbling, and never returned.

11. But the reception continued . . . Knights in armor kneeled before the throne, their plumed helmets in their hands.

12. The rays of the sunset, falling thought the high gothic windows, burned with a scarlet flame on their armor.

1. The young knight returned from the distant northern city. He spent his days and nights in his refuge of solitude.

2. A fountain splashed there. Cold streams of water echoed on the smooth marble.

3. It seemed like the rumbling of a pale fountain morning. The hearty laughter was infectious.

4. But it was just the cold streams of water.

5. From the depths of the basin, a sad countenance nodded at him—a weary reflection.

6. He whispered, "My dear, I know that we will see each other again, just not here.

7. I know that we will see each other again . . . Time will not forget us!

8. Where will this be?"

9. And so he gave himself up to his dreams, and the stream whispered sadly, "It will happen there, not here . . ."

1. One day the knight heard a rustle behind him; there stood the pensive woman in black: an abyss of timelessness was reflected in the deep eyes.

2. And he understood that she was death.

3. She bent over the seated figure and covered him with her black cloak. She led him to his final refuge.

4. They walked along the riverbank. The lead-colored waves reached their feet.

5. Their cloaks, dark as night, billowed like sails blown by the north wind.

6. So they walked along the riverbank, lit by the golden dawn.

1. From that day, the knight was nowhere to be seen. Later they would talk about that memorable morning.

2. That morning they had seen a skeleton.

3. It was dragging itself to the castle at sunrise, rustling the dead leaves.

4. It pressed a fiddle to its ribs and the autumn was filled with the screeching dance of death that wafted from its bow.

1. Cold clouds blew past. The forest underbrush scattered.

2. A stooped colossus rested by the silver stream. He sat with his humongous head in his hands. He mourned for the years . . . the past . . .

3. He was alone in this world. Really, he was just a fairy tale.

4. The stooped giant sighed deeply, his humongous head in his hands . . .

5. The cold stream babbled, "Timelessness . . ." The river creature's carefree head peeked above the water . . .

6. It danced and swam . . . It smiled with amazement. It laughed loudly, loudly . . . It swam away downstream . . .

7. The stooped giant mournfully shook his ancient head. He sat lost in thought for a long time . . .

8. Then he walked among the treetops, alone, inscrutable . . .

9. It was quiet . . .

10. The cold stream . . . babbled, "Timelessness . . ."

1. Eternally young, she sat on the throne. Around her stood gray knights, her trusted servants.

2. Suddenly the setting sun stole in with its golden rays. And the princess's breast, covered in precious stones, blazed with little flames.

3. A strange bird flew in from the open terrace. White, white. With a dreamy squawk it pressed against her fiery breast.

4. Everybody shuddered with surprise: sparks of revelation glimmered in the white bird's clear gaze. The princess said, "She wants me to follow her . . . I will be leaving you for Eternity!"

5. Having said that, she offered her hand to the oldest knight, dressed in his armor, and pearls of tears flowed down his old cheeks.

6. Resting on his arm, she stepped off the throne and blew a sad kiss to the knights.

7. She stepped onto the terrace. She looked at the white bird, showing her the way. She slowly slid forward, carried by the wind.

8. She smiled and whispered, "I know."

1. The distraught knights stood in the hall, resting on their swords and bowing their plumed heads . . . They said, "Do the old days of horror really have to come back! . . ."

2. But then the empty throne blazed with a white glow, and they looked at the glowing throne in ecstasy. The oldest knight cried, "It's a memory of her!

3. She will forever be with us! . . ."

1. . . . .
. . . .

. . . .

. . . .

2. The hall was golden. Along the walls were thrones, and on the thrones sat the northern kings in their purple mantles and golden crowns.

3. They sat motionless on the thrones—gray-haired, long-bearded, their shaggy brows lowered, their bare arms crossed.

4. Among them there was one whose mantle was bloodier than the rest, whose beard was longer than the rest . . .

5. A lamp burned before each.

6. It was a spring night. The moon looked in through the window. . . . .

. . . .

. . . .

7. Devoted servants came out. They carried bowls with intoxicating wines on silver chargers. They brought the intoxicating wines to the northern kings.

8. Each king rose from his heavy throne and took the proffered bowl with a bare arm, saying in a low, halting voice, "Glory to the late princess! . . ."

9. Then he drank the bloody wine.

10. After all the others, the last king rose, the one whose mantle was bloodier than the rest, whose beard was whiter than the rest.

11. He looked through the window, and in the window the red moon was hidden behind the pines. The pale dawn was spreading.

12. He started singing in a coarse voice, praising the life of the late princess . . .

13. He sang, "The starlight fades. Sadness is better.

14. O, dawn!

15. Let the morning flash with the fiery abyss of mother of pearl!

16. O, dawn! . . . Burn off the mist! . . .

17. She was and then she wasn't . . . But all know about her.

18. The tender starlight of the saints hovers above her!"

19. The others joined in, "Let the morning burn with the fiery abyss of mother of . . .

20. pearl . . ."

21. So the choir of northern kings resounded.

22. As the night grew paler, the lamps grew paler and were extinguished, and the kings were shrouded in fog.

23. These were the deceased kings, extinguishing with the night.

24. Only one remained unextinguished the longest, the one whose mantle was bloodier than the rest, whose beard was longer than the rest . . .

25. . . . .
. . . .
. . . .
. . . .

1. The pale morning's horizon was bathed in damp yellow tones. Blue blocks filled the horizon.

2. Block piled upon block. They formed patterns and built castles.

3. Fiery zigzags rumbled in the blue clouds.

1. In the pale morning, the colossus Riza would walk among the clouds.

2. Quietly, Riza would knock over the blue blocks, wading up to his knees in the clouds.

3. At the hour of the foggy sunrise, he sat on a cloud by the horizon, cupping his clean-shaven face.

4. Riza's stony face silently laughed, and he trained his glassy eyes on the distance.

5. He sent his cloak flying toward the heavens and let it float off on the wind.

6. He slid the blue clouds into place. He vanished, burnt by the sun . . .

PART FOUR

1. To the right and to the left were the blue expanses of a lake, covered by white clouds.

2. Sleepy waves poked up in the middle of these expanses and the snow-white flowers of oblivion bobbed on the sleepy waves.

1. Familiar lotuses bobbed on the water, and strange planetary cries carried over the lake's depths.

2. It was the cry of unfamiliar birds dipping their white breasts into the blue waves.

3. On and near the islands they relaxed in their white outfits with their flowing hair, as if they were frozen in place. They nodded to the worried birds with a barely noticeable greeting. They were welcoming their brothers who were arriving to this final refuge.

4. A giant sphinx loomed on the clear horizon. It raised its paws and bellowed a last hymn to insanity and the dark.

5. The men and women in white watched the final nightmare dissipate with exhausted eyes. They sat calmly, bidding farewell to the foul weather.

6. Deep rumblings abounded, and it seemed to be the song of starry dreams and oblivion: it was the lotuses splashing in the murky water.

1. When the last remnants of smoke and darkness dispersed, a familiar and slightly sad figure stood on the horizon in a mantle of snowy clouds and a crown of white roses.

2. He walked along the horizon among the lotuses. He paused and bent his beautiful profile to the depths of the lake, lit with a barely visible greenish halo.

3. He dropped a rose into the depths of the lake to comfort his drowned brother.

4. He raised his head. He smiled a familiar smile . . . Slightly sad . . .

5. And once again, he walked along the horizon. Everybody understood who was wandering through their lands.

1. The clouds spread out and settled. Adam and Eve walked beside the bank, up to their knees in water. Their Old Testament sackcloth robes fluttered.

2. Adam led wrinkled, thousand-year-old Eve by the hand. Her hair, white as death, fell onto her withered shoulders.

3. They were walking to familiar, lost lands. They lit up with ecstasy and laughed with the blessed laughter of the old. They were remembering forgotten places.

4. Red flamingos walked along the bank, and you could still make out his long silhouette on the horizon.

1. Happiness lived here—young like first snow, light like the waves' dreams.

2. White.

3. The horrors were disappearing in the blue sky.

4. A shameful pink glimmer flickered on the horizon at times, like good news about better days.

5. Here and there birds dozed on their long, thin legs—they were dreaming. At times the dreamers spread their light wings and, tearing themselves away, flew off.

6. The surroundings were filled with shrill, sleepy cries.

7. And there . . . high up . . . they folded their long wings and fell back into the cold abyss of oblivion.

8. Barely audible sighs emanated from these sleepy flights and sleepy falls.

9. Ah! . . . Here they forgot about work and captivity! They didn't speak of anything. They forgot everything and knew everything!

10. They rejoiced. They didn't dance, but they flew in graceful, cosmic harmony. They laughed with a blessed aquatic laugh.

11. And when they grew tired, they froze.

12. They froze in chaste ecstasy, entering the sleepy happiness of the cold blue waves.

1. The newly pronounced saint walked in the water up to her knees.

2. She walked along the bank, the water up to her knees, there . . . to the unknown expanse of the lake.

3. From the depths of the lake, somewhere off to the side, the face of a friend, frozen with grief, protruded and looked at her with astonished eyes.

4. It was the head of the knight who had drowned in the abyss of timelessness . . . But the hour of their meeting had not yet arrived.

5. Her saved friend became a little sad and dipped his pale face in the waves, his peaceful profile submerged among the white flowers of oblivion.

1. All around was the blue splashing of the lake.

2. There was just one small island, blessed and overgrown with sedge.

3. In the east was free purity and a shameful pink glimmer. A star flickered. It was reflected in the waves and shook with timidity.

4. That was the evening star.

5. A refreshing breeze blew from the north.

6. Spots of mist disappeared along the western horizon. Fluffy clouds spread out and settled. These were sleepy mysteries.

7. Mystery after mystery floated along the misty west.

1. She sat on the island, dressed in white, in white, and looked into the distance.

2. She had come here from the terrestrial lands ... Happiness was still in store for her.

3. And so she sat, tired and peaceful after a day of wandering.

4. Two birds circled above her.

5. The two birds were two dreamers.

1. The day passed. Sleepy, she rested her head in the sedge. The sedge dripped tears onto her head. She slept.

2. In her dream she followed the two strange birds.

3. They walked near the island along the bank. They spoke of the white mysteries.

4. And then the first miracle in these lands commenced.

5. In her dream she watched as an old man walked along the sandy bank, pounding a heavenly walking stick.

6. It was the night watchman.

7. He walked along the border of the Land of Nod. He called out to the other night watchmen, all old men.

1. She awoke in the morning. A shameful pink glimmer flickered in the east.

2. Venus, the Morning Star, shone.

3. Along the bank wandered a wizened old man in a white mantle.

4. With one hand he held a large key, and he gently wagged the other at the righteous young woman.

5. Stooped over and happy, he pressed her cold hands. In a heartfelt voice he shouted dozy ramblings.

6. He jestingly cried that they all had children, brothers, and sisters.

7. He said that the final sanctuary wasn't here. He advised his sister to keep on the northeastern road.

8. The old porter congratulated his sister on her sainthood. He counted the days of abundance on his fingers.

9. He announced that they don't have name saints, only blessed ones.

10. With his eyes he gestured toward forgotten places.

11. The old jester would have revealed much more to her, but he cut off his tender speech. He set off wandering along the bank with quick steps, hurrying to carry out his task.

12. And she set off to the northeast.

1. There, where she had stood, was now empty. There was just a small blessed island overgrown with sedge.

2. All over there was the blue splashing of the lake.

3. Waves crashed onto the blessed island. Then they returned to the blue expanse.

4. Two white birds sat and vied with one another to sing about what had happened. These were the dreamers.

5. And they flew off into the misty west.

1. In this land were blessed undergrowths of reed. They were scored with canals, emerald green and mirrorlike.

2. Occasionally a wave with a foamy crest broke here, coming from the unfathomable watery expanse.

3. In the undergrowths of reed lived the saints of the reed, not worried by grief, expecting a better life.

4. Occasionally they were transfigured and shone with a silver light. But they dreamed about the Ascension.

5. She wandered there, pushing aside the stems of the pliable reeds, and on the other side of the canal over the reeds was the dull yellow sunset.

6. The sunset over the reeds.

1. Occasionally she met a young hermit, sleepy, sad and reedy, in a mantle of white clouds and a crown of white roses.

2. His eyes were blue, and his beard and long curls were chestnut.

3. Occasionally he looked her in the eye, and it seemed to her that underneath his sad demeanor he hid a smile.

4. Looking at her, he was filled with joyous understanding, and his mantle turned dull yellow from the sunset . . .

5. A homeless cloud roamed on the outskirts.

1. Occasionally, from the depths of the water of the canal, some-one white emerges, white like a drowned man from the abyss of timelessness.

2. She is accustomed to seeing the drowned man, emerging to perch on the evening sunset.

3. Once the reedy hermit said to her, "Do you see the one who sits on the evening sunset having emerged from the abyss of time-lessness, the one who has drowned before his time?

4. The period of his drowning is up . . . If you go to him, the past will be gone . . ."

5. She went to the one who was sitting in sleepy oblivion and recognized her friend.

6. Their deep gazes met. They quietly rejoiced in the unexpected encounter.

1. They smiled at each other, the white children, sadly contemplative.

2. The reedy hermit in a mantle of white clouds and a crown of white roses approached them. He spoke of a great mystery that would be upon them.

3. He broke off his speech with a deep sigh, saying to himself, "White children."

4. He stood for a long time in contemplation.

5. A dreamer-bird wended its way out of the bushes. With a piercing cry it flew off into the pink distance.

1. The day passed. The light water, tenderly foaming, lapped against the green bank.

2. Here they sat and watched the sunset. The snowy-pink foam bathed their feet.

3. Tall reeds grew on this side of the gulf. They watched the sun, still visible through the stems of the pliable reeds.

4. From there came the old man's song.

5. Among the reeds sat the graying Abba,[10] a holy fool with a blessed wrinkled face.

6. Dear sweet Abba cast a long line to catch the water's abundance.

7. His feeble voice praised the reedy land.

8. They laughed loudly. The fool saw them. He giggled and wagged his old finger at them.

1. The evening sky had extinguished its last fire, and the homeless cloud roamed on the outskirts.

2. Dear sweet Abba packed up his rods. He was heading home. He slung the thin rods over his shoulder. He picked up his wooden bucket and made his way back.

3. His singing had faded away when the large red moon floated out from behind a cloud.

4. They were quiet.

5. The homeless cloud roamed on the outskirts.

1. The reedy inhabitants would walk to the garden on the lake shore. There sedge, lilies, and daffodils grew.

2. You could hear cosmic sighs about the rings of Saturn and eternally shining Sirius.

3. Farther were patches of irises. In the evening dusk, the Lord God Himself, wrapped in clouds, strolled along these patches and made the irises sway.

4. And then it was cloudy . . . As if someone blanketed it with a fragrant steam. It seemed that they were singing a cosmic song about the rings of Saturn and eternally rejoicing Sirius into your ear.

1. They often sat on the bank drinking in the sapphire hues with their eyes.

2. A breeze blew. They frowned from the waft of fresh air. They were comforted by the white sigh of the reed. It captivated them.

3. The reedy lands sang and bowed before the onslaught of strong wind . . .

4. Someone was waving a blue iris at them . . .

1. The service was finishing up in the undergrowth of reeds. A smoky cloud rose from there into the sky.

2. At that time, the caretaker of these lands—Iya—emerged from the trees. She went up to the ones who were strolling and directed them as a local, as one in a dream.

3. And when they told her about their white joy, she said, "Is *that* joy?"

4. She was silent and looked off in the distance.

5. The day came to an end, and the song of love and the unity of the constellations echoed even closer.

1. Smoky blue masses moved along the dull yellow horizon.

2. Boulder piled upon boulder. They sketched out plans and built castles.

3. Fiery zigzags rumbled in the blue clouds.

1. And then in between the clouds they saw groups of titans.

2. Silently and majestically, the titans lumbered, misty and smoky blue in glowing, shimmering crowns.

3. They silently parted their hands. They prayed for peace and compassion.

4. Homeless wanderers—for thousands of years they roamed this poor, this northern land.

5. Finally they departed the world, mysteries. They were just a fairy tale!

6. And so silently and majestically, the homeless wanderers lumbered, misty and smoky blue in glowing, shimmering crowns.

1. It was quiet. A star flickered somewhere.

2. Finally Iya said, "That's the old giants.

3. They've given in. They're asking God for peace and compassion.

4. Long ago, the giant would lift his haughty, stony white face crowned with the sunset before the Lord.

5. Long ago they lifted the clouds and moved boulders. Boulder piled upon boulder. They formed patterns and built castles.

6. But they all fell under the weight of the boulders, and the cloudy towers quietly faded into the evening sky.

7. And they were fated to roam for many years among the blue clouds—the remnants of their past greatness . . .

8. That's the old giants . . . They've given in and are asking God for peace and compassion . . ."

9. So she spoke as they watched the blue cupolas, and their clean-shaven white-stoned faces, crowned with the dusk, glimmered among the blue cupolas.

10. That's the old giants who are advancing in a silent crowd to ask God for peace and compassion.

11. The low, threatening clouds blotted them out.

12. Then their smoky blue silhouettes, lit with flashes of the sunset, appeared again.

1. So she spoke. The clouds dissipated. The giants passed by. It was quiet.

2. A light breeze blew. The shadow of an unknown titan stretched over the whole land.

3. The unfamiliar titan stood proud and free in a glowing shimmering crown.

4. This was the most terrible, the greatest titan.

5. In days long past he would lift hunks of blue clouds, flashing with silver lightning.

6. He would flex his muscles and throw the thundering hunks of blue clouds into the evening sky. He tossed clouds into the sky like stones.

7. But he broke down and fell, crushed by clouds.

8. Since then he had stayed clear of people. They forgot about him, and he became a fairy tale for them.

9. He was the one who wanted to be lost in oblivion, to sleep the eternal slumber. He left the world, a mystery.

10. He went straight to God, but along the way he was lost in thought.

11. His legs were covered in clouds, and only his crowned head, lit with a pink luster, stood out.

12. So the lonely titan stood in the distance, wrapped in the evening darkness.

13. The sunset was extinguished.

14. A homeless cloud roamed on the outskirts.

1. Then Iya whispered, "*This* is happiness!

2. It will come on the dawn after the night. It will be unexpected.

3. The old giants have already gone to their God.

4. And He walked among us, like a roaming flame . . .

5. The day of our ascension is approaching . . .

6. The happiness of the dusk will fade before a new, third, happiness, the happiness of the Comforting Holy Spirit . . ."

7. Crimson spots appeared on the white waves. The moon hung over the lake.

1. The night continued. All three of them stood on the shore, shielding the moonlight with their hands.

2. In front of them was water and above the water, the moon; it seemed to them that fear had died.

3. The dreamer-bird sank into the distant lake, lost in slumber.

4. Once more Iya said, "*This* is happiness! . . ." The homeless cloud began to vanish.

1. At midnight, everything became clear and well-defined. They heard something in the iris growths. They diverted their eyes.

2. Distant Saturn shone. They looked at the sky. They were waiting for a new star.

3. An old man in a white mantle holding a key walked along the bank. The moon lit his bald spot. A stranger was with him.

4. They both wore long robes, wrapped in a pale glow. They were deep in conversation. They nodded toward the east.

5. Iya shouted at them, "A moonlit night!" The old man laughed and wagged his key . . .

6. "This is it," he shouted ecstatically, "and just see what will be in the morning! . . .

7. All of your stars, even Sirius and the Moon, aren't worth one single Morning Star . . ."

8. He said that, broke off his tender speech, and ran into the distance rushing to complete his task.

1. They were left with the stranger. In a saintly voice he shouted that the time was near.

2. That this was their last night; that at dawn he would wake them and show them the One Who Has Appeared.

3. Just see what will be, will be—he will be announced and all will fly away . . .

4. This was a powerful old man with the gaze of an eagle, and Iya whispered, "Listen to him. He is the first to know these mysteries. He knows many wonders. He will astound us yet."

5. Deeply shaken, they followed the departure of the strange old man, wrapped in a pale glow, with their eyes.

1. In the morning everything went gray. The red moon had sunk. Iya remained alone on the shore.

2. Iya, the guardian, turned into a white seagull and, with a cry, flew off into the sapphire blueness.

3. The red moon had sunk.

1. They arrived at their reedy home. They were lost in the dream of a sleepy fairy tale. It was the last night.

2. They dreamed . . . A white figure, dressed in a mantle of snowy clouds, strolled along the expanse of a lake, shedding his melting smiles, ever so sad, into the depths of the lake.

3. A greenish halo glowed over his head. They knew He was their reedy hermit.

4. In an inexpressible voice He said to them, "White children!

5. White children, let us ascend into pure joy with the morning wind! . . ."

6. In the dream they heard a bird whistle: the dreamer-birds sat on the bank and vied with one another to sing about what had happened.

1. He whispered to them, "White children! . . ." His voice trembled with sadness.

2. "White children . . . We shall not die, but soon, in the blink of an eye, we'll be transformed, just as soon as the sun rises.

3. The sun is rising . . .

4. White children! . . ."

5. They awoke . . . They saw that their dream was not a dream, because they saw him standing there, pushing aside the stems of the reeds, whispering to them all that they had dreamed . . .

6. In the distance they could hear the strange old man's voice, summoning everyone to the white joy . . .

7. A silver bell tolled.

1. An old man lived on the lake, where the shaggy cliff was covered in pine trees.

2. He woke at dawn. He drowsily climbed to the peak. He rang the silver bell.

3. This was a sign that the Morning Star was already shining in the east.

4. Venus . . .

1. A silver bell tolled.

December, 1900.

DRAMATIC SYMPHONY

(Second)

IN LIEU OF A PREFACE

The unusual form of this work compels me to offer a few explanatory words.

The work has three types of meaning: musical, satirical, and, additionally, conceptual-symbolic. For one thing, this is a symphony, the purpose of which is to express a series of moods that are linked to one another by a primary mood (atmosphere, frame of mind). This gives rise to the necessity of dividing it into parts, the parts into fragments, and the fragments into verses (musical phrases). Frequent repetition of some of the musical phrases reinforces this division.

The second type of meaning is satirical: here certain extremes of mysticism are ridiculed. The question arises whether a satirical approach to people and events that a great many people doubt even exist is warranted. By way of reply, I would suggest they take a closer look at their surrounding world.

Finally, beneath the musical and satirical layers of meaning, an attentive reader may begin to see as well the conceptual meaning, which, as it becomes dominant, does not destroy the musical or satirical layers. The combination of all three aspects in a single fragment or verse leads to Symbolism . . .

Moscow

September 26, 1901

PART ONE

1. The workday was humid. The street shimmered blindingly.

2. Cabbies trembled, turning their threadbare blue backs to the hot sun.

3. Janitors swept up a pillar of dust, unmoved by the grimaces of the passersby, cackling their dust-brown faces.

4. On the sidewalk ran *raznochintsy*,[1] exhausted by the heat, and suspicious-looking members of the middle class.

5. Everyone was pale, and above them all hung the firmament—blue, gray-blue, then gray, then black, full of musical ennui, eternal ennui, with the sun's eye in the center.

6. From it flowed streams of molten metal.

7. Each person was scurrying someplace for some reason, afraid to look truth in the eye.

1. The poet was writing a poem about love and had trouble with the rhyme, but still made an ink blot; turning his eyes to the window, he was frightened by the heavenly ennui.

2. The gray-blue firmament with the sun's eye in the middle smiled at him.

1. Two people were arguing over a cup of tea about important and unimportant people. Their cracking voices were hoarse from arguing.

2. One sat with his elbows on the table. He lifted his eyes to the window. *He saw.* He broke off all threads of the conversation. He caught the smile of eternal ennui.

3. The other leaned a half-blind face, covered in pockmarks, toward him and, spraying his adversary with spittle, finished shouting his objections.

4. But the other one didn't want to wipe his face with a handkerchief; he had plunged into the depths, had dived into the abyss.

5. And the gleeful opponent leaned back in his chair and looked at the silent one from under his gold-framed glasses with kind, dumb eyes.

6. He knew nothing of the uncovering of the last veil.

7. And on the road, where it was humid and blindingly white, the street cleaners drove by in their blue jackets.

8. They sat on barrels, and from the barrels poured water.

1. Big as the mountains, the houses bristled and swaggered like overfed swine.

2. To the timid pedestrian they winked with their countless windows, turned their blind walls to him in a sign of disdain, or mocked his secret thoughts with columns of smoke.

3. At those days and hours, in the proper places, papers and documents were copied, and the rooster led the chickens through the paved courtyard.

4. In the courtyard there were also two gray guinea hens.

5. On a large canvas, the talented artist painted a "miracle,"[2] while in the butcher's shop hung twenty gutted carcasses.

6. And everyone knew this, and everyone overlooked it, afraid to turn their eyes toward the ennui.

7. But it stood over everybody's shoulders, an invisible, hazy outline.

8. Even though the street cleaners comforted each and every person by dispersing the muck, and on the boulevard children were playing with hoops.

9. Even though the blue firmament smiled in everyone's eyes, the gray-blue firmament, the heavenly and frightening firmament with the sun's eye in the center.

10. From there came the sad and severe songs of a great Eternity, the Eternity who reigns.

11. And these songs were like musical scales. Scales from an invisible world. Eternally the same, the same. Barely had they finished when then began again.[3]

12. Barely had they calmed down, and then became agitated again.

13. Eternally the same, the same, without beginning and end.

1. The day came to an end. On Prechistensky Boulevard[4] they were playing military tunes—no one knew why—and out onto the boulevard had come numerous inhabitants of the buildings and taverns, no one knew where from. They walked back and forth along the boulevard. They stood in front of the music, crowding and shoving one another.

2. The shenanigans began; they pawed ladies' dresses; a person with a cane waved it around and around. The horn players, lowering their brows, belted out, "Laugh, clown, at your shattered love, laugh because life is forever poisoned."[5]

3. A pale green hunchback with a bandaged cheek strolled to the music accompanied by his anemic wife and limping excuse for a son.

4. He was wearing a yellow coat, fiery gloves, and a giant top hat. It was the doctor from the city hospital.

5. Just yesterday he had sent a consumptive to the madhouse. The consumptive had unexpectedly opened an abyss in front of everyone in the hospital.

6. At this the madman quietly whispered, "I know you, Eternity!"

7. Everyone was horrified hearing about what was concealed, so they called for the hunchbacked doctor and got rid of that brazen consumptive.

8. That was yesterday, and today the hunchbacked doctor strolled to the music with his anemic wife and limping excuse for a son . . .

1. The fashionable store had an elevator. The operator flew up and down in a frenzy through four stories.

2. Crowds of men and ladies stood everywhere, bursting into the cabin crushing and cursing one another.

3. Even though there was also a staircase.

4. And above this tussle, from time to time, a wooden voice resounded, grandly and mysteriously: "Account."

1. A handsome youth in a worn double-breasted coat and with an excessively dirty neck and black fingernails stood by the window of a bookstore.

2. He looked wistfully at a copy of Maksim Gorky's[6] writings in German translation and scratched his chin.

3. A carriage stood in front of the bookstore. A sweaty coachman with a magnanimous face, a black mustache, and bushy eyebrows sat on the box.

4. Like a second Nietzsche.

5. A fat swine with a snout and wearing an expensive overcoat bounded out of the store.

6. It oinked, catching sight of an attractive woman, and lazily hopped into the carriage.

7. Nietzsche took the reins, and the swine, pulled by the horses, wiped sweat from his forehead.

8. The student stood in front of the bookstore window a while and then went his own way, working to maintain an independent bearing.

1. Many other horrors occurred . . .

1. It was getting dark. There was a blue puff of smoke in the east, sad and foggy and eternally dull, while the sounds of an orchestra wafted from the boulevard.

2. Each person shed their ennui, and little boys and girls ran around the streets with bouquets of forget-me-nots.

3. At that hour one could meet gloomy cyclists going in every direction. They worked their legs and hunched their backs with sweat in their faces; they threatened with their bells and scanned with their eyes, chasing one another.

4. At that hour the philosopher returned home with deliberate steps carrying *Critique of Pure Reason*[7] under his arm.

5. He crossed paths with a gentleman in a cab, with tufts of a red beard and wearing a bowler hat.

6. He was shining the knob of his cane, singing a merry chanson.

7. They exchanged bows. With deliberate carelessness, the philosopher touched his cap, and the man in the carriage spread his lips, revealing rotting teeth, and gave a friendly wave.

8. He wasn't very smart, but his father was known for his intelligence . . .

9. The spot where they honored each other with greetings emptied out . . . To the right, there was the philosopher's back and the spine of *Critique of Pure Reason*, and to the left the hunched coachman drove his nag, carrying the gray-haired man off.

10. Above the empty space, mournful sounds resounded from an open window: "Auuu, auuu."

11. It was the singer from the conservatory warming up her voice.

1. The philosopher rang the bell. When the door opened, he tossed *Critique of Pure Reason* on the table and collapsed on his bed in pointless ennui.

2. His last thought was, "Kant without Plato is a body without a head." He fell asleep, and his thoughts were also headless.

3. And the bust of Immanuel Kant, sitting on the desk, rocked reproachfully and stuck its tongue out at the sleeping philosopher.

4. The philosopher slept. And above him shadows congealed, eternally the same, the same, stern and soft, mercilessly dreamy.

5. Eternity herself strolled around the lonely flat; she banged and giggled in the next room.

6. She sat in an empty chair and adjusted the framed pictures.

7. The bookshelves were already casting stark shadows, the shadows intersected and, intersecting, congealed . . . As if they were hiding in the shadows.

8. But nobody was there except Immanuel Kant and Plato in the form of busts sitting on the table.

9. Kant complained to Plato of the young philosopher's dimwittedness while the philosopher slept in the evening dusk with a pale ironic face and clenched lips . . . Even a small child could have smothered him.

10. A fresh breeze after a hot day crept in through the open window and blew over him.

11. From the open window also came thuds: the basement inhabitants had dragged their furniture into the courtyard and were beating the dust from it.

12. And he woke up: his first thought was about the possibility of unifying the teachings of Kant and Plato; and he lifted his head from the crumpled pillow; and he shuddered from the evening chill.

13. The moon, starkly outlined on dark blue enamel, looked him straight in the eye . . . A red moon.

14. He jumped up in horror and clutched his head; like one madly in love he drank in the pale surroundings.

15. If one were to peek at him through the widow, it would be terrible to see his face: pale, dim with shadows, tired.

16. He looked eternally the same, the same during the spring full moon.

17. His nerves were frayed, and he resorted to valerian drops.

1. And in the next room there hung a gigantic mirror, reflecting eternally the same, the same.

2. The horror of absence and nonexistence was there.

3. The *Critique of Pure Reason* lay on the desk there.

1. It was midnight. The streets were empty.

2. There was one street along a sleepy river. Four side streets ran toward the river.

3. They were First Zachatevsky Street, Second Zachatevsky Street, Third Zachatevsky Street, and, finally, Fourth Zachatevsky Street.[8]

4. It was as if an eternal rehearsal was going on in the sky. Someone's finger played one and then another note.

5. First one, then another.

6. A person in a pince-nez and with a pointy nose ambled along the desolate sidewalk, lit by the flames of the streetlamps.

7. His feet were in galoshes. Under his arm he carried an umbrella, even though it was warm and dry.

8. In his arms he held a folio. This was the lives of the saints.

9. He stepped along silently, floating like a shadow.

10. He came from who knows where, and no one could say where he was heading.

11. A window on the opposite side of the street opened, and some people approached the window.

12. It was two women with indifferent, pale faces; they were thin and wore black caps.

13. They wore black. The elder indifferently pointed at the passerby and commented, "Popovsky."[9]

14. Popovsky had already walked by. No force on earth could say where he was heading.

15. There was desperate ennui. It was as if an eternal rehearsal was happening in the sky. Someone's finger played one and then another note.

16. First one, then another.

17. It had barely finished when it began again.

1. The street opened into a square. Popovsky was already meandering along the square.

2. A kerosine lamp smoked on the square.

3. Standing under the moon, you could see a giant black column of soot over the street lamp.

1. At night they robbed an apartment. Two wise guys broke the locks, but not finding anything better, made off with just an old pair of galoshes.

2. In the morning, before the sun even rose, the stones were glistening white. The cabbies hadn't come out yet. No passersby disturbed the quiet.

3. It was a bright desolation.

1. In the basements they slept. They slept in the attics. They slept in the wards. Rich and poor, smart and stupid—they all slept.

2. Some slept in a disorderly knot, some slept with their mouths open. Some snored. Some even looked like they were dead.

3. They all slept.

4. In the psychiatric ward, the ill slept just the same as the healthy; only one mentally ill melancholic, tormented by colic, walked beside the sickbeds.

5. With an ironic, pale face he shrugged his shoulders, bending toward the beastly dumb faces of the sleepers. Suddenly he covered his face with his hands and rocked with silent laughter.

6. With a cracking voice he yelled, "They can't not sleep or eat! They get undressed so that, covered with a blanket, they can die! They can't not put things in their mouth!

7. What are they doing?"

8. But then a sharp pain in his stomach interrupted his thoughts. He frowned.

9. A pink ray of sun struck the window frame and lit up the dry, mad face with a scarlet blaze.

10. And as if seized with insight, he shook his long skinny finger at the window where the glint of the pink morning shone.

11. Where the healthy slept just the same as the ill.

1. Popovsky was a conservative. Freethinkers hated him for his loose approach to their views.

2. This frail figure caused bright minds to knit their bald brows.

3. He was brazen enough not to be afraid of blank shots, and live rounds flew right over his head, because Popovsky was very short.

4. Popovsky was a churchgoer. He renounced the devil and progress. He supposed that we were in the end of days and anything that glistened with talent was of the devil.

5. He spotted minor demons flying at his acquaintances, and at night he read the Gospels.

6. Popovsky was a joker. His thin lips were always twisted into a barely visible smile. He looked for humor in all ideas and spoiled everything.

7. That was Popovsky, and no force in the world could change him.

1. All morning Popovsky had been going around to his acquaintances to tell them about everything he had read.

2. He was wearing galoshes and carrying a superfluous umbrella under his arm.

3. Carts were being dragged in various directions, and in the sky the gray-blue firmament shone, the frightening and dull firmament with the sun's eye in the center.

4. They were playing eternal exercises above the foggy city. And ennui, like a kind and familiar vision, was dancing on the seven hills.

5. And there ... up above ... someone distant and knowing would repeat day after day, "Pigsty."

6. The same, the same was repeated day after day.

1. At that moment the pale green hunchback, on his way to the hospital, bandaged his cheek: he had a toothache.

2. He bandaged it poorly. Two flaps dangled over his head.

3. And once more, someone *knowing* calmly said "Pigsty," and in a paved courtyard, the rooster grabbed his foe's comb.

4. Then everything was displaced, everything was torn apart, and all that remained was ... *the abyss.*

1. And the minutes passed. Passersby switched out like the minutes ... Each passerby had a minute of passing by each spot.

2. Each did everything at a particular time: you couldn't find a single one who could get by without time.

3. And time passed without stopping, and in the passing of time foggy Eternity was reflected.

1. In the course of the day Popovsky went to five places and in five places discussed five subjects.

2. In one place he developed his idea on the harmfulness of analysis and the superiority of synthesis.

3. In another place he articulated his views on the Apocalypse.

4. In a third place he didn't say anything since everything had already been said; here he played a game of chess.

5. In the fourth place he spoke of earthly vanity, and he was turned out of the fifth place.

6. Little Popovsky hung his head and headed to the sixth place.

1. On a major street, Popovsky met his enemy, the democrat.

2. He was well dressed and his glove-covered hand clasped a scarlet rose.

3. Popovsky was going his own way to talk about parish schools, and the democrat was taking a stroll with a walking stick in hand.

4. They exchanged mutual disdain. They bowed. Just yesterday, the democrat had littered Popovsky with abuses in the offices of a liberal newspaper.

5. And his venerable excellency, the liberal editor, all crimson and respectable, had added his own harsh words to the harsh words of the democrat.

6. That's what they called keeping in step with the era.

7. That was yesterday . . . And today the democrat was strolling down the street with a scarlet rose in his hand, turning his timid, dreamy eyes toward the sky.

8. He was already forgetting about Popovsky; the blue firmament looked him in the eye, no different for liberals than for conservatives.

1. Then the street cleaners arrived, continuing their war with the dust.

2. They were indifferent people, sitting on their barrels.

3. Water freely poured from the barrels, carrying unnecessary liquids away from the street and dispersing the dirt.

4. And the minutes passed. Passersby switched out like the minutes . . . Each passerby had a minute of passing by each spot.

5. And each barrel emptied at the appointed time. A street cleaner went to fill it.

1. Then the democrat caught sight of his fairy tale, the fairy tale of the democrat.

2. A carriage drove along the street, and on the box sat a stiff driver in a top hat and with an English whip.

3. In the carriage sat the fairy tale, the fairy tale of the democrat.

4. She had teeth of coral and blue, blue eyes, the eyes of a fairy tale.

5. She was the wife of a sea centaur who had been granted citizenship since the time of Böcklin.[10]

6. Before that he had snorted and dived among the waves, but then he decided to exchange his sea life for the turf.

7. Four hooves for two legs; then he put on a topcoat and became a person.

8. Her husband was a centaur, and she herself was a fairy tale and a sea nymph.

9. And so the fairy tale passed by, the fairy tale of the democrat, ever so slightly smiling to her dreamer who had lowered his blue gaze.

10. Covering in dirt a respectable old man in an old coat.

11. The respectable old man yelled and cursed the fairy tale, now flying off. He wiped his face, doused with mud, and hissed, "To hell with the rich . . ."

12. And he continued on his way to the editorial offices of the *Moscow News*,[11] carrying the lead article.

13. He had mocked her conservatism often, the democrat—elegant and dressed to the nines.

14. But that was for another day . . . And now he was lost in daydreams with a scarlet rose in his hand.

15. He neither saw nor heard. He remembered his fairy tale, smiled at the image of his blue-eyed nymph.

1. In the giant store with all the fashionable things, the elevator was working hard, and the operator glided in a frenzy through four stories.

2. He had barely arrived at the second floor, and they were already waiting for him on the third floor with their dumb impatient faces; he had barely arrived at the third floor when grumblings of discontent arose from the first.

3. And in the midst of this, Sodom here and there resounded mysterious voices: "Account."

1. A canary chirped in the basement level. A shoemaker worked here, watching the flickering legs of the passersby.

2. Shoes passed by with a squeak, yellow dress shoes, the complete absence of shoes passed by.

3. The crafty shoemaker saw all of this, happily twirling his drill through fresh leather.

4. A freight train rode on the Ryazan railroad carrying Cherkasian[12] bulls; the bulls stuck out their sleepy snouts, and the locomotive, like a madman, shouted.

5. It gloated and celebrated, pulling a train with bulls to the city slaughterhouse.

6. Everyone knew that. Each one was afraid to look truth in the eyes. And over everyone's shoulder stood ennui, opening an abyss among the trifles.

7. And the brave, who turned around, would suddenly tame it with a wag of their finger.

8. It was even more terrifying in the white sunshine of the day . . .

1. The sea centaur, who had been granted citizenship since the time of Böcklin, drove by.

2. His kind and corpulent silhouette wafted an elegant simplicity. Jet-black steeds pulled his carriage.

3. He *thought* . . .

1. The young philosopher read the *Critique of Pure Reason* while sitting in a swing rocking his feet.

2. He was alternately immersed in his reading or would drop the book to his knees and bang his head on the back of the swing while thinking over what he had read and improvising philosophical tricks and psychological jokes.

3. Reading about time and space and a priori forms of knowledge, he began to wonder if it was possible to put up a curtain that hid you from time and from space and let you escape from them into the depths of the abyss.

4. At that moment everything fell apart, all the strings, all the threads snapped, and the blue firmament, the gray-blue firmament smiled right at him, full of musical ennui with the sun's eye in the center.

5. And he quit reading. He went up to the giant mirror hanging in the next room. He gazed at himself.

6. In front of him stood a pale young man, not bad looking, with a head of hair clumped over his brow.

7. He stuck his tongue out at the pale young man as if to say to himself, "I'm mad." And the young man responded in kind.

8. So they stood one in front of the other with open mouths, one supposing about the other that he or they were touched.

9. And who could say that was for sure?

1. In order to settle down, he went up to the worn piano. He sat on the bench and opened the lid.

2. The piano bared its lower jaw so the person on the bench could strike its teeth.

3. And the philosopher banged on his old friend's teeth.

4. Bang after bang. And the philosopher's housekeeper stuffed her ears with cotton even though she was in the kitchen with the door shut.

5. This horror was the twitching of fingers, and it was called *improvisation*.

6. The door to the next room was open. There was a mirror. The mirror reflected the back of the person on the bench in front of the worn piano.

7. The other sitting person played the piano just like the first sitting person. They both sat back-to-back.

8. And so it went on infinitely . . .

1. But the doorbell rang. And the philosopher, closing the piano lid, went into the next room.

2. The room was still empty: only the *Critique of Pure Reason* sat on the table.

3. A woman entered wearing black and indifferently looked at the *Critique of Pure Reason*, resting her wrinkled face on a gloved hand.

4. She held a clutch in her hand . . . The sun was already setting; it went from fiery white to golden . . .

5. On the floor below, someone was having a tooth pulled.

1. But the philosopher, who had straightened up, entered and asked his guest to come into the sitting room.

2. The sitting-room furniture was covered. The black guest had her back to the giant mirror. She was a relative and spoke of sad events.

3. Her son had died. She buried him that day. Now she was alone in the world.

4. She had no one. She wasn't needed by anyone.

5. She received a pension. She had been wearing black for a decade.

6. So she spoke. Tears did not flow from her eyes.

7. And her voice was the same as ever. To an observer, it would seem that a slight smile flickered on her lips.

8. But that was grief.

9. She spoke of the death of her son in the same tone with which she ordered lunch the day before, and two days ago she had complained about the high cost of food in that tone.

10. She had already grown accustomed to sadness; trifles and important things all elicited the same feelings in her.

11. She mourned quietly.

12. She had already finished and was sitting with her head lowered, tapping her clutch with gloved fingers.

13. And he stood in front of her in a deliberate pose, cleaning his fingernails and saying, "You have to look at the world with a philosophical point of view."

14. But then the doorbell rang. Being family, he asked her to wait a minute and hurried off to meet his guest . . .

1. Popovsky stood in the next room with the "Lives of Saints Cosmas and Damian" under his arm.

2. They shook hands. They chatted as if they were both angels.

3. With an innocent smile they discussed the weather . . . Then they were silent . . . Then the philosopher hit the *Critique of Pure Reason* with his hand and said, "There's this one spot . . ."

4. And everything went on as it was written.

5. Soon Popovsky began grinding his thin teeth: this meant that he was a joker; soon he began checking that there weren't any demons here: this meant that he was a churchgoer.

6. And his adversary walked around the room making lovely and deliberate gestures and analyzing Schopenhauer with Kant.

7. Soon everything was muddled: only fragments of exclamations could be heard, "Postulate . . . Categorical imperative . . . Synthesis . . ."

8. And . . . in the next room his black guest sat casting her profile in the giant mirror.

9. She was waiting for her host like family and often squinted her minuscule brown eyes.

10. She didn't understand a thing. She caught fragments of phrases.

11. And next to her in the mirror sat another woman, just as black as she.

12. So she didn't wait for the philosopher and, like family, left without saying goodbye.

13. Putting on her galoshes, she said to the housekeeper, "My Petyusha died."

14. She wasn't thinking of anything. The parish deacon's words rang in her ears, "In the blessed sleep of eternal peace . . ."

15. He was a sonorous deacon.

1. The philosopher spoke for a long time. He spoke heatedly. He spoke to exhaustion until Popovsky left.

2. Tired and pale, he went to his room and collapsed on his bed.

3. His last thought was, "Wrong, wrong . . . Again, it's all wrong . . . Oh, if only I could hide! Oh, if only I could rest!"

4. He slept . . . And above him shadows congealed. Eternally the same, the same, stern and soft, mercilessly dreamy.

5. Eternity herself, in the guise of a guest in black, wandered through the lonely rooms, sat in empty chairs, fixed the framed pictures, eternally, like family.

6. The bookshelves were already frowning; and the shadows were intersecting and congealing.

7. So he slept in the hour of the spring dusk with a pale, ironic face and without a hint of deliberateness . . .

8. Even a small child could have smothered him.

9. His window was open. A warm breeze blew in.

10. From across the way, fat Dormidont Ivanovich looked from window to window, having come back from work.

11. Dormidont Ivanovich drank tea from a saucer and, looking through the widow at him, thought, "It would be interesting to know how much he pays for that apartment."

1. The gloomy cyclists appeared again; they were selling forget-me-nots again; and the music played on another boulevard, "Be daring, clown."

2. The seemingly respectable head of a family stood at the intersection of two streets with gray whiskers and dressed with dignity.

3. Nothing in his appearance was alarming; everything cohered, everything fit into the general plan.

4. He smoked an expensive cigar and discussed a commercial venture; his huge nose hinted at Armenian heritage.

5. This was a transient swindler from the south.

6. And toward him, like a swindler, ran a Moscow University professor coming from exams.

7. Neither one knew why they existed and what they were headed toward. Both were like students writing "extemporalia" but not knowing what mark they would receive.

1. The moon rose. Again, just like yesterday, it rose.

2. So it will also rise tomorrow, and the day after tomorrow.

3. But don't miss its involuntary waning.

1. The philosopher woke up . . . He lifted his head from the crumpled pillow . . . The moon, starkly outlined on dark blue enamel, looked him straight in the eye . . .

2. A red moon! . . .

3. The philosopher leapt up in horror. He clutched his head. Like one madly in love, he looked at the terrible disk.

1. At that time the democrat was writing a critical article for his journal. He caught sight of the moon. He flashed a sorrowful smile.

2. He dropped his pen and his thoughts, bounding and twirling, like excited little dogs.

3. He wiped his brow and whispered, "It's wrong, it's all wrong."

4. He remembered the fairy tale.

1. . . . A silk curtain was raised. Someone opened a window on that side of town.

2. It was a most fashionable and decadent house, and the fairy tale stood in the window.

3. She was fixing her red hair; she smiled, looking at the moon. She said "Yes . . . I know."

4. She looked with sad blue eyes, remembering her dreamer.

5. Jet-black horses stood by the door waiting for her, since it was her driving hour.

1. At that time the pale green hunchback, having returned from the hospital, was dining.

2. His cousin had arrived, complaining about his sufferings; he said how, in the evenings, it seemed to him that objects were moving about.

3. The hunchback patted his nervous cousin on the shoulder and kindly noted that this was nothing to worry about, these were "Dr. Kandinsky's pseudo-hallucinations."[13]

4. Having said that, he opened the piano and began playing Beethoven's *Sonata Pathétique*.

5. But his nervous relative couldn't take this; it seemed to the nervous relative that objects were moving about.

6. These were Dr. Kandinsky's pseudo-hallucinations.

7. But the hunchback continued to play the *Sonata Pathétique*. His eyes were stern. Two flaps dangled over his head.

8. He was a great sentimentalist.

9. And the sounds flowed . . . His limping little son stopped studying for his exam . . . He quietly teared up.

10. The housekeeper was already asleep. The lights in the living quarters were already out, even though there was no set bedtime. The pale green hunchback's mother-in-law stood on the kitchen threshold.

11. Her humongous stomach and swine-like face glowed in the play of the moonlight.

12. She cursed, like a scullery maid, waking up the sleeping scullery maid.

1. Popovsky walked along Ostozhenka Street[14] late at night.

2. No one knew where he was coming from, and no force on earth could alter his direction.

3. Two pale women in black opened a window across the street.

4. The elder indifferently pointed at the passerby and said drily, "Popovsky."

5. They were both mournful, as if they both lost a son. They both resembled one another.

6. One looked like the mirror image of the other.

1. The window of the decadent house was open, and in the window the outline of a Böcklin fairy tale flitted.

2. The fairy tale aimlessly paced around the room, and it seemed dark grief clouded her face.

3. Finally she said, "Ennui!" She sat in a chair.

4. And far, far away, as if taunting the world, there was a cry of "Alarm!" Police whistles echoed.

5. One person had smashed the nose of another because they were both drunk.

1. Late at night, everyone slept. In the sunny morning, rain fell horizontally.

2. The sun playfully chuckled through the downpour. The street cleaners had an entire half day off.

3. In the morning there was a typhoid victim's funeral in the church of "Nikola on Chicken Legs."[15] From there they carried his lilac coffin (the kind that easily fades), decorated in gaudy gold.

4. A priest walked in front with his ginger beard and red nose.

5. There were three carts behind; they were all stretched thin; they aimlessly rumbled along the difficult pavement.

6. The first cart was decorated in faded blue, the second in faded red, and you couldn't make out the color of the third.

7. It was very sad: there weren't enough organ grinders and jesters.

8. In the first cart, they sat and wept.

9. In the second, they just had sad faces.

10. Two old women sat in the third with pretty fat faces; one held a plate wrapped in cloth.

11. This was a dish of kutia.[16]

12. Both old women were talking animatedly, anticipating the memorial dinner.

13. In the procession was one already infected with typhus who was destined to be bedridden the next day.

14. And so the sad procession moved along to a distant cemetery.

1. The streets were all dug up. Some people with beastly faces placed the stones, others covered them with sand, and others pounded them with flatteners.

2. Off to the side was a pile of scraps: there were sheepskin coats, hats, pieces of bread, a soundly sleeping yellow mutt.

3. And there, where yesterday the foul-smelling tramp had sat showing all of the indifferent passersby his fake sore, they mixed asphalt.

4. Fumes wafted. The asphalt mixers would hang on iron rods for minutes on end stirring the black sludge in vats.

5. Then they'd pour the black sludge onto the sidewalk, sprinkle it with sand, and leave it to cool on its own.

6. The tired passersby avoided this stinking spot, hurrying off who knows where.

1. Today the one reading the *Critique of Pure Reason* was in full form.

2. He had found mistakes in Kant and built an entire original system from them.

3. He rooted around in his shelves of philosophical works, raising up an amazing amount of dust.

4. Across the street Dormidont Ivanovich's window was closed since Dormidont Ivanovich himself was at the Ministry of Finance.

5. He was a division head; the clerks adored him.

1. The dreamy democrat couldn't work a lick. Yesterday he had written a letter to his fairy-tale nymph, and today she would receive it.

2. He was supposed to be writing a critique of a conservative work. The democrat was supposed to ridicule the conservative author with withering remarks.

3. But his own thoughts seemed tepid, like lazy dogs. The pen dropped from his hand.

4. The pure blue laughed and joked right in his face. He dreamily stared out the window.

5. What had he done?

1. The blue-eyed nymph received the dreamer's letter. She was troubled with worry.

2. All day she glared at the kind centaur, wishing him misfortune.

3. The centaur fixed his collar and yelled at the lackeys.

4. He was a kind centaur. Misfortune weighed him down.

5. Before that, he had snorted and dived among the waves, and now it was all, all wrong.

1. The aristocratic old gentleman held soirees. Carriages lined up at his door on Fridays.

2. He hosted scholars, diplomats, and the upper echelons of society.

3. He was a kind old gentleman, and he didn't mind differing opinions.

4. Conservatives, liberals, and Marxists all loved the aristocratic old gentleman equally.

5. Here the great writer, a farmer and a count, would come without malice.[17]

6. The old gentleman, with a star on his chest, would pat each person on the shoulder and say to them all, "Yes, yes, of course . . ."

1. In the elegant living room, the old gentleman's stout spouse peppered the guests with pleasantries.

2. There were guests in topcoats and white ties; they were all pleasantly at ease and innocently elegant. They all emitted rays of light and had no idea they were shining.

3. Having gone through three stages of development, they had all become children: you wouldn't meet a mean lion or clumsy camel here. But this wasn't because the magnanimous old man didn't love them.

4. This was because the terrifying servants refused to let them in, no exceptions.

5. The old man's two young daughters moved among the guests, tapping them on the shoulder, "Would you like some tea?"

6. Many accepted, but others did not. Those were asked to go to the ballroom.

7. In the ballroom were young men in topcoats, dapper and feminine, amiably fibbing.

8. The young women, both pretty and not, picked up on the fibbing and took it to extremes.

9. Everyone was cheerful. Nobody worried about anything.

10. It seemed like heaven on earth.

1. The aristocratic old gentleman, tidy and clean-shaven and with a star on his chest, took one and then the other under the arm and led them to his study.

2. This was no banal study, but a room decorated with expensive copies of old master paintings.

3. The old man would sit each one across from himself and say something pleasant to each one.

4. He carried on an intelligent conversation with each one, and in this conversation, free and easy, nothing was off limits.

5. The diplomat agreed with the old man's suppositions; the old man showed the bureaucrat portraits of powerful people with their autographs.

6. He praised science to the scholar and once wept on the bosom of a student, lamenting the state of youth today.

7. To the cynic he showed uncensored French publications, closing the door first as a precaution.

8. The kind old man loved everybody and tried to make everyone comfortable.

1. The moon rose. Again, just like yesterday, it rose. So it will also rise tomorrow, and the day after tomorrow.

2. But don't miss its involuntary waning.

1. Popovsky's teeth hurt.

1. Supported by the plush carpet of the grand staircase, the elegant democrat made his way upstairs in his tailcoat.

2. Two clean-shaven men in tailcoats nearly knocked him off his feet by the entrance to the sitting room: one of them was holding a guitar.

3. They were heading to the ballroom, where the sounds of music echoed and young people, and even old people, blathered to the accompaniment of the piano.

4. The clean-shaven men in tailcoats said "pardon," and ran like mad past the democrat.

5. At the entrance to the sitting room, the democrat flippantly bent his perfumed head, conveying to all his elegant deference.

6. He listened more than he spoke: good manners demanded it of him.

7. But he was a critic and was met with silence.

1. Among the guests was a young man with a long nose and sweaty hands: this was a fashionable musician.

2. A talented artist was there as well, the one who had painted a large canvas, a "miracle."

3. A familiar philosopher was there as well, because he was talented.

4. An important conservative figure was there as well, one who had something to do with the press.

5. The important figure chatted with the brilliant democrat. She made a pleasant gesture with her hands and, gently smiling, said in

a velvet voice, "The difference in our convictions doesn't mean we can't appreciate one another."

6. And the brilliant democrat bent his perfumed head, expressing his total impartiality.

1. The aristocratic old gentleman himself was not there. He was sitting in his study with an old philanthropic prince.

2. The old men bent their old, shaven faces at one other and talked about the nonsense that was popular these days.

3. The philanthropic prince lamented the repeal of serfdom,[18] and his hospitable host chewed on his toothless gums and interjected, "Yes, yes, of course."

1. The fairy tale entered the sitting room with soft, noiseless steps.

2. She was wearing a light gray dress embroidered with pale silver leaves. She wore a diamond star in her red hair.

3. She walked quietly and gently, as if concealing her elegance with simplicity.

4. This was the epitome of aristocratic ease.

5. The young democrat tripped up mid-word, and the ground flew out from under his feet.

6. And behind the fairy-tale nymph grew the outline of her centaur, whose head flowed into his neck, his neck into his shirt, and his shirt into his coat.

7. The hostess said, "I think we're all acquainted here," but, remembering, introduced the fairy tale to the democrat.

1. They shook one another's hand, and the democrat felt the piercing gaze of blue eyes.

2. It was a tender gaze. The democrat understood that she was not cross with him over the letter.

3. Sounds of a piano came from the ballroom. There, elegant youths succumbed to refined pleasures.

4. And they were already speaking to one another in exaggeratedly kind and politely sugary expressions, as if nothing were wrong.

5. Even though every one of the democrat's words contained an accompaniment. This accompaniment meant, "It's wrong, it's wrong."

6. Böcklin's fairy tale listened to this empty speech playfully and empathetically, saying "really" or "go on, how interesting."

7. But under this "go on" was concealed her answer to his "it's wrong": "Yes, yes, I know . . ."

8. This was a refined and playful game with a bit of wit.

1. "Do you like music?" the fairy tale said to the democrat, and he answered, "No, I don't" as if his words were accompanied by three asterisks.

2. These three asterisks meant, "I love music more than anything on earth except you."

3. And the fairy tale replied, "Anyway, such a serious person doesn't need music." And with that were three asterisks.

4. And those three asterisks meant, read instead, "You're a smart one."

5. Then the fairy tale turned with tender nonchalance to the stout hostess saying, "You'll be at the flower festival, of course?"

6. But then the eldest daughter of the radiant old man appeared in the doorway and invited the democrat to join their happy party, pointing her tortoise-shell lorgnette at him.

7. His heart aching, he nodded and followed the thin maiden, knowing that *this* would please the blue-eyed nymph.

8. In the ballroom, young men and young women pleasantly fibbed.

9. Among them was the gloomy philosopher, who was looking through the window at the moon, ringed with smoke, disappearing into the terrifying abyss.

10. He had found awful gaps in his new system. The infallibility of the *Critique of Pure Reason* arose in his mind's eye like a disappointing spot.

11. His nerves were frayed.

1. The stout centaur, all simplicity and accuracy, sat next to the talented artist who had painted a "miracle."

2. He wanted to buy the "miracle" and so, for the time being, patiently listened to a speech about the issues with oil painting.

1. There was singing in the ballroom. A clean-shaven man in a topcoat played on the piano.

2. He danced on the edge of the stool, raising his hands over the keyboard, resting his whole body on his elbows.

3. That's how it was done.

4. A good-natured officer from headquarters with silver tassels played the guitar, keeping the beat with lacquered boots, rocking his graying head side to side.

5. They were having such good fun. It seemed like heaven on earth.

1. The young democrat sat lulled by the gypsy tune and his conversation with the fairy tale.

2. He listened to the music like one enchanted.

3. The officer from headquarters with a black mustache and a kind, but accessible face sang, "Your egchanting tenderness brings me back to life . . . Pgast dweams again nurture me, again I want to love and sugfer . . ."

4. He sang with a deep and passionate voice and clipped the ends of words, like a true gypsy.

5. And a choir of young men in tailcoats and women joined in, "Let us kiss oblivion, heal the wounds of the heart!! Let doubt be dispelled! Revive with a kiss!!!"

6. The men in coats and young women rocked their heads side to side, the piano player danced on the edge of the stool, and the host's daughter, thin as a pole, rolled her eyes at the singing, striking the deft piano player with her tortoise-shell lorgnette.

7. Watching the singers, the young democrat thought, "These aren't people, but the embodiment of my happiness," and the old man's daughter nodded at him, as if saying, "We are ideas, not people." The radiant old man himself, tidy and clean-shaven with a star on his chest, stood in the doorway and smiled kindly at the singing youth, barely audibly whispering, "Yes, yes, of course . . ."

1. The philosopher frowned; a cloud in the window had obstructed the moon. He had found yet another mistake in his edifice.

2. One of the men in topcoats leaned in toward the old man's daughter, asking about the philosopher, "Qui est ce drôle?"[19]

3. The officer from headquarters, with a black cockroach-like mustache and a sweet, kind face sang, "Let stewn weason pwove to me that you'll weave me, betway me! Your chawms are not tewwible fwetters to me: I'm in the gwasp of your beauty!!"

4. He sang with a deep and passionate voice and clipped the ends of words, like a true gypsy.

5. The choir joined in. The men in coats and young women rocked their heads side to side, the piano player danced on the edge of the stool. The young democrat thought, "These aren't people, but the embodiment of my happiness." The old man, tidy and

clean-shaven with a star on his chest, stood in the doorway and smiled kindly at the singing youth, barely audibly whispering, "Yes, yes, of course."

1. At this time the democrat saw the fairy tale and centaur walk by, heading toward the stairs to leave.

2. She shot a strange and wandering gaze into the ballroom, not revealing anything, and smiled sadly with her coral-red lips.

3. Then the fire of her hair flashed. Then the democrat realized that they would seldom be so close again.

4. And once again everything fell apart, all the strings snapped. And from the chaos ennui nodded, eternal like the world, dark like the night.

5. Ennui looked through the window, through the eyes of the horrified philosopher.

6. Something, it seems, had changed. Someone came in, someone was missing. Someone familiar and unseen was standing in the excessively brightly lit ballroom.

7. And the officer from headquarters, not noticing, finished his song, "Even if for that most bewtiful moment I must go to my grave . . ."

8. "Grave," thought the democrat. The choir joined in. The men in coats and young women rocked their heads side to side. The piano player danced on the edge of the stool.

9. The democrat saw that they were all false ideas, and the old man, clean-shaven with a star on his chest, gently approached him. He took him by the arm and whispered, "I am in step with the era, I love today's youth."

1. The democrat and the philosopher stepped out into the dark night together.

2. A thunderstorm was approaching.

3. They were going in the same direction, but they walked silently, listening to the eternal rehearsal.

4. Minute after minute passed, unchanged from time immemorial. Two rows of gaslights flickered their tongues.

5. The young democrat, morose and unhappy, saw the ridiculously rocking old man in front of him. The philosopher's nerves were unequivocally frayed. Insanity crept up on him with slow, but steady, steps.

6. It already stood over his shoulder. It was terrible to turn around suddenly and see its menacing face.

7. So they walked on, doomed to perish, in the dark night.

8. The dust, swirling up, already blew along the sleepy streets.

1. They parted coolly at the intersection. Despite everything, they remembered that they belonged to different factions.

2. The philosopher walked with intentional strides along the lonely side street, terrified and not turning around.

3. It seemed to him that a menacing terror was following him, and he recalled that in his lonely apartment there was a giant mirror and that right now this mirror was reflecting his apartment.

4. He was troubled by the question of whether the reflection was correct.

5. Then he approached the entrance to his building. The resonant door slammed behind him.

1. A stranger in a worn pointed cap was coming down the stairs. The neurasthenic shook like a leaf. His face dimmed like a lamp that had run out of oil when he saw the mark of a terrible mission on the stranger's face.

2. The stranger descended the stairs with his eyes lowered. And passing by him, the neurasthenic philosopher thought, "Now, now he'll look at me! . . ."

3. It seemed to him that at that moment, "everything would be finished."

4. But the man in the cap didn't look up. He laughed tepidly and ran down the stairs. Behind him the resonant door slammed.

5. And the neurasthenic still couldn't recover from that recent horror. It still seemed to him that just now the man would be back.

6. And the door opened again. Someone ran up the stairs.

7. When the philosopher rang at his own apartment, the person had reached the top floor.

8. It was the postman. He was ringing at a neighbor's door.

1. When the madman's door opened, he went straight to his room, not looking at the servant, and locked the door, afraid of letting in the menacing terror.

2. It was pitch black. Blinding streaks of lightening pierced the darkness. A deafening boom shook the walls.

3. The pale stranger with the mark of a wild mission was hiding among the shelves with books of philosophy.

4. This was the menacing terror.

5. The reader of Kant quietly gasped and squatted.

6. He no longer stood up off the floor, but crawled under the bed. He wanted to escape time and space and hide from the world.

7. My brothers, a person who sits on the floor is already finished!

8. Somewhere a clock struck two. Lightening flashed. It didn't illuminate the madman. He was sitting under the bed laughing cunningly at his idea.

9. The menacing terror then came out from among the shelves with books of philosophy, opened the window, and climbed down the gutter.

1. And across the street everything was calm and peaceful. The window in Dormidont Ivanovich's room was shut.

2. Dormidont Ivanovich himself was snoring on his back. He dreamed that it was already Christmastime and he had received his bonus.

1. This was when the young democrat shot himself, not having finished writing the commissioned critical article.

2. Pressing the revolver to his temple, he smiled, remembering his fairy tale, the democrat's fairy tale.

1. And the fairy tale, sad and dreamy, stood by the window of the decadent house, illuminated by flashes of lightning.

2. She was holding the democrat's letter. She wept. Her coral-red lips curled into a smile.

3. With a smile she remembered her dreamer.

4. And . . . there . . . in the distance . . . as if taunting . . . the evening water barrels drove down the streets.

5. They were false ideas.

1. Popovsky's teeth hurt: he was beyond good and evil,[20] forgetting both God and the devil.

1. The elder stood over the river. He rested his elbows on the handrail. His mournful face expressed tortured horror.

2. An exuberant coachman flew down below at the base of the hill, driving his pair of thoroughbreds with all his strength. In the carriage were exuberant stable boys.

3. In the distance the factory glimmered with hundreds of lights.

4. The mournful elder then raised his hands and quietly said, "My God, my God!"

5. His cry went unanswered.

1. At night everyone slept. They slept in basements. They slept in attics. They slept in the house of the aristocratic old gentleman.

2. Some slept in a disorderly knot, some slept with their mouths open. Some snored. Some even looked like they were dead.

3. They all slept.

4. In the psychiatric ward, the ill slept just the same as the healthy.

5. It was already getting light. There was a morose glimmer. A pale and dreary day ominously looked through the window.

6. It drizzled cold, biting rain.

7. No matter how gloomy, the day still grew warmer, and it seemed that this was a message for those who were exhausted, an invitation to new hardships.

8. Just one mentally ill melancholic was sitting on his bed and indifferently glancing at the sleepers.

9. A chill ran up his spine. He felt sick: he felt despicable under the rule of time.

10. He wanted to distance himself from the shape of time, but didn't know how to do this.

11. And time passed without stopping. Foggy Eternity was reflected in the passing of time.

12. The melancholic sadly said, "I know you, Eternity. I am afraid, afraid, afraid!?"

13. And he lay back down to sleep.

1. An express train sped on the railroad, carrying a sleeping Max Nordau[21] to Moscow.

2. Max Nordau snored in a first-class coupe, heading to Moscow at full steam.

3. He was rushing to a convention of scientists and doctors.

4. The zealous Nordau had battled degeneration his whole life. And now he had a speech ready.

5. And the rain drizzled and hit the glass of the carriage. The train sped along carrying the sleeping Nordau along the sad Russian lowlands.

1. In the morning, issues of three journals came out. The democrat wasn't able to skim them.

2. The crimson editor and a starving poet were talking in the editorial offices of a liberal newspaper.

3. The editor informed the poet that the democrat had shot himself out of civic despair, and the starving poet promised to write a "warm" article and "prod" those who deserved it.

4. Flags fluttered on the street.

1. By noon it had stopped raining. The sun peeked out. Popovsky was making the rounds to talk about his studies.

2. He went to five places and in five places discussed five subjects.

3. In one place he discussed the usefulness of synthesis; in another, the Wanderers exhibition.[22]

4. In a third he played a game of chess, and in a fourth he assessed the knowledge of the Gnostics.

5. He was turned out of the fifth place because that very morning the owner of the fifth place had been taken away to the psychiatric ward.

6. That was the philosopher who read too much Kant.

7. The windows of the apartment were covered in paper to indicate that the apartment was for rent.

8. Little Popovsky was disheartened and headed to the sixth place.

1. It was six in the evening. It was getting brighter. Dormidont Ivanovich was coming home from work.

2. He walked past a teahouse and an imported goods shop. A good deal of sausage hung in the windows.

3. Dormidont Ivanovich stopped in the teahouse and the imported goods shop since he wanted to buy a bottle of cider in order to try the favorite beverage of the French.

4. Dormidont Ivanovich went out of his way to be curious.

1. Walking past the philosopher's old apartment, Dormidont Ivanovich saw the papered windows.

2. Dormidont Ivanovich said, "Oh, they're moving! It would be interesting to know how much they pay for the apartment!"

3. Then he strolled on the boulevard, leaning on his walking stick, stout and happy.

4. As a joke, the clerks called him Mastodon Ivanovich, but that was a mistake because he wasn't Mastodon, he was Dormidont.

1. The fairy tale was buying trinkets. Crowds of ladies and gentlemen rushed from one department to another.

2. The elevator was in working order; the operator was flying through four floors.

3. Here and there a metallic echo rang out, "Account."

1. That evening in the hall of the nobility there was to be a concert, noble and special. A famous conductor had come.[23] The whole of Moscow had a ticket.

2. An hour before the concert, a stout man laid out scores on music stands, and ten minutes before the concert, the spectators from the first rows were gathering.

3. A haughty man with vulgar sideburns had arrived and sat in the fourth row.

4. This was Nebarinov, a vital member of the municipal assembly.

5. The countess, the princess, and the wife of a famous writer had already arrived.

6. And the professor with a big beard but short hair from the conservatory, and the professor with a little beard but long hair from the conservatory, and the professor from the university.

7. And the aristocratic gentlemen and his stout wife, and the gentleman with a beard but no mustache who loved Mendelssohn.

8. And the barrister, Ukho, and the young man, Kondizhoglo, and many others who were expected to be there.

9. The centaur and his wife were already at the concert. The fairy tale was chatting with the sweetly dumb city police superintendent.

10. The city police superintendent was from the upper echelons of society. He casually joked and chatted.

11. And the fairy tale responded to inanity with inanity and scanned the room with her wandering gaze.

12. And an important person entered the box. Then the famous conductor appeared.

13. Two people ran up and brought him a garland.

14. And then it began . . . deepened . . . emerged . . .

15. It barely finished when it began again. Eternally the same, the same it rose up in an anguished soul.

16. At that time Nebarinov looked over those who were there and took note of who wasn't.

17. The centaur was attentive. The old man fell asleep. His wife poked him with her elbow and, waking up, he muttered, "Yes, yes, of course."

18. The content countess, princess, and wife of a famous writer all swayed their heads in time with the music.

19. The fairy tale sat like a stern contour.

20. She was sad.

1. And then it began . . . deepened . . . emerged . . . like scales from an unknown world, emerging from no one knows where, fading.

2. This was as if on *its* own accord, and the horns were blown and the bows drawn on their own accord . . .

3. It was as if the lights had dimmed. The hall of the nobility became small and crowded. Something was torn off of something . . . On its own . . .

4. The hall seemed like a strange, gloomy place, and the flickering of the lights was glum.

5. And the multitude of spectators seemed like a row of pale spots on an infinite black background.

6. These faces were serious and stern, precisely as if they were afraid people would learn about their shameful flaws.

7. And *this* was stronger than them all.

1. The sounds sped by with the minutes. Time was comprised of a row of minutes. Time passed without stopping. Foggy Eternity was reflected in the passing of time.

2. Like a strict woman in black, calm . . . calming.

3. She stood among all those present. They all felt her cold breath behind their backs.

4. She embraced each one in her dark contours, she placed her pale otherworldly face on each one's heart.

1. This was like a large bird . . . of sadness. And there was no end to the sadness.

2. The sadness stretched for millennia. And more millennia lay ahead.

3. It encapsulated the solar system. And the solar system altered its course.

4. But it was the same, the same, calm, majestic, mercilessly dreamy.

5. This was like a large bird. And its name was *the bird of sadness*.

6. This was sadness itself.

1. Already among the clearly delineated clouds was the waning, brilliant moon. It didn't live up to expectations and was waning early. It didn't do anything according to expectations, only according to the calendar.

2. And now it was tricking Moscow, saying that it was floating through motionless clouds.

3. It was the opposite.

4. Between the moon and the poor earth, the clouds blew, no one knew where from, no one knew where to.

5. The northern wind rustled, and the young, supple little trees were bent.

6. A drunken voice shouted in the window of a restaurant, "Weeeep, weeep! Don't stooop crying . . . weeeeep, weep, weep! Don't stop cccryiiiing!" . . .

1. At that time the express train pulled in. Max Nordau hopped out of a first-class coupe.

2. Frightful Nordau glanced over the platform, barely audibly muttering, "Die alte Moskau!"[24]

3. People ran around with luggage, and the locomotive whistled like a madman.

4. And from somewhere in the distance the wild hum of the Moscow cabbies, "With me, sir, with me! Here's a cab! . . ."

5. And Nordau was at a loss.

1. At that time the gray-haired elder walked along the boulevard in a cap with earflaps and an open umbrella.

2. The streetlamps blinked dully. From time to time he encountered a suspicious type.

3. It was pouring rain.

4. The gray-haired elder stopped and, shaking his open umbrella, mournfully cried out, "My God, my God!"

5. The lonely passerby turned around in amazement hearing this cry . . . And the trees rustled, leaning over, calling into the unknown distance.

PART TWO

1. Moonlit nights gave way to moonless ones. The new moon was expected from day to day.

2. But for now it was moonless.

3. In the melancholy evening hour, the roofs of the houses cooled off, the dusty sidewalk cooled off.

4. Separate sections of sky could be seen between the buildings. Coming from the right-hand side of an empty side street, you could take note of the delicately yellow close of day bordered by smoky blocks of clouds.

5. Smoke hung over Moscow.

6. A beggar-dwarf, an old bluish pale woman, walked down the empty side street to the almshouse carrying a sack.

7. A man in a gray coat with a black mustache ran behind her.

8. His hand was in his pocket, and in his pocket he squeezed a cobbler's drill.

9. Ahead, the side street intersected with another, perpendicular to the first. There, against a white wall, a black horse bobbed its head, its cabbie hunched over, asleep.

10. Both the old woman and the young man with the black mustache walked past lighted windows. Glancing into a window, you could see an amateur tinkerer sitting at a table taking apart a clock.

11. The tinkerer had taken everything apart brilliantly, but didn't know how to put it together again; he sat there scratching his head.

1. A wagon with the sign "Worker" sat in front of the building's entrance. By the wagon, a man wearing an official's cap explained to the caretaker, who had just run up to him, that he was the new tenant.

2. A minute later, and with the caretaker's help, the mover carried a ton of massive things to the third floor.

3. And the man in the cap watched like a hawk that they were careful with his massive things. He was renting the apartment of the philosopher who had gone to pieces.

1. It got even darker; the infinite expanse of roofs cooled off.

2. The roofs of many houses were connected to one another. Some ran into others and ended there where the others began.

3. Two cats, one black and one white, were fighting by a chimney pipe. They both jumped, scraping the metal, vigorously swatted each other in the face, and yowled with all their might.

4. Holding its breath, humanity watched the fight.

5. The chimney smoked. Standing by the chimney, you could see Dormidont Ivanovich's window in the distance.

1. Dormidont Ivanovich really loved children. He frequently treated them to mint cookies, even though Dormidont Ivanovich's salary was modest and he loved to eat mint cookies himself.

2. But he suppressed his passion.

3. His nephew Grisha had come over today. Dormidont Ivanovich treated Grisha with tea and mint cookies.

4. Grisha demolished all of the cookies, leaving not a single one for his stout uncle; Grisha didn't respect his stout uncle, but tossed a rubber ball at him.

5. And Dormidont Ivanovich kept one eye on the flying ball while the other watched the lights flickering in the philosopher's former apartment.

6. Out of the blue he said, "Well, they're moving!" with a slight sigh.

1. At that time a carriage drove up to the decadent house. Out of it stepped the fairy tale with her sister, the quasi–fairy tale.

2. They were both wearing the spring fashion from Paris, and humongous black feathers stuck out of their hats.

3. The fairy tale didn't know that the democrat was dead. They both chatted in the foyer, discussing Countess Kaeva's dress.

4. At that time in Novodevichy monastery,[25] a devout nun was lighting lamps over some graves but not over others.

5. The democrat's fresh grave was adorned with flowers, and a metal wreath hung from the cross.

6. If you bent over, you it could read the meaningful inscription on the cross: "Pavel Yakovlevich Kriuchkov. Born 1875, died 1901."

7. But the fairy tale knew nothing of the dreamer's demise and continued to chat with the quasi–fairy tale about Countess Kaeva's outfit.

8. And all around stood clean-shaven people whose faces didn't express surprise because they knew everything and had an answer for everything.

9. They were . . . philistines . . .

1. At that moment a young man plunged a cobbler's drill into the back of an old beggar woman and slipped away into the next side street.

2. This was the madman, and the police were painstakingly searching for him.

3. At that moment the cathedral of Christ the Savior imposed itself over dusty Moscow like a holy giant.

4. Beneath the silhouette of its golden cupolas, the waters of the Moscow River flowed to the Caspian Sea.

1. At that time, when the quasi–fairy tale was parting with the fairy tale and a gray cat had beaten the black and white ones,

2. when careless Grisha broke Dormidont Ivanovich's glass with the ball and the old woman mumbled into an empty side street, "Police,"

3. Moscow scientists and doctors were holding a celebratory dinner for Max Nordau; Max Nordau had thundered today, battling degeneration. And now he sat in the "Hermitage," all red from agitation and champagne.

4. He was bonding with the Moscow intellectuals.

5. A worker pulled an empty barrel past the "Hermitage"; it rumbled, bounding on the pavement.

6. This Moscow didn't need Nordau. It lived its own life. The congress of scientists and doctors did not pull at its heartstrings.

7. Today Nordau smashed degeneration, and tomorrow books by Valery Bryusov and Konstantin Balmont will be published.[26]

1. A middle-aged man sat behind a samovar in his lonely apartment on the third floor; his clear eyes watched the open door of the balcony calmly and quietly.

2. From the balcony a fresh breeze flew in and blew steam from the samovar into the man's face.

3. He was neither old nor young, just *passive and knowledgeable*.

4. He finished his second cup of tea, while in the sky the stars appeared, like diamonds.

5. It seemed that he was cold and sat there complacently, shrouded in the fog of ephemeral tenderness.

6. The mystic Sirius[27] burned with love.

7. He threw columns of fire and madness from himself into the black, bottomless space; and not just Sirius—all of the stars were expelling streams of fire into the black cold.

8. This was the astral horror.

1. The *calm and knowledgeable* one wasn't afraid of this and just finished drinking his second cup of tea.

2. It seemed that he was cold and sat there complacently, shrouded in the fog of ephemeral tenderness.

3. It seemed that he was saying, "And so, Lord! I *know* you!"

4. He drained his second cup and poured himself a third.

5. And when it struck twelve in the next-door apartment, he still sat, calm and thoughtful, fixing his tender gaze on the moonless sky filled with constellations.

6. It was quiet. The odd cabbie rumbled by. Cats yowled on the rooftops.

7. Someone with keen ears might be able to hear, in the distance, the beckoning sound of the horn.

8. As if someone stood on a smoky chimney in gray wings blowing on a horn.

9. But it only seemed that way.

1. The heavy interplanetary orb came from who knows where.

2. It streaked into the earth's atmosphere with a whine and, heating up, gave off sparks.

3. From below it seemed like a large glowing star had fallen from the blue sky.

4. A white streak lingered in the sky, quickly melting in the cold.

5. The one sitting behind a samovar saw this, saw the star, and took it into account.

1. The Moscow nights were now full of holy significance.

2. Blue smoky masses walked about, obscuring the horizon from time to time.

3. It was tricky: the question of Russia's holy significance roamed about.

4. The evening barrels drove by answering the question in the negative; haughty people sat on the boxes and argued with the police.

5. Popovsky walked by and answered the question in the negative.

6. But the one sitting with his tea decided the question in the positive, and Popovsky was taken off the streets of the city of Moscow; the door slammed behind him.

1. Max Nordau was very interested in the city's revelries. He was a lively and sociable person.

2. Now he was racing in a Russian troika to the cheery "Mauritania," driven by Russian intellectuals.

3. He hiccuped after a satiating dinner, humming a cheery chanson.

1. A cynical mystic from the city of St. Petersburg[28] was shouting at all of Russia then, and his comrades illuminated the shouter with sparklers.

2. Even Marxists struck out into philosophy, and philosophers into theology.

3. But none of them knew the significance of the mysterious blinking which grew and grew in Russia.

4. The flickering was reflected in Popovsky's acquaintances, who were holding hot May meetings.

5. Each of them paged through the Gospels, read the mystics, and knew Dostoevsky by heart.

6. Some even went so far as to commune with the deceased writer as equals.

7. Occasionally you could see a fanatic pounding on *The Brothers Karamazov*, exclaiming, "Fedor Mikhailovich gave us a puzzle, and we are now working it out."

8. True, they were all joking around, but God help you if you crossed paths with them.

1. The spring was strange and unprecedented. Even after the summer had passed, everyone without exception remembered the spring: liberals, conservatives, mystics, and realists.

2. That year there was an unprecedented surge of pilgrims in Kiev. In May the Ufa forest burned.

3. On the coast they said that a whale repeatedly swam up to the shore in Murmansk and blinked its tiny fishy eyes.

4. The curious whale once asked a deaf old man on the coast, "Hey, good man, how's Rurik doing?"[29]

5. Seeing the deaf old man's confusion, it added, "About a thousand years ago I swam up to this shore. Rurik was your ruler then."

1. At night the sound of the horn most clearly echoed over sleeping Moscow.

2. That was when police detectives caught the crafty one who had stabbed the old women.

3. He passionately wagged his finger at the police detectives and proclaimed, "In Rus we are a multitude."

4. And then, as if in confirmation of his mad words, it turned out that the basement of the Rastroguev house had begun to flood with filth.

5. A city engineer was already on the spot; waving his hands, he explained to the others that the pipes were clogged.

6. The next day there was a piece in the newspapers, "A Sewage Mess."[30]

1. Six hundred old women were agitated. The disgruntled muttering of old women echoed in the wards and in the halls.

2. Vile people had injured one of the old women, plunging a cobbler's drill into her spine.

3. The old woman sat, bandaged, and brewed herself some chamomile tea.

4. They discussed the end of days; they viewed the appearance of the attacker as a sign of the Antichrist.

5. An old man had already come into the old women's section. The almshouse was for both old men and old women, and six hundred old men sent one of their own to offer condolences to their wounded comrade.

6. So he stood with the speech in his hands trying to read: nobody understood anything. All that was heard was a toothless mumbling.

1. The archpriest sat behind a samovar in a brown robe; he wiped the sweat off his puffy brow and chatted with a guest.

2. His guest was a learned philologist. He was an instructor at Moscow University.

3. He was dry and wiry; he constantly wiped his hands with a handkerchief, peppering the archpriest with verses from the Gospel According to John.

4. He relished each text, uncovering its holy meaning.

5. And at his outpouring of eloquence the archpriest was patiently silent, nibbling on a piece of sugar and smacking his lips.

6. Finally he finished his glass, turned it over as a sign that he was done drinking and said to his interlocutor, "Oh, clever! Eh, eh! Oh, clever!"

7. He turned his fleshy crimson face to the scholar, wrung his hands, and, patting himself on the stomach, added authoritatively "Keep going, brother instructor!"

1. An acquaintance of Popovsky's hosted literary soirées for an intellectual array of blinkers.

2. Here came only those who could say something new and original.

3. Now mysticism was in fashion, and Orthodox clergy began to appear.

4. Although, the organizer of the literary soirées preferred sect members, finding them more interesting.

5. All who gathered in this home read Solovyov;[31] in addition to Kant, Plato, and Schopenhauer, they fiddled with Nietzsche, and ascribed great significance to Indian philosophy.

6. They all had at least two degrees and weren't surprised by anything on earth.

7. They considered surprise the most shameful flaw, and the more unbelievable the phenomenon, the more faith this group had in it.

8. They were all people of the highest "*rarified*" culture.

1. That's where Popovsky was going this spring evening.

2. He walked past a fence; on top of the fence dangled a bunch of white lilacs, waving at little Popovsky, but Popovsky didn't see anything and smiled at his own amusing train of thought.

1. When Popovsky passed into the next side street, Drozhikovsky walked by.

2. He saw the white bunch of aromatic lilacs and the tender blue azure.

3. He saw the star shimmering behind a white branch of lilacs, and he saw a cloud enveloped in purple mystery.

4. Drozhikovsky saw all this as he hurried to Ostozhenka Street.

1. The content host wiped his white hands, checking that everything was set and nothing would interfere with maximum literary pleasure.

2. The thing was that Drozkhikovsky himself had promised to speak; he was a fashionable up-and-coming talent.

3. That's what the conscientious host was thinking as guests began to trickle in from various side streets of the city of Moscow.

4. Popovsky shuffled along that same side street, and Drozhikovsky himself hurried behind him, recollecting the white lilacs.

5. The dusk was filled with sadness. Its rosy fingers burned on a turquoise enamel. Precisely as if someone, gray all over, covered in a purple robe, stretched his hands over the city in a blessing.

6. Precisely as if someone was burning incense. And now the smoke from the censer melted into a flaming blue cloud.

7. The bells were ringing.

1. In Savostianova's bakery, the white bread was rising.

2. A stout baker checked on the yeast and, seeing that there was enough, lit the lamp.

3. Treading along the street, you could see in other windows either reddish or greenish lights.

4. This was the glimmering of the lamps.

5. The following day was Pentecost, and Orthodox faithful were filling the lamps with oil.

6. And now these holy tongues of flame were timidly burning before the Lord.

7. More than one atheist complained of an upset stomach.

1. The guests were already gathering. The content host ordered tea to be served.

2. In the well-lit foyer sat caps, fur hats, and pointed caps.

3. But the bell rang. Popovsky entered.

4. He took off his galoshes and moved toward the ballroom.

5. Popovsky had barely arrived when Drozhikovsky himself rang; glancing at the clock and wiping his pince-nez, he entered and was met with greetings.

6. He gave every one his gracious hand. A group of admirers had already gathered around him. Followers of Nietzsche, the mystics, and orgaists came over.

7. Only one didn't come over, but stood by the window, smoking a cigarette.

8. He was tall and fair skinned with black eyes; he had the face of an ascetic.

9. His short golden beard was neatly trimmed, and his sunken cheeks had a reddish hue.

1. A sickly priest in a gray cassock with a golden cross was there.

2. His silken hair, white as snow, was combed; he stroked a gray beard.

3. He listened more than he spoke, but his wise blue eyes scanned the crowd . . . Each one was honored by this ancient silence.

1. The general discussions hadn't yet begun, but the streets were already emptying and the lamps were being lit one after another.

2. The sunset pierced the heavy clouds, which glowed in those pierced spots. The sunset lingered over Moscow all night, just like good news about better days.

3. The following day was Pentecost, and the lovely glow of sunset praised it, burning the smoky clouds, sprinkling the saved and the damned with its rosy blessing.

1. A breeze flew in through an open window, bringing the scent of white lilacs.

2. Drozhikovsky remembered the white lilacs, like the forgetting of illness and sadness.

3. He began his speech amid the grave-like silence of the crowd.

4. He spoke in a halting voice, stopping often to round out his phrases.

5. Then he stopped infrequently, and the phrases flew from his mouth as if carved from ivory.

6. The old priest in the gray cassock was silent, bowing his head, white like the moon, and covering his eyes and brow with his hand.

7. The reddish light of the lamp fell on him. The black shadow of his hand shaded his pale brow.

8. They spread out on the chairs, and the host went up to one and then another on his tiptoes, offering tea.

9. There sat the follower of a Petersburg mystic, scratching his warm face.

10. Popovsky settled in by the stove, and before the presentation even began, he grimaced in advance.

11. A breeze flew in through an open window, bringing the scent of white lilacs.

12. Drozhikovsky remembered the white lilacs. He spoke of the forgetting of illness and sadness.

1. A huge blue cupola blocked the sunset. Its edges glowed and shone. Its shadow fell on Moscow.

2. And Drozhikovsky mentioned the flow of time, and, it seemed, his eyes saw foggy Eternity.

3. He resurrected extinguished giants; he united their thoughts; he saw the movement of these thoughts, noted their twists and turns.

4. And it seemed to everyone that they were sitting in a rickety little boat among the roar of leaden waves, and Drozhikovsky was their able helmsman.

5. He spoke of a volley of rockets and the fireworks of thoughts and dreams; he simply asked, "Where are these rockets now?"

6. He compared the thoughts of philosophers and poets with the fading foam of an emerald sea; he asked the crowd, "Where is it?"

7. The old priest in the gray cassock was silent, bowing his head and covering his pale brow and clear eyes with a trembling hand.

1. A glow flashed from the blue cupola that blocked the sunset. Shadows fell on the faces of those listening, transforming their faces, drawing out folds of sadness and melancholy.

2. But the falling shadows just made it seem that way; in reality, their faces didn't express anything. They were all content with themselves and with Drozhikovsky.

3. Although Drozhikovsky was content neither with himself nor with the intellectual movements of the nineteenth century.

4. He compared them with the flickering of swamp fires: banging on the table, he asked, "Where are they?"

5. White lilacs nodded at him through the window with a wave that was familiar to his heart; this was floral oblivion.

6. The blue cupola slid out of the sunset glow . . . Behind the cupola, the sunset glow laughed with a sincere and childlike laugh.

7. Drozhikovsky banged on the table, and the pink glow was reflected in Drozhikovsky's eyes . . . And Drozhikovsky seemed like a large, kind child.

1. There were streaks of sadness. He stood among the crowd, tugging at his black mustache, and mockingly nodded his head.

2. He was burying philosophy, and on its burial mound he cried and wept, like Jeremiah of the Old Testament.

3. There were streaks of anger. He stood among the crowd in deathly silence. He silently threatened the positivists.

4. He yelled that they had trampled the heavenly pigments.

5. Then he laughed demonically, talking about democrats, the people's party, and Marxists.

6. But it must have smelled of the breeze off of the late democrat's grave because someone whispered to Drozhikovsky, "Let me rest in peace," and the ivory phrases ceased to fly from his fiery mouth.

7. The priest was also quiet in his gray cassock, bowing his white head and covering his pale brow and blue eyes with a trembling hand.

8. His black shadow lay on the floor.

1. Drozhikovsky was silent for a long time, a very long time, and he seemed like a large, kind child. The wind rustled his black hair, and his gray eyes were fixed on the window.

2. An unintentional emotion softened Drozhikvosky's features, as if he were about to pronounce a new truth.

3. At that moment in the Ascension Cathedral they were singing "Lumen Hilare," and the archpriests' miters sparkled.

4. Incense rose to the top of the cupola.

1. Then everybody sensed the distinct babbling of melting glaciers, and Drozhikovsky began his speech with the weighty word: *superman.*[32]

2. Followers of Nietzsche shifted in their seats while the old priest raised his clear eyes to Drozhikovsky,

3. whose words ignited a flickering flame, and in the room a whirlwind of fire and light stirred.

4. As if they felt the nearness of the melting snow, like a cold drink to a fever patient.

5. As if they drowned the hot terror in a foggy, damp swamp while Drozhikovsky showed the holy meaning of *superman.*

6. He inserted nuggets of Holy Writing into his speech and plumbed theological depths.

7. He cited past belief systems and compared them with the burning questions of modernity.

8. He was waiting for spiritual renewal; he was waiting for a feasible synthesis of theology, mysticism, and the church; he showed the three transformations of the spirit.

9. He sang hymns to the children of the tribe of Judah.

10. His words ignited a flickering flame, and—fiery symbols— they blew through the open windows.

11. From time to time he stopped to listen to the waltz of the "snowflakes," which was playing somewhere in the distance.

12. Then everybody saw that a lotus flower hung over Dro-zhikovsky—the tender forgetting of illness and sadness.

13. This was the floral oblivion, and from behind a burning cloud the bright glow laughed with a sincere and childlike laugh.

14. Drozhikovsky banged on the table, and the pink glow was reflected in Drozhikovsky's eyes . . . And Drozhikovsky seemed like a large, innocent child.

15. His eyes reflected a kindness that was too strong; it felt as if the string was wound too tightly and would snap along with the dream.

16. Somewhere the waltz of the "snowflakes" was playing. Each person's soul turned snow white. They froze in a beatific stupor.

17. The impossible, the tender, the eternal, the kind, the old, and the new for all of time.

18. That was how he spoke; the old priest looked at him, friendly and tenderly, gripping the arms of his chair.

19. Everyone was shocked and agitated.

1. The content host offered his white hands to the embarrassed author of the speech; a lively conversation was underway . . .

2. A Marxist who had come here by chance jumped from his seat and thundered in his bass voice, "Permit me to object."

3. But then he was interrupted by a blond man with a golden beard and a stern and thoughtful face; that was the one with the sunken cheeks and feverish red hue who looked like an ascetic.

4. During Drozhikovsky's speech he shot him kind glances that, it seemed, said, "I know, oh do I know . . ."

5. Now he stood like a mighty dictator. His hollow voice soon made even the very educated feel humble.

1. He said, "The Third Kingdom is now upon us, the Kingdom of the Spirit . . . Now the water with its pale-faced cloud is more like sacrificial blood.

2. Although the Kingdom of Heaven is not just water, but also blood, also Spirit.

3. Now we must endure the horrible, final battle.

4. Among us will be those who fall, those who are turned away, and those who are allowed to enter and see and proclaim.

5. The time of the four horsemen has come: white, black, red, and death.[33]

6. First white, then red, then black, and finally, death.

7. Have you not noticed that *something*, or more accurately *Someone*, is descending upon us.

8. This will be the most tender flower from an earthly garden, a new rung on Jacob's ladder.

9. This will be a mountain stream, trickling to life everlasting.

10. It is the secret idea of Dostoevsky, the shriek of a despairing Nietzsche.

11. The spirit and the bride both say: "come."

1. The old priest remained silent, bowing his head full of thoughts, resting his face in a trembling hand.

2. A shadow fell from his hand, and from the shadow peered the priest's blue eyes.

3. In the cathedrals they were already singing "Evening Venerations"; the clinking of the censers echoed with the sighs of the old archpriests, crowned with diamond-encrusted headpieces.

1. The prophet said, "The spirit and the bride both say: come.

2. I hear the pounding of the first horse's hooves: this is the first horseman.

3. His steed is white. He is *white* himself: he wears a golden crown. He has come to conquer.

4. He is male. He is destined to rule all the nations with an iron rod. To crush the heretics like clay vessels.

5. This is our Ivan-Tsarevich.[34] Our *white* bannerman.

6. His mother is the woman clothed in the sun. She is given wings in order to conceal herself in the desert from the Serpent.

7. There she raises a *white* child who will shine with the sunrise.

8. The spirit and the bride both say: come."

1. Then he stood, stern and thoughtful.

2. It was the fair-haired tall man with black eyes. His sunken cheeks had a reddish hue.

3. He was thoughtfully silent, and the Marxist, forgetting his objections, ran like a thief from the *madhouse*.

4. But the white breeze blew through the open window; it brought sweet, lilac kisses to the prophet. And the clear glow laughed, whispering, "My dears."

5. Drozhikovsky warmly shook the fair-haired prophet's hands, and the old priest silently looked over the crowd with his blue eyes and then dropped his gray head to his old man's chest.

6. Then he shielded the light with his hand. The breeze rustled his gray, satin locks.

7. His black shadow fell on the ground.

1. At that time in the Arabian desert a lion zealously roared; he was of the tribe of Judah.

2. But here in Moscow, cats yowled on the rooftops.

3. The rooftops resembled one another: they were green deserts above a sleeping city.

4. You could spot the prophet on the rooftops.

5. He was completing his nighttime ritual above the city, quelling fears and chasing away terrors.

6. His gray eyes sparked beneath eyelashes black as coal. His graying beard fluttered in the wind.

7. This was the late Vladimir Solovyov.

8. He was wearing a gray sealskin coat and a large wide-brimmed cap.

9. Occasionally he took a horn from the pocket of his coat and trumpeted over the sleeping city.

10. Many heard the sound of the horn, but they didn't know what it signified.

11. Solovyov paced the rooftops courageously. Diamond-like stars spread above him.

12. The Milky Way seemed closer than it should have been. The mystic Sirius burned with love.

13. Solovyov alternately called to sleeping Moscow with his resounding horn or declaimed his poem.

> Evil forgotten
> Drowns in blood!
> Cleansed, arisen
> The sun of love!. . .[35]

14. The beautiful glow laughed, red and mad, burning the jasper cloud.

1. A reddish lamp burned in the room. The child awoke.

2. He cried loudly, "Nanny."

3. The nanny woke up with a grumble and calmed the child.

4. And he stretched his arms to her and smiled, saying, "A horn is blowing somewhere!"

5. The nanny made the sign of the cross over him and said, "Christ be with you, my baby! It just seemed that way to you!"

6. And the child fell asleep, smiling. And the nanny went back to bed.

7. In their sleep the both heard the beckoning horn . . . That was Solovyov pacing the rooftops, quelling fears and chasing away terrors.

1. The sunrise was already burning with a new strength when the feeble priest rose from his chair.

2. He spoke of universal love with lowered eyes.

3. A calm breeze rustled his satin locks, and the old priest's lips curled into a sad smile.

4. He neither accepted nor rejected anything that had been said and merely spoke of love.

5. There was a breeze . . . And they didn't know if it came from the exhalations of the sweet lilacs or from the white words of Father John.

6. And the mad glow stomped on the jasper cloud and then laughed, beautiful in the silver dawn.

1. Father John didn't speak long. Then he sat by the window in the predawn glow of the May night and rested his gray head on his chest . . .

1. In the morning Drozhkivsky returned from Ostozhenka Street, sleepy and tired.

2. He frequently yawned because it was already a bright day.

3. An aromatic bunch of lilac oblivion hung in front of the turquoise sky.

4. The purple mystery was performed over a snow-white cloud.

5. Drozhikovsky saw all this as he hurried along Ostozhenka Street.

1. A vagrant with a sack on his shoulder was walking; his narrow, gray, scraggly beard arduously stuck out in front, glowing with the joy of forgiveness.

2. The pine forest was already behind him. Above the green pines, the sun gave out its blessings.

3. Yellowish white clouds, seemingly molded from wax, were inscribed in relief on a backdrop of heavenly blue.

4. And in front of him stretched a ravine. Over the ravine shone sacred caps of gold and silver.

5. This was Moscow, lit by the rays of May. This was Moscow on Pentecost.

6. The gray vagrant examined Moscow's mysteries over the sacred caps and was privately glad.

7. He was of sound mind, and nothing surprised him. He considered surprises *human, all too human.*[36]

8. In the sky the yellowish white clouds floated, seemingly molded from wax, and in his mind the vagrant was placing candles before the Muscovite saints.

1. Father John served in his parish.

2. His clean little white church with its silver domes invitingly buzzed in praise of the Holy Trinity.

3. They sang the Cherubic Hymn. Everybody sweated. A mysterious deacon in a blazing cassock periodically bowed, spreading the incense.

4. Rays of gold burst in through the narrow windows and rested on the glowing cassocks; the scattered smoke of the incense gently dissipated in the sunshine.

5. The Holy Gates[37] didn't conceal the mysteries; Father John raised his arms in blessing, and his satin white hair stuck out from his pale brow.

6. Then Father John bowed deeply before the Holy Throne, and from his pursed lips burst forth a stream of mysterious words.

7. So he finished with an unknown symbol, interrupted the prayers with a dreamy sigh.

1. Then came the great procession; two children, their cassocks flashing, carried the wax candles; the golden deacon shuffled behind them.

2. Father John walked quietly after the rest with the cup in his hands. He eyes shone. His cassock flashed. His hair flowed in snowy waves.

3. And the church parishioners bowed in the May sun.

1. And while Father John was performing services, Father Damian was doing the same in the neighboring church.

2. They were performing services in all the churches; they spoke the same holy words, but in different voices.

3. Without exception the priests all wore gold brocade. Some were gray, others were stout, still others were handsome, most were ugly.

4. In the Cathedral of Christ the Savior an anonymous archbishop in a golden miter performed the services.

5. A church attendant held his staff while he himself was pronouncing blessings from the Holy Gates, crossing the Dikirion with the Trikirion.

1. Dormidont Ivanovich stood through the services. He worked up a healthy sweat and, stepping out, wiped himself with a handkerchief.

2. His fat fingers grasped a five-penny piece of communion bread, taken for the health of the servant of God Dormidont.

3. The clerk Openkin heartily wished him a happy holiday by the door, and at home Matrena put on the samovar.

4. Dormidont Ivanovich devoutly crossed himself and wolfed down the piece of communion bread for the health of the servant of God Dormidont.

5. Brewing the tea, he said to the cook, "Well, Matrena, God is good!"

6. The stout director worked up a healthy sweat in church, and now he greedily took in the steam of Chinese tea.

1. The side street was bathed in sunlight. The sidewalk shone. In place of the sky was a giant turquoise.

2. The house, in a faux Greek style, had six columns, and on the six columns were six white stone women.

3. The stone women had six stone pillows on their heads, and the cornice of the house descended onto the pillows.

4. There was a mound of wet red sand in the asphalt courtyard.

5. On the mounds of sand played children in sailor suits with red anchors and fair-haired locks.

6. They plunged their small hands into the cold sand and hurled clumps of sand on the dry asphalt.

7. A small boy stood on the heap of sand; his face was stern and thoughtful. His blue eyes were the congealed color of the sky. His hair, soft like linen, curled and spilled down his shoulders in dreamy waves.

8. The youth held an iron rod in his hands, sternly and importantly, picked up who knows where; the youth beat his little sisters with the iron rod, smashing them like clay dishes.

9. The little sisters squealed and threw clumps of sand at the self-appointed leader.

10. The youth wiped red sand from his face sternly and importantly and thoughtfully looked at the celestial turquoise, leaning on his rod.

11. Then he suddenly tossed the iron rod and leaped from the mound of sand, running through the asphalt courtyard, squealing with joy.

12. A cabbie drove by with Drozhikovsky. Drozhivkosky was driving to the fair-haired prophet to talk about shared mysteries.

1. A monk walked along the fashionable street; his cowl reached high above his thin face.

2. He wore a silver cross and moved quickly among the festive crowd.

3. His black beard reached his waist; it started right under his eyes.

4. His eyes were sad and mournful despite Pentecost.

5. The monk suddenly stopped and spat: a cruel grin distorted his stern features.

6. This was because the cynical mystic made yet another supposition and published it in the *Northern Lights*.[38]

1. In the window of an artistic store on Kuznetsky Street[39] they exhibited portraits of prophets and bishops.

2. And it seemed like the prophets were yelling from behind the window glass, stretching their bare hands to the streets, shaking their sorrowful heads.

3. The bishops were bright and quietly laughed, hiding a cunning smile in their whiskers.

4. A crowd gathered by the windows, their mouths agape.

1. Golden beams of light penetrated the windows of the decadent house.

2. They fell on a mirror. The mirror reflected the next room. From there were the sounds of muted weeping.

3. The pale fairy tale stood among flowers and silks; her reddish hair flashed in the golden sunlight, and her pale violet garments had white irises on them.

4. On the floral festival she learned of the dreamer's death—and the orphaned fairy tale wrung her delicate white hands.

5. Her coral lips trembled, and silver pearls dripped down her pale marble cheeks, wetting the irises pinned to her bosom.

6. She stood there, distraught and weeping, looking out the window.

7. And the mad glow laughed at her tears through the window, burning the jasper cloud.

8. The fairy tale's tears were in vain because the time of the democrats had passed.

9. The flow of time had washed away the dreamer, carrying him to eternal peace.

10. The mad sunset told her this, laughing hysterically, and the fairy tale wept over the scattered irises.

11. And . . . in the next . . . room stood the shaken centaur. He entered . . . and saw his nymph in the reflection.

12. He stood there shocked, not believing the mirror's reflection, not daring to check on whether the mirror was tricking him.

13. Two sorrowful wrinkles showed on the good centaur's brow, and he thoughtfully tugged at his elegant beard.

14. Then he quietly left the room.

1. The fairy tale ordered them to bring her carriage. She wanted to place a scarlet rose on the dreamer's grave.

2. And the golden Pentecost day passed and was replaced by Pentecost eve.

3. The memory of the dreamer, sitting in a small boat, floated off into the distance on an emerald sea.

4. Other times passed, other things happened: something outlived its time and was put to rest in a cemetery; something mourned in a psychiatric institution; something tugged at the sweet fairy tale's heart.

5. And she, consumed by the sunset, raised her delicate, white arms to the twilight.

6. It seemed as if she whispered, "Let my eternal grief fly off into space.

7. And there echo in order to shine again."

8. The fairy tale stood there so long, conversing with the twilight, that she looked like a holy vision.

9. The memory of the dreamer, sitting in a boat, floated off into the distance on an emerald sea: this was the woman with a necklace of tears.

10. And above the emerald sea was a cloud, burning at the edges.

11. Like a dreamy giant, it melted into the turquoise enamel.

12. This was the nymph's twilight parting with the memory of the dreamer.

13. The memory smiled sadly and rowed off into the unknown distance because other times approached and other things happened.

1. The pale ascetic with the gold beard and a reddish hue gave Drozhikovsky tea.

2. Drozhikovsky sipped his tea with agitation and, taking the ascetic by the arm, gasped, "So you know the woman clothed in the sun?"

3. But the pale ascetic said indifferently, "I don't know anything: it's still all very vague ... Some things are written ... I can't make any conclusions until the summer ..."

4. And through the open window the golden Pentecost evening flowed into the room.

5. The blowing wind flung steam from the samovar into Drozhikovsky's face. The golden-bearded ascetic looked at him, as you would a kind child.

1. A consumptive was dying that golden Pentecost evening. A bouquet of white lilacs stood on a table near him.

2. The shutters were open. Rays of sunlight managed to poke through them.

3. Father John was finally on his way. His white, satin hair vividly contrasted with the dusty sidewalk.

4. Then the door creaked, behind it were hidden the red terrors, and John stood on the threshold in front of the consumptive.

5. His blue eyes were fixed on the sick one, and his trembling hand made the sign of the cross.

1. Then the sick one felt the terror ebb; he raised himself up in his feverish bed; he smiled bitterly to his holy friend.

2. He complained to John of the rotting terrors, and the old priest raised a sprig of lilac to his face.

3. He complained of sin, but when Father John removed his silver cross, the cold metal scorched the dying man's burning lips.

4. The sick one pressed up against his holy friend in fright, crying that he was scared of death.

5. And Father John stood in prayer by the feverish bed. His satin hair was like snow, and his pale brow shone with infinite humility.

6. Then the white priest gladly leaned over the dying man and said with a smile that God was calling him home.

1. The priest opened a window. The golden evening fell onto the sick one.

2. And the sick one died that golden Pentecost evening. His holy friend kissed him for the last time, placing the white lilac on the bed.

3. Servants soon appeared around their late master, but Father John was already walking back along the dusty streets.

4. The little silver church was calling him with its bells for the nighttime vigil.

1. The vigil hadn't yet begun but the crimson lamps were already lit.

2. The Holy Doors were shut and curtained from within with red silk.

3. But here came humble John, making a low bow to the faithful.

4. Now he was sending his wealthy parishioner to the next world; he had been afraid of such a long voyage. John was assiduously equipping him.

5. And in the sky the cloudy giant had gathered, smoky and burning at the edges.

6. The giant burned tenderly in the chill of pure turquoise.

7. In this burning was both the love of old John and the love of the fairy tale for the dreamer's memory.

8. And the memory floated off into the distance on an emerald sea: this was the young woman with a necklace of tears.

1. Inside the monastery loomed a pink cathedral with white and gold domes; marble monuments and iron chapels sprouted around it.

2. The trees rustled over the lonely dead.

3. This was the kingdom of frozen tears.

4. Next to a little red building sat a nun, under an apple tree, showered in white blossoms.

5. Her otherworldly eyes were drenched with the glow of the sunset, and a reddish hue played on her young cheeks.

6. Her black cowl stretched high above her marble brow. And she frantically clutched a rosary.

7. She was in love with the beautiful glow. It laughed in her face, shining on the nun and on the little red house.

8. And the stern mother superior peeked out of the little house, watching the nun suspiciously.

9. The fiery cry of swifts echoed, and the nun idly burned in the twilight's gleam.

10. Her soft hands clutched the black rosary. She raised her shoulders high and froze under the snowy apple tree.

11. Small flames sputtered somewhere on the graves.

12. The black nun lit lamps over some graves, but not over others.

13. The wind rattled the metal wreaths, and the clock marked the time.

14. Dew fell on the gray stone chapel inscribed with the words, "Peace unto you, Anna, my wife."

1. Suddenly the nun heard the rustle of a silk dress and woke from her ephemeral bliss.

2. In front of her quietly passed a young beauty with sad blue eyes wearing a pale violet Parisian gown.

3. Her red hair burned in the twilight's gleam, and her horses snorted, waiting for their mistress by the monastery gates . . .

4. They looked each other in the eye; they both had blue, blue eyes . . .

5. They were both nymphs: one in black, the other in pale violet; one held a scented handkerchief to her face, the other frantically clutched a rosary, and her black *kobluk* fluttered over her small marble face.

6. They understood one another; they both knew the same grief.

7. And the black swallows screeched through the rustling trees, and the mischievous glow glanced at them.

8. It laughed an earnest laugh and sent the wind to the snowy apple trees. And the apple trees showered the black nun with white, fragrant blossoms.

1. And it was already nighttime. The nuns dispersed to their cells with lowered gazes. The flames in the small windows went out.

2. It was the same as always, eternally kind, sadly thoughtful.

3. The wreaths rattled. As if the dead were wandering and fixing the candles in the lamps. They kissed the freshly delivered flowers with bloodless lips.

4. But this didn't happen.

5. And only the silver angel continued to stand over the chapel in frozen silence, and the clock monotonously marked the time.

6. Time flew over the quiet monastery like a light breeze, bending the young birch trees. And the timeless woman in black carried on a conversation with it.

7. Her pale face was petrified in eternal grief and loss, and her gray eyes reflected foggy Eternity.

8. So she stood among the overgrown graves lit somewhere by a flickering flame, barely audibly whispering, "There it is, Lord, one, eternally one!..."[40]

9. The wind, rattling the metal wreaths, carried her otherworldly, holy grief far away.

10. The ancient gray stone chapel was distinguished from the graves by a dark outline, and the undergrowth already covered the stony words, "Peace unto you, Anna, my wife!..."

1. It was a holy night. The last cloud melted in the enamel sky.

2. The enamel sky burned with golden stars; the streets were empty, clean, and white.

3. Stepping out onto the balcony of a three-story house, you could catch sight of two rows of golden flames from streetlamps along the sleepy streets.

4. In the distance the flames merged into one single golden thread.

1. All night the horizon didn't sleep, but glowed. As if a holy candle burned beyond the horizon.

2. As if John the Apostle prayed beyond the horizon all night, performing the purple mysteries.

3. A long, narrow, amber cloud stood on the horizon.

4. The fairy tale sat on the window sill feeling sad. She looked at the amber cloud.

5. Her reddish hair spilled onto her shoulders, and her face was illuminated by the golden stars.

6. The next day she would leave Moscow and part with her dreams.

7. . . . Precisely as if a holy candle burned beyond the horizon.

8. Precisely as if John the Apostle prayed beyond the horizon all night, performing the purple mysteries.

1. It was already Whit Monday. Everybody slept, dreaming clearly.

2. Only a man emerged on the balcony of a three-story house, neither young nor old.

3. He held a candle in his hand. The candle burned on Whit Monday.

4. A whirlwind rose up, even though the sky was calm and clear.

5. The gray dust swirled in long columns.

6. The chimney pipes sang and moaned, and the candle went out in the hands of the man standing on the balcony.

7. The sound of the horn was carried clearly over Moscow, and whirlwinds of light came from on high, streams of light on Whit Monday.

PART THREE

1. The wind blew cold. The emerald fields of grain bowed, offering prayers to the azure morning.

2. The plowed field was black in the distance.

3. Here and there was a horse, and behind was a peasant pulling a plow, turning the earth with deep furrows.

4. The men and the horses were different, but their actions were the same.

5. To the ordinary eye there was nothing to see here, but the careful observer would think differently.

1. A troika drove along a dusty road in the pale green field. The driver, in a velvet sleeveless coat, urged on the tired horses.

2. A fair-haired gentleman in a city frock coat sat in the troika. He was loaded with luggage.

3. The cold made the glass of his pince-nez foggy; so he took it off to wipe and, with black half-blind eyes, glanced around, singing: "Golden, emerald, and black fields . . . You are generous, patient and hard-working land . . ."

4. It was a poem by Vladimir Solovyov,[41] and the man in the troika turned out to be a follower of the late philosopher.

5. And so the golden-bearded ascetic drove and drove to his brother's estate in order to rest after the winter commotion.

6. Now he looked around himself and at the fields of grain with black, half-blind eyes, whispering: "Emerald fields . . . Solovyov put it beautifully . . . They're completely emerald! . . ."

7. But the driver in a velvet sleeveless coat didn't share his wonder; he smacked his lips and encouraged the horses.

1. From time to time they drove past fields. Here and there was a horse, and behind a peasant pulling a plow, turning the earth with deep furrows.

2. The men and the horses were different, but their actions were the same.

3. There was a humongous fellow—a slouching knight—stomping the freshly dug up earth with his bast shoes, scurrying behind the plow.

4. The thin peasant fellow was also digging, shaking his beard enigmatically.

5. The men and the horses were different, but their actions were the same.

1. Sometimes the plain was gouged with deep ravines, making it seem like a high plateau.

2. There was something Buddhist in the alternation of plain and ravine.

3. One remembered the past more than the present. This past was a Mongol past.

4. At least that's what the golden-bearded ascetic thought, sprawled out among his luggage.

5. He whispered to himself, "That's Russian sorrow and Russian listlessness . . ."

6. And from above, the sun was already roasting the back of his head for such an audacious thought.

1. He saw the magnificent fragments of the past, and out of the past came the future, woven from shrouds of smoke.

2. He hypothesized that the realization of the period of synthesis in this or that culture requires a personality; only the hand of a great teacher can tie the last knot, unite the colored threads of events.

3. He thought—the light in the west ceases to shine and dark-winged night creeps out of the murky waters.

4. European culture has said its fill . . . And this word has become a sinister symbol . . . And this symbol was the dancing of death . . .

5. And skeletons began to run around decrepit Europe, shimmering with the darkness of its eye sockets.

6. He thought all this, but was then jolted: the road was one hole after another, and the golden-bearded ascetic said to himself, "Patience."

7. "Patience," because in the east hot blood was already simmering in golden vessels, and around the vessels were hierophants, and blue incense floated to the sky with the sound of the clanking censer.

8. He dreamed of uniting a western skeleton with eastern blood. He wanted to clothe this skeleton in flesh.

9. Sitting among his luggage, he guessed at Russia's role in this great unification, and the driver, turning his dusty face, smiled and said, "You haven't gotten used to our roads, milord."

10. But the golden-bearded ascetic forced himself to smile, sensing the hopelessness of the plains.

11. He asked if it was much farther to *Filthton* and learning that *Filthton* was indeed far, he tore himself from the luggage and flew away on the wings of imagination.

1. The sun became harsh, piercing through with a red-hot cruelty. The cross of a white church shone in the distance.

2. There, where the hunchbacked plain covered the horizon, you could see a lonely cluster heading east.

3. They carried two banners, red with some gold, that fluttered on tall poles.

4. The peasant women wore red sashes, and gold braids flashed on their blue skirts; they carried images of Byzantine saints.

5. They were walking with the icons and banners to the next estate to pray for rain.

6. They walked in a lonely cluster with fluttering banners.

7. They were praying to the prophet Elijah. A holy downpour and fiery arrows.

8. This was a slap in the face to midday skepticism.

9. The cluster of banners soon disappeared into the boundless plain, and the cross of a white church shone in the distance.

1. The ascetic was already driving up to isolated *Filthton*, counting his followers on his fingers.

2. He diligently instilled their hearts with sadness for the fiery whirlwind so that they blazed with sadness and burned with love.

3. Holy days came and called appealingly to the prophets . . . And the prophets slept in people's hearts.

4. He wanted to end this slumber, appealing to the golden morning.

5. He saw humanity motionless, as if in sleepy contemplation.

6. The grazing sheep wandered off in search of a new, still unknown, truth. This was the midday dream amid the summer drought.

7. Everything good, which wasn't still asleep, turned into the madness of the sect and the ravings of delirium.

8. Oh, he knew, the golden-haired ascetic knew a thing or two! Now he was going to the village to rest after the winter commotion.

9. He had to put a dome over the walls he had built—to make conclusions from the material he had collected.

10. He wanted to burn with prophesy in front of the Moscow scholars; these were daring people who had attained the wisdom of science and philosophy; the morning star flickered here, as it did for Drozhikovsky.

11. This was the dough, put into the oven by a crafty baker.

12. Many of them had already wiped reality from their eyes in order to immerse themselves in dreams with a pure heart.

13. A cascade of diamonds would soon shower the impoverished land. Soon the stars of prophesy would fall down from the heavens.

14. The heavenly firmament seemed to be drawn on porcelain.

15. Whirlwinds of black dust rose up on the horizon.

16. The black-dust funnel rose and then, dissipating, sent the dust to the indifferent heavens.

1. The golden-bearded ascetic *saw, saw* and he *knew* a thing or two! . . .

2. How on this dreary autumn day the titans of destruction, overgrown with thoughts, like the fluffy fur of a beast, were burying Europe.

3. It drizzled, and the wind howled mournfully, drowning out the tears of poor mothers.

4. They walked behind her black casket wearing clothes that looked like the night, with images of skulls on their gloomy hoods and horrific torches in their hands.

5. They carried pillows with silver braids, and terrifying regalia lay on the pillows.

6. The largest, most terrifying gravediggers walked behind the casket.

7. There was also a Norwegian lion whose roar rattled the corpse and thick-skinned Emelian Singlethought: in one hand he held a wood chip, in the other an axe. He was planing the wood chip muttering, "Like a man, like a fool! Chop, chip, you get a ship!"

8. And Zarathustra—a hungry black panther who gobbled up Europe.

9. There was a Belgian hermit and a French monk in a bat skin suit holding a magical censer.

10. A black cat sat on his shoulder, licking its paw and beckoning guests to the funeral.

11. There was the singer of lies, stewing in a dungeon, and the Parisian magus.

12. And the Milanese, and Max—a curly poodle yelping about degeneration, and Sir John Ruskin who confused the meaning of good, truth, and beauty and cooked a sweet stew of modernity.[42]

13. And an inappropriate parody of the Christian superman, called *super-impotent* and carried by Swiss Guards on a rotting litter, wearing a paper cap.

14. This was a wind-up toy, meant to parody Christianity.

15. Barren thistle! Heir of the roadside stone! Roman wastrel! His holiness, glowing with electricity!

16. Behind the large gravediggers trudged a crowd of small ones. What they lacked in quality, they made up for in quantity.

17. There were gnomes, regressed back into childhood; lisping old men barely two feet tall.

18. They carried green torches covered in black crepe, and on their mourners' ribbons you could read, "neurasthenia," "depravity," "indifference," "mentally deficient," "mania."

19. But the most dangerous mania was the mania of false learning: it consisted of a person gouging out his eyes and sticking convex lenses into the bloody sockets with his audacious fingers.

20. The world had fractured; the result was its inverted, diminished representation.

21. This was a horror, and it was called exact science.

22. Future sowers of destruction were also there, indescribable in their horror.

23. All eyes were focused on the black cover of night, silently spread over the North, the Germanic, Sea.

24. It looked like a giant bat, blocking the sun.

25. The leaden waves crashed on the sandy shore and ejected a beast with seven heads and ten horns.

26. And the great and small teachers of filth all shouted, "Who is equal to this beast?"

27. Lit by the gas flames of its horns, it slouched toward dying Europe which opened its dead eyes and mumbled through its toothless mouth.

28. It preened and powdered for the beast and its words were more than sinister, and it opened its dead eyes and mumbled through its toothless mouth.

29. And then every one of the great gravediggers and great scoundrels (which was what the teachers of filth were called) decorated their night crowns with false gems.

30. Here they placed Zarathustra's red ruby and Huysmans's black diamond.

31. Sir Ruskin's Carrara marble and Russian Singlethought's cobblestone.

32. But these were all false gems; they glimmered strangely over the great whore's wig.

33. Then the crimson moon plunged into the noisy ocean, and all felt a rush of instinctive terror.

34. And they said to the hills, "Tumble down on us!" But the hills didn't tumble. And one's face couldn't be hidden from the horror.

35. And every last one of them was horrified.

1. And while he had these thoughts, they were praying for rain in the neighboring estate.

2. Red banners with some gold fluttered among the emerald-yellow grain, like holy, beckoning signs.

3. The priest dipped a birch branch into a dish of water and sprinkled the grain, praying for *bountiful winds*.

4. A lone peasant, barefoot and dirty, got lost in the grain.

5. And just his doleful voice echoed in the fields.

1. The ascetic continued his fantasies. At the zenith of the dark-winged night, he tripled its northeast illumination.

2. The Sunday light had already entered the sky, and its holy fire chased the horror of infection from the east.

3. In the east they weren't horrified. A happy anxiety had long been present there, as if the seraphim stirred up unseen outrage.

4. And when the beast ascended to the throne with the great whore, the fires of the prophets appeared over holy Rus.

5. Its apostle was John, whose gaze penetrated the depths of previous centuries.

6. Then a sign appeared in front of the expectant faces: the woman clothed in the sun flew on two eagle's wings to the Solovetsky monastery,[43]

7. in order to give birth to a male child who is destined to rule all nations with an iron rod.

8. The ancient prophesy about the white horseman who emerged victorious came to pass.

9. And there was a great battle between the legions of the beast and the woman. And when the battle reached its apogee, an angel could be seen rising in the east.

10. He stood between the Tigris and Euphrates; he poured a chalice of the Lord's fury on the west, chanting, "It fell, it fell, Babylon, the great city!"

11. He vanquished the whore and the beast, chaining the demon for a thousand years.

12. This was the first resurrection, the premonition of the second resurrection, and it was the first death—a likeness of the second.

13. This was the sign, read by the prophets.

14. The golden-bearded ascetic *saw, saw* this and he *knew* something!

1. He whispered a prayer, "Woman clothed in the sun, reveal yourself to your standard bearer! Take heed of your prophet!"

2. And his terrible face suddenly expressed extreme indignation.

3. He remembered a familiar image: two blue eyes framed by reddish hair, a silvery voice, and the sadness of an otherworldly mouth.

4. With one hand she waved a fan, answering nonsense with nonsense.

5. That was how he had seen her at the formal ball.

6. Unsettled, he whispered, "woman clothed in the sun," but her troika had already pulled up to the entrance.

7. The golden-bearded ascetic's brother, the landowner Pavel Musatov, stood on the porch, wafting intoxication, with his bogatyr's[44] shoulders and large beard.

8. His wide-eyed face laughed and glistened, framed by his blond beard, soft as linen . . . In his left hand, a cigar was smoking.

9. The wind rustled his white silk coat, and he waved a handkerchief at his brother.

1. His niece Varya stood in the cool entryway, staying at her uncle's with her consumptive mother.

2. This was a pale-skinned blonde with dreamy eyes, a small nose, and freckles.

3. The Musatov brothers embraced and kissed.

1. A lone peasant, barefoot and dirty, got lost in the grain.

2. And just his doleful voice echoed in the wide steppe.

1. Breakfast was laid out in the dining room. Here Pavel Musatov joyfully drank six glasses of cherry liqueur.

2. Then he grabbed his giggling niece and danced the mazurka.

3. He masterfully performed in front of his shocked brother, stomping his glossy boots.

4. He had been a Guardsman.

5. The girl giggled, and so did he, making his stomach shake and the watch chain on his stomach shake, sweat pouring from his crimson face.

6. The golden-bearded ascetic was surprised since he had come to the village to sort out the fate of the world from the material he had gathered.

7. But everybody was happy . . .

8. And now his brother Pavel had already unbuttoned his silk coat and was wiping his wide-eyed face with a handkerchief.

1. Over breakfast, the golden-haired ascetic explained his arrival to those present while cleaning a fresh radish.

2. He said that he was tired of the bustle of the city and intended to rest in the bosom of nature.

3. His niece Varya paid reverent attention to the speech of her learned uncle and Pavel Musatov, pouring his eighth glass of cherry liqueur rumbled, "And for the besssst!"

4. He was huge and crimson, having penetrated the mysteries of farming, and his brother was skinny and pale, crammed with knowledge.

1. The landowner Musatov led a life full of village work and village fun.

2. He drank and caroused, but he looked after the farming.

3. He had romantic secrets, as attested by the scar on his forehead, which appeared after being struck by a walking stick.

4. He would speak often, rumbling, "Once, carousing in Saratov, I spent a week as a coolie loading steamers."

5. Then he would roll up his sleeves, baring his furry arms.

6. Such was Pavel Musatov, the cheerful lord of enticing *Filthton*.

1. On a hot June day, the pale ascetic was wandering in a shady alley, book in hand.

2. He was leafing through an article by Merezhkovich about the union of paganism and Christianity.[45]

3. He sat on a bench. Cleaning his nails, he said to himself, "Merezhkovich has made a ton of mistakes here. I'll write an objection to Merezhkovich!"

4. But Pavel Musatov slipped onto the bench next to him and covered the odd article with his broad palm.

5. He spoke through his teeth, clenching a cigar, "Later. Now it's time to swim."

1. The ascetic sank into the cold water by the willow, giving in to the calm.

2. He bathed with dignity, remembering the holiness of the ritual, and his stout brother cooled off on the bank, pounding his bare chest.

3. Finally he dove into the water and vanished.

4. He wasn't gone long. His soaking wet head soon popped onto the surface and, snorting, said, "How delightful."

1. The wind howled in the endless plain, whistling through the ravines.

2. It flew to the Musatov estate and mourned with the birches.

3. They stretched into the distance, but couldn't fly off . . . and just rocked bitterly.

4. This was time passing, flying into the past on its cloudy wings.

5. And in the distance the great sun bowed, flanked by its burning robes.

1. The golden-bearded ascetic paced quickly in the shady alley.

2. He was making conclusions from the material he had gathered, and his black eyes burned into space.

3. A straw hat was on his blond curls, and he swung a walking stick with a heavy handle.

4. He had already figured out most of it and was now getting to the main idea.

5. Eternity whispered to her naughty child, "Everything returns . . . Everything returns . . . One . . . One . . . in all dimensions . . .

6. Go to the west and you'll arrive in the east . . . All essence is visible. Reality is in dreams.

7. The great sage . . . The great fool . . . All are one . . ."

8. And the trees latched on to this hidden dream: *once more it returns* . . . And a new gust of flying time went into the past . . .

9. That was how Eternity joked with her naughty child, embracing her friend with her dark outline, resting her pale otherworldly face on his heart.

10. She closed the ascetic's eyes with her thin fingers, and he was no longer Musatov, and so *something* . . .

11. *What, where,* and *when* were equally unnecessary because *they* had put the stamp of otherworldliness on everything.

1. The ascetic already knew that a great and fateful mystery was coming at them from unknown constellations, like a fiery-tailed comet.

2. The orchestra had already struck up the overture. The curtain would rise any minute now.

3. But the end of the drama flittered off into the distance because it would still be a good millennium before *they* untangled the Gordian knot of time and space. Events flow with the stream of time, obeying foundational principles.

4. The trees roared about new times, and he thought, "*Once more it returns.*"

5. He was feeling bitter and sweet playing a game of blindman's bluff with his Beloved.

6. She whispered, "All is one ... There is no whole, no parts ... No born, no seen ... There is neither reality nor symbol.

7. Each may play a part in the common fate of the world ... There may be a common and a personal Apocalypse.

8. There may be a common and a personal Comforter.

9. Life consists of prototypes ... One hints at the other, but they are all equal.

10. When time is no more, there will be that which replaces time.

11. There will be that which replaces space as well.

12. These will be *new* time and *new* space.

13. All is one ... And all returns ... The great sage and the great fool."

14. And he grasped, "*Once more, once more it returns ...*" And tears of joy fell from his eyes.

1. He went to the field. A cloud blushed on the horizon: as if a shaggy Cossack froze while dancing with his leg pointed at the sky.

2. But it dissipated. Bits of clouds were scattered on the horizon . . . There were dark gray spots on the yellow-red backdrop.

3. As if a leopard skin were spread out in the west.

1. He smiled, seeing his dear Friend after days of separation and sadness.

2. And in the distance Pavel Musatov was riding in a dog cart with a cigar in his teeth, masterly holding the reins.

3. In the distance, someone's deep voice sang, "Parrrdon, parrrdon my looooove, my dearrrr."

4. Pavel Musatov rode off into the hazy distance; only dust remained on the road.

5. The voice sang, "In a farrrr off laaand, I think of yooouu."

6. A lone peasant, barefoot and dirty, got lost in the grain . . .

7. The voice sang, "And yoooouu are my saaad lot, saaad lot . . ."

8. The leopard skin stretched out in the west.

1. A lone peasant, barefoot and dirty, got lost in the grain . . .

1. The landowner Musatov sat in the evening chill.

2. He rested after the hot day, his blond beard singed.

3. And now he slammed his fist on the table, shouting at Prokhor, the village elder, "Fiend and scoundrel!"

4. And Prokhor bowed his neck, wrinkled his brow, and tugged at his giant beard.

5. And to the threatening exclamation, he blurted out, "We ain't knowed! . . ."

6. But this was a little while ago, and now stout Pavel was resting in the evening chill.

1. Varya, the niece, was eating a scarlet wild strawberry in the brightly lit dining room; she stabbed the berries with a skewer and,

laughing, said, "Uncle, you're a real pagan priest . . . You should put on a cloak . . ."

2. He seemed oddly cheerful and giggled for no reason.

3. Now he laughed, "Wait, give us a chance to build temples . . . Clothes, that's nothing . . . Is my walking stick not a rod? Is the straw of my hat not gold?"

4. And raising his arms over his niece, he jokingly pronounced:

> I am a high priest, with my tufts of gray
> Onto your head, my fragrant crown I will lay!
> And with the unspoiled salt of speeches aflame
> I will sprinkle the luxurious innocence of your mane![46]

5. So Sergei Musatov, golden-bearded ascetic and prophet, joked.

6. Then he opened the newspaper and read about the Tibetan Dalai Lama's state visit.

7. Then he asked Varya's mother if he could have a lemon.

8. Then Pavel Musatov gave him a lesson in farming and poor harvests.

9. They placidly smoked on the open terrace. The moon shone on them.

1. In the blue of the night, the niece Varya stood by an open window; her eyes sparkled and, with a book of Fet's in her hand, she pronounced:

> I am a high priest, with my tufts of gray—
> Onto your head, my fragrant crown I will lay! . . .
> And with the unspoiled salt of speeches aflame
> I will sprinkle the luxurious innocence of your mane! . . .

2. But the bright moon was setting, and the sky turned blackish blue.

3. Only toward the east was it pale green.

4. The shadows intersected and, intersecting, congealed. Pavel Musatov snored somewhere in the distance.

5. A familiar woman was in a soft chair in the sitting room.

6. Her deathly face shone white in the darkness.

1. The trees roared with a roar about the new times over the sleeping house.

2. Gust after gust blew by. The new time passed.

3. The new time didn't bring any news. God only knows why they were worried.

4. And the light of life already sparkled in the distant firmament. The familiar woman in black with the white face was no longer in the sitting room.

5. Only, on the spine of the chair there was someone's forgotten lace handkerchief . . .

6. The screaming time proclaimed, "*Once more it returns*!?" And half the sky had already turned pale green.

7. A piece of yellow Chinese silk was unfolded at the very edge of the horizon.

1. These were the days of working in the fields, the days of drawing conclusions from collected material, the days of forest fires that filled the surrounding area with smoke.

2. The days when the fate of the world and Russia was being decided, the days of objecting to Merezhkovich.

3. And the familiar image with blue eyes and a sad mouth become brighter and clearer.

4. It was a snowy silver banner raised over the fortress at the moment of superstitious anticipation.

1. In the morning the golden-bearded ascetic drank his fill of tea, debated with his brother, and joked with his niece.

2. Then he made conclusions from the material he had collected.

3. Then he and his brother gave themselves over to watery relaxation and dove among the waves. Then he composed spiritual epistles to scholars in Moscow and elsewhere.

4. They included revelations about Christianity and hints about the viability of mystical anticipation.

1. The circle of Moscow disciples grew, and a net of mystics covered Moscow.

2. One mystic lived in each district; the district government knew this.

3. They all considered the golden-bearded ascetic an authority as he prepared in the village to pronounce his word.

4. One of them was a specialist on the Apocalypse. He had traveled to the north of France to conduct an inquiry on the possibility of the coming beast's appearance.

5. Another studied the mystic smoke congealing over the world.

6. A third had gone in the summer for fermented mare's milk; he was trying to ascertain about the resurrection of the dead in practical terms.

7. A fourth went around monasteries to interview their elders.

8. Another was battling in the press with the St. Petersburg mystic, while another was fanning the sparks of grace.

9. Drozhikovsky traveled around Russia and gave lectures in which he blinked and winked with all his might.

10. He gave the impression that he *knows* while he attributed his knowledge to the golden-bearded prophet.

11. For others, who didn't know, his lectures resembled a dresser with valuables locked away.

12. He had already given six lectures and was now preparing a draft of the seventh.

1. A foppish carriage approached, carrying Pavel Musatov to the neighboring estate.

2. A familiar family greeted Musatov by the door and inquired as to why Pavel Musatov had neglected the hospitality of their hearth for so long.

3. At which Pavel Musatov bowed pleasantly and clicked the heels of his lacquered boots. He took the hostess's hand to his crimson lips and mentioned, "My learned brother is staying with me! . . . You know, we discuss this and that . . . And the time just flies by."

4. To the question of why he didn't bring his learned brother along, Pavel Musatov laconically replied, "He just sits around . . . busy with his extensive investigations . . ."

5. The curious family understood.

1. Their niece Varya strolled in the berry orchard with her friend Lida Verbliudova.

2. She suddenly kissed Verbliudova's long neck[47] and said, "Darling, come quickly to visit *Filthton* . . . I'll show you my learned uncle . . ."

3. Verbliudova asked what this learned uncle looked like, and her friend, screwing up her eyes, fiddled with the end of her braid and cunningly smiled . . .

4. She didn't answer.

1. Villages burned. An agent from the rural insurance company traveled around the district.

2. Dropping into an estate while chewing on some ham or spreading mustard on it, he would invariably say, "And Pavel Pavlovich is running around with his brother, the scholar . . ."

3. When asked what sort of creature he was, he would answer with a telling glance of his crablike eyes, "He just sits around in *Filthton* . . . busy with his extensive investigations . . ."

1. Two residents of a provincial town were having a feast.

2. There were empty bottles on the table, and the eyes of those sitting there were intoxicated.

3. One of them grabbed the other by the knee and said, "Let's each raise another glass . . . ha, ha . . . but what . . . ha, ha . . . are we compared to Sergei Musatov's learning . . ."

4. At this his companion dryly noted, "He's coming."

1. The house was dark gray and very old. A stone mask was hanging over the open terrace.

2. The stern face was still and pale; it looked warm and pink from the evening sun.

3. Pavel Musatov was sprawled on the open terrace, dappled with scarlet specks of light.

4. His stout stomach puffed out from under his coat, and his right hand was sunk in his beard.

5. With his left hand he played with his watch chain, and an ashtray and matches sat on the table in front of him.

6. Two young poplars bent over, as if enchanted, shaking and hiding from the never-ending fairy tales.

7. The cries of mournful lapwings echoed by the river.

8. Wide-eyed Pavel was lost in sad thought in the evening sun.

9. Finally, he sneezed and walked down from the terrace, having caught sight of a guest.

10. The mask laughed in his wake with a stony laugh.

1. A storm approached. A boom and roar lingered over the estate.

2. Deep-rooted trees, buffeted by the wind, were torn away.

3. Sheets of rain approached, already over the plowed fields.

4. Gray herons flew over the leaden river.

5. The village schoolteacher was stooped and wiry. His sallow face was darker than his bald spot, but lighter than his beard, and his squashed nose jauntily jutted out from under his blue glasses.

6. He was a young man, drawn to the folk.

7. He and Pavel Musatov were walking along the yellowing alley; the teacher's yelping voice battled with the noise of the trees.

8. His sallow faced seemed to grimace, and his long arms made awkward movements under the leaden vault of the sky.

9. Deep-rooted trees, buffeted by the wind, were torn away.

1. The golden-bearded ascetic sat on a painted bench and made conclusions from collected material.

2. And the schoolteacher squeamishly thought, "There sits a *rotting* mystic!

3. He's drenched in *lamp* oil and his *kvas*[48] patriotism sickens me."

4. The mystic, who was not at all rotting and didn't drink kvass, rose to greet them.

5. He was trained as a chemist, and the young schoolteacher had more than once disgraced himself in his eyes by his ignorance of the empirical sciences.

1. They went to dine. The village schoolteacher amassed a battalion of intellectual warriors from his readings and mounted an attack on the *rotting* mystic.

2. For now there was just the occasional cannon fire. Things hadn't yet progressed to muskets.

3. A store of personal insults remained as yet untapped.

4. The pink glow on the windowpanes died out; a deathly pale face looked out through the window at the passersby.

5. As if great Eternity pressed up to the window.

6. But this was just a bouquet of white feather grass and nothing more.

7. Pavel Musatov didn't participate in the argument. With his eyes wide open, he sang, "Night flies on the edges of the cloud, the ominous cloud covers the dawn!"

8. The cloud was terrifying and spread out high in the sky with two low swirls, sinister and white, trailing off somewhere to the side.

9. In the clearing by the house, two young poplars whispered with the storm as if they were enchanted.

10. The glow of dusk on the windowpanes died out. A bouquet of feather grass sat on the windowsill.

11. The village schoolteacher grew animated from the ascetic's silence, and Pavel Musatov quietly sang, "The brilliant happiness dims, like the dusk; grief, like a storm cloud, comes on all of a sudden . . ."

12. They had already entered the house and slammed the door when a scrawny mutt wailed with its tail between its legs, its narrow snout pointed to the sky.

13. It was horrified and seemed to cry out, "*It returns, once more it returns*," and two swirls, sinister and white, were already over the house.

14. The cries of mournful lapwings echoed by the river.

1. The ascetic was silent before the huffing schoolteacher because he was on another plane of existence.

2. It was a pure waking dream.

3. It was a revelation: Eternity was joking with her naughty child, her favorite. These eternal jokes were sweet music that echoed in the prophet's despairing soul.

4. The prophet knew that he was being torn from the trap of three dimensions. People called him mad—that was a good sign.

5. The prophet already knew that he was Eternity's apostle.

6. He had studied too much for that, grieved too much, rent too many veils, loved Eternity too much.

7. His dreams were too vivid: it was a sleep that shrouded Russia like sweet madness.

8. It was Eternity joking with her naughty child, her favorite.

9. The stone mask on the terrace laughed, and in this laughter went mute.

10. The cries of mournful lapwings echoed by the river.

1. This dream incinerated reality. It dissipated into black ash.

2. "Let, let this just be a dream," thought the prophet, "but let the world just this once take part in these dreams, lose itself in fantasy.

3. What then would stop these dreams from being real?"

4. That's what he thought, and his heart froze from sweet sadness and into his eyes other eyes, blue . . . And the poplars, with their deep basses, were already moaning under the pressure of Eternity's passing flight.

5. These waking dreams flew by in a roaring torrent. and the old poplars raised their bony arms in joy and cried out in song, "The groooom comessss at midniiiight."

1. There were shouts and howls outside the window. Unknown voices cursed and yelled and prayed.

2. He saw Moscow and the masses of clouds with icy edges over Moscow, and in the clouds the *woman clothed in the sun* holding the holy child in her embrace.

3. And the elder prophet and apostle of Eternity himself was sprawled at her knees.

4. Diamonds flashed on his miter and cross, and his golden beard disappeared in the cupola of clouds.

5. From beneath the clouds, like lightning, the blade of the Lord's sword was cutting down the unworthy.

6. And in the distance the Antichrist ran back to northern France.

7. Amid the general shouts, the elder poplars, like steadfast archbishops, raised their bony arms in joy and cried out in song, "I seeee your palacccce, my Saaaavior."

1. And again, as always, two sad blue eyes, framed with reddish hair, stared at the ascetic.

2. There was a smile and sadness. There was a question, "Is *this* really the truth? . . ."

3. They stood by the window and watched the storm with curiosity.

4. The hail pounded. Broken branches flew by. Somewhere in the house there was the cracking of glass.

5. Here and there the bloody blade of the sword poked through for an instant, and a resounding deacon's voice proclaimed, "*The Daaamned!*"

6. That wasn't yet The Blow, but just the blade of the sword among the clouds.

1. In the evening, the samovar hissed. They sat around the table in silence.

2. The night gaped in silence, pressing up against the windows and looking at the people.

3. The ancient clock marked the time with steady beats.

4. Their sister poured tea. The golden-bearded ascetic stirred his glass with a spoon.

5. Varya fiddled with the end of her braid. Pavel Musatov picked up a guitar.

6. Suddenly the stooped schoolteacher spoke up in a yelping voice. Opening his mouth, he let out volley after volley.

7. His squashed nose zealously flashed at his opponent and Varya's cheeks flushed bright crimson.

8. But the jealous schoolteacher wasn't looking at Varya. Pavel Mustatov watched, strumming the new strings of his old guitar.

9. Then he coughed, sighed, and shook his head.

10. But his brother didn't notice any of this.

1. The samovar hissed.

2. Someone pressed up against the windows with gaping eye sockets.

3. But nobody was there.

1. The schoolteacher shouted, "This is madness!" Varya fumed with displeasure at the schoolteacher.

2. Pavel Musatov plucked a string with his fat finger.

3. The ascetic's gaze flashed like lightening because he was thinking of his long years of studying science and philosophy.

4. In a piercing wooden voice, he said, "If I'm mad, then it's only because I've progressed though all stages of sanity!"

5. He stood and, with a yawn, walked to the window.

6. Suddenly Pavel Musatov strummed a *Persian March* on the guitar.

1. The mail came. The golden-bearded ascetic read a letter. He said to his brother, "Tomorrow I'm going back to Moscow."

2. Stout Pavel stood behind Varya. He said to his brother, "Good for you!"

3. With his eyes, he pointed at his wilting niece.

4. Varya quickly left the room.

5. The schoolteacher's pale lips were twisted, even though he was calmly smoking a cigarette.

6. But the ascetic, lost in thought, didn't notice anything.

7. He went out into the garden.

1. Night spread out. The bottles rattled. Pavel Musatov was getting the schoolteacher drunk.

2. The schoolteacher's head lay on the table. He cried, "Love your neighbors!"

3. Pavel, who was turning crimson, laughed merrily. His face glistened with sweat.

4. With one hand he banged the table; with the other he raised the dregs of his glass over his head.

5. There were wine stains on the table cloth. Flies circled overhead.

6. The guitar, with broken strings, was toppled on the floor.

1. It was dark in the next room. Varya was there.

2. Tears flowed from her eyes. She was biting a small handkerchief.

3. She dropped the handkerchief onto the back of a chair and went out into the garden.

4. And the handkerchief glowed white on the back of the chair as if it was someone's face, malignant and deathly pale.

5. But nobody was there.

1. The ascetic strolled in the garden the whole night, wrapped in darkness.

2. His hot breast heaved from the eternal fairy tales.

3. They wrote to him that the family of the coming *beast* had been found and that the *beast* was still in diapers.

4. For now it was a normal boy, blue-eyed and living in the north of France.

5. And the ascetic cried into the nighttime alleys, "We will march on the beast with the *woman clothed in the sun* like a holy, snowy silver banner!"

6. The night watchman banged on a sheet of iron.

1. Time flew over the mournful trees in a roaring stream.

2. The dispersed clouds went off into the hazy west.

3. As if someone, evil, were escaping back to the north of France.

4. And the ascetic stood on his knees in the mud with his arms raised to the sky.

5. He cried in exhaustion, "Tat Tvam Asi!"[49] and beat his chest . . .

6. It grew light.

1. And when he went back into the house, it was already light outside.

2. The morning drinking was underway in the dining room, lit by an overhead lamp.

3. Black flies swarmed around the schoolteacher's mouth, and Pavel Musatov unsteadily walked toward his brother.

4. His intoxicated breath wafted over him as he beat his chest.

5. He muttered, "That scoundrel Proshka . . . Across the road . . . Envious devil . . ."

6. And collapsing onto his knees before the ascetic, he cried, "Sergei, I'm madly in love, but she's a peasant . . . The elder Prokhor is jealous . . ."

7. He was red as a beet. The ascetic said to him, "Stop drinking; otherwise you'll burn up from drunkenness . . ."

1. The ascetic looked at his brother and at the scrawny schoolteacher. Black flies swarmed around the schoolteacher.

2. The overhead lamp battled with the daylight. The guitar was toppled on the floor.

3. In holy terror, the ascetic thought, "Then she's *apocalyptic death*!"

4. It grew light. Looking out the window, you could see an old man, the night watchman, dragging himself off to sleep in the bushes.

5. In the east you could see a piece of yellow Chinese silk.

6. And above it the sky was pale green.

7. It grew light.

1. It was getting on in the evening. The rain drizzled. Rooks cawed over the willows.

2. Pavel Musatov stepped out onto the porch to see his brother Sergei off.

3. The troika rumbled, its bells ringing. Pavel Musatov remained alone on the porch.

4. He stood in a blue silk coat and waved a handkerchief to his brother.

5. His face was redder than usual. He had bags under his eyes.

6. He went to the barn.

1. The women were sweeping the barn. One of them saw Pavel and blushed.

2. Pavel wasn't looking at the women.

3. He had even turned away from the elder Prokhor, who was standing in front of him with his cap off.

4. It was cold.

1. In the evening he stood on the terrace with Varya and silently smoked a cigar. Nobody spoke.

2. Varya understood his silent sympathy.

3. Out beyond the river, they sang, "Parrrdon, parrrdon my looooove, my dearrrr . . ."

4. Eternity stuck her head out from the wall and sadly hung over them.

5. It was just a mask.

1. A funeral shroud spread over the fields.

2. Sergei Musatov rode through the fields, cloaked in fall fog.

3. He thought, "It's nothing . . . It's just a glimmer of fear . . .

4. It's foggy death floating in from the west . . . But we'll keep fighting . . .

5. It's not over yet . . ."

6. In the west, the clouds fragmented. A fiery crimson finger rose up over the foggy fields.

7. The ascetic's glowing face smiled, even though it was cold.

8. But clouds covered the horizon.

9. The day was extinguished like a sad candle.

PART FOUR

1. Summer flew away on the wings of time. It was carried off into the melancholy distance.

2. The autumn crept up. Everything it touched scattered, was soaked in foggy tears.

3. The old woman winter had long skulked along the Russian lowlands; she mumbled and threatened.

4. At that time Mrs. Nikolaeva was shooting fire from her mouth, like a musket.

5. Two millionaires went bust, cut down by Death. One famous writer[50] almost gave his life for his friends.

1. A great stir took place among the Moscow mystics: Drozhikovsky, fighting, went after Sergei Musatov, incited by Shipovnikov, the St. Petersburg mystic.[51]

2. There were a multitude of words . . . And people were drawn to Drozhikovsky, who was puffed up and on the rise.

3. Drozhikovsky's party merged with the party of the wily Shipovnikov . . . And Merezhkovich joined them.

4. Those remaining crowded even closer around the golden-bearded mystic and looked to him with hope.

5. They waited for a sign.

1. The horizon opened up from Voronukhin hills. A fiery triangle glowed from the dark clouds.

2. Crowds of people gathered and saw a sign in that.

3. They stayed for a long time, interpreting.

1. One came to another, flushed from the walk.

2. He shouted from the front hall, not taking off his boots, "Holy days have begun over Moscow! . . . Let's go, pal, and take a look at them in the frosty night! . . .

3. A new star shines in the heavens!

4. With its appearance we await the resurrection of the dead . . . The late Vladimir Solovyov was seen recently riding in a carriage wearing a fur cap and with his collar up!

5. In front of *witnesses* Solovyov threw open his fur coat, revealed himself, and shouted from the carriage, 'The end is near: that which we await will come to be.' "[52]

6. They both stepped out into the frost, and the frost turned their noses red.

7. They stepped quickly and turned into an empty side street. Like experienced sleuths, they examined the goods.

8. They peered into windows and other people's courtyards. Their eyes flashed.

9. The pipes wailed. The house gates squeaked. The bare trees whistled, scraping their branches.

10. The Milky Way descended lower than it should. A white cloud hung over their heads.

1. The snow crunched under the feet of passersby. Where in the day there had been a puddle, there was now black ice . . . And the chance passerby would go flying, feet in the air, parodying the course of European civilization.

2. A pair of trotters chased her along the bright street . . . And she, bright, drank in the white snow with her gaze.

3. Her cheeks were red from the frost, and her eyes reflected eternal striving.

4. Her coral-red lips paled.

5. There was a party yesterday, and today they were preparing a ball . . . But just now she was indulging in a snowy pleasure.

6. Like an empress, she flew on the wings of fantasy, and the wind whistled, bathing her in cold.

7. There were timeless fairy tales about that which never was and that which could have been but wasn't.

8. And her gaze was fixed on the infinite. and the infinite shone in her gaze.

9. And so she flew, like a holy vision that blew up a snowy dust.

1. The Church of the Burning Bush was locked. Nonetheless, they opened it from the inside.

2. They stood on the portico, unnoticed.

3. One was wearing a huge fur coat and fur hat, and the other was wearing a cotton overcoat and winter cap.

4. Both were tall, thin, and stooped. One would have looked like a church deacon if not for the gold-framed glasses, which he took off from his nose and wiped with a handkerchief.

5. A gray lion's mane of hair stuck out from under his cap. His gray beard was trimmed.

6. He looked at a bright star from which a golden thread extended and said, squinting, "So, Vladimir Sergeyevich? It's the blazing day!"

7. Kind wrinkles appeared around his mouth and eyes. He locked the church.

8. They both strolled along Poluektov Street while having a lively conversation.

1. At Maiden's Fields they sat on a bench covered with snow. They craned their necks toward the sky, risking losing their hats in the snow.

2. They looked at the sky with kind, nearsighted eyes.

3. They gazed at the Milky Way, and the Milky Way shone white with fog, irretrievable dreams, and lost youth.

4. The one wearing the fur hat said in a deep bass, "What more they'll see in the aftermath!"

5. In the distance, the bared branches of the trees shook their black arms, pleading for the holy breath.

1. They were silent for a while, performing a sacrament. Finally, the one wearing the cotton cap suddenly wailed like a child.

2. He pounded his hand on the frozen bench and, tugging his lion's mane of hair and gray beard, yelled, "Ah! . . . They caaan't do that, Vladimir Sergeyevich! They are completely compromising us with their uncooouth conclusions! . . . This is just savage! . . ."

3. Then he began to recount Sergei Musatov's conclusions, and the one next to him broke out in laughter like a madman. He stomped his foot with laugher, opening his coat.

4. His black but graying beard fluttered in the wind, and the trees shook their black arms, pleading for the holy breath.

5. The Milky Way shone white with fog, irretrievable dreams, and lost youth.

6. Finally, overcoming his laugher, he said, "It's nothing, Bars Ivanovich:[53] practice makes perfect."

7. A pair of passersby shuddered from this holy laughter, but they didn't bother to look into the face of the one laughing.

8. If they had seen it, their worried souls would have been wrenched with horror and tears.

9. They would have recognized old friends.

1. They sat on the bench a while longer, quietly talking among themselves.

2. Then they walked around Moscow, peeping into windows at their friends. They pressed up to the cold glass and blessed their friends.

3. More than one friend heard the storm knocking at the window; more than one friend raised his confused eyes to the dark window, squinting from the lamplight.

4. They didn't know that it was their old friends knocking, that their ghostly hands were blessing them.

5. So both wanderers walked around Moscow.

6. Finally, with a melancholy sigh, they quit their surroundings with a parting glance . . . They headed off to a joyous meeting.

7. Among the graves of Novodevichy Monastery, they shook hands and departed in peace.

1. Behind a broad table sat the founder of neo-Christianity himself, the one making conclusions from collected material, passing through all stages of sanity, receiving on the highest step the crown of holy madness.

2. Alongside him sat an enigmatic individual, returned from India—a participant in enigmatic mysteries.

3. It was a tanned man with a long nose, clean-shaven and with a golden earring.

4. There was also a theosophist[54] there, come from London, with red whiskers and wearing a fashionable tie.

5. There was someone else there, familiar, frozen in an affected pose; he said little and listened much.

6. The beaming host walked among his guests, wringing his white hands, and the mystics circled around him, asking, "Who's that sitting in such an affected pose?"

7. At which the host replied, cupping his hand to his mouth, "It's a former Kantian, disenchanted with his ideals . . . A seeker

of truth who spent time in a mental asylum but didn't find it there ...

8. He was recently discharged, and he came to learn about our views. We'll snatch him up in our net ..."

9. The mystics looked at the seeker of truth, and he at them.

1. In one corner they debated about the appearance of Solovyov, and in another an ardent mystic taught them how to raise the dead.

2. He swore that he had done a lot of work in this area and had already achieved some results.

3. They had their doubts.

4. New guests arrived with faces red from the frost. Father John came in a black silk cassock and smoothed down his velvety gray patch.

5. He silently sat behind the green table, silently examined the noisy group; in his blue eyes, the eyes of a child, you could see sadness.

1. Sergei Musatov spoke, "It's approaching . . . It has come back again . . . It's begun . . .

2. You were all witnesses, looking at the star which shone just as it did 1900 years ago . . .

3. It shines again now!"

4. The man with the earring exchanged glances with the red-whiskered theosophist, but Musatov continued:

5. "He grew in obscurity until that hour when the world needed him to appear . . . We have waited for him to announce himself from hour to hour . . .

6. But I won't mislead you about the cup from which we must drink: it is the battle with the Coming Beast.

7. Now it grows in Western Europe.

8. Now the whole world quivers looking at the lands surrounding Belgium, Holland, and northern France . . .

9. Therefore let the holy mother of our white banner man come—*the woman clothed in the sun! . . .*"

1. The prophet's speech was brief. His expressions more than odd. But even more oddly resounded the voice of the mysterious figure from India.

2. "Dreamy visions . . . Familiar to me . . . *I know* . . . You are drowning in dreams, cursing deceptive reality . . .

3. But dreams are the same reality, the same deception . . . You haven't yet slept without dreams . . ."

4. How bowed his shaved head, his earring glimmering, and cawed like a black raven at the entire assembly, "For so long, so long will they not recognize you, oh karma!"

1. The mystics went off to drink tea, the priest checked his watch, the theosophist straightened his red whiskers, and the figure from India immersed himself in the ephemeral . . .

2. The prophet raised his head, gazed at the frost patterns on the window, and spoke in a steady voice, responding to the objections, "Only sleep without dreams?

3. It would be odd if we did not pass through this stage, sleeping and not dreaming . . .

4. But when we saw that which no one had seen before, then *we awoke and returned . . .*"

5. Father John took his black glasses out of his pocket, put them on his sickly blue eyes, and examined the papers lying on the table.

6. Having turned around, Musatov waited for the bald man with the earring to object, but the man wasn't even listening to Musatov.

7. He was immersed in the ephemeral, studying the dreamless state.

8. The priest objected, saying timidly, "You're wrong!"

9. And when the enraged ascetic was ready to pounce on the insolent priest, the black diamonds of his eyes shining,

10. the priest wasn't afraid in the least but merely took off his glasses and studied the ascetic.

1. Then the theosophist of Jewish heritage intervened. Twisting his red whiskers, he struck up a mewling song.

2. In his fashionable tie he looked like a wily cat as he shook the prophet's hand, explaining, "We have much in common . . . We're fighting for the same thing . . .

3. Our emblem is pansynthesis . . . And we don't separate morality from knowledge. Religion, science, philosophy—they're all distinguished by quantity, not quality . . ."

4. But the disgruntled prophet freed his hand and haughtily said, "We know your interest in synthesis . . . We know what it means . . .

5. We don't need Gnostic ramblings, and your friends, the Hindus, aren't very flattering to us.

6. We aren't children: we love pure gold, not an amalgam . . .

7. In building a temple, you compare the cupola, crowned with a cross, to the foundation . . . Who has seen such a building?

8. Unite yourselves, and we'll heed you . . .

9. But we haven't really explained ourselves yet . . . Drop by for a cup of tea . . ."

10. Here the golden-bearded ascetic stopped because a familiar image sent a shiver down his spine: it was *the woman clothed in the sun.*

11. *This* he saw . . . And he caught John's blue gaze on himself, the gaze of a child, shining with condemnation.

12. But the priest made out as if he were examining papers . . .

1. Sprinkled with diamonds, *she* stood by the frosty window.

2. The starlight was shining somewhere over there, and she looked like a holy vision in her white dress, lit by the starlight and the moon.

3. She was going to a ball and remembered that which wasn't, which could have been but didn't happen.

4. Her soul mourned and, mourning, rejoiced . . . And, mourning, grew to the heavens! . . .

5. And there her diadem with twelve stars sparkled on her head . . . And she, tearing herself from the frosty window, continued to get ready for the ball . . .

6. And in her blue eyes there was such clarity and such strength that two stars fell from the moonlit sky, trembling with friendly compassion . . .

1. The theosophist was already riding in a carriage with the mysterious figure from India . . .

2. The mysterious figure from India yawned indifferently. And the theosophist sanctimoniously espoused:

3. "This is all nonsense . . . They're going against reason . . .

4. Reason teaches patience: the unexpected will only occur in five years . . .

5. Another five years . . . For now it's impossible to speak of anything with certainty, not before 1906."

6. The mysterious figure from India indifferently listened to the voice of reason . . .

7. And yawned.

1. Father John had already put on his wide boots, wrapped himself in a fur coat, and stepped out into the moonlit night.

2. . . . . He thought: "Trifles . . . But dangerous trifles."

3. There was a frost. The snow crunched under foot.

4. Lonely courtyards sang out of hidden dreams, "*It returns . . . Again it returns.*" And the priest pulled his coat even tighter.

5. He knew *much*, but for the time was silent.

1. They slept at night. Someone had a dream.

2. The Hindu stood on the banks of the Ganges with a lotus flower in his hands.

3. The Hindu taught, "Our knowledge is not an amalgam, but pure gold . . ."

4. And we have had our Kant, our Schelling, our Hegel, our positivists . . .

5. Really! . . . Shocking! . . .

6. Go study wisdom with Sri-Shankara-Ashra and Potangali! . . . What do you know of the *brahman* Vedas and *purusha* Samkas . . ."

7. That was how the Hindu taught the sleeping as he was reflected in the water upside down with a lotus flower in his hands.

1. Maslenitsa[55] came. Muscovites baked buttery bliny.

2. The weather was snowy. The jingling troikas vanished in the blizzard.

3. They awaited the announcement of the holy child. They didn't know who the child was, nor did they know who was clothed in the sun.

4. They deferred to the ascetic's knowledge.

5. He had studied too much, grieved too much, rent too many veils, loved Eternity too much.

6. Eternity lit a new star for her naughty child and favorite one, and now the whole world wondered at the novelty.

7. Eternity revealed the marked child and the woman clothed in the sun.

8. And as he thought and doubted, blizzards came and went.

9. Troikas, jingling their bells, vanished in the snowy dust.

10. Something tender whispered, "I haven't forgotten you, my dears . . . Soon we will see one another! . . ."

1. One sat by the other. They had both descended into the depths of theosophy.

2. One said to the other, "White light is comforting light, representing the harmonious blending of all colors . . .

3. Purple light is holy and Old Testament, and red is the symbol of martyrdom.

4. You mustn't confuse *red with purple*. Here they break apart.

5. The color purple is the noumenal, and the color red is the phenomenal."

6. They both sat in the depths of theosophy. One lied to the other.

1. The dawn burned through thick white smoke, bursting into pink laughter. The ascetic woke up and, yawning, reached for his watch on the night table.

2. He hopped out of bed and, remembering his upcoming appointment, blew a kiss to the frosty dawn.

3. He laughed, like a small *child*.

4. Then he was given a letter from the north of France. He ripped open the envelope and read it, rubbing his sleepy eyes.

1. They wrote to him that the *Beast* had been overcome with a digestive ailment and had given his soul to God, not reaching five years of age, frightened of his terrible fate.

2. The ascetic tugged at his golden beard with agitation and whispered, "And the Apocalypse?"

3. Putting on his pince-nez, he reread the letter.

4. Finally, he quickly got dressed, his hand shaking with worry.

5. And in the window, above the white snow, the crimson dawn laughed, mad and erratic, like a small *child*.

1. In the white of day, someone was chatting with the old woman Death, listening to the intimate songs of the blizzard.

2. Through the widow you could see a courtyard, covered in snow, and from the edge of the roof hung massive icicles.

3. He was neither young nor old, but *passive* and *knowledgeable*, and in conversation with the old woman he expressed unhappiness with the conduct of the Moscow mystics.

4. He said that disappointment awaits them because they chose the wrong path.

5. He was sad and regretful, and with his cloudy gaze he watched as the pale whirlwind of snow swirled and hid the icicles from his view.

6. It seemed that he said to himself, "Lord, they *don't see* themselves!"

7. But the old woman Death didn't want to understand his intimate fairy tales and suggested he write a letter.

1. The fairy tale stood in the sitting room. Looking at the card, she said, "Please . . ."

2. She automatically fixed her reddish hair, automatically went to meet the golden-bearded ascetic with a charming smile!

3. The chief of the neo-Christians was pale. His black diamonds didn't sparkle from under his drawn eyelashes.

4. The golden fluff of his hair fell onto his knitted brow. Wearing a long coat, he seemed to be shrouded in mystery.

5. He shouted to himself, "*The woman clothed in the sun.*" In his mind he raised his hands, performing the rite.

6. And in front of him stood the fairy tale, smiling inquisitively. Surprised by the ascetic's arrival, she kindly invited him to sit.

7. The ascetic informed her that he came to decline the centaur's invitation to lecture on mysticism at a charity evening for widows and the elderly.

8. His time was fully booked, and he couldn't take on any additional work.

9. The fairy tale only half listened to him, hoping to see him out quickly.

1. "And now we'll place this cylinder," said the wiry general and, cleaning the dust out of the cylinder with a small brush, put it down and started the gramophone.

2. Guttural sounds came from the horn, "O, if ooonly it were pooossible to expressss the full fooorce of my suffffferings . . ."

1. The evening dusk laughed over Moscow, and Musatov worriedly said, "Don't be shocked . . . I have something important to tell you . . . When I'm able to come to you . . ."

2. He blushed, and the shocked fairy tale hastily said, "Well, we receive guests every day between two and four! . . ."

3. At that moment the curtain was moved aside. In ran a handsome boy with blue eyes and curls down to his shoulders.

4. This of course was the male child destined to rule all the nations with an iron rod.

5. "Sweet boy," said Sergei Musatov, making a superhuman effort not to give himself away. "What's his name?"

6. But the fairy tale laughed, turned her memorable face to the little one, straightened his locks, and with feigned sternness said, "Nina, how many times have I told you not to come in here without knocking."

7. Nina pouted her lips, and the fairy tale happily told the ascetic, "My husband and I dress her like a boy."

8. The dusk laughed, like a small child, all red and mad.

9. The edifice, built on a shaky foundation, fell; its walls collapsed, raising a cloud of dust.

10. The knife plunged into the lover's heart, and scarlet blood flowed into the mournful chalice.

11. The heavens were rolled up into a useless bundle, and the fairy tale kept up a mundane conversation with charming kindness.

12. All of his blood rushed to the deceived prophet's head, and, barely standing on two feet, he hurried to leave the bewildered fairy tale.

1. "And so, if I put this cylinder here, then you can listen to Petr Nevsky, the lively accordion player and singer," shouted the general, excited and wiry.

2. Guttural sounds already came from the horn, words full of platitudes, and after each verse Petr Nevsky would say under the sounds of the accordion, "Goooootttt, dddis is very gooooot . . ."

1. "This is how the cookie crumbles," said the chef in a white hat looking at an unsuccessful cookie.

2. "Oh well, there will be others . . ." And with these words he tossed the cookie to a greedy mutt.

1. At Savastianov's bakery they asked if they had any yeast left and, learning that the yeast had run out, asked if they had ordered more yeast.

1. The matinee of the Public Artistic Theater was finishing . . . Behind a foggy cover, the gray dreamer was leading the white woman to glaciers in order to clothe her in the sun.[56]

2. An avalanche tumbled with dust and a roar and carried them off to eternal peace.

3. And Eternity herself stood on the cliff in her black robes, and her voice rang out like a string pulled too taught.

4. This wasn't reality, but its representation . . . And *they* quickly lowered the curtain because there was nothing to represent.

1. One sat by the other. They both said intelligent things.

2. One said to the other, "If the color red is a synonym of God the Father, and red and white is a synonym of Christ, His Son, then what is white a synonym of? . . ."

3. "We have already lived through the color red, have already seen the One Who Has Arrived *not only by water but also by blood* . . . Now we will see the third kingdom, the *white* kingdom, the *new* word . . ."

4. One excitedly wagged his finger in front of the other's nose . . . The other believed the first.

1. Popovsky's teeth hurt . . .

1. A tramp stood on the corner and showed passersby his nakedness, revealed it before them.

2. To the left walked a student, and to the right, the ascetic . . . And to both the tramp pointed to his nakedness.

3. The student abhorred personal charity, and Musatov didn't notice the tramp.

4. Eternity whispered to her naughty child, her favorite, "I was joking . . . Now you joke . . . Let's all joke . . ."

5. The deceived prophet was haughtily silent at Eternity's playfulness. He raised his beaver-fur collar.

6. This wasn't the *woman clothed in the sun*; it was a deceptive fairy tale. But then why did her image set Sergei Musatov ablaze? . . .

7. He whispered, "Don't, don't! . . ." And the tramp scurried after him, holding his vile breath, trying to slip his hand into Musatov's pocket.

8. For ten years the tramp had battled with capital, regulated property, and more than once been thrown in the clink.

1. It was already evening. The Muscovites were already raising a complete ruckus.

2. In the boardinghouses, the scammers and the fast talkers were tussling.

3. In the puppet booths the tambourines were jangling, and the painted clown ran out into the cold to dance in front of a gathering crowd, urging them into the den of disrepute.

4. This kind of entertainment was different from the genuine sort, which was harmonious like a well-tuned orchestra . . . *Here* there were just flakes.

5. Someone banged on a Turkish drum, and the carousel spun wildly, flashing stripes of red cotton, gold leaf, and tinted lamps.

6. Wooden lions spread their jaws, and hatmakers rode on their backs chewing sunflower seeds.

7. The suburban restaurants shimmered with ominous lights, attempting to conceal their mortality with gas and electricity.

8. In the theater Omon, naked singers shouted obscenities.

1. A terrible lifelessness hung over the city. Torches of horror and madness flickered on both sides of the sidewalk.

2. The feverish movement didn't hide the horror and revealed its wounds even more.

3. It seemed that avengers were flapping their invisible wings over the city.

1. They awaited a *comforter*, and instead came an *avenger* . . .

1. Lit by the streetlamps, the prophet was still staggering down the street.

2. He went into a restaurant in order to drown his nagging grief in drink.

3. He had never done that before. He thought of his brother Pavel.

4. Swallowing chilled champagne in a separate room, he cried out, "Don't . . . Don't . . . Where are we flying off to? . . .

5. Isn't it time to stop? . . ."

1. There was a concert. Shlyapin[57] sang. He sang about fate, how it looms.

2. They called for Shlyapin. They talked about Shlyapin. Shlyapin came out for an encore.

3. During the intermissions, the crimson Nebarinov performed, twirling his chestnut sideburns, bowing to those in the audience, and noting those who were absent.

4. The charming fairy tale smiled at the aristocratic old man, as if she were an angel and the hall her heavenly kingdom.

5. Tall, gray Kandislavsky stood there, with his black mustache, and here the stout centaur was leading an elegant brunet with a curled mustache by the hand through the cultured crowds, and all around they whispered, "Look, there goes the famous writer Drozhikovsky! . . ."

6. Silk dresses rustled.

1. But then everybody took their seats, and a singer came onstage, her dress covered in diamonds.

2. The fairy tale listened to the singer but was exhausted by life's vanities.

3. Today was a formal dinner, and yesterday morning she had received guests, but now she could stop smiling and fantasize.

4. The singer, sparkling with diamonds, stretched her neck as she sang, "Where werrre yoooou, happinesssss? . . . Oh, the tiiiired get eeeeven more exhausted."[58]

1. Still as a sculpture she stood in a black cowl, and in her raised hands could be seen the eternal rosary.

2. The pale marble face had frozen in tearless weeping. Like the fairy tale, she languished under the moonless sky.

3. They both suffered, they both languished, they were both drawn to the otherworldly.

4. They both had the same grief.

5. The wind, blowing through the quiet sanctuary, rocked the metal wreathes on the snowy graves . . . And the wreathes rustled, "Where werrre yoooou, happinesssss? . . . Oh, the tiiiired get eeeeven more exhausted! . . ."

1. Flushed and drunk, he paid his tab and, swaying slightly, left the restaurant.

2. The image of the *woman clothed in the sun* laughed in his face. He heard the familiar words, "My husband and I dress her like a boy . . ."

3. Then drunk Musatov slipped and went flying, feet in the air, parodying the course of European civilization.

4. He picked himself up, brushed off the snow, and whispered, "Where are we flying off to . . . Don't, don't!"

5. He raised his beaver-fur collar.

6. And death hung over him, the sound of its invisible wings echoing.

7. Avenging cries echoed.

1. *They* showed him the open door. He listened to *their* advice.

2. Don't reproach him, good sirs! *They* themselves whispered to him, "Here your misunderstanding will be resolved."

3. And he went into the damned place, and the sleepy doorman didn't ask what he wanted.

4. *They* showed him the door, and on the door *they* had attached a sign.

1. There was a hanging lamp over the table, just as in any public building.

2. A pitcher and glass were on the table.

3. A stout red-nosed, red-haired man sat on the floor in a white cap and underwear.

4. He raised his index finger and read a lecture to an invisible audience in a clear voice.

1. "Say that I have at my disposal a metal pipe.

2. I bury it in the ground, covering the opening with an oven door. I bring some morons to the spot and remove the oven door in front of their eyes to reveal the hole."

3. The blob finished his lecture and looked around with satisfaction. But then the door noisily opened. In hopped a skinny invalid with bushy black eyebrows, and frightful gaze, and a shaggy head of hair.

4. He was barefoot and in his underwear. He coughed like a consumptive seeing Musatov enter. He hobbled to the cawing stout man and in whisper commanded him to be silent.

5. At which the barefooted lecturer wailed in a mighty voice, "Petrusha, let me belt out just one more little horror!"

1. "I take it that you have come to ferret out our mysteries, my dear: I am at your service." With these words he bid Musatov take a seat and sat down in front of him, pressing his hands to his chest to hold back his hacking cough . . .

2. "People rarely come here. I think it's unforgivable frivolity: the fact that you are seeing us is, sir, a great honor for you . . .

3. Well, sir? . . . What do you have to say? . . ."

4. By that time the dumbfounded Musatov, understanding *the heart of the matter*, asked, "What are the world's great truths?"

5. "Everything comes into focus, differentiates . . ."

6. "I know that very well myself," said a disappointed Musatov, at which the cripple was suddenly indescribably happy.

7. "Really?" he shouted, "you've made it *that* far!"

8. "Of course: any grade-schooler knows that . . ."

9. "And do you know that everything returns?" cried the cripple with explanatory gestures.

10. "Certainly, I know that too," complained Musatov, "that's not why I came . . ."

11. "In that case I have nothing more to teach you, wise one," squealed Petenka, twisting into a sinister grimace and crossing his arms in feigned exhaustion . . .

12. "Well, I can tell you the mystery of mysteries to reassure you: *there are no mysteries.*"

13. The hanging lamp sputtered, just as in every public building. The stinking soot made Musatov sneeze.

14. Musatov was fed up with the cripple's lies, and, banging his fist on the table, he surprised himself by bellowing, "No need to see me out, pals."

15. Drunk and haughty, he now resembled his brother Pavel.

1. "You don't dare to disbelieve," rustled Petr, like the autumn wind, leaning his threatening head to Musatov's face and sprinkling him with saliva like the rain, "because *I am the essence, the thing itself!*"

2. Musatov gulped down several glasses of water, grabbed his head, and was burning up as if he had a fever. The words of the babbling stout man rang in his ears, "Say that it's hot like in Africa . . . I completely undress and plop down on an anthill . . . A multitude of small insects sink their teeth into my body! . . ."

3. The stout man crawled on the floor and laughed, laughed until he collapsed.

1. "Have I really discovered the fourth-dimensional world?" thought Musatov, horrified with the structure of this world, but the essence of things, in the form of Petrusha, added, "Yes, yes, yes, yes, yes! A million times yes! This is the so-called fourth-dimensional world! . . . But the thing is that it doesn't exist at all . . . People have traveled up and down the three-dimensional world. They know everything, but knowing this, haven't calmed down. Like alcoholics, they need more and more vodka, even though the vodka is gone and the bottle is empty . . . And so they've invented for themselves some fourth dimension on the other side of the wall . . . And now they're pounding holes in the wall trying to break through to this fourth dimension . . . Let them pound!" he shouted, making the walls shake, his teeth and the whites of his eyes flashing. "Let them pound, because the *Avenger* lives . . . Hark! The sound of sinister wings is above us, just as it was above Gomorrah on the day of its destruction! . . ."

2. "But is there anything on the other side of the wall?" whispered Musatov, frozen.

3. "The same room with the same wallpaper as in every public building, with the same fool who beats his fist against the wall imagining the there is something different on the other side . . . Let them pound; like a giant furry spider, the Tormentor stretches its web for the madman in order to drink with pleasure his inflamed blood! . . ."

4. Done speaking, Petr furrowed his brow, and green lightning flashed in his wild eyes with horrifying brightness. But he quickly extinguished these flames, lowered his gaze, and looked like a spent volcano.

5. Deathly pale, he sat in deep silence.

1. "Well, what about death?" inquired Musatov.

2. "Death is like relocating a resident from room number 10000 to room number 10001, if they have the necessary paperwork," said the malevolent Petr, perking up, waking from the dead.

3. The hanging lamp quietly went out, and the servant in uniform brought the gentlemen each a cup of tea with bagels.

1. "Perhaps the union of East and West?"

2. Petr the Terrible replied, "What kind of union: the West stinks of decay, and the East no longer stinks only because it decayed long ago!"

3. "Then on whom does the future smile?"

4. Then there was a small problem: the heart of that matter grabbed his falling drawers and sat down in shock. Then he tapped his high forehead with a finger and shook his head reproachfully, "Eh! . . . What are you saying, friend? . . . You've poked around in our mysteries and still don't know your ABCs! . . ."

5. Then he poured a pitcher of cold water on Musatov's head, muttering, "And the blacks? . . . And the blacks? . . ."

6. "So, the blacks," said the prophet in an utterly dejected voice, fixing his wet hair.

7. "The blacks, the blacks! Of course, the blacks! . . . The dark-skinned, red-lipped blacks are the future masters of the earth!"

8. Then Musatov dropped his head to the table and froze in a fit of drunken despair.

1. The amusing stout man started a new lecture for the invisible.

2. "I cut open my gut . . . I pull out and clean my intestines . . . Cutting out the part I need, I sew the ends back together,

3. and that's that," he ecstatically concluded his lecture. And barefoot Petr already pounced on him, whispering feverishly, "*At it again*, you gray old purveyor of sin!"

4. But the stout man piteously implored, "Dear Pierre, let me belt out just one more little horror!"

5. At which Petr said, like the eye of a storm not portending anything good, "Quiet, and don't open up old wounds!"

6. But Musatov didn't hear any of this, running down the stairs.

7. He whispered, "Lord, what is this? What on earth is this?"

8. He nearly knocked over a black man who was haughtily walking down the well-lit street in an elegant top hat and dressed to the nines.

9. The curious black man looked around and audaciously thought, "What does Moscow have on Chicago!"

10. Under the influence of this revolting thought, he smiled his thick-lipped mug.

11. And the sinister kites flew over this Sodom, diving for the stinking carrion, happy for its wished-for demise.

1. And after Musatov's departure, the barefoot oddballs sat peaceably around the table. Each was stirring a glass of tea with a spoon.

2. Over their heads a strange particularity was forming: a pair of real horns, growing God knows why or where from . . .

3. The stout one said to the skinny one, "And are you an artificer, and are you a cheat, and are you a liar, Petenka?"

4. At that he laughed.

5. But Petr didn't share his amusement, twisting around, "Please, don't try to guess where power lies . . . *For they are tricky . . .*"

1. It seems to me that you, gentlemen, would have seen the two of them sitting on the graves.

2. They were tall, thin, and wiry; one of their beards flapped in the wind, and his gray eyes looked out sadly from beneath his eye lashes, black as coal.

3. The other was in a winter cap and gold eyeglasses.

4. One said to the other, "Bars Ivanovich, I still feel sorry for Musatov, despite his vanity and self-assuredness!"

5. And the other shouted, "Eh! Vladimir Sergeyevich, you can't forgive such bumbling!

6. After all, Musatov's conclusions are the conclusions of a shoemaker!"

7. Perhaps it just seemed that way to me, gentlemen, and among the graves stood only a beautiful woman, grieving with tearless weeping, wearing a black cowl and holding an eternal rosary . . .

1. At night, everybody slept. The poor and the rich. The stupid and the smart.

2. Everybody slept.

3. Some slept in a ball. Some with their mouths open. Some slept like the dead.

4. Everybody slept.

5. And the bright day was already angrily knocking at the windows. It seemed that it beckoned anew to the exhausted.

6. An awakening to new struggles.

1. In the morning they rang the bells because the time of joy was over and the time of great depression had come.

2. At the markets they sold dried mushrooms, and it was a bit slushy outside.

3. Wetness dripped from the roofs. The sinister sky threatened a cloudy spring.

1. In the office sat a famous scholar, stretched out on a leather chair, sharpening a pencil.

2. His white hair haphazardly fell on his high forehead, honored with many famous scientific discoveries.

3. In front of him was a young professor of literature, standing in an elegant pose and smoking an expensive cigar.

4. The famous scholar said, "No, I'm not satisfied with youth! . . . I find it impure, and here's why:

5. Fully armed with the empirical sciences, they could rebuff all feasible conclusions of mysticism, occultism, demonism, etc. . . . But they prefer to flirt with darkness . . .

6. A love of falsehood has taken root in their soul. The straightforward light of truth burns their weak eyes.

7. All of this would be forgivable if they believed in this nonsense . . . But they don't even believe it . . .

8. They need only catchy absurdities . . ."

9. The young professor of literature rested his elbows on the back of a chair and politely listened to the gray celebrity, although his mouth curled into a slight smile.

10. He offered a self-satisfied objection, "That's all true, but you must agree that this reaction against scientific formalism is purely temporary.

11. Without overlooking the extremes and absurdities, at heart we see here the very same search for truth.

12. After all, Spencer's differentiation and integration encompass only the formal aspects of the perceptible world, allowing for other interpretations . . .[59]

13. After all, nobody can contradict evolutionary continuity. The issue is just in finding sense in that evolution . . .

14. The youth are looking for that sense!"

15. The famous scholar let out a sad sigh, closed his penknife, and imposingly replied, "Then why does it all always fall apart! What a lack of honesty and integrity in all this affectation . . ."

16. They were both wrong.

1. In the archpriest Blagosklonsky's clean little room the golden-bearded prophet poured out his complaints.

2. He had run here pale and distraught, and Father Ivan held his cold hands.

3. "What is *this*, Father, what on earth is *this*? *This* wasn't a dream or reality?

4. My heart is overflowing with blood, and I'm burning up!"

5. The white priest quietly bowed over the horrified man's head. He caressed him with his blue gaze, the gaze of a child.

6. He silently stroked his golden curls. The ascetic's heart contracted painfully from the old man's caresses.

7. The caressing priest asked in a whisper, "Do you love her very much?"

8. And the distraught child shared all of his deceptive dreams with the priest, as if with another child, old and innocent.

9. Outside the slush was melting, and the overcast clouds made the priest's face seem wrinkled and yellowish.

1. "But what on earth was that yesterday? Who were they? Do such horrors really happen in reality?"

2. Then the priest lowered his head as if he had been caught red-handed. It seemed that he was ringed with a subtle foggy bit of crepe.

3. He tugged at his curls, hopelessly waved his old man's hand, and finally he said, "Don't think too hard about it.

4. All sorts of things go on . . . But about *that*, it's best not to say anything . . .

5. Do I not see that we're all flying somewhere at breakneck speed!

6. Do I not comprehend *what that* means!

7. And even now: do you not see that between us there is something alienating, harmful, horrifying!"

8. The ascetic looked at the old man's despondent image, draped in foggy crepe. The old man nervously tugged at the cross around his neck.

9. The golden-bearded one looked around and understood that *not everything was as it should be.*

10. They silently stared at each other, and Sergei Musatov whispered, "*And so it flows . . . And so it flows from everywhere!*"

11. They silently crossed themselves, and the priest whispered, "May God restore to life!"

12. Then Father John sat Sergei Musatov down and quietly lectured him about their common mysteries:

13. "Now, when you're dejected and your soul burns with love, *they* gather around you in an invisible cloud, a horrible cloud, driving you to despair, unfurling a scroll of horror . . .

14. Love and pray: universal love always wins."

15. John said a bit about universal love, neither accepting nor rejecting anything, and a white breeze blew from these words, chasing off the *horrible herd.*

16. He and the white priest stood on the slushy sidewalk, wrapped in a dark fog.

17. The priest left to perform vespers, and Musatov got a cab home, intending to pack that very evening and head to his brother Paul, who was burning up from drunkenness in the village.

18. At the intersection of two streets the cabbie stopped because a funeral procession was winding along.

19. They were taking a departed government official to his final resting place.

20. The servant of God Dormidont had died after a brief but painful illness.

21. And so passed the funeral processing, with a capless worker from the funeral agency at its head.

22. In his hand he held a small icon wrapped in a white cloth.

23. The day flickered out, like a sad candle.

1. "I'm bored . . . This life doesn't satisfy me . . .

2. I smile like a doll, and my soul wants that which never was and that which could have been but wasn't."

3. The fairy tale wept by the window, pressing a scented handkerchief to her blue eyes.

4. And the drooping centaur was silent, biting his nails with chagrin.

5. He did everything he could to amuse his beloved wife.

6. And here she wept by the window, whispering, "Dull, dull!" She absentmindedly watched the caretakers sweep the dirty slush outside.

7. Outside they lit the streetlamp . . . And her diamond star sparkled in her brilliant hair.

8. And she looked like a holy vision.

9. The day flickered out, like a sad candle.

1. The railroad tracks stretched along the snowy plain. A train raced along the tracks.

2. It was cold in the train car. Musatov sat bundled in a fur coat.

3. The fairy tale appeared before him. She smiled sarcastically in his face with her coral-red lips, and he whispered "I love . . ."

4. A couple of people were talking in the next compartment, on the other side of the partition.

5. One shouted, "Don't say it . . . We *know* a thing or two, we're *waiting* for something . . . We're interested in the Gospels . . ."

6. The other retorted, "Nonsense . . ."

1. Mystical assertions muddied the press. The liberals, the Populists, and the vestiges of former Marxists united and bowled over their few opponents, relying on popular opinion.

2. One article in particular gained notice, and its author became popular.

3. It was titled *Mysticism and Physiology* . . . And there was nothing in it objectionable to the mystics.

4. Earlier, they had become distraught on learning that Musatov had fled Moscow, seeing in that the flickering out of a newborn star.

5. Only Shipovnikov, the Saint Petersburg mystic, took up the gauntlet and responded with a comment that began and ended with the words: *well, so what?*

1. These were new times.

2. But the new times didn't bring any news. God only knew why they worried.

3. A horrible wave of poverty nearly broke out over Moscow.

4. An old woman arrived to Moscow on a freight train. Stepping out onto the platform with a basket in her hand, she stopped the chief conductor and pulled a black rooster from the basket.

5. When the stunned conductor asked what it meant, she replied, "Last year someone had a dream: the icon doors in the church were opened three times, and three times a rooster came out: white, red, and black.

6. The white signified the harvest, the red was war, and the black was sickness.

7. We have eaten bread, we have fought the yellow Mongols, and now we shall die . . ."

8. The malignant old woman was expelled from Moscow, and they forgot about the rooster.

9. It started to run around Moscow, and from that time a plague spread.

10. But active measures averted a catastrophe.

1. In the evening, the sun set. The sky turned crimson . . . An intangible tenderness coursed through the land.

2. Someone *calm and knowledgeable* stood on Voronukhin hills, the collar of his cotton coat raised. He was wearing an official's cap with ribbons.

3. He looked at the factories and the city outskirts, spread out in front of his gaze, and there was such strength in this gaze and faith in his features that it seemed to vanquish all fear.

4. The end of his nose was red from the cold, and he said, "So, Lord! *I see You.*"

5. He went to the old woman Death for a cup of tea.

1. Father John was with the old woman Death. The doorbell rang.

2. One who is neither old nor young, just *passive* and *knowledgeable* had come.

3. She introduced her guest to John, kindly noting, "This is Aleksei Sergeyevich Petkovsky . . . You've heard tell of him, Father."

4. And the priest smiled, and the priest extended his old hands and joyfully said, "If only there were more like you! . . ."

5. They sat with the old woman Death at a round table. The samovar hissed and blew warm steam in their faces.

6. The darkening blue sky could be seen through the window, with the diamonds of the stars appearing one by one.

7. The old woman Death served them tea, and they quietly talked among themselves.

8. Father John said, "This was just the first attempt . . . Their failure doesn't deter us . . . We are not faithless; we have learned *much* and anticipate *much* . . .

9. They were not on the true path. They perished . . . We draw no conclusions and do not speak of it . . . We are only waiting, O Lord, for Your Glory.

10. And do you not see that it is *close* . . . That it already *looms over us* . . . That we have to abide only a short while longer . . . That the unexpected is approaching . . ."

11. And Father John's interlocutor finished a second cup of tea and replied, "So, Lord! I know You . . ."

12. And they were silent . . . And they silently listed to the *eternal approach* . . . And it seemed that *something was flying, making a noise and singing* . . .

13. And it seemed that somewhere on the other side of the wall *someone's steps approached* . . .

14. And the old woman Death was also silent, also listened to the *eternal approach* as she washed the cups.

15. And it was already night . . . The diamonds of the stars had appeared.

16. The Milky Way descended lower than it should have. It shone white with fog, irretrievable dreams, and lost youth.

17. And in the garden the trees stretched their bony arms in a gust of fresh wind, rejoiced, and shouted in chorus, "The groooom will cooome at miiidnight! . . ."

1. And again it was early spring. A bunch of gold and red roses hung inside the house. Around it were marble monuments and chapels.

2. The trees rustled over the lonely graves.

3. It was the kingdom of frozen tears.

4. And again, as it had a year ago, the young apple tree blossomed its white, fragrant flowers by the red house.

5. These were the flowers of forgetting illness and sadness; these were the flowers of the new day . . .

6. And again and again under the apple tree sat a nun, grasping a rosary with trembling hands.

7. And again and again the red dusk laughed, sending a breeze to the apple tree . . .

8. And again the apple tree sprinkled the nun with the white flowers of forgetting . . .

9. The cries of the swifts echoed, and the nun idly burned in the glow of the sunset . . .

1. And again and again a beautiful young woman walked among the graves in a spring dress . . .

2. It was the fairy tale . . .

3. And again and again they stared at one another, she and the nun, smiling, like old friends, at one another.

4. They wordlessly told one another that all was not yet lost, that many holy joys were ahead . . .

5. *That it is approaching, it is coming,* the sweet, the impossible, the sadly contemplative . . .

6. And the fairy tale stood among the graves as if under an enchantment, listening to the rattling of the metal wreaths, shaking in the wind.

7. The future spread out before her, and she was bathed in joy . . .

8. She *knew*.

9. Small flames puffed smoke somewhere on the graves.

10. The black nun lit lamps over some graves but not over others.

11. The wind rattled the metal wreaths, and the clock slowly marked the time.

12. Dew settled on a gray stone chapel. On it were etched the words, "Peace unto you, Anna, my wife!"

THE RETURN

(Third Symphony)

PART ONE

I

The bottom of the ash-gray cloud puffed and flashed on the horizon.

Above it the sky was a golden green, and below it a discolored yellowish pink ribbon unfurled.

A child played on the bank, digging in the velvet sand with a mother-of-pearl shell . . . From time to time, he laughed slyly. And clapped his hands.

And blue sparks shot out of his eyes.

The rippling, undulating waves scattered Bermuda pearls.

Done playing, the child sat on the bank and called his friend Crab from the depths of the sea until the blue wave delivered his friend to the child with a splash.

Crab was humongous and stout. They began to play with one another.

The child clapped his hands. He tossed round stones at kind Crab. And catching him, Crab put his fat claw on the child's head and dragged the runt along the sandy beach.

Then, finished playing with one another, they shook their limbs, and the stout crab went back to the depths of the sea.

And it was almost evening . . . The foam sparkled like rubies . . .

Everything around was shrouded in pale blue fog . . . A smattering of stars jingled . . .

Vicious evening lightning already blazed twice from behind the cloud.

A white stone that resembled a person could be seen on the bank in the distance—as if an old man had frozen in place, hunched over and immersed in thought.

Squinting his blue eyes, the child laughed, looked at the stone, and said, "I know you . . . You're just pretending . . ."

But the white silhouette didn't move. Because it was only a stone.

And the child yawned . . . Watching the outline of the shore, he whispered earnestly, "Come quickly . . ."

The child was afraid of lightning and clouds . . . He went off to a heap of rocks.

He lived here. He slept here. From here he laughed at the clouds.

The black, nighttime snipes landed . . . They ran along the shore whistling, "Waaiit . . ." He fell asleep to this sound . . .

The ash-gray sea ebbed in snowy silver, as if cleaned of all filth.

A low wavy cloud hung over the sea, covering the crescent moon.

Crab crawled up, shook his whiskers, and snapped his claws. He was warming himself on land, watching the sleeping child with sly, tender eyes.

The past, long forgotten, eternal like the world, wrapped the distance in a moist shroud . . . Sweet weeping echoed in the sea: ecstasy was driving the universe.

The low cloud, agitated and puffing, lingered over the sea and then, bursting from ecstasy, flew off somewhere to the side in holy fragments.

There, where the stone once was, sat an old man. He turned his expressionless face to the sleeping child, and in a velvet bass voice he shouted to the sleeping one, "Your quiet happiness exudes silver . . .

That's good. That's for the best . . ."

The old man walked along the shore, drawing mystical signs in the sand with his blinding iron rod.

He was noting the speed of the interplanetary dances; he had already noted them for millennia, but he never ceased to be amazed . . .

He muttered, "So commands the Lord God." Dull underground thuds accompanied his words in a strange harmony.

A giant white hump hung between the earth and the sky, and the crescent moon, piercing it in one spot, sent its soft rays to the old man.

II

The child woke up. He was lying on his back. It seemed to him that the blue of the sky, speckled with sonorous gold, had descended closer to his face.

And he lifted his head, but the sky retreated, and nobody knew how high it was.

The child looked around with sleepy eyes. The tide was in. The sea approached. Now it licked the gray rocks.

In the distance a cherub rushed by like a crimson meteor, leaving a streak of fire on the sea.

And the sea whispered, "Don't, don't . . ." And the cherub dissipated in a shower of sparks.

198 \   **The Return**

It seemed to him that the universe included him in its worldly embrace . . . Everything toppled around him.

He was hanging over the black abyss, in the unmeasurable depth in which the constellations raced.

He was drawn toward this black universal embrace. He was scared of falling into the abyss . . .

It just seemed that way.

Everything was calm. It remained as before. Cries could be heard in the distance: the mysterious old man was completing his calculations, rejoicing in the motion of the planets.

The child began to walk along the gray stones. He reassured himself, "These are just dreams . . . And I am not afraid . . ."

The sea roared. A flock of black snipes rushed by, brushing the child with their resilient wings.

He sensed a familiar nearness. He didn't have time to turn around, when his shoulders were bundled in warm goat fur and an old man's hand began to stroke his silky hair.

The old man had come. The child smiled at him, "You've come again. You're not stone . . ."

The old man interrupted him in a thundering bass voice, "That's good. That's for the best . . ." The old man sat next to him.

The thin, stooped half-moon was lost in the blue expanse, pierced by cloudy needles that were carried up and away . . . The old man was glowing and looked like snowy silver.

At times he leaned toward the sleeping one, raising his hands over him in blessing; at times he turned away and sat motionless, full of radiance.

Gray hair streaked with white covered his stooped shoulders. His beard reached to his waist.

His gray eyes, two abysses resting in huge sockets, burrowed into the calm distance.

The pale blue clouds were extinguished. They hurried off to the west. The emerald-gold sky turned pink.

The child wiped his dark blue eyes. He whispered, "The old man is still here." He dozed off.

The old man's silver and white cassock and his blinding iron staff trembled with orange sparks.

A mysterious diamond necklace swayed on the old man's chest. It looked like little flames sputtering on his chest . . . And hanging from the necklace was a symbol of unchanging Eternity.

The old man was silent, but a suppressed ecstasy burst from his fiery chest.

It was as if he whispered, "The constellation Boötes has lived for a hundred million years. It will live another hundred million . . . But a terrible comet nears Canis Major . . ."

He was taking stock of his accounts.

The child woke up. The old man vanished. He remembered the nocturnal visit with sadness.

He glanced at the spot where the white stone had protruded. The stone was gone.

The tide had suddenly swept it to the sea in order to toss it back out again . . .

The child strolled along the shore in thought. He gathered pearls. Sometimes he stomped on the pearls. They crunched under his feet.

The wind blew in his face, spraying him with velvet sand.

III

A white-winged eagle rattled the surroundings with its victorious shriek, and the child heard this shriek, huddled in the black cliff . . .

In each of its eyes was a giant turquoise stone, and azure-blue rays emanated from its eyes because, from time to time, the child heard a call coming from Eternity.

He was sad and excited. He knew that the old man wandered in these parts.

A kindly centaur floated on the backdrop of the orange horizon, splitting the transparent waves with its hooves . . . A fiery ruby orb rose above the sea.

An obedient cloud floated alongside him with its long, thin fingers of molten gold . . . Soon it was all covered with a white hump.

The hunchbacked edges shimmered.

Crab crawled up to him. He sat in front of him, sitting bowlegged. They discussed current events with excitement.

The inhabitant of the sea hurried to inform the child that there was a disturbance in the depths: just last night an unfamiliar serpent had crawled up to him and was now lying low in the coral.

That's what Crab said, opening his claws in the warmth of the sun. With tears in his eyes, he begged the child to be careful and not to stray too far from the gray rocks.

But the child wasn't afraid of snakes: he knew that the old man was here too.

The curious child clambered up the black cliff hanging over the sea. The clear water hid no secrets.

The sea stars seeded the depths. In the depths, the child also saw the sleeping serpent and the pale pink coral with little fish flashing brilliantly above it.

It was an enormous serpent with a small head, like that of a calf, crowned with golden horns.

The child laughed at the sleeping horror and whispered in his pearly voice, "You don't scare me, monster: I'm high above you. I like this! I'm safe from your attacks!"

So the little one shouted, sometimes going pale, sometimes flaring up, but his light blond hair quietly stood on end from the unfathomable horror.

Suddenly the sleeping reptile raised its calf's head—licking its lips, it instantly disappeared into the growth of coral . . .

Turning around, the child saw the old man.

The old man's cassock didn't shimmer like the night, and on his marble brow you could just make out a wrinkle.

The old man approached, not looking at the child and from time to time bending toward the ground.

He was collecting pearls.

Watery fragments of clouds—snow-white and blown by the wind—floated by low over the cliffs.

A fast bird, rising up, occasionally pierced them with its cry.

The evening stealthily crept up. The dusk again glowed with a noxious and insidious flame. A giant cliff stood in the distinct clearness of the east.

There, a stern man paced back and forth in the evenings, guarding Eden. A burning sword flashed in his hands.

Occasionally he lifted the fiery blade of his sword over the world at dusk: then it would seem like flashes of lightning.

A thin, curved streak of silver rose above the waves, and the diffuse clouds shimmered like familiar threads of silver on pale blue velvet.

The child didn't return to the gray rocks but instead spent the night on the black cliff. He wasn't afraid of anything since, from time to time in the distance, the cloud flashed silver and then vanished once again.

The child looked lovingly at the far-off flashing cloud, whispering, "That's the old man. His cassock is shining . . ."

In the distance a cherub dashed by like a crimson meteor.

When everything was asleep, when everything had quieted down, something that looked exactly like a giant stick rose to the sky from the depths of the sea. It was the sea snake.

Its horned calf's head stretched up and quickly turned in all directions, gazing and sniffing.

Then it dove back into the deep as quietly as it had come up.

Looking at the surface of the sea, nobody could tell what horrors lie beneath.

The child had a dream. He thought that giant serpents were suffocating him in their powerful embraces.

He woke up, but everything was calm. In the distance, in this peaceful embrace, rambling and black, the cherub dashed like a crimson meteor, leaving a flying streak of fire on the sea.

And the sea whispered, "Don't, don't . . ." And the cherub dissolved in a shower of sparks . . .

From then on, the child would meet the old man on the steep slopes and in the shoals.

His silent silhouette was wreathed in mystery. The impression was magnified when the child looked at the old man's stooped shoulders.

Then it seemed to him that the old man was *completely exceptional.*

Once, turning around suddenly, the old man caught a blue gaze fixed on him, filled with misunderstanding.

But the old man had no desire to clear up the misunderstanding: he didn't say a word to the child.

In those days, the air was transparent, like radiant azure, like a leopard skin. In the evenings the crimson gleam of a giant sword flashed particularly brightly, rocking on the waves.

Sometimes echoes of thunder flew to him. They were carried on the breeze, which didn't let one hear the meaning of this thunderous rumbling.

Here it was clear, but elsewhere it wasn't. A storm cloud loomed over there, and it seemed to the child that the day was coming when the cloud would make its way here . . .

IV

Black stones were piled one on top of another. Masses grew from nobody knew where, surrounded by chasms and holes.

The old man made his way along the slopes, raising his iron rod toward the clefts in the cliffs, and the child scrambled behind him, following the mysteries ascending over the earth.

It was as if he was delirious. His eyes glowed. His cracked lips whispered, "Upward."

The flickering old man's outline ceaselessly rose upward, fearlessly overcoming both chasms and cliffs.

His gray head, resting snugly on his powerful shoulders, was thrown back with his beard extended and flapping in the wind, and his back was stooped: the old man was hunched over and clawing with his hands at the grass and bushes growing in the cracks of the cliff.

The black rocks jutted to the sky, breaking through to the sea . . . The wind whispered in their ear, "Upwards . . ."

They ascended. Their ridges hung over the sea. Vertigo—the insidious inhabitant of the heights—spun their heads. They thought they were in heaven.

The sea rumbled below, its waves tiny, and the beatific semicircle of the crimson sun quickly retreated into the boundless depths.

The old man wasn't afraid. Head-spinning words burst from his flaming lips, tossing his gray hair.

The diamond necklace sparkled with flowery worlds, and he gave the sun lofty commands:

"I doom the constellation Hercules to the flames, and Saturn I will freeze . . ." He was keeping tabs on his domain.

Standing up high, the old man could tumble down any minute, and the child shuddered from the danger. He wanted to shout, "Save the old man . . ."

The fiery crimson semicircle retreated into the depths. All that was left of it was a glowing dot.

The old man threw up his hands and tumbled from the jagged crest of the cliff. He didn't fall into the watery green depths, but rather vanished into the space between the peak of the cliff and the sea.

The evening transparency was intoxicated with sadness . . . A huge *white* bird pierced the expanse with the heavy flapping of its wings.

Screeching quietly, it flew off into the distance.

It turned its long neck right and left. It screeched, it quietly screeched, laughing at the impossible.

A necklace with multicolored points of light flashed on its feathery neck, and the mysterious sign of changeless Eternity swayed, attached to the necklace.

It seemed to be flying far, far away, to other worlds, toward other constellations.

The child said, "There's a reason for all of this . . . The old man is *completely exceptional* . . ."

Then he was touched by vertigo, and the golden threads of his hair danced around his head, and, gasping, he clutched at the stones.

The fiery fingers—the fingers of ecstasy—were gently extinguished one by one.

In the distance a flying white point was still visible.

It soon vanished in the distance, rushing to other worlds, toward other constellations.

The child looked down, where there was no bottom, just placid eternity.

A black cliff hung between the two skies.

Two children dangled, one above and one below. Each fixed his gaze on his twin with his unfathomably blue eyes, sometimes going pale, sometimes flaring up.

It grew dark. The wind blew along his sleepy vertebrae, tossing and twisting the child's puffy curls.

Suddenly a bright streak of lightning flashed in the east, from a mist that had sneakily crept up.

The dull rumble of thunder rolled through the foggy crevices. The cliffs shuddered, shaking the rocks.

The frightened child noticed the silhouette of a stern figure guarding Eden, shrouded in rambling clouds.

From time to time he raised his burning sword over the world at dusk and struck it against the cliff.

At night the child slept, worried and quietly moaning. And down below, the terrible serpent crawled from the sea and dragged itself along the shore, rustling and curling into a circle.

Its small calf's head, crowned with golden horns, quickly turned from side to side, gazing and sniffing.

It crawled past the heaps of stone debris where the child was sleeping and soon disappeared into the night.

Then the air seemed to be made of smoke, and the child's burning agitation grew.

In fright, he set off looking for the old man, hiding and hazarding glances as if he sensed the nearness of the serpent here.

V

The night was dark. The worried child, tormented by that which could not be seen, quietly stole after the old man, who was flittering along in the fog.

The old man marched holding a burning torch high above his head.

He soon lost sight of the old man and wandered in the fog, despondent.

Suddenly, a blood-red flame blazed in the fog. A sweet voice tenderly rumbled, "Who is this troublemaker spying on me? . . ."

The child broke into tears for some unknown reason. And the white-stranded old man bent over him, and the white strands of his locks tickled the child's cheeks, like silver ringlets of goat's fur. He took the child into his peaceful embrace, letting go of the torch.

The fiery torch went out and lay on the ground, scorched and stinking.

Old man: There are tears in your eyes . . . You are scared and crying . . . What's the matter? . . .

Child: I'm scared . . . It's not safe anymore to look from the cliff into the depths. A sleepy horror lies there among the red coral.

Old man: That's nothing . . . It only seems that way.

Child: The wind whispered to me that I would die and that you had come to save me from sleepy dangers . . . The wind whispered to me that the future can't be changed. I'm terrified, terrified, that you've already come back to these lands . . . I'm afraid that this has happened sometime in the past and ended tragically . . . I'm glad that you're here . . . I love you, old man, but I'm terrified.

Old man: Calm down. Go to sleep. Forget. Before I even came, the horror had already crawled away on underwater paths, and now I don't think it would dare to rise up from the depths.

Then a foul wind blew, and the old man was horrified. He went silent.

He sat there glumly.

The distant past poured down on them from the constellations shining in the sky.

And the water snake swam to the sandy cape, deafening the foggy surroundings with its roar.

A vagabond sat on its back, deferentially holding onto its golden horns so as not to fall off.

It couldn't bring itself to murder the child, so now it carried an assassin, capable of anything, on its back through the boundless ocean . . .

Child: Old man, who is it that roars for so long and so sadly in the ocean? . . . I've never heard such a voice before . . .

Old man: That's an inhabitant of the sea who pulled himself from the depths . . . Now he's wringing the water from his green beard and trying out his voice since he fancies himself a singer . . .

Child: I know the voices of the inhabitants of the sea, and they don't sound that plaintive or that strange.

But the old man was silent. He shuddered from the malevolent cold that enveloped them. He muttered to himself, "No, he can't be saved . . . He must return . . . Another of these needless returns will come to pass . . .

The day of the Great Sunset is coming."

The distant past poured down on them from the constellations shining in the sky . . .

A foul meeting took place on the sandy cape. The serpent, twisted into a disgusting ball, stretched its neck and bellowed dully. The louse from the cloudy ocean obediently heeded its master's command . . .

He plucked at his shaggy beard, his green eyes flashing, and crumpled his felt cap in his hand, not daring to put it on in the presence of a serpentlike monstrosity.

Finally, the serpent crawled to the sea and, with a heavy plop, disappeared in the waves.

The unfamiliar louse was left alone on the cape.

He lit a crimson light and killed time waiting for morning.

VI

It was night. On the giant black cliff, reaching into the sky, the stooped old man stood, stretching toward the sky while leaning on his iron rod.

Gusts of cold wind buffeted the nocturnal old man, and his cassock was as black as night. And it blended into the night.

Gusts of cold wind buffeted the nocturnal old man, and his dark-winged cassock flapped behind his back like blades of an oar.

These were precisely the wings of the night, and they blended into the night. And it looked like the old man, in the darkness on the giant black cliff, wasn't standing, but flying like a bat over the world.

And it looked like his beard stretched out into the darkness like a silver cloud, like the fog preparing to multiply the fiery tears of the constellations and dash off into the dark river of time.

And a shining necklace glittered on his chest, and it looked like stars. Sometimes a glittering star—a diamond torn from his chest—swirled into the dark of night.

And the old man scattered the diamonds. And the diamonds, like seeds of new worlds, swirled brilliantly in the dark of night.

It looked like new life had arisen on them, new types of creatures had finished their life cycles.

And the old man kept flying, beating his wings. He flew and shouted, "The child will return. On every extinguished diamond he will make his eternal return."

It just looked that way. In the darkness, on the giant black cliff, the old man wasn't flying, but standing. Gusts of cold wind buffeted him, and his dark-winged cassock flapped like blades of an oar.

And as the white day rose in the sky, his dark cassock glowed purer than the snow.

The transparent green sea's surface winked, loudly splashing on the shore. The soft, delicate, glassy sky looked golden green . . . The horizon alone burned crimson and purple.

Otherwise, everything else was green.

But greenest of all was the sea demon who rose from the depths in order to shout at the sunrise.

He reached his webbed hands to this unobtainable but dear dry land, rolling his dark red eyes . . .

This was a kindhearted demon—an inhabitant of the sea.

Circles raced around him, flowing crimson and purple.

Above the green waves the pale pink satin garments of the sea beauties shone as they approached the surface and then retreated back into the depths.

However, this wasn't the beauties' garments, but patches of the tender dawn's light.

Now the green sea demon, having shouted and swum, dove into the depths, his scaly silver tail splashing.

Everything was empty and quiet.

Only a stooped old man was immersed in thought on a high cliff.

His eyes—two gray abysses sitting deeply in their sockets—looked *completely exceptional.*

The mysterious symbol of unchanging eternity hung on the old man's chest.

He quietly rocked . . .

VII

The Wind King had appeared in these parts that morning.

Now he blew into a large shell while sitting on a block of granite.

And mournful sounds flew out, bitter and despondent.

A storm raged.

The old man appeared like a whirlwind. His hair was tossed about. His clothes were torn away.

Restrained indignation sounded in his voice.

The child understood that he wasn't the object of the old man's ire. Someone else, someone who made their way *even here,* aroused his indignation.

The old man took him by the hand and said, "Your destiny will be decided today."

And he led him on.

The infinite blue expanse indifferently laughed over the travelers' heads and accompanied them with a long gaze.

There was a grotto at the bottom of the gulf. Dark gray stones loomed over it.

The hunchbacked giants lay on the opposite shore and stretched their hunched chests.

This was the granite.

A shock of blue, resting sumptuously like cupolas of water, drunkenly laughed at the granite.

Inside the grotto it was dark and wet.

Streams of water fell from above and flowed from the grotto in diamond trickles with an upside-down infinite blue expanse.

Somebody hurried over the grotto in a felt cap, tugging at his brown rags and spritely beard, reaching his mossy arms into the blue distance of the gulf.

In one hand he held a large yellowish red shell, and at times he pressed his blood-red lips to the shell's opening, making noise and furrowing his brow; at times he squeezed it to his long ear to listen; at times he hopped repulsively on his lame legs.

He praised the storm with a grimace. From time to time his wolfish thirst for blood made his sallow face flush.

This was the Wind King—mentally disturbed.

The old man brought the child here.

The Wind King quickly hid among the rocks. Only his felt cap poked out from behind the gray rock, and there was the occasional echo of a muted sneeze.

And because of this sneeze, silver white dust scattered, swirling and settling again along the shore.

The roaring waves foamed, and a shoreside breaker leaped.

A black petrel spread out over the sea.

The old man said, "This is the grotto of contemplation. Here are the *first ones to know*. From here *the first ones descend*. They set out on *their travels* . . .

Now *it has come . . . You must . . . It is necessary . . .*"

And when the child asked what had come, the old man turned away and left the dark grotto.

He sat *to think* by its low entrance, enveloped in his cloak. The old man's bowed shoulders were raised up high. It looked like worlds orbited around his holy beard.

A breeze played with his soft white curls. The fluffy locks stood on end over his giant brow and then again plastered themselves to his old man's cheeks.

Exactly as if they were fiddling with the eternally blue idea that was burned into his eye sockets. As if they were pleading, "Easier, easier . . . Not so seriously . . ."

And from behind the gray rocks came an indignant whistle and sneeze: silver-white dust scattered, and, swirling, flew along the shore.

Occasionally from behind the gray rocks belemnites and driftwood flew toward the stationary old man.

Occasionally the head of the mentally disturbed one in the velvet cap showed itself, twisted into a grimace and completely pale . . .

Occasionally the one in the cap shouted from an excess of indignation, like a cat whose tail had been stomped, and then hid behind the rocks.

Then something odd happened by the entrance to the grotto. The sun broke through the clouds, pouring over the old man, who had stood up from the rock and was frozen in a mute fit.

The old man's necklace blazed on his white chest, and the sign of Eternity rocked in the wind.

But the old man smashed the necklace on his chest, and the diamonds fell to the sand like fiery tears.

Then he left, no one knew where, and the sun went dim.

VIII

As soon as the old man disappeared, the stranger stood over the grotto and started tossing driftwood and belemnites into it.

And when the child left the grotto, he quickly hid among the rocks.

The stranger finally tired of playing hide-and-seek. He peered into the grotto.

The child managed to notice his velvet cap and pale, sallow face framed with a wolfish beard.

The one in the cap soon grew impatient, and his silhouette blocked the light at the grotto's entrance.

He hesitated, checking if the old man was in there someplace, and when he was certain that the old man was far away, he walked into the grotto as if it were his home.

His green eyes, like two nails, bored into the child.

He sat silently on the gray rock and stuffed his pipe with a foul-smelling powder.

He offered the child a pinch of the foul stuff and matter-of-factly noted, "Well, so let's sit . . . have a chat, this and that . . ."

But the child pushed the stuff away.

Then he lit his pipe and began to puff smoke while the child watched the new arrival in amazement and wondered, "Who could this be?"

Mournful sounds came from every direction. As if in every crevice someone was playing the bagpipes.

They began talking about the child's incomprehensible fears, which then turned into curiosity.

The stranger called fear a shameful weakness, but he encouraged curiosity.

The pure rays of the sun finally stopped breaking through: pale, gloomy sadness was all that constantly peered into the grotto's opening.

The stranger mentioned the old man and with a squeamish grimace noted, "A terribly clever little old man." He accused him of concealing secrets.

The child listened to the green-eyed one in the cap's strange assertions with an open mouth, shocked by this mixture of insight and humor.

A stream of laughter—hopeless and sad—echoed in the cave, and under the sound of this laughter flowed the speech of the one in the cap.

He began to tell the wise tale of Khandrikov and, as the tale became clearer, the color drained from the shivering child's cheek.

The tale was finally over. The one in the cap with a pipe clenched in his teeth turned away from the child and indifferently raised his wolfish beard, making it seem that he was indifferent, but the green flame flickering in his eyes told a different story.

And when the child cried, "*I don't believe that this is true,*" the one in the cap said, "If you don't believe, look into the hole gaping in the porous stone . . ."

Then he shifted his soft cap in his hair, put one leg on the other, making a twisting motion with the sock of his right foot, and fiercely inhaled the noxious smoke.

Then he made a funnel with his blood-red lips, and blowing blue rings of smoke from his mouth, he impaled them with a stream of smoke.

He got up and left.

The child was alone. He thought, sometimes going pale, sometimes flaring up.

Then he pressed up against the black hole gaping in the porous stone . . .

The child sensed something terribly familiar, as if he were swallowed by the muck of Eternity.

A pitiful sadness echoed in the waterfall's torrents of laughter, hundreds of pearls cascading down . . .

IX

The old man was already approaching him, piercing him with the depths of his eyes.

He held his hands over his head, and in his hands was a crown of red roses—a crown of bloody flames.

He calmly kissed the pale white child, placing these bloody flames on him.

In a bitter, loving whisper he said, "I crown you with suffering..."

But a wind rose up and blew the soft, aromatic petals from his fair-haired head. It carried them into the boundlessness.

These burning flames were soon extinguished in the leaden distance.

And then a strange sight was revealed to them both.

A tall feathered man with a bird's head walked along the foggy shore.

White feathers fluttered on his neck when he opened his yellow beak.

The old man pointed at him and said, "That's the eagle: when the time comes, I'll send him to you.

You will leave. We won't see you. The desert of suffering will stretch above, below, and in all directions.

You will cross its expanse in vain—the endless desert will keep you in its cold embrace...

Your cries will be useless...

But the hour will come. *The climax will arrive. I will send you the eagle.*"

The child looked at the feathered man and whispered, "Eagle. Kind..."

It began to pour. Streams of water obscured the eagle, and he plunged into the fog.

They were silent for a while longer, holding one another in a parting embrace.

The old man said, "Good bye . . . There, in the desert, wait for the eagle . . ."

The old man went into the clouds, heading toward the constellation Hercules. The streaming dampness enveloped him.

The lonely grotto, like an open jaw, gaped in the cloudy darkness, and black masses with veins of pale marble protruded above the grotto.

Clumps of clouds raced along their stone chests, licking their chests, getting snagged on them.

The Wind King was fooling around on the masses, shaking his rags and howling. His wet velvet cap, soaked by the downpour, was sad and crooked.

He held a gnarled shell in his hand. Waving it around, he smashed it against the rocks in celebratory joy.

Occasionally a tattered clump of clouds blocked the Wind King. But he would tear at it with a shriek, thrusting his shaggy, wolfish head out and sounding like a stormy petrel.

X

The storm passed. The sunset was cleansing.

The surface of the sea looked like an overflowing abyss of emeralds mixed with crimson rubies.

The child sat on the wet shore, his head in his knees.

An endless desert stretched above, below, and in every direction. And the old man was no longer there . . .

Stout Crab crawled up to the child and squeezed him in a dry, leathery embrace, as if parting with him forever.

And then he returned to the depths.

A sail appeared in the distance and was then hidden from view.
And the old man was no longer there . . .

The inhabitant of the sea, bald, green-bearded, and snub-nosed, led a litter of his low-browed sons to the nearest cliff and taught them to plunge into the ocean depths.

Then he stood on the peak of the cliff. His fiery face burned in the rays of the sunset. Roaring, he beat his engorged stomach.

Then, with his arms spread, he plunged into the emerald ocean depths, causing a ruby-colored whirlpool with his fall.

The low-browed sons of the inhabitant of the sea stomped their feet on the cliff, shaking their hands with their feathery fingers spread out. Scared of heights, they quietly screeched.

And the fat-bellied old man, diving into the emerald sea, yelled to them, "Well, well, my sons . . . Who is brave enough? . . ."

His green beard floated around him, and his bald head glowed in the sunset

. . . The child watched life, which had until recently been shut from his gaze, with amazement, sadly remembering his former acquaintance who had gone away.

The old man was no longer there . . .

It grew dark. The red disk, cast from beyond the horizon by the hand of a giant, smoothly rose into the abyss of the evening.

Long snow-white needles, frozen high in the heavens, formed a feathery cloud. Like a forgotten net, it moved through the sky.

The shining moon fell into this net and went dim with sadness, caught in a trap.

The child fell asleep. It seemed to him that *everything had remained the same.*

And the old man was no longer there . . .

The shining moon, tearing itself free from the tricky net, continued to rise into the pure tranquility.

PART TWO

I

He woke up. The grotto was gray and gloomy. The familiar sound of
the sea echoed.

But it wasn't so: his spouse woke him up. She ran around the little
rooms. She tramped about in her slippers. She shouted at the servant.

Everything reminded him that his dream was over. It had irretrievably disappeared.

It was gone until the following night.

The familiar sound of the sea echoed as usual from behind the
partition, decorated with cheap wallpaper.

But it wasn't so: there was no sea behind the partition. The samovar hissed on the round tea table.

He jumped up as if he had been scalded. Amazed and confused
about where he returned from, he carefully remembered where he
had been.

He remembered when it was and where it was and that he himself was Khandrikov, M.A.[1]

"Yesss," he said, scratching his head, and he put on his boots.

The Khandrikovs sat over their morning tea. An unpleasant child
with a capricious and flabby little face walked around them.

Sofia Chizhikovna[2] burned herself on the tea. She was hurrying
to her lesson.

The little one stumbled. And fell. It was splayed out on the floor
like a sea star. It yowled like a cat.

Khandrikov comforted the little one. He crawled on all fours. He played horsey.

But the little one turned away its flabby little face. Tears were shed. His eyes became bloodshot.

And the M.A. himself, Evgeny Khandrikov, astonished himself by crawling around in this place because in his heart he harbored the secret hope that everything around him *was all a dream, that none of them are real*, that the endless desert stretched above and below and in every direction, that he was wrapped in misty ephemerality, and that starry worlds quietly revolved in his room.

That's what he thought as he crawled on all fours.

And Sofia Chizhikovna pointed at him, crawling and pleaded, "Don't cry, Grishenka: here's a horsey."

It was all so alien. The samovar quieted down. Someone howled in the pipe because it was windy outside, and it seemed to Khandrikov that this was a signal from Eternity giving courage to him who was lost so that he didn't let go of his last shred of hope.

He ran through unfamiliar places, past the usual buildings with his collar raised, wiping either his nose or his ears.

The wind blew into his cold overcoat, trying to tell him something.

It smelled of smoke. A telegraph pole mutely rumbled. The gloomy doormen sprinkled passersby's feet with sand.

The frost settled, like misty ephemerality, and assorted servants flitted by, covered in frost.

They were rushing to their work dens, trailing steam and recognizing one another in these morning encounters.

A pale-faced youth, thin as a stick, was rushing there too. Taurus Lambovich Cutlet looked like a dolphin in a raccoon-skin coat with a briefcase under his arm.

But Khandrikov wasn't bothered by banal sights and ran off to the lab.

The street stretched out before him. A horsecar squeaked plaintively, complaining about timelessness.

The chimney pipes emitted an abyss of smoke, and a frozen fire stood over the smoke.

II

In the haze of the lab, gloomy student silhouettes dimly glowed, having dragged themselves in all morning from every corner of Moscow.

They all merged into one: they all gave off smoke, making a stench.

Although one sniffed the test tubes and another washed them; one lit a crimson flame and another put it out.

Dull desperation wasn't reflected in their colorless eyes.

Khandrikov ran into the lab. Lighting a small flame, he distilled the pliant liquids from one dish to another, paying no attention to the planetary race.

The earth orbited the sun. The sun flew nobody knows where, approaching the constellation Hercules.

No amount of learning could draw the curtain on this appalling uncertainty.

A deadened face leaned over, and two eyes, like green nails, bored into Khandrikov. The blood-red lips were about to smile, but a wolfish beard concealed this smirk.

The trembling M.A. sensed something terrible and familiar. He quietly screamed.

But the only one there was the associate professor of chemistry, who had come in unnoticed and was now watching Khandrikov work.

The associate professor was aiming for a full professorship. He was skinny and positive. He would speak about a new method of manufacturing sulfuric acid, and it seemed that his deadened face concealed bursts of fury.

At the current moment he was in a dispute with the psychiatrist Orlov,[3] which explained the deadened hue of his face.

"A mask," thought Khandrikov, observing the associate professor's terribly familiar face, in which, for everybody else, there was nothing peculiar.

He listened to the calmly flowing speech, in which you could find a terrible mixture of insight and humor.

They did not care for one another.

III

Khandrikov, M.A., had been hustling to the lab for eight years already and was already coughing blood.

He was frequently lost in thought. His colleagues called Khandrikov a philosopher as a sign of their dislike for his thoughtfulness.

The associate professor doubted that these thoughts concerned any empirical science.

Khandrikov was of a short stature and had a slim build. He had a pointed nose and a light beard.

When he was lost in thought, his lips drooped and blue sparks flashed in his eyes. He looked like a child who had grown a beard.

In the lab, Khandrikov ran around in a jacket with a burn spot. The same at home, but when visiting he put on a black suit coat and looked even smaller for it.

Khandrikov was mostly silent. Sometimes he would have an outburst. Then the spittle would fly, and he'd shout abuse after abuse in his howling tenor while pressing his thin hand to his heaving chest.

Things happened to him. Things were *foisted* on him. Then he would escape from the world. Flitter off.

A misunderstanding arose between him and the world. Gaps emerged.

For all of this, his colleagues called him eccentric.

Hearing the signal from Eternity, now he rushed through the transparent visible world. He froze with a burner in his hand, heating a flask filled with liquid.

The flask burst, its glass tinkling. And his colleagues laughed when Khandrikov, who had flitted off, returned from the void. Came back. He wiped the noxious smelling liquid off himself.

Holding their noses, the lab assistants said, "Khandrikov broke another vial." And they opened the windows.

Stooped Sofia Chizhikovna shuffled from lesson to lesson. Seeing a wall plastered with notices, she put a pince-nez on her red nose.

There were announcements for lectures: "On Improving the Health of the Russian Woman," "On Germany," and many others.

There were announcements that Fritch would read "About All That Is New"; Grach,[4] "On That Which is Old"; Mech, "On the South Pole"; and Chizh, "On a Sick Talent."

Reading it all to the end, Sofia Chizhikovna planned to attend the lectures of Chizh and Grach.

IV

It was evening. Professor Griboedov[5] finished his lecture "On Buddhism," and Professor Corpsov "On Mushrooms."

They both gave lively talks, but their audiences were equally placid. They both resembled ancient centaurs.

It was evening. The students dispersed in their ratty coats, hurrying to cafeterias. Harsh shadows flickered on their tired faces as they mutely exchanged words.

Their dull eyes didn't reflect desperation.

Khandrikov walked through the room and vainly addressed his colleague, who was silent as a ghost.

He was shaking a liquid in a test tube.

Khandrikov felt as if he were alone. He was afraid—he was afraid in his solitude.

And he deafened himself with his own voice to drown out the appalling calls of the universe he heard in his soul.

He said, "Who lives a lively life? Who makes use of our labor? To what end are we laboring?"

"We are dragged from city to city and, dragging us there, they again fix the yoke on our shoulders. They heal us when we're ill only to ruin our health once again.

We surrender ourselves, our very selves, to labor and servitude. They don't kill us, freeze us, or let us die from hunger.

Where is the *yes* that we surrender?"

The ghostly pale laboratory worker gloomily whined, worn out by labor and exhaustion. Covering a test tube with his thumb, he shook it.

The moon crawled out from behind a cloud over the heavy black hulking buildings. It was obscured by smoke, like a bridal veil.

As if it wanted to say, "Here is the evening and here am I . . . The night will come . . . And you will sleep . . ."

The square onto which various apartment doors opened was lit by a faintly gleaming streetlamp.

One of the doors was open. Stooped Sofia Chizhikovna dashed out like a madwoman and flew down the stairs.

She was starving. She was tired. She missed her husband.

And so stooped Sofia Chizhikovna rushed down the stairs and hurried to her cold home.

Khandrikov felt as if he were alone. He was afraid—he was afraid in his solitude.

He spoke. He deafened himself with his own voice. But Eternity beckoned him in his soul, in the windows of the lab.

It said, "I'm working on Ivan. Ivan on Peter. And Peter on me. We will surrender our souls to one another.

We'll remain without souls, receiving just the minimal right to exist . . .

Getting nothing, we will become nothing. The sum of nothing is nothing . . .

This is the horror . . ."

Everything was horrible and yawning, gaping. Jaws hung over his head—Eternity's chasm. The lab's gray walls were like an underground cave. The sound of the sea echoed in the distance. But this was just an electric stove.

Then Khandrikov calmed down. He felt as if he had been lost in the desert.

The moon laughed from behind a cloud above the hulking buildings, wreathed in a bridal veil.

It wanted to say, "Here I am, round like zero . . . I am also nothing. Don't be sad . . ."

Then the ghostly laboratory worker rushed to make his presence known. He shook the test tube. He suddenly thrust it under Khandrikov's nose and uncovered the opening.

He violently snapped, "What's it smell like?"

V

Khandrikov jumped onto a trolly. He stood on the platform and leaned. He observed the passengers through the pale window as they were pressed into one another.

They sadly hung their heads in the light of the streetlamp.

They were undeniably all of different mindsets, but they all merged at a single point—by the Ilinsky Gates.

Now they were engaged in a single common task: racing along Vozdvizhenka Street to the Arbat.

In that enclosed space, it seemed, was a special world randomly appearing by the Ilinsky Gates, replete with stars and patches of cloud, and Khadrikov, pressed up to the pale window, observed this universe from another world.

He thought, "Maybe our world is just a trolly pulled by sickly horses along endless tracks. And we, the passengers, will soon head off into different universes . . ."

The frozen conductor, warming himself from the cold, stamped his feet next to Khandrikov. Like he was mocking this wild fantasy.

With fiendish concentration, the conductor fixed his face, frozen with cold, toward the hazy distance of the street.

Familiar and unfamiliar figures rushed around, all covered in fur. Like bears and fawns. But no, they were people.

A centaur raced by, wildly neighing and waving a stick, and alongside him raced a horse. But it was just a boy on a hobbyhorse.

And Khandrikov remembered that this had all happened already and that even before creation trollies rattled along in every direction.

VI

The worn-out Khandrikovs ran back home. After their labor, they ate. They were served sausage with sauerkraut.

They looked like corpses seated at a table.

They related to one another the dull impressions of their day. Khandrikov choked on a sausage as he erupted in affected laughter.

The night lurked at the window. It reflected their dull figures— faded, as if shrouded in fog.

An attentive observer would note that Khandrikov's reflection didn't laugh: horror and despair contorted his reflected face . . .

And the whole reflection trembled with tearless cries and weeping.

The blue night pierced the airy blackness of the space. The blue night blinded passersby.

A man with a deathly pale face and blood-red lips, not blinded by the night, jutted a wolfish beard from under his fur coat.

He stomped his boots on the thick ice.

On his head was a gray woolen military cap, sticking out like a pointed hat. The one in the cap rang a doorbell.

A little while later he sat in Professor Corpsov's cozy office, rubbing his frozen hands.

This was associate professor of chemistry Tsenkh.

The venerable and gray Corpsov, with a giant bald spot and wearing gold-rimmed glasses, soon came in. Soon they were sitting in front of one another, and the associate professor was talking about his case against the psychiatrist Orlov, about the state of chemistry, about the new blood working in the field of chemistry.

Counting on his fingers the lab workers and M.A.s, some he praised, but most he disparaged.

When he mentioned Khandrikov, he hopelessly waved his hand and said with annoyance, "A hack." His face concealed bursts of fury and looked like a mask.

He lit a cigarette and continued talking. He made smoke rings with his blood-red lips curled into a funnel. He impaled them with a stream of smoke.

His tale was a shocking mixture of insight and humor. But Professor Corpsov didn't notice that.

Taking his glasses off his thick nose, he wiped them with a handkerchief, looking like an ancient centaur.

Sleep crept in. It nursed Khandrikov like a sick and frightened child.

The chemist smiled at these fairy tales, which had appeared to him in the night, and his sallow spouse put her hand on Khandrikov's shoulder and whispered, "Why aren't you being tender with me?"

Khandrikov didn't answer her. He swatted her away like a fly. He went to sleep.

Pulling up the blanket, he thought, "Well, now it will all be over. Everything will flitter away. Now you're done for."

A sleepy Khandrikov got out of bed when the child cried. He saw the crying child on his shoulders and walked around the apartment in his underthings, like a ghost.

The moon doused ghostly Khandrikov in its sad light. Someone, tired and ingratiating, muttered, "It's night ... Why aren't you sleeping?"

VII

The next day was a holiday. It was getting milder. Everything had thawed out. Khandrikov went for a shave.

They swaddled him in towels. A man in white grabbed Khandrikov's cheek and lathered it.

Khandrikov looked into the mirror, and from there a Khandrikov looked at him, and in front of this one another mirror reflected the first one.

A pair of Khandrikovs sat there. And even farther, another pair of Khandrikovs, with greenish faces, and in the infinite distance you could spot another pair of Khandrikovs, now completely green.

Khandrikov thought, "This isn't the first time I've sat here, watching my numerous reflections. And before long I will see them again.

Maybe somewhere in another universe I'm also being reflected and another Khandrikov, like me, lives there.

Every universe has a Khandrikov . . . And throughout time, this Khandrikov has been replicated more than once."

But the one in white interrupted this prophetic fantasy. He freed Khandrikov from the towels and customarily noted, "Forty kopecks for the haircut and shave . . ."

It dripped from the roof. The sparrows chirped happily. The bookstores sold Chirikov's[6] stories.

A spring breeze blew on Khandrikov, chilling the spot where he was shaved.

Low, ashen clouds blew in from the west.

His lonely heart sensed someone nearby, someone who had been gone a long time and was now back to see him.

He went to the bathhouse.

VIII

The public bathhouses were luxurious. Naked, distracted people, covered in soap and in improbable positions, sat on the marble benches.

Here the gray-haired old man with a paunch doused himself from a silver basin and said, "Ooof..." A fierce bathhouse attendant was scratching the head of a young skeleton.

In the next hall was a marble swimming pool decorated with ironwork depictions of inhabitants of the sea.

Emerald-green waves continued rippling in the cold pool, igniting waves of rubies.

The gray-haired old man came here with his son in tow after dousing himself with scalding water from a silver basin. Standing over the pool, he taught his son how to plunge into the pool.

Then, giving off a roar, he pounded himself in the paunch, illuminated by the blood-red lights. Then with outstretched arms he plunged into the waves, his dive resembling a ruby waterfall. From it, rings of red light scattered on the waves and crashed into the marble bank.

Khandrikov washed in the bathhouse. Now he was standing in the shower, and warm streams poured over him, flowing down his body like drops of pearls.

They flowed. Everything flowed. And there was no apparent end to this flowing.

Khandrikov thought, "The other Khandrikovs are also washing in the bathhouse. All Khandrikovs scattered across space and periodically appearing in time are washing identically."

However, it was now time to stop the flow, and a naked Khandrikov turned the handle.

Khandrikov dressed. There were couches. A well-steamed stout man, still young, sat in front of Khandrikov, watching Khandrikov with sly, crablike little eyes.

He sat with his legs crossed. He looked like a giant crab.

He suddenly cried out, "Khandrikov! Greetings, friend." And the chemist recognized his physicist colleague.

They were soon chatting happily, and the physicist said to him, "Come to the pub later. We'll make a night of it. Your wife won't know."

Khandrikov left the bathhouse. He walked along a hallway decorated with porous stones. He bumped into a tall old man in a beaver-skin cap and a hooked cane.

The old man's tall shoulders were raised, and his eyes could be seen under his bushy gray eyebrows—two gray abysses sitting in enormous sockets.

He looked like *a completely exceptional old man.*

In the old man's hand was a parcel—a blue box with a picture of Hercules. Hercules lifting weights.

It seemed to him that he had seen this old man before more than once, but he forgot where.

He turned. He followed him with his eyes. He was disturbed by a prophetic premonition.

And the blizzard began whistling as if the roaring river of time was completing its eternal cycle, its eternal revolution.

It flew and flew: this pillar of wind—the tornado of the world, circled by planetary orbits—rings—flew into the terrible unknown.

Ahead was an abyss. And behind as well.

Khandrikov stepped out into the street. Blue boxes with pictures of Hercules were on display in the window of the imported-goods store. Khandrikov remembered the old man and said, "The sun is rushing toward the constellation Hercules . . ."

Ravens flew in front of him and cawed about eternal return. Golden rings were for sale in the jewelry store.

Ashen gray clouds blew in from the far west, and above them flapped an unseen flamingo's fiery feathery wings.

And such was the proximity of these unattainable heights that Khandrikov unexpectedly said, "The climax approaches." Surprised, he thought, "What did I say?"

A gray veil of clouds blocked the fiery flock, and cold white flies circled around.

The mysterious old man, having been washed by the bathhouse attendant, wandered around the changing rooms wrapped in a snow-white sheet.

He circled around the couches, making invisible orbits. He circled and circled and returned to his orbits.

While circling, he rotated.

His majestic silhouette showed up here and there, and drops of pearls shimmered in his silver beard.

He circled and circled and returned to his orbits. While circling, he rotated.

Two people were undressing. One asked the other, "Who is that majestic old man who looks like Asclepius?" And the other told him, "That's Orlov, the famous psychiatrist. The one who's in a dispute with associate professor of chemistry Tsenkh . . ."

The old man dressed. He left the bathhouse. Attached to the button of his fur coat was a parcel with a picture of Hercules.

And now this parcel was swaying on the old man's chest like the symbol of unchanging Eternity.

IX

In a certain basement establishment, they were feasting disgracefully—Khandrikov and three others.

It was his colleague the physicist, his colleague the zoologist, and his colleague the thief.

The first studied radioactive substances and cryogenics, was stout and confident, and looked like a crab. The second spent his days immersed in rabbit intestines and at night became rowdy and drunk; he had a cheerful head and long legs, but his torso was short.

The third behaved with dignity and had no legal occupation.

They were drunk and boisterous in this gloomy basement, like a cave—they were boisterous and red, enraged trolls.

They toasted with mugs filled with golden sparks. They spilled these sparks on one another, not beer.

Even though the barman assured them that he served them beer, they didn't believe him.

The physicist, looking like an enormous crab, shouted, "Radioactive substances destroy electrical forces. They cause boils on the skin."

The abyss, resounding with darkness, forced its way in through the high windows. The barman, who looked like a fat toad, scowled at the drunkards from behind the counter. It seemed to Kkhandrikov that this was a warlock's lair.

And his colleague the physicist shouted, "There is no time. Time is intensiveness. Causality is a form of the thermodynamic process."

And it blew and blew, the whirlwind of worlds; the race of the constellations lured both the drunkards and the lair into the great unknown.

Everything turned and spun since everyone was drunk.

Sofia Chizhikovna was racked with fever. She couldn't finish reading "The Foundations of Physiological Psychology."[7] She lay down. The fever overcame her.

She started raving. She whispered, "Let my husband, Khandrikov, invent psychology while Wundt holds meetings in taverns . . ."

It was two in the morning. They were carried on the wind. They staggered and shouted.

Their overcoats weren't buttoned, and their boot covers were off, even though it was a biting and freezing evening.

Khandrikov threw his head back. The night's jaws loomed over his head—the horror of Eternity split by the Milky Way.

As if it were a row of teeth. As if the sky bared its teeth and threatened misfortune.

It seemed to Khandrikov that he was surrounded not by streets but by gray cliffs with the eternally foaming river of time babbling through.

Someone sat him in a boat, and Khandrikov sailed home on the waves of time.

Something carried him into his rooms, where his sick wife was delirious.

X

With the servant's help, a drunk Khandrikov put his sick wife to bed. The servant grumbled, "Where have you been?" and Khandrikov stumbled and answered, "Matrena, I was sailing on the waves of time, sprinkling the world with golden stars." Without undressing, he sat by the patient's bed.

His leaden head rested on his chest. He was sick from wine and the unexpected misfortune.

The flame of the candle danced. Dancing along with it was Khandrikov's black shadow, cast on the wall.

He closed his eyes. Around him someone began to weave a silver web. And Eternity's whistle resounded outside the window—a signal to the drowning man so he didn't lose the last shred of hope.

Someone said to him, "Let's go. I'll show you." They took him by the arm and led him to the seashore.

The blue waves scattered Bermuda pearls.

They walked on the shore barefoot. Their feet sank into the silver dust.

They sat down on the warm sand. Someone wrapped his shoulders in lamb's wool.

Someone whispered, "This is nothing . . . It will pass."

And he answered, "Do I have to linger here long?" They said, "Soon I will send the eagle to you."

The wind rustled his curls. A silvery dust settled on the dreamers.

A thin, curved stream of silver rose above the waves, and the wisps of clouds sparkled like familiar silver threads on a pale blue velvet background.

He woke up. There was crimson-lily smoke on the horizon. Everything was fragile and delicate as if made of golden green glass.

The old man walked away, laughing into his beard. The blue waves scattered melting rubies.

The servant woke him up. He jumped up in front of the patient's bed as if he had been pricked.

And he remembered everything.

He was green like a young leaf in the forest, and she was crimson like a glowing ember of wood.

XI

The white-winged day banged at the windows with gigantic flaps. The old man's glasses shimmered, and he adjusted his long snowy beard.

This was Dr. Orlov, the famous psychiatrist, heading to Khandrikov's apartment (who knows why) wishing to treat his wife.

He stood by the patient's bed. Dr. Orlov doomed her to perish, stretching his reverent arms over the bed.

His stooped shoulders were raised high. Streams of Eternity flowed from his gray eyes.

It all felt terribly familiar to Khandrikov, and he wasn't sure whether the old man knew it.

But the old man knew everything. He grinned into his beard.

The white-winged day banged forcefully at the windows.

During associate professor Tsenkh's lecture, Khandrikov lowered the glass tube with a curved end and tipped the glass beaker collecting gas over the water.

Khandrikov remembered the patient. He was sad that he was now dependent on Tsenkh, and Tsenkh curled his bloody lips into a funnel as if he weren't impinging on anybody's rights and joyfully announced, "Gentlemen, you see how the lit match was extinguished. We conclude that the resulting gas was nitrogen."

And Khandrikov thought, "Will Orlov, with his dispute with Tsenkh, not save me from this servitude?"

Hardly had he thought this and Tsenkh's two eyes, sparking like green nails, bored into Khandrikov's soul, and in them a long-standing hatred glowed.

Everything blew and blew, spinning and twirling to the other world: the wind stormed outside.

He ran to his sick wife, to Sofia Chizhikovna. The moon had risen.

A white bell tower, as if made of lace, stood out in relief on the clear blue background. A golden cross flashed over the horror in its unattainable heights.

The pipes belched out a mass of smoke. The smoke spread into flashing white threads.

Khandrikov greeted these familiar threads with a kind gaze.

At home, his wife's ravings and his stout mother-in-law awaited him—a runt speckled with warts.

At night everyone was racing around, and sleep was out of the question. The little one was sent to the neighbors.

The severe outline of an unknown woman was on the partition.

XII

Khandrikov looked blankly at the waxy face. A coffin loomed. It flashed gold. It was surrounded by heavy candles in mourning crepe.

An infinitely fiery sunset lit up the brocade and the frost patterns on the windows into millions of rubies.

In the semidarkness everything looked frightening. It seemed that Eternity was approaching.

But it was just Orlov who arrived and stood in the dark corner. From there his glowing face could be seen, bowing reverently while his glasses glowed.

His glasses were fiery from the sunset. Two crimson spots rested on Khandrikov.

The merciless nun's voice quietly pronounced, "O Lord, O Lord." As if frozen leaves were rustling and flying off into lonely timelessness.

And Tsenkh lectured in the classroom, "One might have thought that the cross section of currents creates not only an equivalent quantity of electricity but also an equivalent quantity of ions."

The dark street was visible through the window. A cab was moving in the distance—a black mass with a flashing mystical eye.

It was still crimson over the buildings.

And a white bell tower, as if made of lace, stood out in relief on the crimson background of evening. A golden cross flashed over the horror in its unattainable heights.

While Tsenkh continued, "However, Kirchhoff[8] has shown that that isn't true."

The sunset was over. The rubies were extinguished. Now there was just a blue darkness.

"O Lord, O Lord," resounded from somewhere in the distance like an October breeze.

And the invisible leaves were rustling and once again flew off into lonely timelessness.

XIII

The child grabbed its grandmother, Pompa Melentyevna. Identical days flowed by for Khandrikov.

He was enveloped by the roaring stream of dreams. More and more often he was coughing blood.

He didn't go to see Dr. Orlov. Just once, while walking by an unfamiliar doorway, he heard Eternity's signal. He raised his eyes. He read the golden letters on the plaque, "Ivan Ivanovich Orlov, Doctor. Patients received between two and five."

The sun was setting in the distance. The reflection of the crimson gold blazed on the plaque and roof. All of the buildings seemed to burn crimson gold.

In those days, he was working on a scientific brick—his master's thesis.

A year passed. The thaw had again begun. The crimson of sunset was scattered in the pale blue sky like a flamingo's wings.

You could sense its proximity. The climax approached.

His thesis was finished. The two-hour-long slog was rewarded with applause.

The venerable professors stoutly flowed from the room.

Khandrikov glowed, and he was approached by a correspondent for a serious newspaper. Khandrikov answered his questions, "I was born in 1870. I graduated from Moscow University. I was assigned to a laboratory to continue my scientific investigations. For my research "On the Structure of Hexahydrobenzines" I received my degree. My parents are poor . . ."

But here the respected correspondent politely interrupted him, "I won't trouble you any further."

The dark university corridors looked like underground passageways. There, two gray professors collided, venerable to the extreme.

They looked like ancient centaurs, and they were each holding a weighty brick.

The professors greeted one another. They exchanged bricks. They wished one another the best. And they parted ways.

One brick, the red one, was titled "Poisonous Mushrooms" with an inscription in the author's hand, "To the most respected Nikolai Savvich Griboedov, from the author."

The other, the color of dried leaves, was titled, "Citizenship in Every Era and Nation," and someone old had scratched "To Dusty Petrovich Corpsov, in friendship."

The venerable scholars were already heading off in carriages—one to Hunter's Row and the other to the Church of the Ascension on the Graves.

They were sitting in a restaurant, celebrating and feting Khandrikov with a dinner.

Associate professor Tsenkh had tucked a napkin into his collar. He casually chatted with his neighbor. He spoke sensibly and optimistically, but in that sensibility you could detect more horror than in foggy mysticism.

A careful observer would take note of a subtle irony concealed in the professor's whiskers. There were barely visible wrinkles around his blood-red lips.

Nobody noticed that and the professor successfully hid this frightening significance under the guise of a scholar.

Khandrikov *saw*. He was afraid and outraged. Tsenkh understood this outrage. His evil little eyes suddenly looked up.

There was something cruel in these side glances, vaguely familiar, forgotten but occasionally flaring up.

As if they knew each other in times long ago. As if they had already been carried away by hatred. As if once one of them had committed an act of violence against the other and now the recollection of that horror flitted by like a black cat when Tsenkh's eyes met the intoxicated gaze of the M.A.

Khandrikov was drunk. He was filled with fury and insolence. He wanted to throw a gauntlet at Tsenkh, on whom he depended.

XIV

The opportunity arose for Tsenkh to make a toast. He stood, showing off, and said, "I would like to propose a toast to those cultural phenomena that, closely tied to science, proudly advance human genius along the endless rails of progress. I'm allowing myself to say this because these phenomena are distinguished from one another not qualitatively, but quantitatively. I have in mind not so much a representative of one of the most empirical of sciences, but rather a cultured person. I drink to scientific, artistic, and philosophical development. Finally, I drink to the development of our common interests, purified in the crucible of knowledge and promising humankind a peaceful and happy future . . ."

A drunk and furious Khandrikov asked to say a word, and it was clear that they were about to hear insults and insolence.

He said, "Addressing me as a representative of empirical knowledge, you drink to the development of science, art, philosophy, and our common interests. Deeply touched by your toast, I nevertheless decline this address. I think about a lot and may be right about this and that. But my ideas are developing in opposition to what you are accustomed to call culture. I don't see a peaceful future for humankind fueled by science, art, philosophy, and social interests without changing our formulas."

People shifted their chairs. People sneezed. People blew their noses. People shrugged their shoulders. One said to one another, "I told you so." The other replied, "You told me so." A smile of pity froze on Tsenkh's greenish face.

He said, "Social interests . . . The organization of relationships between governments, classes, and individuals—can that regulate the relationships between people, change the forms of these relationships by overlooking the individual? And really any model of social order founded on social equality reduces the productivity of the members of that society . . . In thermodynamics the work capacity of heat is determined by the difference between the sources of heat and cold. The capacity will disappear if the amount of heat is equal in both."

Khandrikov began to fume and furiously threw a gauntlet at Tsenkh. He screamed in his hoarse tenor, clutching his heaving chest with his hand.

He didn't see anything except two green little eyes boring into him like nails and bursts of fury occasionally flushing the dead cheeks of associate professor Tsenkh. And Tsenkh whispered,

"Orlov's opinions. We can't delay. We must root out the old man's influence from the very beginning. I will send a cautionary telegram to *The Snake's Nest* today."

He had recently lost his legal dispute with Dr. Orlov.

Khandrikov continued, "I don't see a future for existing forms of art. Some say that art serves life, others that life serves art. But if art is a copy of life, then it is superfluous in the presence of the original. You won't sway my opinion with objections about ideology. If life serves art, then it is for the reflection that meets me every time I approach a mirror . . . Anyway, I don't know . . . Maybe those who say that life serves art are right since we may turn out to be not people but merely their reflections. And it's not we who approach the mirror, but someone's reflection, a stranger, who approaches *from the other side* and grows bigger in proportion with the surface of the mirror. So we aren't going anywhere, aren't coming from anywhere, but just expand and contract while remaining on one and the same surface. Maybe we're standing upright, maybe upside down or running at a forty-five-degree angle. Maybe the universe is just a flask in which we have been planted like crystals, and life with its movement is just the sinking of crystals in formation to the bottom of the container, and death is just when the sinking stops. And we don't know what will be: will we decay, will we pass on into other universes, will sulfuric acid turn us into sulfates, will we wish to dissolve or be ground in a mortar? You say that this is a decline. Maybe you're right and we are decadents in our development, but maybe all development leads to decadence. And life is the last degeneration that prepares us for death."

They hissed. They rumbled. They banged. They wailed. One bald bacteriologist earnestly cried, "I don't want to be planted in a flask: my parents were respectable people." Tsenkh's fury—his volatile sneezing—had no limit because even he was once mentally unwell.

And now on his face were traces of mental disturbance, but he concealed his stormy rage while threatening the incessant Khandrikov.

And Khandrikov continued, "Maybe everything will return. Or everything will change. Or everything will return, but different. Or just appear to be the same. Maybe that which has returned changed from its previous state will be better than it was previously. Or worse. Maybe not better or worse, but the same. Maybe progress moves in a straight line. Or in a circle. Or both straight and in a circle—making a spiral. Maybe the parabola is the sign of progress. Maybe the spiral of our progress isn't the spiral of the atoms' progress. Maybe the spiral of the atoms' progress is wrapped around the spiral of our progress. And the spiral of our progress, as much as we can detect, is wrapped around the single ring of the spiral of a higher order. And so without end. Maybe these spirals circle one another, making bigger and bigger circles. Or the circles are contracting, getting closer to a point. Maybe each point in time and space is the intersection of the spiral orbits of many different orders. And we live simultaneously in the distant past and in the present and in the future. And there is neither time nor space. And we use these categories for the sake of simplicity. Or this simplicity is the resulting synthesis of numerous spiral orbits, and everything in time and space should be just as it seems. Maybe our capriciousness will shatter against the iron laws of necessity. Or the laws of necessity are just habits that took root over the centuries. Everywhere is the solution to a single equation with many variables.

However we change the coefficients and exponents, the variables remain unsolved.

Everything is unclear. The most empirical of sciences gave birth to *probability* theory and *polynomial* equations. The most empirical science is the most relative. But relativity without things in relation is nothing.

Everything flows. Flies. Races in foggy circles. The huge tornado of the world holds all life in its stormy embrace. In front of it is emptiness. And behind it too.

Where is it flying?"

It blew and blew. A blizzard banged at the windows. And the blizzard's white wings circled over the forest, the city, and the valley.

XV

They put their coats on. One of them was too agitated to get his feet into his boots. Shaking his finger at the bald bacteriologist, he explained, "I told you he was a dangerous person with no place among scholars."

"I don't want to be planted in a flask," wailed the bacteriologist.

At that time the botanist Corpsov was hunched over his desk, skimming *Citizenship in Every Era and Nation*.

His bald spot was lit by a yellow flame. The lenses of his glasses obscured his dead eyes.

And the philologist Griboedov read *Poisonous Mushrooms*.

They both thought, "How many different specialities there are in the world, and how capacious is each specialty!"

The night was sad and cloudy.

A pale, bitter man with a pointed wolfish beard and wearing a cap walked along the slushy sidewalk with the collar of his coat raised.

Passersby involuntarily avoided him, and arriving at the telegraph office, he sent the following telegram: "Samarsk Region. Snake's Nest. To Vladislav Denisovich Dragonov. Come. Khandrikov is putting up a fight. Tsenkh."

A giant black snake with fiery eyes flew along the endless rails with an unimaginable rumble.

It lifted its trunk to the sky and made a prolonged roar, giving off a heap of smoke.

It was coming from the Samara Region, from "Snake's Nest," knowing that the final battle approached.

Many people in the neighboring villages heard these sinister moans in their sleep, but they thought it was just a train.

XVI

The next day Khandrikov dared to go to the lab, notwithstanding Tsenkh's challenge.

Opening the door to Tsenkh's lab, all he saw was a foggy gray grotto. In the middle of the grotto sat an unfamiliar man in a cap with Tsenkh's face but wearing brown rags and threatening Khandrikov with an ancient horror.

Khandrikov ran from the lab in terror. He understood—his final battle for independence from Tsenkh had begun.

And associate professor Tsenkh, standing amid chemical fumes in a brown jacket with a towel over his shoulder, didn't understand a thing.

Khandrikov didn't sleep that night. He paced his room. He knew what he was getting into. He paced, waiting for the sunrise.

He knew that last night's gauntlet was more than a simple disagreement. Something bigger was concealed in it.

He knew that Tsenkh wouldn't forgive him. He would pour out his fury on him for the rest of his life.

Throwing that gauntlet, he issued a challenge to fate. He knew that it would result in a reshuffling of cosmic forces. He was planning to visit Dr. Orlov—Tsenkh's enemy.

He knew what he was getting into. Golden stars were watching him through the window. It was a moonless night. The horizon reflected the darkness. You couldn't tell what was there—sky or cloud.

Suddenly on the horizon was the blue-black sky above the clouds ringed with silver. The moon rose belatedly and filled blank spots of the clouds with silver.

The chimneys on the houses were given away by their black edges, and there, where before was only darkness, you could now see the contour of the roofs.

He knew that this wasn't by chance and that this very night similar contours would give away the greatest of horrors.

It was previously unknown, and much had flowed into it, like rivers to the sea, and now it must come to light, bringing to life many unknown terrors and delights.

And the moon was already above the clouds and was shining in the sky. An airy golden finger stretched above and below the moon.

He went outside.

The night felt damp. The melting snow was streaming. It flowed along the sidewalk and fell into black holes—urban abysses. The sound of lonely Eternity's song echoed in the fog, "I will come after the darkness of the city, the difficult times."

The warm spring breeze rattled the telegraph wires. Khandrikov thought, "Something is about to happen."

When we he was walking home, a rumbling carriage crossed his path.

In it was a tall old man, slightly stooped and with a long beard. Seeing Khandrikov, the old man removed his wide-brimmed hat and yelled as he passed, "Wait for the eagle, Khandrikov" . . .

It was Dr. Orlov. Something awfully familiar wafted toward Khandrikov, as if the pit of Eternity had opened in front of his face, but the rumble of the carriage had already died down in the next street.

He wandered until daybreak. The golden sky glowed red with heat. Rows of buildings ran past like gray cliffs.

In the distance, one street intersected another street; a section of the other street could be seen from this one. That's where he was looking. He saw something alarming.

It was a chain of unbroken links, like squat gray barrels connected to one another. The spot where they were connected bent and, with a crash, the whole chain was being dragged down the street.

You couldn't see the chain's end or beginning, but only a row of linked barrels crashing and twisting between two rows of buildings.

Then the barrels began to thin out and ended with a disgusting dark gray tendril which quickly disappeared, pulled by the torso.

Khandrikov understood that this was a snake summoned by Tsenkh to frighten him.

Horrified, he whispered, "There . . . It's begun . . . And we can no longer go back to peaceful times."

The fat red sun had leaped into the orange horizon and was silently laughing and playing with the light.

He thought, "I must flee to Orlov and his sanatorium to calm my nerves."

At home he began to pack his suitcase, and the sun's golden rays were beating at the windows, beating their way in.

He squatted in front of his suitcase glowing in the golden stream.

XVII

He calmed down by evening. Tsenkh had only gathered a fog of delirium against him. Nothing had begun yet. The horror was still congealing.

He could rest and gather his strength.

He drank his evening tea, not without concern for the future.

Upstairs a musician played on a horn, "I walk alone on the road,"[9] and Khandrikov thought, in order to drown out his concern, "I would sit with my wife and he'd play the same thing upstairs.

Sofia Chizhikovna would complain to me. Where is she now? No one is complaining to me now, but I'm sad and afraid."

Across from his window the four windows of an empty apartment still gave off the golden glow of the dawn.

Her dear plain face was wreathed in a bridal veil, and she was wearing flowers.

He adjusted his white tie. He squeezed her hand and said, "So death was just a dream. So we're inseparable."

All around were the joyful faces of familiar men and women.

The priest led them from the church. The white church stood on a cape lit by a thin crescent moon.

Bits of fluffy clouds flew around. Whitish and smoky like ash, they were low and floating toward the holy place.

They floated under the moon and glowed. The bridal veil twirled over the world. There was a blue expanse and the silver glimmer of small cupolas.

They sat on the porch of the church. In the moon they cast black shadows, and the snowy foam was broken up at their feet.

They waited. The servant woke Khandrikov saying, "Wake up, sir. It's time for the memorial service."

Khandrikov opened his eyes. The samovar sputtered. Upstairs they had stopped playing the horn. Khandrikov thought, "I recently defended my thesis. Now I have to defend myself."

He looked through the window. It was a cloudy night. The black windows of the empty apartment still gave off the golden glow of the dawn.

The bell rang. Khandrikov shuddered. It was Tsenkh.

They opened the front door. Someone took off their coat. Blew their nose. Took off their boots.

The door creaked.

It opened.

A strange creature stood in the room. It was a man of average height in a gray coat and trousers.

A feathery head popped out of the starched collar.

Khandrikov noted how clearly the collar contrasted with the white feathers with black spots. Prehensile eagle's talons protruded from under his shirt front instead of hands.

Lit by the lamp, the stranger offered Khandrikov a talon, threw back his feathery head and shook the room with a sharp screech.

Khandrikov flushed. He laughed, wept, and cried out, "Dear eagle . . . You've come . . . You've come back."

He took the eagle by its prehensile talons and shook them for a long time in happy oblivion.

The eagle sat in a chair. He took a cigarette from a case and smoked with his legs crossed. You could see that he was resting from a long journey, while Khandrikov paced around the room and quietly whispered, "The eagle has come. He's come back."

Then the eagle said, "It's time for you to go to Dr. Orlov's sanatorium. You should take the train to the *Eagleton* station.

I'll bring your suitcases later.

When Tsenkh comes, you'll already be gone." They put on their coats and boots. They took umbrellas: the weather was changing.

Khandrikov trustingly leaned on the eagle. The eagle hailed a cab. They sat in the carriage and rode off.

XVIII

The train boarded. The eagle shut the door to Khandrikov's coupe. They talked to one another through the carriage window.

A man passed under the train, banging and oiling the wheels. The sound of the hammer echoed, "Ten-teren"...

Standing on the platform, the eagle parted with Khandrikov saying, "My role is done. You will now ride through Eternity to *Eagleton*, to the sanatorium for the mentally unwell."

Khandrikov warmly shook the eagle's outstretched talon, and he became sad that he had to part with the eagle so soon.

But the eagle said, "Don't be sad. You'll feel better there. But it's my fate to liberate people from the yoke of horror and ease their burden.

It's my fate to lead them to *Eagleton*." With these words the eagle raised his hat. The train departed. Khandrikov stuck his head out the window to bid the eagle farewell.

The train flew through the fields. The laughter of the uncertain, the cry of the lost, fully merged into one mournful plaintive cry.

As if a hyena loomed on the horizon.

The platform was empty. The train flew on.

The eagle stood and stood on the platform and then went into the waiting area for first- and second-class passengers.

PART THREE

I

The terrace curtain blew in the wind. The residents of the sanatorium looked warily at the terrace. Khandrikov watched their wary glances through a slit.

The wind made cool ripples on the blue lake. Above the lake, the wind carried flowery pollen from the trees with a whistle.

It blew and blew—the cloud rose high. Ahead was an abyss. And behind too.

Orlov walked toward Khandrikov, winding along small paths between round flower beds.

His beard fluttered. His summer jacket strained against him. He held a wide-brimmed hat in his hand.

With a wave, he threw a kerchief over his stooped shoulders.

A neurasthenic sanatorium patient passed by and, indicating Khandrikov's terrace with her eye, said to Orlov, "And is he a hopeless case, Ivan Ivanovich?"

"Progressive," he answered, adjusting his beard. And again he wound along the round flower beds heading to Khandrikov's terrace.

It blew and blew—it rose high—the flowering cloud, twisting above the light blue lake in an uncharted expanse.

Khandrikov jumped back from the slit formed by the blowing curtain.

And the curtain parted. In front of him stood Dr. Orlov in all his glory.

It was almost evening. An ashen gray cloud puffed in the uncharted expanse, while its bottom half flashed in the horizon.

Above it the sky looked green, and a yellowish-pink ribbon of satin unfurled below it.

And it was fading.

II

"You're crafty, Doctor!" laughed Khandrikov. "Accepting that they could catch neither you nor me, you cut the Gordian knot and diagnosed me as a progressive paralytic."

Somewhere off to the side they were playing lawn tennis, and the ball flew through the air and was carried off. Orlov leisurely put his wide-brimmed hat on the table. He stood his walking stick in the corner. Rubbing his hands, he said,

"Yes, otherwise no one would understand anything."

Wanting to change the topic, he said, "Well, how are you doing here?"

The yellowish-pink cloud stretched out and turned red—like a flamingo's wing. Khandrikov's lonely heart sensed its nearness—its approach.

"Excellent," he said. "I'm happy." They sat side by side. They smoked in silence.

The golden reflections of the sunset were everywhere. The horizon burned with the golden sunset. There was a sea of gold.

They tapped the ash from their cigarettes. The past, long forgotten and eternal as the world, wrapped the distance in damp towels. Tender weeping echoed on the lake.

This joy outgrew the universe.

They forgot about time and space. The old psychiatrist bowed his inexpressive face over Khandrikov. He yelled at the distraught one in a velvety bass, "I speak to each in a language he understands.

That's good. It's for the best.

Isn't it all the same? Whether we sit here in mantles or in sport coats. On the shore of the sea or a lake."

Orlov was quiet, but the two abysses sitting in the depths of his eye sockets spoke.

Sounds of a trumpet resounded from the facade of the main building, "I walk alone on the road." Khandrikov said, "I once had a wife. Where was that? What was her name?"

Some kind of face, vaguely familiar, flashed in the chaos. It nodded and then disappeared again.

Orlov struck a match and suddenly shouted, "What do my sanatorium residents' opinions about you matter in the face of the universe!"

Muted joy flared from his chest. He raised his eyes to the heavens. The heavens, speckled with sonorous gold, descended to their faces.

But all you had to do was move and everything flew back up. And nobody knew how high.

A thin curved strip of silver already hung over the lake. The taut clouds illuminated the silver threads, like friends, against a blue-black velvet background.

The splashes of oars streamed silver. In the boat, they sang of the moon. The tender breeze whispered, "What does associate professor Tsenkh matter with his nastiness and mean looks?"

Orlov said, "What does your insanity and my sanity matter in the face of the phantasm of the world? The universe engulfs us all in its embrace.

It caresses. It kisses. Be still. It's good to be silent."

And they were still.

In the distance a crimson meteor flew by leaving a fiery trail on the lake . . . And the water danced, "Don't . . . Don't . . ."

And the meteor dissipated in a shower of sparks.

III

A gong sounded. Dr. Orlov, fully buttoned, offered Khandrikov his reverent right hand in parting. He said something to him in his deep voice. He took his stick and hat and headed off to stroll around the lake and make swizzles in the sand.

It spins and spins and returns to its orbit.

Khandrikov thought, "Tsenkh—you don't scare me. They will defend me from your attacks. Orlov is with me."

A velvety soft, intoxicated, sad, quiet, clear happiness was beating in the depths of his heart.

The soft velvet of the abyss surrounded him and kissed and caressed him.

The abyss itself called out to him, "I am yours, yours. Yours forever."

He tenderly watched the old man Orlov circle the shore. A huge white hump hung between the earth and the sky.

The crescent moon, breaking through in one spot, sent its rays to the old psychiatrist.

Khandrikov moaned, "My dear abyss . . . I will recognize your quiet caress."

And the abyss responded, "I am yours, yours. Yours forever."

From the open window of the sanatorium's main building, a mournful voice sounded:

> With fiery caresses,
> I will inflame and smother you.[10]

The abyss quietly crept in. It stood over everything. Everything watched it and languished deeply.

The voice sang, "Come be with me, come be with me!"

IV

One day Khandrikov's colleagues visited him: two gloomy laboratory assistants. They patted him on the shoulder and awkwardly encouraged him, "Be strong, friend. You'll still write your doctoral dissertation . . ."

Khandrikov thought, "These are Tsenkh's spies." He walked with them in the green garden.

The dark velvet arboreal flora murmured about the abyss. And spots of sunlight swayed on the sand.

When they left, they confided in one another, "Khandrikov is hopeless."

And he was still standing in the garden alleys worried that his presence had been given away.

And above him echoed the dark green trembling and the noise of the velvet abyss, "Come be with me, come be with me!" And on the sand, the spots of sunlight flew off in fright.

At that time the air was transparent, like a radiant azure. In the evenings the sunsets flared like a hazy red sword that cut the horizon.

Khandrikov noted that Orlov was completely exceptional. This impression grew stronger when he looked at the old man's stooped shoulders.

Once, turning around unexpectedly, Orlov caught Khandrikov's confused blue gaze watching him through a slit in the curtain.

V

They parted. Orlov went to the house where the lights were on. It was as if the windows of the house were smiling with light. Khandrikov pressed up against the smiling glass.

Orlov was talking with his young wife. His back was reflected in the mirror. The wall clock somehow bared its teeth and marked his departure.

Booming notes flew from the bright windows, and now they were shining happily and the whole house smiled tauntingly. But Khandrikov didn't pay any attention to these smiles. He watched through patches of glass. There, on the other side of the panes, they were gesticulating.

From the gestures, Khandrikov understood that someone was leaving.

He stood indecisively for a while. Low black clouds slinked along in the sky.

Orlov went into the next room. And the clock marked his departure.

The wind blew at Khandrikov's back. It dusted him with velvety sand.

A rush of cold come from somewhere. A looming line of hailstorms quickly moved in from the north.

Worried and tormented by the unknown, Khandrikov quietly crept to the door that led to the old psychiatrist's room.

He pressed up to the keyhole.

Orlov, holding a candle and not wearing a coat, was packing a suitcase. He was getting ready for the train. Khandrikov's heart sank.

Then the door creaked and opened. A yellow flame was blazing. The uncomfortable silence was broken by a tender voice, barely containing its disappointment, "Khandrikov, you're still spying on me."

They sat in Orlov's room. Orlov said, "Go to sleep . . . Why are you worrying over nothing: I have to go, and for a very important reason. Nothing will happen to you."

The flame of the candle flickered, nearly out. Silver streaks of wallpaper—not streaks, but streams of water—silently flowed down the gray walls.

Orlov was on the suitcase in the shadows. Now the lenses of his glasses glimmered in the darkness.

Khandrikov: "I'm afraid. Without you Tsenkh will show up. He'll force me to renounce my beliefs. They say that he's conspiring against us."

Lightning flashed. Thunder began to rumble but then stumbled.

Orlov: "That's not important. It just seems that way. And if it is true, my trip abroad will upend these intrigues."

White hail began to pound at the window with regularity, and Orlov said, "Hail." There was a cold breeze. It died down.

He sat dejectedly.

The hail stopped beating the window. The moon was shining.

The silver wallpaper—not streaks, but streams—silently flowed from someplace. Someone filled the surrounding area with a protracted roar.

Khandrikov: "Ivan Ivanovich, who is roaring so protractedly and sadly over the fields? Where have I heard that voice?"

Orlov: "That's the postal train speeding north. The engineer pulls some levers and the train begins to whistle. Go to sleep, Khandrikov. It's not good for you to sit up too long."

And when Khandrikov said, "You've calmed me down, Ivan Ivanovich," the old man silently took a cigarette from a silver case and, smoking it, took a candle to light Khandrikov's way.

He left. The hail stopped. A piercing cold overwhelmed him. The cloud that had burst through from polar lands went off to the south.

The cloud was blackish blue and gloomy. And above it was a chain of snowy caps and sharp icy peaks. These were the lofty glaciers, foretelling a coming frost.

They flashed blindingly. The moon, a familiar evening friend, strolled in front of the heavens, a bit turquoise and soft gray.

A distant hum disturbed Khandrikov. In the distance flew the crimson-eyed serpent with its trunk raised—it flew through the valleys. It flew—speeding away.

With chattering teeth, Khandrikov made his way home whispering, "I'm not afraid of you, monster . . ."

His heart was beating from the approach of the abyss.

And again it stood there and lovingly whispered to him about the possibility of happiness. Its frozen smile mocked Khandrikov.

One of the residents of the sanatorium sang:

> In vain do I wish to mute
> Bursts of mental anguish
> And calm my heart with reason.

And laughing and despairing, he kissed the air—that sweet, fresh clarity. And they sang:

> My heart doesn't listen to reason
> When I see you . . .

The cloud flew off. The snow caps were blurred and the icy peaks tumbled.

VI

He walked with the psychiatrist. The quivering and vague noise of the velvety-green abyss echoed above them. Spots of sunlight scattered in fright on the sand.

The wind made dusty circles on the bank. They spun and spun and returned to their orbits.

The crystal-clear lake shone in Khandrikov's eyes. His lip protruded, and he looked utterly childlike when he asked Orlov, "In the newspapers they write that distant countries have been discovered somewhere."

The old man blew his nose in a batiste handkerchief. The wind poured in from the lake. You could see a velvety abyss of leaves and frightened spots of sunlight. And Orlov objected with gravity, "Well, it's too early to think about that . . ."

And he added, "What are you imagining? Tomorrow I'm going abroad. Let's row around the lake and say our farewells."

They sat in the boat, rocked by the waves. Khandrikov set up the oarlocks. Orlov took the oars.

He pointed toward the distance on the blue lake with the paddle and said in a deep voice, "The distance, Khandrikov . . . the distance . . ."

He rowed, making foamy blue waves. A pearly eddy formed. His back arched. He threw his head back with its silver hair blowing.

The wind whispered in his ear, "The distance . . . The distance . . ."

The door to the men's changing room flew open. An attorney, bald with a long beard and a snub nose, recovering from a nervous attack, stood naked by the lake.

The sun was setting in a ruby backdrop. A fiery face burned in the rays of the sunset. He gave off a roar and patted his paunchy stomach.

With outstretched arms he plunged into the abyss, causing a ruby-red eddy. And naked boys stomped their feet in the door, "Well, well, folks. Who's brave enough?"

His bald spot glowed. His head rose above the blue lake with the sunset in the backdrop. The ruby orb set over the lake. An obedient cloud floated up to him from the side with its long thin fingers of molten gold.

The lake reflected the sky. It seemed to them that they were flying between two skies. Vertigo—the insidious inhabitant of the heights—spun their heads. But Orlov wasn't afraid of anything.

He rowed. Head-spinning words burst from his mouth. He expounded on his theosophical ideas. He nodded to the sun, shouting, "Set."

And it set. The fiery crimson semicircle went into the irretrievable abyss. Just one shining point remained.

The psychiatrist said, "Calm down, Khandrikov. Everything will pass. It's all for the best." He stood up, holding the wet oar. Straightening his beard, he sang in a velvety voice, "My blessings to you, woods, valleys, fields, and mountains."

The transparent evening was filled with sadness. Here and there a white-breasted angler split this transparency. Quietly screeching, it flew off into the distance.

And then he flew back again, smiling at the impossible.

Khandrikov stared at a spot where there was no bottom, just calm infinity. He expected to see his own reflection, but he saw a child looking back at him from an overturned boat, sometimes going pale, sometimes flaring up.

And Orlov's velvety bass resounded powerfully between the two skies, "My blessings to you, freedom and the blue sky."

The day grew dark. Fiery fingers—fingers of joy—were quietly lit one after another.

Khandrikov stared at the rippling mirror. The boat floated on an ocean of air. The shore made a ring around the airy blue expanse, which looked like a lake.

But it wasn't a lake—it was a mirror reflecting the sky: it was the sky itself into which he and Orlov had plunged along with the boat.

Everything seemed better there.

Khandrikov exclaimed, "Ivan Ivanovich, is this the border?" With these words, he dipped his finger into the pale turquoise surface. And his finger disappeared into something cold and soft.

"Will you not be going abroad and crossing that border?"

Orlov laughed in his beard and rowed, "And if it is *that* border, what does it matter to you . . ." But Khandrikov was silent. He was calm and content. He began to understand something.

They rowed until late at night. The glimmering constellations were so clear, so well defined. Orlov pointed his pale finger here and there. His beard trembled as he said, "This is the constellation Cassiopeia. That's the Corona Borealis. And over there is the constellation Perseus.

Today the Perseids are in motion . . . Their path is long . . .

It stretches far beyond Neptune . . . But they aren't afraid of their long path . . .

They bravely fly onward, onward—and then return to their former orbits."

Here and there were golden points descending. Then they went out.

Their heads flew back. Orlov said, "That's the Perseids in motion. They don't fear the expanse in their mad flight.

They fly onward . . . far beyond Neptune in the dark embrace of space . . .

Terror is unknown to them, and they overcome everything through flight . . . Today I'll fly away, and tomorrow you will, and there's no need to be afraid: we will meet again . . ."

They watched the flights of the Perseids for a long while. Here and there were golden points descending. Then they went out.

Orlov whispered, "My dears, give my regards to Neptune."

White feathery clouds stretched out in the sky, smoothed by the wind high in the air.

VII

Khandrikov was gloomy all morning. Dr. Orlov said a heartfelt goodbye to his young wife and then left for abroad.

He was wearing a black traveling coat and a plush hat. He was painstakingly supervising the packing of his travel things and not paying attention to his wife's request that he let her do that.

Finally, the Orlov household minded Russian custom and sat on the edge of chairs arranged on the terrace.

And Orlov mercilessly ended this ritual: he planted a kiss on his sad wife's lips and gingerly hopped into the country cart. Waving his hat, he rode off for abroad.

Orlov was standing by the booth, getting his ticket. Tsenkh was on the train that just pulled in. He walked past Orlov. They coldly bowed to one another.

Holding a yellow ticket in his hand, Orlov turned and watched with derision as Tsenkh walked away. When he got his change, he caught up to Tsenkh and took him aside . . . "Are you going to see Khandrikov?"

And Tsenkh answered, "I've come to do my duty and visit the sick."

But Dr. Orlov furrowed his brow and suddenly banged his walking stick and haughtily straightened up. His bass voice rumbled like a peal of thunder, "You're lying again, you deceitful creature."

He raised his hooked walking stick and threateningly shook it at Tsenkh. A gendarme came up and lazily said, "Gentlemen, no rowdiness here."

But Orlov majestically turned his back to him. He took the receipt for his baggage from the porter.

VIII

Orlov left for distant lands, and Khandrikov wasn't sad. He knew that he had to face the abyss without fear.

He knew they would meet again.

Autumn was coming. The leaves shone with gold. The sunsets bathed everything in lily and crimson. The autumn wind rustled the dry leaves on the shore of the lake. They made golden dances.

It flew and flew and twirled—the tornado of leaves. The shore was ahead. And behind.

In the evenings Khandrikov would take out the boat. He would row to the middle of the lake. The fog rolled in. The dew settled. Everything seemed mysteriously miraculous. Khandrikov would stare into his reflection. It looked like he was hanging in an abyss surrounded by the heavens. Pointing at the water, he would say, "Orlov went there—beyond the border."

From there a thin child with azure eyes watched him and quietly laughed at him.

The joker was laughing at him from there—from far-off lands.

And Khandrikov thought, "Well, if I tumble out, I'll be there, beyond the border, and this joker would emerge here with his boat . . . Well, now."

And the more he stared into the depths, the more beautiful the upside-down far-off lands seemed to be.

Somewhere someone was singing, "Come to me, come to me." It seemed to him that the old man's call rose up again, sweet and familiar.

He said to himself, "Orlov is calling me . . . Again he calls . . ."

He began to have visions. One time he was strolling in the woods. There was the echo of horses' hooves and a flabby voice, "Chapter 26: Citizenship Among the Papuans."

On the path were two centaurs—they were both old, were both venerable, and were wearing black wide-brimmed hats and cloaks. They were holding hands.

Watch chains dangled from their vests, and glasses shimmered on their broad noses. They waved their tails and rustled the rotting leaves. One was holding a thick book in front of his nose. The other caught sight of a fiery beauty, a poisonous mushroom, in the moss and bent his stout torso toward it.

He became flushed and picked the mushroom, looking it over in celebration with squinting eyes, having pushed his glasses onto his forehead as a precaution.

His colleague exclaimed, "Dusty Petrovich, this spot doesn't agree with me." They started to argue.

One, waving his arms, flung the mushroom at the other's head, and the fiery beauty was smashed to pieces on his high brow.

Turning to one another, they began to neigh and kick, waving their tails.

That made Khandrikov laugh.

IX

Orlov wrote from abroad, from far-off lands. He described the riches of those spots in colorful language and beckoned his wife to join him.

The young lady relayed the contents of these letters to Khandrikov in ecstatic terms.

And Khandrikov thought, "Yes, I already know." He laughed and winked to himself. He remembered his lakeside strolls and flights through the air between the two heavens.

More and more often he wanted to tumble in the air so that he would be carried to far-off lands and cross the threshold. To be abroad. To push his reflection out from there.

To return to Ivan Ivanovich.

That desire became acute after the old psychiatrist's letters.

It was autumn. The lake was clouded by fog. The leaves glistened with gold.

The sky and the waters of the lake seemed soft and delicate, as if they were made of golden green glass.

Khandrikov readied the boat, rattling the chain. When he got it out, he rushed to the middle of the lake. It seemed to him that he was rushing between two skies. He was accompanied by his overturned reflection.

It grew dark. The red disk unleashed from beyond the horizon by a giant's hand was now steadily rising into the evening abyss.

The foggy tenderness of the abyss overwhelmed his heart, and he said to himself, "Time to leap."

A white angler flew over the emerald gold abyss, quietly screeching and laughing at the impossible.

As if in a dream, Khandrikov saw the bench on the shore, and on it was the attorney with his long beard, distractedly watching the glimmering boat.

The shining moon was caught in a net of sharp and feathery snow-white clouds and dimmed dejectedly.

Something made a sound, "Come to me . . . Come to me . . ." The boat rocked. From it radiated circles streaked with purple and crimson. He made his decision.

"I'm coming to yo . . ." In an instant: the emerald and gold water rumbled and poured into the boat, which was taking on water and was streaked with molten rubies. He flapped his arms and plunged into the abyss of emerald gold. His reflection rushed at Khandrikov, defending its border from his attack, and he fell into its embrace.

A white angler screeched over the drowning man's ear and laughed at the impossible.

The attorney distractedly watched the glimmering boat. What he saw was the boat rocking and quickly growing smaller. Looking harder, he saw its overturned bottom.

Jumping up from the bench, he waved his arms, "Help: Khandrikov's drowning..." The autumn wind rustled the dry leaves on the shore of the lake, and they made golden dances. It blew and blew...

No one returned his cry. The bottom of the boat floated. The shining wind continued to rise.

In an instant: the heavenly depths touched Khandrikov's face, but he moved. The heavens reached upward, and nobody could say how high.

He sighed with relief. The boat rocked. Black nocturnal snipes flew by, brushing against him with their outstretched wings.

He looked down: the upside-down shore was reflected, with an upside-down bench. The attorney stood on the bank, waving his arms, head over heels. Waves arose.

The reflection grew hazy.

X

He lifted his head. He saw a strip of dry land. From the ocean's endless expanse, waves pushed the boat to the shore.

The extinguishing sky glowed with purity. Far, far away a blue unsettled titan of clouds floated in the distant west.

The waves tossed the boat. The wind picked up the silvery sand and formed dusty dances. A stooped old man stood on the shore, leaning on his blinding iron rod. He was happy to be meeting again.

In his hand he held a crown of white roses—a crown of silver stars. He kissed the child's light hair, placing the silver stars on it.

He said, "You have left and returned many times, led by the eagle. Returned and left again.

Many times I have crowned you with suffering—with its burning flames. But now for the first time I place these silver stars on your head. You've returned and will not set again.

Hello, my sunsetless child . . ."

They stood on the shore. The child trustingly pressed up against the old man, taking stock of the starry expanse. The old man embraced the child. He showed him the constellations.

"There is the constellation Cancer, and there is the Cross, and there is the sun."

Over them the blinding stars illuminated the silence with invisible splendor.

These were the stars of Hercules.

The old man said, "Today the Perseids are in motion. Their path is long. It stretches far beyond the earth.

They bravely fly ahead, ahead. In their mad flight they aren't afraid of the expanse and overcome everything with their flight."

They both put their heads back. Here and there golden points flew by.

And went out.

They watched the motion of the Perseids for a long time.

The old man whispered, "My dears . . . Bow to the earth . . ."

1902

A GOBLET OF BLIZZARDS

(Fourth Symphony)

It is with great admiration
that the author dedicates this book to
Nikolai Karlovich Metner,[1]
who inspired the theme of the symphony,
and
to the author's dear friend
Zinaida Nikolaevna Gippius,[2]
who made this theme possible.

"I knocked at the door. Embraces smother.
A kiss—again and again.
Look, sister and brother,
How our love glows!"
M. Kuzmin[3]

IN LIEU OF A PREFACE

Finishing my "Fourth Symphony," I find myself in a bit of a quandary. Who will read it? For whom is it meant? I worked on it for a long time; I tried to depict certain lived experiences as accurately as possible, things that, as it were, lay under the fabric of everyday life but could not be incarnated in depiction. These experiences are dressed in the form of repeated themes infused thorough the whole *Symphony*, shown as if through a magnifying glass. Here I encountered two types of problems. In depicting an experience that can't be incarnated in depiction, should I privilege the depiction's inherent beauty or its accuracy (i.e., allowing the depiction to convey the experience to the maximum degree)? Additionally, how do I incorporate the inner connection of experiences that cannot be incarnated in depiction (which I would call mystical) through connected depictions? There were two paths in front of me: the artistic path and the path that analyzed the experiences themselves, that broke them down into their constituent elements. I chose the latter and for that reason have my doubts: is the *Symphony* before you a work of art or a record of the contemporary soul's state of consciousness—interesting, perhaps, to a future psychiatrist? That is what concerns the substance of the *Symphony* itself.

Concerning the method of the writing—that's also where I have my doubts. I was interested in a structural mechanism for that vaguely conceived form in which my previous *Symphonies* were written: there, the structure begged the question and I had no distinct idea of what a literary *Symphony* should be. In the *Symphony* before you, I have attempted most of all to be precise in the exposition of themes, in their counterpoint, coherence, and so on. In my *Symphony* there are really two groups of themes: the first group is comprised of the themes in Part One. Even when they differ from one another in the construction of phrases, they all nevertheless have an inner kinship. The themes of Part Two form the second group which, in terms of structure, is in essence one theme, outlined in the chapter "The Blossoming Wind." This theme develops in three directions. One direction (which I call theme "Alpha") is most clearly expressed in the chapter "In the Monastery"; another (theme "Bravo") in the chapter "Wheat Foam"; the third (theme "Charlie") in the chapter "Golden Autumn." These three themes of Part Two—Alpha, Bravo, Charlie—act in concert with the themes of Part One and form what might be called the fabric of the entire *Symphony*. In Parts Three and Four, I attempted to introduce a structure of phrases and images such that form and images were predetermined by their thematic development and, as much as possible, make image subordinate to the mechanical development of the themes. I admit that such structural precision makes plot subordinate to technique (I was often required to make the *Symphony* longer for entirely structural reasons) and that the beauty of an image doesn't always coincide with the regularity of its structural form. Which is why I viewed the *Symphony* as a purely structural task when I was working on it. I still don't know whether it deserves to exist. But in general, I don't know if the majority of contemporary works of literature deserve to exist. I attempted to be more of a scholar than an artist. Only the objective judgment of the future will decide whether my structural calculations make sense or if they're paradoxical. But that's the state of those who toil for pure knowledge: the future decides if there is any practical application for their labor. For precision's sake I could offer a structural overview of all of the chapters here, but who would be interested in that? For example, I'll just say that the Part Three chapter "Dewy Tears" is comprised in the following way. If we call the fragments, excluding the first, of the Part Two chapter "Golden Autumn" $a, \beta, \gamma, \delta, \varepsilon,$ and so on, and we recall that (1) the main themes of Part Two are Alpha, Bravo, and Charlie and (2) one of the themes of Part One is "ρ," then the general structure of the chapter looks like: $a \rho \beta \gamma \delta$ and so on. The reader will understand what that means. And that's how the rest is written as well.

Finally, there's another difficulty in fully understanding the *Symphony*. The meaning of its symbols becomes more transparent with an understanding of its structure. In order to fully examine an experience that can be seen in a given image, you must understand which theme the image is part of, how many times the image's theme has already been repeated, and which images accompanied it. If with a superficial reading the sense of an experience is conveyed with 50 percent accuracy, then with the reader following everything that's been said above, the sense of an experience is clarified with 99 percent accuracy.

This leads to a conclusion that saddens me: I must recommend that my *Symphony* be studied (first read it through, then examine the structure, then read it through again and again). But what right do I have for my work to be studied when I myself don't know whether my whole *Symphony* is a paradox or not? Without careful attention to my literary devices, the *Symphony* seems dull, bloated, and written merely for the colorful tone of a few disparate scenes.

In conclusion I'll speak about the point of the work's plot, even though it's closely linked to its literary technique. In the *Symphony* before you, I wanted to depict the whole range of that particular type of love which our era vaguely anticipates, as in earlier times Plato, Goethe, and Dante anticipated sacred love. If a new religious consciousness is possible in the future, then the path to it is through love. I should say that I have nothing in common with contemporary prophets of the erotic, who not only erase the boundary between mysticism and psychopathology, who not only infuse mysticism with pornography, but who give the esotericism of vaguely religious experiences the flavor of advertising and charlatanism. I should say that for now I don't see a reliable path for the realization of the vague call for turning loving into a religion of love. That's why I wanted to portray the promised land of this love with the blizzard, gold, the sky, and the wind. The theme of the blizzard is a vaguely enticing flight . . . but where? To life or death? To insanity or wisdom? The souls of lovers dissipate in the blizzard.

The theme of the blizzard came to me long ago—back in 1903. At the time I wrote a few excerpts (which have subsequently been revised). The first draft of Parts One and Two were finished in 1904 (I subsequently revised them). By that time, the leitmotif of the blizzard had fully come into shape. I read those excerpts to a few writers in Moscow and Petersburg. At last, the final draft of Part One was finished in June of 1906 (I hadn't been able to work on the *Symphony* for two years for a variety of reasons). In rewriting it, I added just a few satirical scenes—nothing more.

I write all of this knowing that many people may reproach me for rehashing some contemporary themes. After all I've said, I decidedly reject this potential reproach.

The Author

Moscow, 1907

PART ONE: THE SNOWY PAW

The Blizzard

The blizzard blew pale whirlwinds off the roofs.

The snow drifted up and, like a lily, swayed above the city.

Melodious ribbons of silver swooped down—flying by, enveloping everything.

They collided and shattered into snow.

And the snow was sprinkled in handfuls of diamonds. It danced, flittered around, rested on the ground like hundreds of buzzing gnats.

And the gnats faded.

But then, buzzing in the light, they flew back up again.

Giant lilies again swept up and began swaying above the city, swirling with the snowstorm.

It was the first blizzard of winter.

On the street, the passersby seemed pale and odd as they bumped into one another, clutching their hats.

A familiar mystery passed through the soul unexpectedly. Familiar wailing echoed enticingly from afar. A familiar mystery swam through the soul unexpectedly.

But they kept walking, just the same, just the same . . .

Here a passerby flitted past, there a passerby tipped their plush hat.

Walking, he would bump into someone coming from the opposite direction.

Everything swirled in front of him in a pale whirlwind—a snowy whirlwind.

And the word of the wind became stormy flesh.

Passersby flickered by, carriages and carts collided with the wild blizzard like shadows.

A single face showed itself, blizzard-like and full of desire—it moaned, smiled, and leaned over.

Again. And again.

He was tempted by one and the same mystery.

A white sleeve moved up along a wall. And behind it grew another.

The white sleeve, oozing out of the fence, grew, unnoticed.

It licked the walls of the building.

And slipped away.

White sails puffed above the buildings.

Airships flew above the buildings with a song.

White-winged flyers raced through time: to their motherland, their unknown motherland.

A white corpse stood by the window. And behind it another white corpse stood by the widow.

The white corpse, oozing out of the cemetery, knocked beneath the widow, unnoticed. It opened its shroud.

And the white corpse flew by . . .

The City

And so. The moon rose.

Someone, familiar, offered a glowing dandelion. Someone, familiar, set everything ablaze.

He offered, and he burned.

Everything unfolded in puffy feathers of brilliance, and the feathers settled tenderly on the windows of the buildings.

The carriage's shadow, growing slowly, fell on the buildings and fractured, lengthened, and slipped away.

The evening was stormy, vigorous.

Someone, familiar, sat in the carriage. A crimson streetlamp, reflected in the melting snow, splintered.

The reflection raced in the puddles and on the rails ahead of the carriage. It outlined the stones in a crimson glow, splintered, and disappeared.

The carriage's shadow, growing slowly, fell on the buildings and fractured, lengthened, and slipped away.

Crowds of participants ran out from the lecture, set off into different streets, thrust their bookish knowledge into the blizzard, and became dumb and snow-covered.

Clouds of snow flew above the buildings and broke off into hundreds of rustling pages, flickering and scattering under the student's nose.

Someone, the same one, was on a bender, and the drunk showered the lackey's hands with silver, icy rubles. Everything from his change purse streamed into the blizzard, and the snowy money shimmered in the streetlamp.

A thief's shadow grew slowly, stretched out his hand, plunged it into someone else's pocket, removed it, and slipped away.

Someone, the same one, a banker and a cheapskate, put his bag in the blizzard. Snowy rubles poured into it, their silver droning on the roofs, signs, streetlamps.

A prostitute, still attacking, dragged first the banker, then the drunk to her place, undressed, dressed, and ran out again into the blizzard.

Someone, the same one, offered a glowing white dandelion over the city: everything unfurled in puffy feathers of brilliance blooming in the streetlamps.

And the feathers gently tickled the passersby under their warm collars.

And so on.

The wind was stormy, singing.

A white sleeve grew slowly, attacked the buildings, fractured, lengthened, and slipped away. And after it another sleeve rose up, and after that one rose another, and another, and another.

All of the sleeves roiled with laughter, fell on the buildings, scattered fierce stars, frosted the windows, and then—flew off.

And again. And again.

A Pearl in Scarlet

An invisible deacon bent over the buildings and swung a creaking, fluttering censer, pouring out tenderness, airy and snowy.

An invisible choir sang, "Rejoice, bride of the blizzard!"

The ones in white stood up. They flew and danced.

But they were tickled by sunny stalks of wheat, and the blue worlds smiled at the distant expanse like lowered silver eyelashes.

The lace of the iconostasis fluttered in the flames of wax candles.

There was a golden velvet dusk, dotted by fifteen lamps.

A woman with fiery hair bent over, and the deacon poured the tenderness of the incense over her, fragrantly azure.

And a swarm of boys rang out, "Rejoice, unbetrothed bride!"

And so: the woman with fiery curls bent over: the crimson fire of the lamps glimmered over her portentously.

Her face was shrouded by the veil's snowy cloud.

She bent over.

And rose up again.

Her softly swishing silk sang sweetly when she turned toward the exit.

A storm cloud shrouded the glimmer of the lamp.

And then it dispersed once again.

And the purple flame shone portentously, lighting the image of the Virgin Mary.

Everything twirled in front of her in a pale whirlwind—a snowstorm, a snowstorm.

She remembered, "And the Word became Flesh."

The woman with the golden hair had been searching for incarnation her whole life—in smiles, in words, in deeds.

A single Face showed itself, Desired—it smiled before her and bent over.

Again. And again . . .

It was tempted by one and the same mystery.

The awakened chaos noisily rioted. A white pillar flew up.

And, like a ghostly bow, it slid over the telegraph wires as if over strings.

And the strings sang, "Our happiness is with us." Whirlwind horns sounded.

The snow flashed by, flying off like fluff, flying by like happiness, like a dream.

The days flew by.

Shocked, she flew along with the days in the expanse.

She called her dear one, called and called. And now he summoned her, he summoned.

With a sly tiger's smile from under her lace veil, from under her black, black eyelashes, from under her long almond eyes, her gaze took in the dark blue velvet sky, stunned, sweet, exhausted.

The more greedily she drank in the sky with its calls, the faster the stormy stallions flew over the city, the more adamantly one and the same clattering of hooves echoed, ceaselessly thundering over the roofs.

The blizzard spread its light whistling hands over the city.

The chimney pipes of the buildings—loud with piping—piped out smoke, an ancient call, sad and easy.

The blizzard's snowy claws stroked it and then painfully scratched it with its needles.

The velvety soft day, covered in snowy white spots, floated over the buildings.

The velvety soft sunset, dotted with smoky clouds, flickered out over the buildings.

The Velvet Paw

Adam Petrovich ran urgently on urgent business. Passersby flitted past.

The familiar outlines of buildings loomed unchanged. They spoke of one and the same thing, always the same thing...

Everything will leave. Everything will pass. Leaving, it will bump into that which is coming in the opposite direction.

And so universes spin in eternal rotation, always the same rotation.

The familiar outlines of buildings, the fences, the white walls, the twists of curved streets—he has long known your mysterious call.

The velvety soft day, covered in snowy white spots, flickered out over the buildings.

A fatal grief swaddled him in its fierce paws.

It swaddled him in a crimson tiger—in a skin that was slightly terrifying.

The storm tore his heart just so.

He never had a sweetheart. And now the blizzard called him.

Adam Petrovich smiled with a sly tiger's smile from under his chin, golden like a clump of ripe wheat; from under the dark fields of his hat his gaze flew to the dark blue velvet sky, stunned, beckoning, exhausted.

White swarms circled above the city.

He watched: white swarms flew past with a buzz and covered his eyelashes with dampness.

The snow was sprinkled in handfuls of diamonds.

It rested on the ground like hundreds of buzzing gnats. And the gnats faded.

A tall woman with fiery hair walked from the storm with uneven and slyly sad steps.

Her appearance, like the sky, was distant yet close.

Her eyes—unbearably damp scraps of azure—like other worlds, were draped by black eyelashes and looked up at him temptingly from distant places.

They offered hope. They spoke about the impossible. They conveyed an exhausted tenderness that clenched the heart. The more tenderly her eyes caressed, the more ardently and steadfastly the outstretched strands of her veil, ash black with flecks of scarlet, tore from her hands.

The more madly he tried to reach her, the more enticingly and appealingly the softly swishing fabric of the blizzard twirled and scattered helplessly.

Had she not guessed his strange ideas?
Why is she looking so sadly at him, almost smiling?
Is her sadness a comfort, always asking about something?
Now she's quietly approaching him.

Had the blizzard not assailed him with snow?
Why did the city melt into a softly swishing dance of crumbled ghosts?
The blizzard comforts sadness and carries off the poor heart.
Now the world passes in snow.
Poor heart: the world is passing.

His face, with the sadness of the clouds, was torn apart by his soul, the sunset—his soul, the sunset floated by uneasily.

His soul imbibed an ancient drink—that which no one drinks: feasts floated through his soul uneasily—feasts that had long ago been extinguished, had sweetly exhausted themselves.

The scarlet wine, scarlet, flowed to his cheeks. It tore apart his chest, always the wine.

A moaning sigh—the snows of the clouds—twirled in a storm: snow—snow, whipping with the cold, turned silver.

The blizzard sang an ancient ditty—that which no one sings, no one sings.

The white silver, white, fell into his eyes. His chest was starred with silver, brocaded.

But she flashed by without responding. Her dress rustled by like the flight of withered leaves, like a current flying in the wind, like the nights and the days.

She bent over. She straightened up. She was still straining to listen to something.

She turned around oddly and nodded to him in the middle of the street.

Again. And again.

But her ash-black dress, but the azure of her eyes, but the honey-gold of her hair all went out, blending their hues into a single vague inexplicable sadness.

And so he burned softly in the tongue of a fierce flame.

The flame swaddled him in a crimson tiger, in a skin that was slightly terrifying.

The velvety soft day, covered in snowy white spots, floated over the buildings.

The snowstorm—a web of silver threads—abated: the winds began to calm.

And a brocade of silver entangled the streets and buildings in a gossamer web.

From behind the fence a row of silver threads rose up and flew off into the heavens.

Calls echoed, "Laas . . . Laas . . .

Alaas . . ."

An airy stallion reared above the roofs.

The stormy flyer neighed wildly, and its hoof pounded resoundingly on the iron.

Its white mane shook, fluttering in the wind.

Above the roofs it reared, neighed, and pounded.

Adam Petrovich was returning.

The fiery yellow sky spread its velvet sunset embrace over the buildings.

He thought, "I'm returning. Will she not also return?"

A carriage appeared from behind the bend. It stopped.

A soft yellow plush fabric, speckled with gray rings, was wrapped around her legs.

Red banners waved in all of the windows that were facing the sunset.

These were the dusky reflections of eternally strange thoughts.

Unchanging.

It was her . . . no, not her.

An airy stallion reared above the roofs.

The stormy flyer flew up wildly. It rocked in the air.

And it fell, torn apart by the wind.

It reared, flew up, rushed by, neighed.

A winter coat was draped over a dress that was orange, like the hide of a lynx.

The brim of her hat cast a shadow over her face.

Her lips—slices of crimson peaches—curled into a tiger's smile—slightly terrifying.

She stepped out of the carriage. She gazed at him with dreamy cruelty.

A soft cat will stroke you with its velvet paw like that: stroke you and then scratch.

The dusky reflections slinked from one window to the next.

And so she flashed by without responding.

The rustle of the leaves echoed, flying by like spots, spots of the nights and the days: the rustle of her silk dress.

He turned around. He followed her.

The streets were woven into a single mysterious labyrinth, and the protracted wails of the distant factories (the dull groaning of the minotaur) troubled his heart with its prophetic foreboding.

Calls echoed, "Laas . . . Laas . . .

Alaas . . ."

From all of the chimney pipes facing the sky, smoky calls piped out.

There was a battle going on.

These were the snowy banners of the eternally white legions— the ascending ones.

A soldier, flying by, threw open his coat and, waving his cap, yelled to someone, "Quite the little blizzard!"

His spot of gray hair shimmered for a minute, tussled by the wind, and then he was hidden in a snowy maelstrom.

They met at the bend in the road.

He walked with uneven steps, thoughtful and sadly quiet.

She slid by with arrogant ease.

Her gaze was inquisitive, and he responded; she calmed down, and he was silent.

They raised their eyes to one another—blue worlds—and froze, as if they didn't notice one another.

Then he smiled, and she, without smiling, made a sign with her hand and her carriage came.

Exactly like two approaching waves crashing into one another in a tempestuous sea of old.

And again running off in different directions.

And all that was left was something ancient, something eternally sad.

Always the same.

The sky went dim.

The velvet-soft sunset, speckled with cloudy spots, was extinguished over the buildings.

An airy stallion reared above the roofs.

Flying into the sky, it waved its tail and neighed to someone, shaking its mane.

A stormy rider was sitting on it—eternally white and strange.

His spear glistened for a moment; then he was hidden in a snowy maelstrom.

A ringing trembling echoed: the storm had torn the number off a streetlamp.

Beads and Pearls

He arrived at the editorial office.

A mystical anarchist with golden hair and an obsequiously parted beard ran to meet him.[4]

His coat, green as a bottle, was unusual.

The sweeter and tenderer he was to the guests, the more ardently and steadfastly his eyes, dark blue with greenish specks, were fixed on them.

The purple of his mouth, the azure of his eyes, the gold of his hair blended their hues into a single, vague, inexplicable sadness.

It reminded one of Correggio's depiction of Christ[5]—it was the same image.

Here he was walking around all the same, all the same . . .

He wandered around and talked. He shook his golden and slightly parted beard.

And he had an unrequited love for music: before, he listened to Wagner.[6] His eyes would burn green like peridot.

Sometimes, before, his eternally strange, fleeting thoughts would make him weep.

Unchanging . . .

As if in a dream . . . no, not a dream . . .

Now he was pale white, glowing slightly, spilling out beads and pearls, sighing and insolent.

The green of his eyes didn't shine—forget-me-nots.

His voice ran through the scales—velvet, like snow.

From ceaselessly searching for a mystery, his eyes, from behind his flaxen hair, from behind his pale brow, right and guilty, softly, agilely, and steadfastly fell in love with a slightly sad bliss.

The snow didn't sparkle in the windows of the editorial office—chitons.

The snowstorm, like Kuzmin, ran through the scales—velvet, like snow.

From the inexhaustible sparkle of an evening "Chablis," as if in the restaurant "Vienna," from behind the storm's cakewalk, as if the white foam of champagne with the terrible bliss of a rosy dusk, they fell in love with whomever they encountered, passionately, steadfastly.

Words of love, like dark yellow butterflies, flittering around the lips—the mystical anarchist pelted these to the first one he saw from a distance, enthusiastically, quickly, fiercely.

He aroused hope. He spoke about the impossible.

His voice went up and down the velvet scales, and he clutched galley proofs in his hand:

"Are we not running through a fiery belt of passion like Siegfried's? Why did the ancient dragon scowl at us? We will unsheathe our sword and all seek Brunhilde.[7]

There, she flies with the dawn . . .

She sprinkles forget-me-nots. She breathes colors, she breathes tenderly.

As if covered in greenery, she oozes the honey gold of timelessness, and the trees that comprise her sway from invisible embraces and kisses.

They cast out their celebratory green liturgical garments, like the deacon's worldly service—they revel, breathe, and bath in them, chasing off midnight."

Nulkov[8] hopped down. He pressed his ear to the door and listened to the mystical anarchist's prophesy.

Seized with horror, his hair standing on end, agitated, he quickly wrote in his pocket notebook, "Now, I'll write a feuilleton about this!"

The mystical anarchist spoke, hopped, cursed the darkness, prayed, with shoulders lifted high and a pearl face and long locks of hair—a sea of yellowish buttercups—that faded in the tide of the evening.

The snowstorm—a web of silver threads—swayed toward the window: the winds began to calm.

And a brocade of silver entangled the streets and buildings in a gossamer web.

From behind the fence a row of snowy fuzz rose up and flew off into the heavens. From behind the fence crests of gray hair rose up and shattered in waves against the heavens. From behind the fences a row of snowy threads rose up and flew off into the heavens.

But it fell. It lay on the ground in a single starry net.

And again flew up, and everything was lost . . .

Adam Petrovich, searching for an answer, came to the mystical anarchist: he was woven from words, just like a giant piece of linen.

And so the beautiful lie entwined, his mysterious meeting in a web.

The mystic stood in front of him and jumped to the sky. But he flew down. He spoke such beautiful nonsense.

Adam Petrovich squeamishly screwed his eyes: from the fiery amber shaking in the window a row of piercing needles flashed and pierced the heavens.

He squinted.

The needles crisscrossed and broke into a single starry net.

And he opened his eyes: and everything was lost . . .

He opened and closed his eyes: the needles broke and flew, like finely sharpened blades of gold.

Snowy Honey

Adam Petrovich returned home from the mystical anarchist.

Adam Petrovich's shadow grew steadily and rushed ahead of him, lengthening and fading on the pavement.

And yet another shadow slipped along the wall, and another rose up behind it.

All of these doubles grew and faded and floated off ahead.

Grew and faded. Faded and grew.

So he walked, ringed by a mass of ghostly doubles. So he walked, with a throng of white old men. So he walked, ringed by cold swarms—ancient, unchanging, eternally stormy.

When he walked in the other direction, all of the doubles that had faded reappeared and floated back: they grew and faded—faded and grew.

The lacy wings of a moonlight bird tore through the swords of oncoming clouds. The wind blew the pale cap of a dandelion, scattered its fluff. The wind scattered.

The moon dimmed.

And so: he thought that strange rumors were circulating in the city.

A pale swirling current settled down softly: like snow, in the hearts of the Decadents. Their words bloomed like rhinestones and burned out.

Decadents were rushing around the city, expressing horror and shock. The goat herder Georgy Nulkov spun mystic circles in sitting rooms.

He smiled with a cunning mouth, "Who can speak with more ecstasy than me? Who can collect all insolence in a jar, like honey, and use it to make a mystical soup?"

The blizzard mocked him, "Well, of course, no one!"

It took him in its arms: took him and tossed him—tossed him into the emptiness.

And swarms of printed books flew from the presses, blown by the blizzard and scattering a flurry of unread pages at the feet of passersby.

So he thought.

Yes.

Dark feelings—wasps—swarmed in his heart.

The scarlet velvet of blood flowed from the crucifix where the horror of nonexistence was trampled and nailed. A king dressed in the scarlet silk of his own blood.

Someone renounced his soul and then beckoned him again—covered it, as if with a mantle.

As if he extended a sponge with vinegar, "Who can take You down from the cross?"

He pressed up to the Crucifix, and the Crucified, "Well, of course, no one!"

Someone kind took him down from the cypress tree, tenderly kissed him, and tossed a heap of nails at his feet.

Let thousands of sharp stingers drain the poor feet drenched in purple blood.

He thought.

Decadent society was at war with the world.

The social democrat fled for anarchism; hordes of anarchists raced to mysticism; like an Assyrian king, the large black theocrat reconciled God and man.

They all made fun of the social democrat,

"We are more leftist than you!"

Over tea they threw verbal bombs, expropriating other people's thoughts. They all swerved to the left and disappeared beyond the horizon, bathed in mysticism, and rose up again, like the sun, to the right.

And the throng of mystics grew and grew, purposelessly ambling from one to another, raising a blizzard of words.

He thought.

The happiness of Christ left Adam Petrovich. He let out a sleepy cry, and his cheeks faded, as if burnt out.

His eyes were at times sad and at times sparked with rage, "Who would leave me in these red silks?"

Someone, Invisible, whispered, "Well, yes—it was Me." He meekly bumped into the jaws of nonexistence and tossed a handful of diamonds at its feet.

And a flock of buzzing worlds distantly rushed by under Adam Petrovich's feet in the black velvet of nonexistence.

"Oh, nobody will help me get back!"

He hung there in the dark. Worlds flew by him, humming; bright stars, glowing, cast their rays.

Helpers came.[9]

Fedor Sologub approached him from a side street.

Black shadows loomed, cooled by starry crystals of tears: shaking his gray beard, he noted sarcastically, "Bright stars burned in the sky, too!"[10]

Remizov ran out from beneath the gate, "Do you want to play a game of snowy Boogie Man with me?" He looked at Adam Petrovich from under his glasses.

The great Blok arrived and proposed making a snowy bonfire from the icicles.[11]

Hippety-hop to the bonfire went the great Blok: he was shocked that he didn't get burned. He returned home and humbly said, "I was burned on a snowy bonfire."

The next day Voloshin went around to everybody singing of "the miracle of St. Blok."

Black crowds waited for Gorodetsky on Nevsky.[12]

The good people waited for a long time. Gorodetsky snapped his fingers. He flicked somebody on the nose with his fingers.

Thunderous wailing accompanied the boy.

Georgy Nulkov flew by in a carriage and shouted, "Us, us, us."

Shestov sighed dejectedly, "I don't love chit chat!" . . . "You are ours," shouted the mystics and carried him off to the "Vienna."

Really? Really.

That's what Adam Petrovich thought.

He walked by.

He stopped by a window.

He was doused with light from the window. "No one will help me treat these angry sores!"

Gnats flew by with a buzzing sound, as if vibrating in the light, and the fierce gnats bitingly plastered themselves to his face.

He walked along the walls of buildings and looked, gazing into the windows of light.

Who sat in the window under a lamp?

And the window of light quietly went out, and the gnats went out: who left, taking the lamp with them?

He came to. He gazed into the window.

Then the yellow lace grew cold on the ceiling. Then the yellow lace started to crawl.

Then they returned to the room, holding the lamp.

Its velvet, stormy embraces scattered in the sky. The unknown soared above it. What was it? . . .

It blew the storm clouds around sumptuously, chasing off the new. Blew and chased; chased and blew.

Then the storm answered this sigh with a sigh. The white blizzard answered this desire by shimmering near the light.

A stormy pillar began dancing above the fence. The unknown one raised its pale depths. What was in them?

But it ran, and the stormy pillar collapsed onto the hinge of the fence: there, airy flyers—pillar after pillar—sumptuously swooped up and sumptuously fell.

They nodded to one another from behind the fence, they were transported past the fence by the sweetness, the sweetly gasping storm.

Past the fence, columns flew up past him, unnoticed: but past the fence it was beckoning him, as in childhood, somewhere.

He turned. He went back.

The snowy pillars grew—then shrank, and shrinking—melted.

They met. Their eyes flashed. They bowed to one another in the silver shadows.

They met where the lamp's flame sprinkled the snow with purple, illuminating the image of the Virgin Mary.

Her eyes flashed with love when she bent over it in gossamer veils, wearing silver sable; she bent her golden head invitingly, oppressing with a purple sigh from her lips: all this sang in her joyfully.

This wiped the sleep from his black eyelashes. Yes, he answered sigh with sigh, desire with desire.

They bumped into one another. But they parted ways. But their steps died down in the distance.

She was anguished, the sleep was wiped away; she answered with a sigh: but they parted ways.

He thought about her. She thought about him. The snow sumptuously flew up and sumptuously fell; now it pelted bitingly, now it tickled tenderly under the collar.

He recognized his mystery in her. What did she recognize in him?

She was kind to him, and he—to her.

They longed to meet, they sought to meet, they prayed to one another to meet, they dreamed to meet.

A circle of light rested above the streetlamp.

You just had to get closer and the streetlamp pulled the circle of light, trembling on the snow, to itself.

He was walking.

Snowy circles—circle after circle—were pulled into the glass of the streetlamp, unnoticed, melted before him, unnoticed.

Then behind him, they formed again.

It was sweet to think of her, the Lord's sweet mystery: it meant that the Lord was with them. He sadly beckoned, as in childhood, somewhere.

He turned. He went back. No one was there.

The circles of light grew—and melted, grew—and melted.

He turned. He went back.

The circles of light melted—and grew, melted—and grew.

Who was standing there and watching him with a long, blue gaze?

Stormy swarms whirled up by the buildings. The gates softly creaked when the mounds of snow swooped up and fell. Everything was covered in a dull frost.

There was a sigh in the window, "Who can cover everything in snow?"

The storm answered, "I can, of course!"

It dejectedly exhaled and tossed more snow under foot. New swarms of screeching dust adamantly rushed from behind the fence into the blue velvet of the night, flying past with a buzz and coating and chilling the windowpanes.

White bees swarmed by the street lamps.

The white velvet crunched softly under his feet: handfuls of diamonds bloomed and burned out.

His eyes were first sad and then joyful with azure, and his golden beard was covered with a dull frost.

He smiled at the white snow, "Who can stop me from just thinking about her?"

He ran past the streetlamp. Someone unseen whispered to him, "Well, of course, no one! . . ."

He tenderly kissed and tossed a handful of diamonds at his feet. Yes: a blooming heap.

Swarms of buzzing gnats flew blindingly from under his feet on the white velvet snow.

He twirled his golden whiskers by the doorway, "No one can stop me from just thinking about her.

Thinking about her."

He rang the bell.

Swarms flew past him with a buzz: white bees coated and chilled his face.

Windows of light floated along the blank wall.

It was the servant coming to open the door—she passed through the room holding a lamp.

The window of light froze on the blank wall: it was the servant putting down the lamp to open the door for him.

"I'll just think about her.

Think about her."

He lay in bed. Thoughts raced by. He opened his eyes.

Spots of light raced along the ceiling: it was someone walking with a lantern outside at night.

Different thoughts perked him up—mournful thoughts, "I am the one who seeks, and she is Brunhilde, circled with a ring of fire!

Brunhilde from the fire."

He opened his eyes.

The spots of light ran the other way on the ceiling.

In the White Foam

Bending her head, wreathed in flame, over a porcelain cup of coffee, she teased the bichon frise with a butter knife, flung herself back in the chair, leafed through a book, and then dropped it on the tea table.

Rustling the delicate lace under the window, she stirred up a storm, tore the lace, and knocked at the window.

Yes, knocked.

His snowy face, as if tearing through the blizzard, smiled at her through the window like a chill, nodded and flew off.

And Svetlova[13] ran up to the window covered in crystal, in ice, leaned over and kissed them, stretching out her hands and freezing.

Her lace fell from her hand and, bunching up, wrapped around her dress; wringing her hands, she went back to her coffee.

He stood, all in flowers, all in snow, in crystals, and laughed by the window, as he once laughed in childhood.

He raised up his hands and tossed a swarm of snowflakes, a bouquet of wildflowers at her window: just as he had once tossed petals in childhood.

He beckoned her, as once in childhood.

The crafty mystic, blushing like the young dawn, brought her a volume of stories.

His words, wreathed in clouds and speckled with mysteries, stormed over her.

Her velvet slippers lightly carried her away from her guest, and she plugged her ears with her hands.

The stout puffy man, an engineer who happened to be her husband, casually walked in on the enamored mystic.

But the embarrassed student, tripping over symbols and the rug, manage to slip away from the yawning stout man.

There, in the flowers by the door, he watched as she flew away somewhere in a sleigh.

After her, after her, into the snowy laughter of the blizzard, he rushed after her somewhere.

From behind the black door, they rushed somewhere into the mortal cover of night.

The chilled corpse of the storm, enveloping everybody, whispered in the pale moiré of the cover, unwound the cover, loomed over the cornice like an icy bone.

The light sleighs slipped into the infinitude of the storm, making the snow soar, spreading smoky silver, screeched, and disappeared.

A call, growing mournfully from the storm, beat on the silver-streaming trickles, mournfully tender, mournfully carrying.

In a fashionable dress shop she was choosing moiré, digging through sad-fleecy satin, bending over and straightening up.

His pale hands reached for the storm, as once in childhood.

His friends smiled; he didn't see his friends: he ran past them going somewhere.

As if they beckoned him somewhere, as once in childhood.

Her friend bent her head with ostrich feathers toward Svetlova, pressing her muff to her face and whispering to her enticingly.

Svetlova bent her head with ostrich feathers toward her friend, touching her furry hands with the small muff.

They bent toward each other with enticing laughter and ostrich feathers. Glancing at a passerby, they whispered to one another, "It's him, it's him!"

A pale, kind face turned to them as if it wanted to approach, but walked past.

The velvet-soft day, covered in snow by the storm's whirlwinds, sang over the buildings.

Plucking the sad-fleecy strings from a silver lute, someone pale was sad, just as before, was sad, just as before.

Auguries

The storm hummed.

The storm flew in the window like an icy skeleton, wrapped in a burning mantle, flying up and hurling.

The storm's horn thundered, "Here I am, here I am coming for you!"

The blade of a scythe screeched, dripping snow above the buildings. A stallion's diamond hoof clattered on the telegraph wires.

It reared. It broke the wire, "Misery unto you, misery!"

The perfumed aesthete sidled up to Adam Petrovich, "We've had a revelation . . ."

He lisped sacred words, putting on airs, pompously.

He beckoned him there, there, "Everybody will come. Everybody will be enveloped. When you leave, don't speak of this."

A wide-brimmed hat, swaying flowers, a gossamer veil, a dress rustling with silk—he looked, he looked through the open door.

A blonde entered with a velvet-soft stride, a brunette entered with a velvet-soft stride; wrapped in veils, they rushed to Adam Petrovich; they embraced; they looked into the other's eyes.

"We will induct you into our society. We will fill you with pleasures. We will—we have sweet, sweet fantasies, come to us, come to us!"

The perfumed aesthete, the blonde rustling with silk, the brunette rustling with silk—he recognized them, he recognized those bitter delights!

Someone's nervous cry flew over the city; someone was calling someone somewhere.

A well-groomed lackey took her fur coat, "The master has returned for dinner!"

And the words entwined her with disgust, "They'll all sit at the table. They'll all lie like rats at the table. They'll leave and come back. Come back and leave . . ."

The familiar depravity of the days, the taunts of perverse pleasure—oh, if only he hadn't given in to temptation!

Someone's torn shroud whispered under the windows: someone was calling someone somewhere.

Adam Petrovich spoke to the blonde. The brunette blushed jealously, the aesthete blushed jealously. He spoke to the brunette— the blonde blushed jealously, the aesthete blushed jealously: these were the prophets of eroticism.

The blonde, the brunette, the aesthete—the aesthete, the brunette, the blonde: they stood up, breaking the stifling ring.

Someone's cutting blade, like a scythe, sounded in the windows: someone, growing pale, threw up their arms.

Svetlova flew back home and flailed her gloves in front of the mirror. The rooms escaped into the mirror. There he was, dear, dear. She turned around—her husband was running by; she dropped her gossamer handkerchief.

The flabby puffy engineer, panting into his chins, put his sweaty, sweaty hands on her shoulders.

Adam Petrovich put on gloves in front of the mirror. The rooms escaped into the mirror.

There she was: dear, dear.

He turned around—the lackey stood in the foyer: he picked someone's gossamer handkerchief up off the floor.

They gray, dead lackey, standing there with the fur coat, put the heavy, stuffy fur on his shoulders.

A pitiful oak coffin floated out of the crest of the blizzard: someone's funeral was shuffling somewhere.

Her husband caught Svetlova. He tormented Svetlova with caresses, "Our friends promised to be here without fail!"
And she said, "Well, nevertheless (stop it) those philistines will come too!"
She spread open the swishing wings of her shawl (just like a swan sensing the cold), and, running back to her room, with her breast she broke the green stems falling from above the door.

The bacchant caught Adam Petrovich. He tormented him with questions. Familiar answers echoed out of habit.
He spoke like that, like that . . .
The crystal wings of snow—swans, singing with the cold—shattered on his chest, falling from the heavens.

Someone's nervous cry wept over the city; someone was calling someone somewhere.

A Flight of Gazes

It welled up. It welled up.
Snowy leaves frothed up—pale flowers of puff.
It spoke, "Again it approaches—again, again it begins: it begins!"
It tapped on the telegraph wires, "Again . . . it's coming . . . again! . . ."

A flood of snow rose up.

He entered the feathered women's box. He smiled distractedly, quietly.

A stern-looking beauty turned her lorgnette on them.

The bright blue distance outlined languid eyelashes—they were oppressed with bliss.

The glow, the gold of her hair, swayed.

It aromatically sank, sank—in the dress of forget-me-nots, like the sky, in the white-foamed storm of muslin and cream lace, as if in a soft, snowy dust.

A pink diamond shimmered in her hair, glowed like the morning, and like the day, a dull pearl swayed like a tear.

A fan just barely ruffled the light feathers—careless waves.

The storm sang, whistled.

Pearls of songs poured down—snowy soft fairy tales, stormy.

They whistled, "Happiness approaches—again, it's coming, again!"

A sleeve moved along the telegraph wires like a taut bow along iron strings, "Dear . . . stranger . . . dear!

Our happiness is with us!

Yes, yes."

The cello gave an unanswered sigh: the rustle of violins hung in the air, just like the flight of snowy foam, just like a stream of swans in the sky, foamy from splashing in the wind and stretching out in the night.

She turned to him: she looked with surprise—she stared in a frightened stupor.

In a stupor, she was intoxicated with the turquoise wine of her blazing eyes.

She lowered her eyes. She waved her fan.

A storm cloud rushed at her, as at the sun; she was swept up in lacy snowflakes.

He breathed the dawns.

His chest was splashed with a sweet flame, sweet.

He nodded, he nodded with embarrassment at friends and acquaintances in the orchestra seats, as if he were shooing her coquettish, her tender glances: as if he was sighing about something.

Out of tedious worry, he pointlessly played with a woman's feathery boa, from under the velvet of his eyelashes, he caressed his dear one with his gaze, just so, just so, stupidly, pointlessly, distractedly offering someone his binoculars.

He chatted with the woman next to him about things, about things. His gaze was fixed there, there.

She got up, and her shawl, roiling in satin, fell from her like the gossamer, fluttering pillar of a blizzard.

The blue waves of her eyes stealthily flowed over him, around him, the painful blueness painfully tormented him, sweetly.

The intoxicating wine of gazes, intoxicating, tortured with this one thing, always this one thing.

In the air they waved branches of snowy lilies of the valley: there they drank in the expanse of the night with a frenzy, breathed the frozen whirlwind, bathed, gently bent down to sing above the pipes.

And the pipes sang:

"Days flow by. The snow is scattered. The indefinite, the undusky became snow . . .

It poured out its storm—its frozen caress—with its white mouth it lavished icy kisses . . .

It oozed a snowy whistle . . ."

And the trees, enveloped with snow, waved their rejoicing boughs like deacons of the night, bathed in the snow, and sighed with relief, growing pale in the snowy embrace.

People flowed by. The intermission was coming to an end. And now she was close.

She moved in black clouds of coats, like a blue streak of sky veiled in lace, turning bitter despair into gold and a storm.

Azure tenderness flowed from her eyes. A smile swept over her mouth, like petals, aromatic.

She scattered forget-me-nots on the shining parquet like the train of her dress.

Locks of her hair oozed by like a honey flame when she playfully pulled the gossamer silver lace over her face and bestowed her bright gaze.

Her beau, an old colonel, stuck out his arms, twirled the tails of his uniform coat, glimmered with his aiguillette and gray hair, laughed with his shaved face, was taken with her coquetry, flapped at her jokes, ate, drank, and breathed her, sighed sweetly in her aroma, and—a clergyman of delight—cast his profile up higher and higher, like a proud, frozen sphinx.

The storm turned bitter despair into joy and snow.

Gossamer lilies of the blizzard swayed—censers of the cold.

The icy deacons cast their incense into the sky with a roar, a roar.

Adam Petrovich entered the box, entwined with the glow of eternal love, unspeakable . . .

He went to his friends. No, not his friends.

Like a flowing waterfall, streaming, singing, folds of silk crashed into her soft body when she stood up haughtily.

Ever so slightly smiling. Ever so slightly blushing. Ever so slightly bowing. Ever so slightly stepping away.

She said something to her friend.

"Pardon me, pardon me!" "Not at all!" He realized that he had it wrong.

He left her box flustered, wreathed in the eternal, always the same. The haughtily thundering colonel's loud laughter struck him haughtily.

Again. And again . . .

And she smiled, too.

These were the pleasures of the suffocating happiness of their momentary nearness, barely noticeable: the breezy, snowy flights of coquetry.

It was a game. No, not a game.

The expanse wept.

The abbot flew along on a wild mother-of-pearl stallion—the mother-of-pearl abbot, strange.

Wearing an icy miter woven with coldness, the priest of the frosts carried the sweet, sweet lute higher and higher in his arms.

Moiré snowflakes streamed from his sleeves. With his pale fingers, he strummed the light-colored airy strings.

He sighed, "Happiness, happiness!

You are with us!"

She ran down the stairs. They swarmed by the door. The light velvet of the rug crunched under her feet; her slightly lifted skirt bloomed with silk and then burned out.

Her eyes were now sad, now happy, now laughing, now crying, now shining, now dim.

Her shawl, like a dandelion, puffed with lace above her golden head.

Above the staircase, hanging, one of the men in coats lewdly laughed at her, "Who says I can't admire her shapely legs?"

She slid away without a word: the rustle of her skirt passed like a sigh of dying sadness.

But she plunged into the snow without a word: the rustle of the snow passed like the flight of a silver bird.

But she had already sat in her sleigh.

The soft snow kissed her and tossed a handful of diamonds at her feet.

The sleigh drove on determinedly, crushing the fragile velvet.

Silver lutes, as if made of snow, strummed above her.

The singing of her snowy bridegroom echoed, "You, storm, are a vintner: you turn bitter despair to silver and snow.

Rejoice, drunkards, rejoice and drink wine—white wine:—the wine of the frost."

And she gulped down the frosty wine.

Odious Pest

She undressed thoughtlessly.

The rustle of the forget-me-not waves of silk—a waterfall of cascading garments—echoed from the slipping movements of her naked arms.

The more tenderly the garments clung to her, the more steadfastly she tore them off, stepping out of the blue silk foaming with white, as if from the waves of the sea, crashing against a cliff—she stepped out in gossamer batiste.

Her breasts rose like two light clouds, swirling in the yellow dawn of her hair, dividing her cloudy body.

Rose and fell.

The desired one smiled at her, the eternally sad one smiled, just like that.

She swirled in the dark shadows: she beckoned him with a festively sweet kiss from the darkness.

In this incessant languor, glances from behind her eyes, long like almonds, from behind her black, dark eyelashes, drank in the velvet, cruel and blue in the night, powerfully, sweetly, oppressively.

But the stout one came in, flittered by in the darkness, and lay on the bed, calling his wife in a whisper.

Yes, she fell into the sheets debased, yes, despairingly she fell, and the stout one bent over her in excitement—he panted and burned with sweet desire.

The wind danced in the window.

Everything was bubbling there with the pearly foam of the cold, as in a flute of intoxicating champagne.

Flute after flute bubbled, and the snow struck the window.

She froze with sorrow in the odious embrace, eternally odious.

The engineer lay next to her. The engineer whispered to her, "I love you!"

He flaccidly clung to her warm lily body in saccharine exhaustion.

Tighter. Even tighter.

And she was silent, debased.

The wind died down. The blizzard quieted. The rooster crowed.

Its zealous guttural cry echoed strangely in the silence of the night.

Again. And again.

And roosters crowed everywhere.

And then the triumphant chaos rose up again, scattering a deluge of snow.

First Blizzard Litany

The dead circles of extinguishing faces, the hiddenness of gazes, the curves of twisted thoughts—she had recognized this terrible nightmare long ago.

So she thought, falling asleep: she raised her golden, exhausted head from the pillow.

The undulating smoke of her shirt wrapped around her body when she threw the heavy blanket from herself, like a golden purple mantle spotted with stains.

The blizzard laughed at her through the window.

You, blizzard—white ball, roar of snow, laughter of foam, sound of the wind.

Like a flittering bird, like a swan, you flew up.

Flew up over the bells, towering over us.

Like a bright feather—with a snowy pillar—rattle into the azure.

Yes: the world's bell will roar, summoning to the worldwide litany.

Let us pray to the blizzard.

You, foamy-white blizzard.

You smoke into the distant azure like swishing white snowy wine.

Rise up above the world, lightly flying snow, drunken snow, rods of snow.

With a roar, a roar, cast your vestments into the heights, blizzard-serving deacons.

Let us pray to the blizzard.

The stout philistine sighed sleepily, snared in the sheets—sleeping, still sleeping.

Yawning, she held her knees with chiseled arms.

She stepped a white foot on the carpet, lined with ermine.

The blizzard laughed at her through the window.

You, blizzard—the color white, a cloud of fluff.

Like a giant dandelion, like the fleeting moon, rising over the world, fruitlessly nourished on azure by the winter day.

Like fluff—with biting snow—whirl higher, whirl higher.

Screech like a lacy, snowy fountain.

Gush with happiness, baste.

Let us pray to the blizzard.

You, blizzard—a hive of white bees: imbibe in the sea of heavenly bells with your stinging bees.

Honey-bearing bees, who tore themselves from blue flowers.

They crawl under your collar and buzz about the irretrievable.

Turn your faces to the blizzard, to the blizzard in prayer, stretch your hands out to it.

Let us pray to the blizzard.

Her eyes despondently fell on her husband: her husband was stout. Her husband flew off into the void.

Swimming down low, he dreamed of lofty things.

His puffy, sleepy head smothered the pillow.

She listened with disgust to his loud breathing, like the breathing of a blacksmith's bellows.

Oh, storm—resounding horn, voice of God!

You are like good news, you speak into our hearts, you speak to us.

Resounding horn, resounding: stay in the heavens and speak, and pronounce.

Tell us, O prayer book of ours, O benefactrix:

"The Lord is with you."

Thunder, thunder, stormy horns!

Louder, louder bride, louder testify, louder—blizzard bride!

The bride is coming, clothed in snow and roaring wind.

The blizzard is coming with snow, unbetrothed.

Let us pray to the blizzard.

Her golden weary head showed itself in the window.

The undulating snowy smoke still whirled in front of her: as if still scattering fluffy fur before her.

She loved the blizzard.

Fly, white swan woven from snow, fly.

Flap your stormy wing along the azure sea.

Winged one, winged one—sing to us, O sing to us the song of the storm as you fly off to the sun!

And the swan sings. The swan flies. Sings and flies. Flies and sings.

"You, O sun, are a heavy sphere—the world's golden temple!

Golden temple, raised up into the azure . . .

I fly to you, to sacred places—to the golden pillar—to the rays— to the universal Mass!"

Carry our prayers.

Fly away, stormy swan!

Muddle

Adam Petrovich walked to a noisy meeting in order to see his clearheaded friend, an old mystic who had long ago retreated into silence.

The familiar contours of the buildings rose up unchanged. The familiar shrouds of the dead flew by like snow.

The familiar contours of the buildings rose up from under them unchanged.

They spoke of the same things, the same things . . .

Everything goes. Everything comes. Leaving, it bumps into that which is coming.

So the universe spins in eternal rotation—one and the same rotation.

The stormy pillar flashes, the snow swirls, the snow sighs. The pillar merges with the storm hurtling toward it.

So the columns spin in eternal rotation, in the snowy foam—all the same, all the same, the snow sings about the same.

The mystical anarchist greeted his guests. He shook their hands.

He led them to his study, lit with a pink lamp. He led them to his study, scented with perfume.

Here they chatted just like that.

Everybody shouted. Everybody was impudent. The anarchist shook his golden, slightly parted beard, happy with himself and his guests.

He vaguely resembled an image by Correggio—the very same image.

Pillars of blizzard swooped down. They pounded the windows. They flashed by the windows. They sang in the windows.

And the anarchist had an unrequited love for music: before, he listened to Wagner. His eyes would burn green like peridot.

Sometimes, before, he would weep from his eternally strange, fleeting thoughts.

And now—never.

Now that he had become a prophet of higher logic, higher-energy eroticism, he spewed fog that no one understood from his mouth.

As if on purpose. No, not on purpose.

His voice ran through scales, velvet like a carpet of snow, listening to the stormy scales of the snow.

From constantly catching something new, his eyes—from under his linen hair, from under the pale brow of sun worshippers, planetary worshippers, orgaists, Dionysians—tempted with caresses slyly, nimbly, with calculation.

Sweet words flew from his mouth with excitement—the saccharinely sweet words buttered up the guest.

Nulkov hid in the corner, jotting down other people's thoughts: he had already jotted down a lot of words. He thought, "It's time to publish a book."

Adam Petrovich's old friend sat off to the side—the gray mystic.[14]

He was more profound, more profound than the others. His knowledge surpassed, surpassed everyone, surpassed everything.

He had recently published a tremendous volume—the volume was deeply considered and had become a well from which everybody drank.

Like a stone, like a stone it plunged to the bottom of Russian literature (splinters of books floated on the surface).

The volume was called, "One, Always One."[15]

He didn't shout about mysteries.

But he knew all the mysteries.

From time immemorial, the time of Christ, he had collected a wealth of Gnostic wisdom about love, out of the chaos of shouts, and he concealed under a mask this loving knowledge of Christ, powerfully, wisely, steadfastly.

He didn't rise to the top. He didn't give lectures. He said, "The end is coming."

The gray mystic fought off the universal racket alone. He waited. Again. And again.

But around him they ran off into the abyss.

And around him was noise. In articles, they howled, "Us, us, us!" But the dawn of a new life glowed strangely in the old man's eyes. There. Again.

But the morning light wasn't glimmering anywhere.

Around him they hurled mystical rockets. They formed gangs.

They babbled mystical babbling ceaselessly—they talked about the same things, the same things. That they will be impudent, they will kick the world: they stand on their heads in order to threaten the world with their heels.

That's who gathered around the mystic—anarchists, babblers of eternal babble.

The golden-haired anarchist reared above his guests' heads.

A swarm of heads obsequiously bowed before him, and his words flared up and burned out.

His hands flew up and then fell to the table, and an icy spear pounded at the windows.

He shouted, attacking everyone, "Who forbids me from scrambling everything?" Nulkov wailed, "But no one, of course!"

They grabbed Dal's dictionary[16] and obsequiously gave it to the golden-bearded mystic.

Snowy avengers covered the windows, howling.

Red shafts of light fell on everyone. Bright spots fell on their faces.

So bunches of spots bloomed and burned out.

The old mystic first spilled his gray hair onto the table, then whispered to Adam Petrovich:

"The golden age of modesty is racing by. Who can now return the past to me?"

"Well, certainly not the shouters!"

"And That One still, That One still calls us there!"

He nervously smoked and tossed a bunch of flames on the ground with a match.

And a flock of spurting smoke aromatically swirled off the cigar in the blue velvet of the evening.

"No one knows what goes on in the mind."

"They are blind. They perish, and the ghosts of death advance from all directions."

"They talk about the same things, the same things—they talk about love and don't know about love . . ."

"They turn lines of depth into a point on the surface."

"The labyrinth's walls are bare: the minotaur awaits!"

And while they were all making a rattle around him, Adam Petrovich opened his soul to him, "I love her."

"All love brings us closer to Christ!

My dear, let Christ's love carry you off, as if on wings . . .

To you it is given: oh, be bold, desired one!

You are heading to death!

The more tender the love, the more unspeakable, frightening, terrifying the reviled moment will rise up in the image of man . . .

You love that which is holy, oh, be afraid, desired one: a third will come between you!

Sacred love is strangely beckoned to battle the dragon of time.

Beckoned. Always beckoned . . .

Love conquers all!"

And off to the side they shouted, "The more holily, more unspeakably the mystery sighs, the more subtly we distinguish it from the mystery of Sodom.

Alongside Christ's bright white, azure, and purple, other purple compels us with a whirlwind of temptation.

Angelically, angelically they peer into our soul, alone, forever alone."

The abbot reared over the buildings—the stormy abbot, white.

He pronounced, "Temptation is destroyed!"

He waved the wind, howling above the buildings, like a sword.

"Here I . . . you . . . here I!

My fury is with me!"

And he shined with snow.

Fires bloomed in front of him, above him, around him: behind him rushed the avenging warriors, shackled with silver, with ice.

They fiercely, fiercely shook their spears—they cast snowdrifts like swords, like swords.

Like two oncoming waves, two aesthetes bumped into one another in a dark corner.

One whispered to the other. Yes, to the other.

"You're just the same, you're sweet, just as eternally desirable!"

"Just the same."

"You're my reflection of a smile, my velvet of a desired quest."

"You love the beautiful lady. But no, love me."

"Love me."

"The more tenderly the black curls lay on your brow—the more boldly and steadfastly I love you, love you."

Then the lips of the aesthetes curled into a forbidden smile. Yes, painfully forbidden—curled, curled.

So.

The snow princess roiled in the window, crying angrily—flying.

He bent over so angrily, so angrily, and lowered his eyes: it was as if she was crucifying him, the mystery of the cross was crucifying him.

As if torn from a cypress tree, torn.

Ah, yes, yes! The old mystic spoke to him, "They're talking of the mystery, but temptation has ensnared them in the mystery."

Adam Petrovich stood up. He stood up—his lips froze in a mournful twist.

And he stood up . . .

He raised his hands, snapped, and lowered them: he cracked his knuckles.

His lips were frozen, frozen.

Very well: they were frozen.

He returned home. And swarms were swarming: by the streetlamp swarms were swarming—and the swarms settled at his feet.

They swarmed.

The white velvet of the snow crunched softly under his feet: ah, little flowers of sequins bloomed and withered.

His eyes bloomed and then closed their lashes, and his brocaded beard was covered with velvet frost.

Crunching past her house, he laughed into his golden mouth:

"Who can stop me from just thinking about her?

Thinking: yes—about her."

He ran, he ran—ran by.

Someone unseen whispered to him in snow and wind:

"Think about her? Well, no one of course."

It kissed him snowily, tenderly tossed—dropped a handful of diamonds at his feet.

Tossed.

Flocks of buzzing sparks blinded him and already flew: flew—flew from under his feet in the white velvet snow.

Someone, the same one, tickled him for a while, brightly, like a blinding dandelion—yes, and stretched everything: stretched out like a flash of puffy feathers, blooming by the streetlamp.

And the feathers gingerly tickled the passersby under their warm collars.

The wind was winding, singing, sweeping: winding fibers.

The cold silver flower pressed up to the buildings, as it grew into the sky, unnoticed.

Flew around and slipped away: and slipped away.

Let another slip away behind it: another slipped away. Let it rise up behind it more, and more, and more . . .

All of the sleeves, twisted with laughter, fell on the buildings, showering them with snowy stars.

They covered the windows in diamonds and flew off, flew.

The distance grew dark. The distance flew.

"I will live only for her."

He lay in bed. Thoughts raced. He opened his eyes.

Spots of light raced along the ceiling: this was someone walking with a lantern outside at night.

Different thoughts perked him up—his different thoughts, "Am I the one walking: and her? Yes, yes!"

He opened his eyes. A tear streaked.

The spots of light ran the other way on the ceiling: they escaped irretrievably.

The Fortune-Teller

In a room facing a three-legged stand, the fortune-teller waved a blue silk scarf.

The fortune-teller's dress fiercely fluttered around the room when she passionately stretched her bony fingers to Svetlova: her powerfully prophetic, fateful embrace.

Svetlova's face, transparent like a cloud, was gaunt with burning ecstasy here.

Her eyes—languid dots of azure—like sharp blue nails—bored into the fortune-teller.

They shook hands and spoke of the impossible.

And they spoke to exhaustion—sending kindness, heartfelt kindness to someone.

The more ecstatically Svetlova gasped about her dear one, the more shamelessly the fortune-teller crouched over the embers, the more steadfastly her lace, black on blue, twirled and danced, like dust scattered in the sky.

Their sinful ideas grew, "I see your bright encounters in the embers, growing and dissipating like smoke, like a puff of smoke."

The sinful ideas that oppressed Svetlova grew and dissipated, dissipated, grew, like their shadows dancing on the wall.

They sprinkled the embers like velvet: first they bent over the heat and then they stood up.

A red web of stains: like a bright beast in the sky, it put its flying paws on them.

They bent over and then they stood up. The light put its paws on them.

The purple reflection first crawled up from below: then the reflection crawled down from above.

The fortune-teller raised her eyes to Svetlova in the passionate darkness, lowered them, flashing in the passionate darkness, extinguishing in the passionate darkness.

The thin fortune-teller bewitched his soul in the passionate darkness, fell to the three-legged stand in the passionate darkness, stood up, and froze.

A necklace jangled on her chest, hung between her chest and the floor, scattered sparkles from her chest, and went dim.

The fortune-teller said,

"The sweetness of mystery, the sweetness of mystery—because even before meeting you he answered your sigh with a sigh, your desire with desire. He has been searching for you his whole life.

You are his.

Before even meeting, you prayed to one another; before meeting, you dreamed of one another. Your love is sweet, sweet. But someone will come between you.

Only by praying to an angel, only by wise deeds, only by the enchantment of lit lamps will the image overcome fate for you.

You prayed to the angel. You saw him. You understood.

That he isn't mortal—he's an angel.

You've made for yourself, you've made a mortal image: for new deeds, you've made it.

Him, only him. You're burning with intense passion.

Only."

Svetlova stood there sadly, thoughtfully, quietly.

The fortune-teller—with coquetry, with sinful gentleness—brought her powdered, wrinkled face to Svetlova's face.

Svetlova questioned with her gaze, and the fortune-teller, with coquettish gentleness, only sweetly pointed with her eyes—only. The one wanted to be assured; the other just tormented her.

With only their gazes, they bored into one another.

And the two ideas blended in a monstrous ordeal.

Two ideas.

Only in their gazes something ancient and eternally mournful arose.

Arose. Just the same . . .

Suddenly the old woman's lips burned the young beauty's face, beaming with a sinful smile. Her bony hand, like a bird's claw, gently stroked her, gently burned her with the purple of her breath.

And Svetlova staggered back in horror.

The mad abbot carried his avenging sword over the buildings and his mouth gaped with a dark opening—a dark wail.

"I'll smother them with snow—shred them with wind."

He lowered his sword. He tore at his robes. He brimmed with tears of rage.

And the tears fell, fell like diamonds, pelting the windows.

He flew up.

And from the heights he fell like a horse: pissing a stream of snow over the city.

The City

The carriage's shadow, growing slowly, fell on the buildings and fractured, lengthened, and slipped away.

The wind was stormy, vigorous.

Someone, familiar, sat in the carriage. A crimson streetlamp was reflected in the melting snow.

The reflection raced in the snow—on the melted snow in front of the rails. It outlined the stones in a crimson glow: splintered and disappeared.

The carriage's shadow, invariably growing, fell on the buildings and fractured, lengthened, and slipped away.

Crowds of people ran out of the buildings and hurled themselves into the blizzard, breathed the snow, drowned, and again floated away.

Someone, the same one, was on a bender, and the drunk in the restaurant showered the lackey's hands with silver, icy rubles. Everything from his change purse streamed into the blizzard, and the snowy money shimmered in the streetlamp.

A prostitute, still attacking, dragged him to her place, undressed, dressed, and again ran out into the street.

Her friend bent her head with puffy feathers toward Svetlova, pressing her muff to her face and whispering to her enticingly.

Svetlova bent her head with puffy feathers toward her friend, touching her furry hands with the small muff.

With enticing laughter they bent toward one another with puffy feathers, watching a passerby, tenderly and shamelessly.

Yes: in the fashionable dress shop they were buried in satin and silk, first plunging in with their heads and then expanding.

A mournful cry, growing from the snowstorm, beat with a snowy stream, caressed the heart and then carried it off, carried it off.

His pale hands stretched out to the snowstorm, as once in childhood.

His friends smiled. He didn't notice his friends: he ran past them, going somewhere.

As if he was beckoned somewhere, as in childhood.

The Third One

The gray mystic bowed, like a stormy old man, from the pale whirlwind, and his icy stick lashed at the pavement. Adam Petrovich bowed in the blizzard, and its icy hands fell on his shoulder.

The snowy hands of crystal skeletons first waved above him and then pelted him with white hailstones.

The mystic said,

"It sweeps: the snowy smoke of time sweeps away the image of fate, and its snowy curls blow in your face."

In a stormy laughter he sang out, "Someone will come between you and her."

The venerable colonel ran toward him.

His wings sang, hissed, and flared up, and the venerable colonel burst into the snowstorm with his beaver-fur collar.

And there—a clean-shaven face whirled at them from white-hued clouds of snow.

Whirled from the snow.

Now the colonel covered the old man storm with the beating wing of his coat. Laughing, he looked at him askance—laughing, he looked at him askance.

Laughing, he looked at him askance.

Over the buildings, the whirlwind abbot reared his stallion, reared his stallion.

Reared.

The snowy smoke swirled furiously, swirled at his feet; and mounds of radiant snowy lightning bloomed and faded.

He first waved the spear in his hands, then shook the spear, and the spear, the icy spear pounded the roofs.

He shouted in stormy rage, "Who will come at me?

I'll demolish him, I'll skewer him, I'll slash him with biting snow."

He flared up with foam and doused passersby in foam, in foam.

As if a flock of buzzing spears blindingly flashed by from the frozen smoke of snow.

The colonel stood among them, as if made of snow, covered in snow.

All he said was, "The blizzard is raging."

He waved his cap, which flew over Adam Petrovich's head as if threatening, "I'm coming . . . coming for you!

Me."

He shrugged his shoulders. He ran off into the snow. Snow danced in front of them.

He came from the snow and returned to the snow.

The abbot rose over the buildings—the swirling abbot, flying up.

He roared, "All will be destroyed."

He swung the wind, wailing over the buildings, like a sword, "Here I come: for you.

Here I come."

And he snowed brocades. The snow blew. He rushed into it.

He came from the snow and returned to the snow.

The mystic said,

"Now fate has brought you the colonel, like an avenging sword.

Be afraid of him: yes, be afraid of the colonel."

The mad abbot slung his avenging sword over everything.

"I'll smother them with snow—shred them with wind."

This was the stormy abbot, rearing his stallion above the buildings—wearing diamonds, faded . . . and blooming.

His icy hands shook the spear threateningly and pounded the window.

As if sprinkling stormy vengeance, he stood up again. And sprinkled again. And he carried a forest of horsemen's spears, ancient, eternally stormy, avengers, always the same.

Second Blizzard Litany

A radiant pilgrim walked in the snow.

The frozen velvet crunched under his feet, and bunches of diamonds went flying in the snow.

But the forsaken city first sadly looked back, then sighed and carried its prayerful honey to the expanse.

"There my hive is swarming. There they await me, thinking only of me."

The wind sighed, "Well, they're just waiting."

It kissed him: ah!—it tossed a golden swarm under his feet.

Tossed.

And a flock of sun bees rushed at him: they covered his feet in gold.

In You, oh Lord, is the snow; in You, oh Lord, is happiness.

Like the sky, You are a swan; like the sky, You are white; conquering death with death, You have risen above us all.

Beat the azure with feathers, the robes with the snow—winnow, strike.

Yes: they sing snowy psalms at the stormy Mass.

Let us pray to the Lord.

The crimson blood of the sunset boiled like snowy wine: communicants approach.

Spill out, stormy foam, stormy foam, foam.

Spill out, foam.

With thy voices, thy voices proclaim unto the earth, sigh about the Lord!

Your vestments, deacons—

throw your vestments, throw them into the sky, snowy deacons.

Let us pray to the Lord.

The radiant pilgrim went to the woods.

He knocked softly at a hut; there in the window, diamonds of flame bloomed in bunches and then scattered.

This was the elders first lighting candles then handing those in prayer packets of candles.

They questioned him from the door:

"Who is standing there by the door and knocking for admittance?"

The pilgrim said, "I am your joy."

They placed their hands on him and clothed him in fine white linen.

Ah, a flock of fiery bees flew from the censer when he blew on it!

You, oh Lord, You are unfading color, oh Lord.

You, oh Lord, are snow, You pass by like the snow: snow pierced by azure, like the flesh of the sky pierced by an eye.

Snow pierced by azure like a gossamer dandelion.

So the snow is pierced.

Put it on like gossamer white lace.

We know no other clothes; we understand the storm.

We pray to the storm.

We see the hive of white warriors: the honey-bearing bees of the Lord: sweet, fragrant honey of the soul—they collect prayerful honey.

To the storm, to the storm open your faithful hearts; give your prayerful sweetness to the hungry bees.

Bees, carry the honey to the hive, carry it; and before the Lord we kneel in zealous prayer.

You, oh Lord, have mercy.

The royal pilgrim, radiant.

He deferentially took a book, lifted it up, and sprinkled their hearts with it.

Those in prayer prostrated themselves.

Burning candles flew to the ground, just as if they had tossed a handful of diamonds at his feet.

But he remained standing.

In the air, golden from the candles, he turned first to the right, then to the left, and swung the censer.

Of You, oh Lord, it is a mystery and, oh Lord, of you the word is spoken to our hearts like a kind whirlwind.

In a snowy cloud, in a pillar, stormy, come to us, to us.

And to us, to us, say, "I am with you."

Say it to us.

Bridegrooms, confess louder, louder—like white snow, louder.

Thunder, thunder, oh stormy horns!

Wail louder, louder, wail still louder: the bridegroom has been clothed in snow, he comes like the blizzard.

Come, blizzard, come!

The pilgrim read them an unknown prayer:

"That in the sky is not a swan, made from the snow.

That is not a swan, but the sun.

Oh Lord—our sun.

The blizzard storms in our hearts so that we can enshroud in prayer and snow the Bright Throne.

Oh Sun, accept our supplication and, oh Lord, bring us to You!"

1906

Serebriany Kolodez[17]

PART TWO: GOSSAMER VISAGES

The Marble Genius

O water—the roar of foam, O silver lace!

Above the pool, like a fleeting bird, you sprinkled with flight.

Sprinkled in flight: became a crystal shield. Exhausted, you fell like cracking crystal.

Ah, cracking!

Thunder, thunder, golden crystal!

Thunder louder, laugh louder, thunder louder—fall like a fountain, fall!

And weep triumphantly with sprays of laughter.

From behind gossamer crystal, lacy, lacy, gossamer, a sad white head froze and floated above the spray of the marble block.

From behind the laughter, the watery laughter, laughter he stood up, like fate, with a face gone mad.

The white low-hanging tunic, embroidered with fountain pearls, flowed on the old one. He bobbed his big head, white, from under the pearly current of water in a bitter burst, like unchanging time, arising like laughter of momentary streams: watery moments flying upwards.

Ahead there seemed to be a marble emperor crowned with a silver crown of laurels.

His wide brow was extended by a bald spot, which swept from the top of his head in streaming gray spots of snow.

His giant silhouette, wearing a pale glowing tunic like a heroic sculpture, went snowily dim from spurts of water.

A gray spot fluttered palely from cracking splashes, a cap fluttered palely: the cap of the dandelion of the emperor of the moment palely fluttered.

From under his upturned nose, from under his wide nostrils, his withered lips smiled at foggy time.

His clean-shaven powdered visage, not that of a woman, not that of a genius, rose above the splashing of the fountain like the weary morning moon.

The reflection of his exhausted visage, daintily falling into the ripples and glass, danced lifelessly and nodded mockingly.

The steel cog, the spear of time squeezed by fingers, glowed like feathers, flashing brightly, and by the steel cog, the spear, a lifeless head sighed.

A lofty pile of years floated away on pearls, but he stood there, unchanging but the same, clothed in pearly time.

In purple, the purple of roses, dimly burning with pearls, as if with a halo of fire, his face grew lifeless, his face: bitter, it grew lifeless, like the face of the lofty moon, vainly drinking the azure of a summer day and, like a clump of frozen snow, dripping azure at the edges.

The fountain is a marble swan spreading its wings, gushing crystal time from its larynx.

The swan song of crystal time.

The laughter of flowing tears, bits of silver, little tears; a childish sadness and, flowing out, an eternal sadness.

The fountain is a marble swan spreading its wings in order to spray crystal time into the heavens from its larynx.

Colonel Svetozarov[18] stood there, like a giant, in his morning robe, speckled with spots of light and with a spear instead of a walking stick.

From under his dark black brows, bitter gray eyes peeked into the expanse: they drearily sank; sad, from the side he looked like a fish, looking at the sun from the water—not a plain one, a silver-scaled one.

From the water, from the green vegetation, from the purple clusters ahead he appeared, and like a marble beast in a metal crown, he rushed into the waterfall of the sun.

And it seemed that this was time, this was a cloudy Legate: that's what emerged from the pearls, from the ripples, from the sunny leaves.

That's what.

The colonel plucked tearful clouds of flowers (clouds of ancient gusts) with his hand and outlined a diamond zigzag with his finger on a bush.

His mother sat by the marble arch, bent over her knitting—a century-old woman, ancient.

It seemed that this was a crimson dress and shawl made of fluff.

It seemed that this was a crimson dwarf with the head of a dandelion.

Grieving, she drooped like a crimson rag, a petal, oh, like nasturtiums buried in the sand!

There in front of her, like big chords, like big ones, rose up columns: the columns of the marble, pointlessly clear like the blue of a lake.

The moon was pale—the fleeting dandelion was sad, fleeting with pointless azure like a summer day.

The whistling wind—wandering little bells—swirled like prickly bees above the fir trees, swirled above the fir trees.

The old woman, bitten by a bee, looked up, gossamer, lacy from old age.

She whipped a fiery blade and hunched over the crushed, dead stinger.

From under the crystal torrent, above millions of splashes, the old colonel fell over like an ancient relic above an exitless exit.

From under the swan's larynx, crystal fireworks, weeping a golden spout of water, cascaded down the marble.

From under the static life of old man Svetozarov, arms of love stretched out like a large beggar.

From under the folds of the times of love his face floated up, her face: like the sun from a cloud. Beckoned and called.

Beckoned and called.

From beneath the crystal lace of ripples he threw himself into the waterfall from the wind and sun in order to catch her glances, smiles.

He saw—high up in the glowing streams of sun, feathery clumps flew, like lilies pale like the dawn: high up, her hands flew, hers.

So: she was playing the harp of the sun.

So: it flew past her, flew past, the song of the strings.

And the old woman mournfully hung her head there in the distance, as if the feathers of her housecoat were waving off the future.

So: Svetozarov threw himself into the waterfall of sun, blue and falling from the cliffs of the sky:

"I hear, I hear. You are portending resurrection to someone because you are in love with someone.

Enough—because soon your laughter will fly around, fly by.

It's time—because the sun will set: it will set when love withers."

There, sensing, the old woman squinted in fear—and the sun pierced her gaze like needles: soft peacock feathers danced in her eyes.

His hands, his waterlilies, deceitfully stretched out ahead, deceitfully flashed their diamond rings, as if deceitfully threatening a rival.

Clumps of the centuries fell like a tunic from his shoulders—clumps of years of shadowy carousing—and he shook his spear.

His hand was draped in a streaming cloth of pearl: he couldn't break the pearl of the fountain's laughter.

Thousands of silver specks flew around his balding head as if in horror, as if swirling in the air, water kicked up by the wind.

A marble swan rushed to him with a bent neck and doused him with an icy crack of biting crystals.

The colonel's eyes grew wide, flashing like two powerful emeralds, when he stabbed the white-winged swan with his spear.

The stone swan, with a golden stream blasting from his larynx in a column, also lamented about time:

"There is no wife for you, not for you, time.

There is no wife for you, not for you, but there is for me: the sun is for me.

Not for you, for me."

He stretched his neck and shouted, shouted:

"I am her life—a winged angel. I am unchanging for her.

I am the one who was called from time.

Me, me: this is me."

So: the sun's rays jingled high up as if her cloudy hands rested on them—on them, pale and in the azure, like withered lilies.

So: silky golden threads of hair were sprinkled on the turquoise mantle of the sky.

So.

And she shouted, "You, swan, you—white one, you: fly to me, you who are made of the snow.

Lash my turquoise with your heavenly feather.

Winged one, winged one!

Sing as you fly away!"

And Svetozarov shook his spear and proclaimed,

"Passion is a resounding grief: gray passion is a deceiver, death.

The roar of the avalanche, crashing through the emptiness."

The white old man loomed in green, speckled with gold spots, as if a lofty golden cheetah had been thrown at his golden body.

His beard flowed to his waist, and his piercing blue gaze was directed from under his straw hat at the bushes when he walked toward the pool in his summer coat.

It was the famous mystic. He bade farewell to the expanse: for he wanted to sink into seclusion.

The fierce golden cheetah, appearing from specks of the ether, put its airy paws on his chest and, like the wind, they tore at the old man's coat.

But the old man parted the drooping bushes, and the airy golden cheetah was torn apart by shadow and light.

Then, like silver fabric, his head fluttered like white dust flying from a carriage.

A golden net danced on him through the linden trees, sunny.

It's time. Soon the sun will be everywhere and it will get hot.

The children met him with a shout, "Hello, hello. Was it you hopping like white sand by the entrance to the garden because the wind makes the sand dance there?"

Joking, he said to them, "Yes, yes."

Soon the children flew away wearing pale pink—pink muslin.

Then, like lilies, hands grew from the grass and a butterfly sat on them, a pansy.

Then the tired mystic drew colonel Svetozarov to himself, like wise death, muttering:

"It's time, it's time to pull back the covers of ambivalence. To fly like the wind: to reveal the mystery of death.

It's time—because otherwise it will be too late."

From beneath the bubbling, dancing tears, from beneath fabric weeping with a watery cry, they flitted by like pale, distended silhouettes.

A humongous giant, like a crystallized statue, waved his flashing spear in profound silence, and his hand flew to his face with a shudder, and a pointed crown of gray hair poked out from the palm covering his face, and you could see his upturned nose and the bright teeth of his mouth, open wide.

So he stood, like a crystal king. And he danced in the pool, slicing the watery blue with the teeth of his crown.

The haughty newcomer adamantly froze from beneath the stream, and his beard bubbled like a foamy waterfall in the pool.

His eyes, dispassionately raised over the silver genius, coldly measured him from head to toe: as if calm death, from age immemorial defeating the memorial, measured time. Their foggy outlines danced under a roiling stream of tears.

But it just seemed that way.

From beneath the lace of time, as from beneath the lace of water, they spoke of something unknown, like an endless end, like timeless time.

Then the palely sculpted giant, like a marble fighter of fate, covered the newcomer's clean-shaven face with his chest and grabbed him, trying to burst into the bubbling time of the pool.

But it just seemed that way.

Svetozarov fell on the marble of the pool and plunged his face into the stream, washing away pearls of tears and dousing himself with pearls, and the old mystic, standing dispassionately still, raised his eyes to the heavens.

But it looked like he was dipping his beard in the pool causing a white foam cascade, because the colonel was alone.

Then a red hunched hill tore aside the green curtain of bushes, and under its red hunched spine, as if under the peak, a wrinkled face rocked in a halo of Lyon lace.

She cast her bespectacled eyes toward the colonel, and from the lenses thousands of needles of sun twinkled at him.

Svetozarov said to her, "You're worrying again, mother. It's nothing—a famous mystic who is leaving these parts and retiring to a monastery was just bidding me farewell."

Like a big dandelion flying over the old woman, he pressed his stubbly face to his mother's hand, a snowy fountain of hair fluttering over her nose, just like the foggy visage of the clean-shaven genius of time in a halo of silver leaves.

From beneath closed eyelashes, moist emeralds fell on the marble railing, crammed with tears, and from the pool he winked to himself with tempting fear.

His white robe flowed into the pool like marble folds, and he looked like a statuesque genius carved by the side of the pool.

Broken branches of purple roses, outlined on the pale marble, swayed and burned with bright spots.

So the carved genius sat, speckled with blood, like a crystal outline. From the pool where the stern newcomer was sinking, someone foamy roared, and his streaming beard fluttered in the sky like watery smoke.

A web of sunlight danced at his feet like a big golden cheetah.

The airy cheetah dove with his paws onto the crowned genius's chest, but he didn't turn his head toward the golden beast meowing like the wind.

Thunder, thunder, watery crystals, thunder, thunder louder—dancing crystals like a crystal umbrella!

Blossoming Wind

A shaft of good-tiding light rose up above a thick grove and flew off into the turquoise.

It fell on the young birches: it lay under the birches in a single radiant web.

The birches swayed, and everything vanished.

You, birch tree, are a green sunny web.

It threw its top into the wind: it caught the sun.

And little golden fish leaps by its roots.

You, sun, are a clump of brocaded thread.

It rose: they began to unravel—and the brocaded yellow of the gossamer spider web entwined meadow and wood.

"Hello, hello.

It is I who have flown in to sigh about resurrection, because we all shall be resurrected, because we all shall see one another there."

She opened her eyes.

A brightly shining stream of light broke through a glowing crack in the shutters and rested on the wall in an oddly pale patterned spot.

You could hear a deep sigh that began long ago and had no end.

That was the noise of the trees.

It was a very windy day.

And the lilac bushes, rustled by the wind, eased sadness as if they were inquiring about something.

And she, rustled by the wind, spread the bushes and ran off somewhere.

And the lilac bushes, rustled by the wind, brushed off the unseen embraces and kisses.

She walked in the garden, pacified—motionless.

She walked wearing a lace hat, like the sun in foamy white clouds.

She stood still, doused in sunny sheaths—resoundingly singing strings.

Doused in color, she plucked the sunny sheaths—resoundingly singing strings.

She stood still, doused in plucked sounds—sun and memories.

With a turquoise train, like a lake, she tore herself from time and brushed off the days with her hands.

Enough.

Soon he will shine—he will arrive.

Her sumptuously sweet lips dried up and whispered enticingly like the wind.

It's time—because he will arrive and time will be extinguished in him.

It's time—because there is a breeze, like a harp with taut golden strings.

It's time—because he will run his hands along the sunny strings and sing a swan song to her.

Unexpected fluff, like snow, flashed at her feet and flew up in the air.

She was reaching for him, for him.

Because he will say the word to her, and golden time will form.

Such was the noise of the trees.

Such was the very windy day.

And so she devoutly raised her gaze to the expanse where a dissolving cloud brushed off gusts of honey wind, shaping it surprisingly, and breathed out its fluff into the turquoise sky.

There someone dear, dear was calling her somewhere, as in childhood.

"Hello, hello.

It is I who am sighing above you about resurrection, because we all shall be resurrected, and we shall see one another there."

And with surprise she asked him about something.

The sun! . . .

It is everywhere, the sun. The golden sun. The kind sun. The ring of the sun.

The sun!

Sun, stretch out your strings of light faster, your golden-spread strings, stretch them everywhere!

Now touch it with your brocaded yellow, like a gossamer spider web and, like a veil, fly over the sea of trees.

Golden pheasant, touch it with your scarlet feathers!

Intoxicate us with the morning light!

Soon the sun will wither and lower in the west.

And so, burning, the image of this world will pass.

And the sunsetless will approach, that without limit. It will say,

"It is time for me to go to the old world."

Sun, sun, it is you who will rock the web under the birches because you will drown and the reflections will fly by.

Those are your golden fish from the birch web, shining and flowing to the ocean.

Adam Petrovich was strolling, lost in thought, with a spring in his step from ecstasy, like a bird.

The turquoise lake, like a princess's bridal veil, like a pale sapphire dream about her, rippled at his feet turning first black then gold.

And foamy white waves ran along it.

Just as if a silver swan with wings stretched out had been tossed onto the waves and now he swam toward the horizon.

A trail of silver stretched behind it.

Dragonflies flew by . . . Their crystal wings drowned in the sky.

The sun beat on the light-catching webs of the water, like a fishing net.

And she wandered in the expanse, first growing pale and then blazing up over him.

And on her dress, turquoise like the lake, was a silver swan—it looked like it was swimming when she toyed with her chain, like she was brushing off embraces and kisses.

And her gossamer buttons, like dragonfly wings, shimmered like crystal.

And he whispered, "It's time for me to recognize her.

It's time to pull off the covers and stare into her face.

To tell her about the Word.

Our life is a cloud floating past.

There, like a white swan, it flies, flies.

She, like me, now sees the swan—the cloud, because it rose up above us into the unchanging.

It floats: floats and sings."

So, dissolving, the image of this world will pass . . . into our motherland . . . into our unknown motherland.

You, cloud, are a gossamer clump of fluff.

It rose up: the winds began to swirl, and it breathed its fluff into the turquoise sky.

You, cloud, are a big fleeting dandelion.

It rose up: the winds began to swirl and it stretched out like a veil of snowflakes.

But a big gust of wind picked up, a big waft of honey, and cleaned the heavens of fluff.

It fell on the dandelion and scattered it: and it spread the pale twirling seed heads over the meadow.

And that was the noise of the trees.

And it was a very windy day.

And the many-branched bushes, rustled by the wind, shook mutely, and someone spoke to him tenderly in his ear,

"Hello, hello!

It is I who have flown here to whisper about resurrection because we shall be resurrected—dear, my dear—and we shall see one another there."

He turned around.

The young birch tree quivered, and a thin-legged mosquito danced dumbly and fell from the light above him and buzzed in his ear.

And she whispered,

"Resurrected, we shall be resurrected . . ."

And the wind blew a new cloud, as white as the one that had dissolved.

And her hands flailed in the shining strings of sun and rested on the strings like miraculous lilies.

The blue harpist tore at the strings like shining diamonds and bent over the harp like she was freeing airy singing birds.

She played the harp of the sun.

The song of her strings flew to him.

And there, in the expanse, he was silent, overwhelmed with the sounds, not brushing away the melodious splashing of the invisible heavenly birds that flew to him, the ones born in the air.

"I hear, I hear.

You are singing to me about the coming resurrection because you too will be resurrected: we shall see one another there."

He stood still. The sun pierced his gaze like needles: soft peacock feathers danced in his eyes.

These were the feathers of the airy birds because when he opened his eyes everything disappeared.

The heavenly birds called him to the eternal feast with voices like the air.

Unconsciously, quickly she plucked a dandelion from a patch of grass, raised its gossamer head in the air with a smile—and blew on its pale cap.

The airy cap sprayed the air with its soft fluff, like a sigh.

She said, "Dear, like everything, let this fluff fly to you . . .

It's time—because if the soul doesn't catch a chill from the sky, like fluff, then the sun won't flame up in the body.

It's time—because if everything isn't given, everything will be extinguished.

It's time—because we love one another."

With hurried steps, seized by dancing flowers, she brushed away the butterflies.

Unconsciously, helplessly, she bent over the streams of the water jets. The fountain whispered, glowed,

"It's time—because if everything isn't given, everything will pass, everything will be extinguished.

Because the sun will set, the water will fall like a rolling pearl, and the golden crystals will fade in the streams.

It's time—because love will pass, and life will be extinguished.

Because even love falls into light-battling darkness."

The wind swirled the pale seed heads of the dandelion around him.

The honey fragrance touched his cheek with its fluffy snowflake, like a kiss.

The seed heads first danced in the air, then settled on him like lace.

And golden rings ran around the lake: as if a lofty summer princess threw her silks into the turquoise sky and her hair—serpents of light—now these serpents of light blindingly twisted in the broken mirror of the dancing water.

Dragonfly wings drowned in the water.

The swan flew by, the swan screeched.

White and winged, it emerged on the land. It yelled,

"It's time for me to go."

It stretched its neck and yelled, yelled,

"I am this—life, a bird flying away, sweet, sweet.

I am this—a bird—I will rise up and drown in the air."

The swan looked at him unchangingly.

It seemed to him that before him was an image of the world, flying off to the motherland.

The wind twirled her silks, honey, like streams of pineapple juice.

It was as if her hands caught the air, floating, first going pale and then blooming with light.

And a ring of hair danced on her dress.

As if the sun cast its rays on a lake—serpents—and they glowed like crystal.

She waved the swan—a compact mirror—and the little mirror's chain jangled.

It flashed in the water like a bird, like light.

She shouted, "It's time for me to love." She tore off two golden sunny strings and flashed them in the air.

She stretched her neck, waved her arms, clutching the strings, and sequins flew through the air.

She stretched her neck, flapped her arms, spread out the gold of her hair, and sang, and sang,

"I will kiss you, my dear, with my sweet red lips.

Love me, my dear—I am your life, a bird flying off.

Catch the bird—otherwise it will fly off.

I am part of the unchanging, for you I am the same, the same, dear, my dear."

It seemed to her that the image of this world carried them to the motherland—to the motherland.

A shaft of good-tiding light lay over the birches. It flew off into the heavens.

It lay under the trees like spots of light, flowing like the light of dawn.

But the trees swayed. The apples ran off.

Everything disappeared.

The sun, a clump of brocaded threads still wrapped the birch trees in a gossamer web.

He saw it unexpectedly.

Someone flew at him in a gallop, shining.

There was a white Arabian stallion racing over the sea of wheat, like a bird.

And on the field its upside-down shadow floated along with the stallion, unchanging.

He thought,

"This isn't her racing on a stallion at the hour when the sun goes down."

So, she rode on the stallion's back as if she were racing in the fields like an image of the world.

As if she flew again—she moved like an insane vision.

He thought, bitterly, "Hello, hello.

Again, it isn't you who fly by to mock resurrection, because you know that isn't possible."

The Amazon, dazzling like sapphire lightning, jumped from the stallion and lay on the stallion's milky-white back like an azure spot.

The stallion's gallop could be heard. It began long ago and had no end.

This was her rushing by the country estate where he was staying.

It wasn't her . . . no, it was her.

His blue eyes asked the galloping woman something, but she flew by, as if swatting away his gaze with her whip.

Soon she had flown by. It grew dark . . .

The strands of her train whispered quietly like the flight of sighing leaves.

It grew dark—and the old sun was extinguished.

And he returned home and sighed.

He enticingly called to his friend, in a voice like the wind,

"It's time, because when everything has flown by, then time will be extinguished."

"You, sun, are a clump of brocaded threads: you set, and they began to unwind.

And the yellowing dust—the bloom of rays—was swept from the birches and dusted the clouds.

The moan of good-tiding light was above the world. But it dissolved.

The birches rocked. The bloom was extinguished.

Aerial Foray

The carriage stopped.

Africans in red livery got down from the footboard, opening the door: the pug-like Africans, with prominent scarlet lips, like peony leaves, first bowed and then shone with their bright braids.

A graceful white statue stood up from the carriage, showering flying sparks like silver.

Bent, bowed, shone—the Africans: she stood up and showered a spark-like silver.

Like a genius sprinkled with light like gray feathers, they dressed him in a tunic flowing with a trail of flying sparks—his aiguillette—and now he took off his cap.

The horses' snouts, brightly reflecting gold, haughtily bent down when the driver pulled the reins.

And red sleeves led colonel Svetozarov from the carriage; he was surrounded by faces with red lips.

They opened the doors. The butler met him and bowed his head: the foamy gray of his sideburns brushed up against his chest.

And he led them. And he led them.

He led them down—opened the doors. The butler met them with foamy gray hair. And led them. And led them.

When the butler slid away, having put a card on the tray, Svetozarov fixed his dashing breast, where everything shone with the glimmer of engraved medals and ribbons.

When the butler slid away, a marble profile proudly grew among the potted palm trees.

When the master of the house floated out from waves of moiré drapery, the streaming curtains of the doors, like green shafts of wheat, shuddered, and oblique rays of sunlight, splintering the shafts, broke through to the white coat of the swimmer, stout like a dolphin, with a heavy jangling watch chain.

A guttural voice hung and floated strangely on the waves of silence in the room. The dolphin strangely rocked his snout from the waves of moire. His puffy fins strangely thrashed and beat against his scaly vest.

Echoed, rocked, and beat—strangely, strangely: echoed and beat, strangely.

A strange, strange head strangely rocked like a scaly crest heading off to the folds of the chin.

The dolphin humbly grasped the colonel's outstretched hand with his fin. He humbly shook it with scaly scales and scaly fins. The engineer Svetlov humbly met the millionaire.

The guest's lips flared up in a smile—like a spike of foam covered in a saccharine smile. He was an underwater grotto with big nostrils on its face, with stalactites, when he sniffled with his spurs.

His nostrils trembled, his face, icy like crystal, trembled when he scanned the door to the boudoir with the emeralds of his eyes as he walked into the study.

The heavy curtain to the boudoir trembled, and the face of a young mermaid looked out from there. The young mermaid trembled as she walked by the closed door of the study.

One took the other by the hand, shook, greeted; the other sniffed and scanned with his emerald eyes; and the third trembled, she trembled.

When the stout white dolphin squirmed and his ruffled coat burst off him like gossamer rustling scales, first twisting silk and then untwisting, the flabby face of the engineer rushed toward the colonel alongside the malachite desk, lowering his chest to the desk and, as if pleading, raised his fingers, speckled with the flames of diamonds—

then Svetozarov's face—a moon filled with the glow of silver money—haughtily rested on the back of the carved chair, the white locks of his hair pouring out, rustled by the wind. Then the engineer's words flew at the colonel, flew past his ears.

Like the wind, pounding against a marble statue.

And there, in the garden, she strolled.

A stinging bee bit into her petal of a finger.

With a scream she tore the honey-bearing bee from her lily finger.

It will still crawl under her collar to buzz about the impossible.

She threw her hands to her dear one in the wind, to her dear one with a prayer; she stretched her hands to him, asked for his help, oppressed with foreboding. Stretched her hands, tore the bee from her finger—strolled, sighed.

And when Svetlov stopped talking, a marble giant with nostrils flared widely grew before him. When he stood up and put his hand on his breast, everything there shone with helplessly gossamer medals, like glimmers of shredded clouds on the moon's breast.

When Svetlov walked up to him, the greenish palm trees under the open window, dried out by the sun, tossed about and babbled, and the oblique rays of the sun's fire danced on them like an airy herd of spotted cheetahs.

The colonel said, "You're buried in debt, your affairs are shaky, and one minute you're one your feet and the next you're down again.

And throughout your past there are dark spots that cause worry in the engineering community. Exactly: I sank my gold into your venture and you fizzled out—and now I can ruin you.

My participation in your affairs will continue. I will obtain monetary support for you, and your shaky reputation will sink into oblivion.

But you, your wife, are in my hands—and that's enough about that, enough. In my hands: for you it's rough, for me the joy is enough, and 'nuff about that, enough."

When the sun ran off behind a cloud, the airy beasts escaped into the window.

When the sun ran off, the engraved medals and ribbons stopped glimmering on the colonel's breast.

When they turned to the door, emerald streams of her dress, like green shafts of wheat, rushed to the door, and her sidelong glance, split by a smile, turned to the colonel.

Golden flaps of lace flapped from her exposed bosom like columns of thick gold on a green streaming mermaid.

She cast her bright gaze to her dear one through the window, gave him her soul, beckoned him.

And there, in the expanse, Adam Petrovich sighed and flinched.

Ah, wind—a moaning horn—what are you groaning in my ear?

A windy voice: look—a storm in the sky rips the strands of the sun. Rips and proclaims.

Tell me, oh tell me, how to help her, tell her, "The Lord is with you."

Go now, go—the stormy horn calls you to battle: it rips and proclaims—it groans.

From beneath his gossamer crystal gray hair, Svetozarov's bald spot bowed to her satin hand like time, foggy and approaching, like a cloud.

Her drooping emerald tunic, speckled with golden fish, seemed to pour out a train of green water.

He offered her his hand and led her from the terrace, looking like a marble emperor crowned with silver laurels of old.

Gusts of flowers flew at him in the wind, and he pushed these red caps from her with a hand blazing with rings, like a king of old.

Fly, white stallion, as if made of snow! sound out, rider, with an agile lash to the stallion's back!

Brave, brave, slash through space, flying off to battle!

And he gallops on the stallion: gallops and flies.

Hurry, stallion-bird!

Svetlov—the loud stout man waved his hands over the colonel with a roar of laughter, like a ridiculous bird, like a rooster. His chestnut brown comb flapped; he rattled his claw in Svetozarov's palm.

And a dusty-foamy stream of words burst forth.

Svetozarov's silver-white balding head boiled and bubbled: when he foamed up with a passing glance at her in the distance like the rustling lace of white thunderclouds—the past boiled, the gray spot bubbled.

He said to her, kissing her hand, "Fly up above us, like a little bird."

He took her by the hand: like a corpse, powerless, she walked in a pale emerald mantle, her shoulders entwined in the lace of swept-away leaves, melting in the distance.

Thousands of bright needles sprayed from her dragonfly beads, but they didn't look like sequins: these were thousands of wasps crawling on her and stinging her, crawling in a swarm.

The colonel bent his festively sweet lips over her, he bent his oppressively thunderous face: like a big dandelion, futilely blowing through her emerald silks, his gray hair touched her subtly fragrant locks. His snowy stinging spurs inadvertently touched her legs.

And the stinging wasps, covering her in sparkles, crawled into her soul, where little bluebells tinkled for him.

They crawled under her collar to buzz and sting. Now, hurt by the swarm, she shrugged her shoulders.

She cast her gaze with a prayer to her dear one, her dear one, entreating him to help her.

She prayed to him.

They passed by a stone statue. Her winged husband lowered his marble visage.

The opening of his horn pointed straight at the sky.

And the horn rumbled,

"Time does not wait. It flies.

The cup of charms overflows. No matter how the charms splash.

The world has never been this dangerous, radiantly deceptive."

They walked in the garden reconciled, powerless.

She wore a lace hat like the sun in foamy white clouds.

They stood still by a column covered in branches; they reached for her shoulder strap, pulled it like a bright string.

The colonel said, "*Pardon*—
I want to fly up with giant steps—fly up, fly."
And she put her strap back.

The colonel jokingly said,
"Like a steady spiral, we're all flying around now.
We'll return to our circles later.
So the universe spins in one and the same rotation: so the image
of this world flies."
And they flew up.

The clatter of feet echoed. It began suddenly and had no end.
Unhappy, she slipped away from the colonel like the sun descend-
ing into timelessness, but Svetozarov, like the moon, smoothly flew
behind her.
That was the abbot of the fields, rearing his white stallion in the
distance—diamond dew dripping from his shoulders . . . blooming
like lightning bugs.
These gossamer hands of his menacingly tossed the wind; the
tree trunks rocked in the wind.
"Who is with Sodom . . . I will ride . . . Me . . ."
Like stormy vengeance, the hundred-branched trees rushed at
the colonel with a roar.
And then calmed down again.
And the sound of the horseman's clatter carried, carried—the
ancient rider, the rider of the fields: the harvester of the grain.

The colonel bent over her in the air steeply, like death, and
silently said to her,
"Hello, hello!
It is I, time, rushing after you to whisper about death because we
shall all die and be laid out in the grave."

She turned around as she flew up.

Gray-haired death danced above her, spurring a golden spotted beast with his jangling boots, and descended above her from the evening shimmer.

It was the colonel.

She suddenly cried, "Enough, too rough . . . Oh, enough!"

She waved the lacy leaves of her fan as if struggling with time in the wind, and the wind sprinkled her with gray time, aromatic, honey-sweet.

She waved the lacy leaves at her face, struggling with the fiery sun, and the beast jumped into a goblet at the colonel's feet.

And a clump of leaves of her fan, blown by the wind, splashed upward, like a dusky shaft of rays of the sun as it slipped away.

The colonel went flush and leaped even higher: his old face gazed in the air like the heavy disk of the moon and hung there like a dead circle.

At her wit's end, she flung herself away, first going pale and then flaring up.

Like a pointy stone, his head hit her shoulder and fell into her emerald dress.

Its greenish folds streamed and splashed in his face, washing his bald spot and flying off like a cloud of twisted leaves.

The horseman rode in the fields . . . And Svetozarov shouted, caught by the black branch of a shaky tree.

Bodies in shoulder straps fell to the ground. The madness was over.

The moon rose.

It stretched over them like a glowing dandelion: everything was shrouded in fluffy feathers of glimmering light.

And the feathers tenderly tickled with their powerlessness.

Svetozarov whispered to her, "You have never been so beautiful, never so vibrantly lofty.

Never before."

She obediently breathed in the poison and sleepily bowed down in the invisible net.

They went into the house.

Greenish knotted threads gathered and hung down from the trees like shafts of unripened wheat.

They plunged into the streams and went into the sitting room.

The horseman galloped on his foaming stallion.

He hopped off the stallion, tired and pale.

He waved the whip like a sword, making a nervous screeching sound in the air,

"Here I am . . . Here I am! . . ."

The lackeys cracked a smile in front of him.

He asked, "Is the mistress home?"

And went to the garden.

Svetozarov said to her, "You have never been so beautiful, never so vibrantly lofty.

Never before, never."

Clouds of light rays flew from her beads.

These were wasps leaving her and flying off into the darkness.

Svetozarov squinted: her gold threads crisscrossed into a single starry thread.

It was armor, put on her by someone's hand.

He opened his eyes. Everything disappeared.

She went to the garden.

The greenish knotted stems on the door shook, streaming with a rustle, and the dull fires danced, splintered by the stems, like sunny columns of gold on water above someone gasping.

Adam Petrovich's blue, long-beloved gaze shone clearly at her. His golden locks, which she had kissed in dreams long ago, flashed clearly from under his straw hat. His white face bowed down clearly when she reached her hand out to him.

He quietly handed her a letter from the neighbors where he was staying.

He quietly said to her, "Pardon the interruption." She quietly reached out her soft hand to him in the moonlight. Quietly looked in his eyes, unrequitedly, powerlessly.

It was cold and clear.

Nothing happened. They met. A calm, bright as the dawn, settled on their souls.

She lowered her head and said, "Adam Petrovich, I've heard a lot about you."

He raised his eyes to her. Rustling the leaves with the whip, he said, "Really?"

And Svetlova smiled, "I'm so lonely. Let's be friends."

They walked toward a lonely open spot over a ravine.

Walked . . .

And crunched the dry leaves.

The vast distance spread out before them.

And stretching out her arms, she said, "How nice it is over there—how nice!"

There, where there the sun was, the uneasy extinguishing light still remained.

The minutes stretched on. All of life rushed by them. Everything seemed eternally familiar.

The bright wine, poured out on the horizon, faded in the distance. As if it was being mixed with the night.

They sat on a bench. She spoke, "Sometimes I would sit here just like this.

Sit and think about one thing.

The days passed . . . And now I'm sitting here again.

Sitting and remembering the past."

The fountain next to them whispered and glimmered.

He leaned his flaxen beard over her clearly, like a bundle of ripe wheat. He smiled at her clearly and bade her farewell. She called to him clearly. She followed him clearly with a loving gaze has he walked off into the greenery.

The moon's feathers were torn to bits by the diamond of an approaching cloud, but edges of the cloud were debased by the evil charms of their black border.

The wind blew the pale seed head of a dandelion, blew, twisted, scattered the fluff.

She saw that in the house people were passing by with lamps, glowing palely, like a dandelion.

And from the lamps light fell and floated on the flower bed in a strange patterned web.

As if a ghostly cover of light and shadow had been thrown and it dashed around the flower bed.

She saw that the colonel carried a lamp, dead, pale as a ghost, glazed over.

She saw, but didn't recognize: she thought it was a corpse.

Svetozarov bade them farewell: he raised his old face to her. There was emptiness in his eyes.

His aiguillette flashed like lightning on his white tunic.

He waved his cap, now squashed, without a sound, as if laughing at her, "Breathe, take it in, love it: you are now in my—you are in my power."

But it just seemed that way.

The colonel blew his nose, and they couldn't tell if he was laughing or crying.

He blew his nose, and they couldn't tell: everything seemed that way, appeared.

They brought his carriage.

The Africans in red livery rushed at him from the darkness like pugs with bloody mouths to open the door and stood there, shining from the darkness with the whites of their eyes and their bright, bright braids.

A white statue came from the house and walked down the steps in the bright moonlight.

The horses haughtily thrust their snouts from the spots of moonlight into the heavy dark night.

Something just like the head of a genius crowned with silver laurel rushed into the darkness after the horses—and then he waved his hat in parting.

And the fiery Africans flew after him on the footboard when the driver started the carriage.

The sound of galloping horses could be heard on the wooden bridge, a little off in the distance but still not quieting down.

He stood in the carriage, and the Africans helped him down, and he had spent the day with them, strolled in the garden, and joked, and threatened, and prayed.

Yes, he loved unlovingly.

He forgot.

Easy come, easy go.

Prayer for Wheat

You, field of grain, gold. You—writhing ripe wheat.

Marked with a purple mantle—winnow, thrash.

Let us pray to the field.

The sweet ruby blood of the sunset boiled with the foam of the golden-stinging wheat: communicants approach.

Taste the sweet foam, ruby foam—taste the foam.

Pour forth, foamy wheat, pour forth.

Proclaim your voices, voices over mother earth, yearn for the Lord, plowers of the earth—deacons of the wheat.

Collect the wheat from the fields.

That was what the call to those asleep sounded like, but everything finished in the distance with the plaintive rooster's song.

And the call flew, swirling the smoky dust of the earth on the way.

The moon rose—a clump of icy snow melting, like azure, on the edges.

Here the menfolk—the salt of the earth—here the menfolk pass through the many-grained field, the golden flowing field: their clothes are infused with the earth as a dandelion is infused with the air.

They pass through the field.

You, menfolk, are the bees of the Lord, you, menfolk, open your hearts freely to the earth and heed the call, collect the honey of the field with languor.

Cover your huts, menfolk, with straw.

Cry out, "You, field, are ours!"

It was cold and clear. Waves, bright as the dawn, washed over their faces.

They walked, and their packs bounced on their shoulders.

They walked along the plains. Nothing touched them, and nobody stopped them.

It was quiet. The azure sky wept in the distance. A radiant old man lamented, "The image of this world will pass."

He rested his hand under his chin and fixed his gaze at the earth.

They came to a hill with many crests over the sandy ravine.

Tall weeds slapped them with their big bright-red stinging tops.

Stone after stone fell into the ravine.

The radiant old man lamented, "Blind men cannot see."

The wind wafted gold-bearing honey, and the azure sky laughed in the distance.

The wind wafted gold-bearing honey.

The many-faceted black, spreading shadows of clouds broke apart on the spine of the ravine.

The wind wafted gold-bearing honey with the black, spreading shadows of clouds:

"The days flow by. The ages build up. The sunsetless, that without limit, approaches.

It pleads:

'It is time for me to go to this old world: time to pull off the covers, to unravel, to fly like the wind, to hiss in their ears about that which is premature.

My lofty embrace of the world opens wide without trepidation.

I carry the brocaded robes of all things.' "

The wind wafted gold-bearing honey with bright flashes of the sun's lightning into the marked shadows of the clouds, and they were now carried away into the distance.

The radiant old man lifted his exhausted gaze. He stood on the many-crested hill with outstretched arms:

"Yes, the blind shall see: yes, the blind will see the light."

The wheat rumbled. A quail, caught in a tenuous shadow flying on the sharp wheat, screeched.

All this happened: it came and went.

Come, field hand, come!

For you—field hand—there is a mystery, and the word about you will be spoken in our hearts by a beneficent whirlwind.

In a dewy cloud, in streams of air, wafting of flowers, descend to the fields and unleash your sickle[19] on us—unleash your sickle on us, your sickle on us.

Say, "I am with you."

Field hands, workers, confess even louder—like the day is louder than the white.

Thunder louder with your sharp scythe.

Louder, avengers, louder, cry out even louder, "Now the field hand comes with the sharp harvest."

Come, harvest, come.

Riding the Wind

The noble Arabian stallion, as if soaring into the wind, resoundingly jangled on the flint, and it took the bit, first dipping into the waves of greenery, then popping out with its swanlike snow-white neck. And its mane, disheveled by the wind, flowed like milky streams into the azure.

The horseman, flaming silver as if molded from tin, was tossed onto the stallion—and now he made the whip swish while bent over like a graceful, taut figure.

His head, seething with gray, bowed low to the wild stallion and was brushed by its mane when he took off his cap.

His bright, pointed gray hair stood up like tongues of white flame lapping the air.

The stallion brought him to the hedges—he flew through them: flowers pounded against his chest with a whine.

And they flew . . . and they flew . . .

When the hedge offered a dewy, pink flower, Svetozarov plucked it at a gallop, and behind the horseman's back, the flower streamed a trail of pink butterflies.

When his stallion flew up, flashing its rear hooves on the red sand, the horseman, frozen for a moment like a cast-metal statue, jabbed the stallion in the side with his sharp spurs, pressing it with his lacquered boots.

When the deathly pale horseman flew over the bushes like tongues of gray locks, he looked like the laughing image of death, covered in pink flowers and derisively slashing the azure.

When it was, so it will be; when it will be, so it is. Is, was, will be.

But the world will forget death.

Ahead there was a loud clatter that had already begun and would not end.

The blue Amazon was staggering, drifting, flew by, staggering, into the bushes, first going pale and then flaring up like the sun.

As if Svetlova had been thrown to the wind—and now she was etched in the air because her stallion, white as the day, blended into the day.

Ahead bushes rushed at her like waves of noisy peaks; they rushed at her and threw themselves at her breast: behind her they closed ranks and ran off into infinity.

They rush at her, they rushed at her—they will rush at her again. When it was, so it will be; when it will be, so it is.

Death will not forget the world.

Let it!

Then the white air covered her airy stallion, and the airy stallion flew into the greenery covered in golden spots. This was the sunny purple mantle dancing distinctly beneath the raging leaves: airy gold cheetahs, as if made from fierce coals of the sun, staggered, blown around by the wind, first crouching and then leaping onto the stallion.

But the bushes flew by. The golden airy cheetahs ran to meet her (infinity had tossed them out), molded from light and shadow, as if an airy howling pack had been unleashed on her by the wind—and now the cheetahs threw themselves at her, shattering into her chest like waves of leaves, like pink flowers, like spots of sun and cold, cold dew.

These were the moments flying by—flying by and shattering.

This was her flying through time, desperately grasping for blue freedom.

When she turned around, time—a cloudy Legate in a halo of silver leaves—rode off smoothly behind her on the heavy stallion.

When she met his grinning face, the grinning face nodded to her from the helplessly gossamer leafy lace, the grinning face nodded to her, the grinning face nodded to her.

When she flew by and left the roiling dewy bushes behind her, the roiling greenery of a veil unfurled behind her, the green lace streamed on the galloping horseman, and the grinning face nodded to her, and shreds of lace, torn by the stallion, pitifully splashed in the fiery sun, like the green spray of waves that had crashed into marble.

When she flew out of the bushes, the golden airy snapping beasts drowned like spots in an ocean of light and trembling.

When she flew in the wide-open expanse, her stallion, white as if sculpted from wax, silently melted in the white wind; the wind took her stallion, and now she flew in the air like a blue bird sprinkled with feathers.

But it just seemed that way: the stallion had carried her to the ravine; the lake shimmered below; she kindly turned to the colonel who had been chasing her with a laughing call, "You couldn't catch me!"

When death wasn't able to, then it isn't able to. Death doesn't know what it can't do.

Time scatters death, time forgets death, time will vanish. The blue firmament will exist without time.

The lake, burning with sparks, looked like a mirror; when they went down the slope, dragonflies flew up from reeds shaken by the wind; they danced over the young sylph.

The obedient giant, like a slave, took her horse and stood there like a marble statue when she, stepping on a stone, twirled the agile, melodious whip under his nose: "Colonel, I'm hot: take the horses while I bathe over there, behind those green reeds."

The blue, blue sylph stood on the shore of the blue, blue lake.

It seemed to the giant that her dress merged with the lake into one cold deep as she plunged—and now her face and the wrists of her lily hands stretched out to him from the depths of the lake because her hair had dissolved in a bright dance of sunny serpents and a foamy white cap rocked on streams of snow-white waterlilies.

But it just seemed that way: her white wrists danced; the foamy white cap rocked with flowers tauntingly under the slave's nose, and her dress could be distinguished from the lake's blue blueness as a vague outline.

Then she hid in the green reeds: there she threw off her clothes; there the dancing dragonflies landed on her shoulders and breast, and she waved off their ticklish kisses.

Soon the splashing of waves echoed, which had already begun and had no end: she walked up to her knees in the water, twisting like a crystal veil sewn from dragonfly wings.

And the sedge rustled. And it was a very windy day.

And the shuddering colonel, seized with passion, quietly followed her in the green stalks.

"Hello, hello.

I will talk to you about passion because I can wait no longer."

From beneath the green thorns of the stalks his old, sultry, dead face popped up.

He didn't see anything: the sunny lake—the princess—cast rings on its glass, and now they rolled and expanded.

A sunny serpent danced on the shore. The white waterlilies bloomed on the shore.

Her golden curls popped up from under the water, her two hands—two flowers, her face—a bouquet—rose up from the depths of the lake. Soon she stood up entirely in the crystal lace of dragonfly wings.

He rushed at her.

His outstretched arms tore off the naked sylph's crystal lace when he fell to his knees, first bowing and then straightening up.

The cold velvet of a passing cloud covered them, and they took in one another with stunned eyes.

The cold velvet of a passing cloud.

Time is the cold velvet of a passing cloud. Death is the cold velvet of a passing cloud.

Sorrow, joy, life, oh, it's all the same, all the same.

If it was, so it will be; if it will be, so it is.

Here are tidings for the world: take the cold velvet of a passing cloud.

Like a beast, he devoured her with his gaze, and she lowered her head in horror.

He said to her,

"My sun—eternal, eternal gold—give yourself to me willingly. I will shower you with my riches like waves of burning, intoxicating sunlight.

When you come to me, I will build you a crystal palace as if made completely of air. The sun will shine on me in this world."

But she stepped back.

Upset, she grabbed the batiste shirt, shamefully covering her nakedness, and first tore herself away from him and then helplessly crumpled.

Suddenly she lifted her face: a many-crested sandy peak rose before her.

There the silhouette of the frozen horseman grew with a twisted, pale, insulted face. A sunny beard and strangely pained smile were etched in his soul.

The horseman's face exhaled an aromatic ether in the pale heavenly turquoise.

This was him—her vague dream.

Suddenly he raised his pale hand and threatened her with his agile, flashing whip.

His straw hat looked like a copper helmet, and the feathery cloud floating above his head looked to her, from below, like a clump of scattered white ostrich feathers.

He hurried to her in order the tear her from the hands of time and now sadly drooped, like a horse over a precipice, covering her in the old man's embrace.

His agitated chest heaved heavily.

The silk of the sun raged around his gossamer pearly face.

Then he stopped, seized by the wind—by time flying by irreversibly.

Then his face, distorted with torment, took in his desired one with his blue eyes for the last time, and he hid behind a hill like a cloud that floated off with two spots of azure.

So we were, so we will be: but time approached, and in time are birth and death. Between death and birth is life, a cloud floating off with two spots of azure.

The children of the light—those are the two spots (birth and death)—spots shining on the firmament.

Oh, passing cloud!

When she pushed the colonel away wildly, he, breathing heavily, stood to the side and lowered his gray head.

When she buttoned her blouse, the palely shining lace on her chest ceased to be transparent.

When she ran to the horses, the Amazon splashed her with rage and despair, and the sunlight danced on her with its flames.

The sun set. The sky became a large golden mirror, and the palely shining lace of the clouds turned blue and ceased to be transparent.

The wind whispered to her,

"Enough.

Love has flown by, and the large, ancient sun has been extinguished.

Farewell, farewell!

I will never return to astound you with resurrection because you will not be resurrected; you will die."

Death, enough: there we'll find only a vale of tears, but we are many, we are many. We shall never walk the wide-open road.

No—yes.

The blue road of the blue palace.

Death, enough: we're free.

To us this joy is rough.

Again her noble Arabian stallion, mad with sorrow and slander, clattered resoundingly, carrying her along the fields.

Again it melted into the whistling wind.

Again the wind molded her a white waxen stallion when the sea of shrubs attacked her.

When she flew by and left the shrubs behind her like a gossamer endless green shawl falling on her shoulders, like the crashing green of the sea's waves smashing on a cliff, and the green lace and the spray of the shattered waves danced on the horseman galloping behind her—Death.

And Death tore the lace—the cover over the abyss.

Death crushed the hissing waves of forgetting.

Death laughed mockingly behind her.

But it just seemed that way: behind her Colonel Svetozarov pleaded for forgiveness in a weeping voice.

Golden airy beasts attacked them as they returned.

The wild pack, groaning like the wind, was thrown on the greenery, and now the cheetahs tore at them with sharp claws, gnawed at their chests with bloody, dusky, airy wings, pounded them in the chest with waves of leaves, flowers, spots of the sunset, and cold, cold dew.

They appeared again at their shoulders.

So the cheetahs flew, carved out in the greenery by spots of light, along with the flying bushes from horizon to horizon.

The future threatened like a roaring pack of beastly moments; the past ran away like the very same pack; the present tore up the moments like waves of leaves, like color and shadow, and like a cold, cold stream of tears.

Wheat Foam

The foam was turbulent.

It was as if the uneasy wheat was swaying, bending, turning first black and then gold.

And spots of a shadow ran along the field, creating turbulence.

As if a spotted golden mantle had been thrown onto the field and now it rushed toward the horizon.

The sun—a chalice filled with gold—quietly tipped over into timelessness.

And time spilled out like waves of intoxicated grain.

They flew up—and flew by: shattering against the boundary wall in a big foamy rustle.

And it flew, and it flew.

When the sun ran off, the sky became a large mirror.

When the sun ran off, the palely glowing lace of clouds turned blue and opaque.

When the sun ran off, they sang in the distance,

"Be a liittle kiiind, deeaaar looove . . ."

The accordion ringed the deep purple bass with a fringe of gold.

And the high melodious tenor flew over the fire, and gold like a sleek azure arrow shot high.

The weeping colonel flew by somewhere in the distance, in the distance, bent over, first growing dark and then flashing with tears.

And the spots of his shadow ran along the field.

And flying . . . and flying . . .

Low purple streams of the sunset poured into the sky ringed with a fringe of golden clouds.

And the high, melodious azure flight shredded the lace of the clouds like a sharp, cold arrow.

In the distance it froze,

"Straaaaighten uuup, taaall rye . . .

Keeeeep your hoooooly mystery . . ."

The lofty embrace of the world spread open unhesitatingly.

The wind carried the brocaded robes of all things.

The horseman flew, and a quail screeched, caught by the shadow flying on the uneasy wheat.

Our life is a shadow flying away.

And so it flies over the sea of wheat like a black bird.

It flies along with us, unchanging.

And so the image of this world flies, rocking . . . to the motherland, to the unknown motherland.

Suddenly the horse stumbled on a many-faceted stone, and the colonel plunged into the stormy rye.

The greenish, knobby stalks streamed around him, and the oblique rays of the sun, broken up by the wheat, splashed above his head like sunny columns of gold above one who is resigned to drown.

When the sun ran off, the sky became a large mirror.

When the sun ran off, the palely glowing lace of clouds turned blue and opaque.

When the sun ran off, the wind carried the brocaded robes of all things with a hiss,

"The days flow by. Time gathers. And the sunsetless approaches, that without limit.

It pleads: it is time for me to go to this old world. To pull off the covers. To unravel. Time to open their eyes. To fly like the wind. To whistle in their ears about that which is premature."

An old man appeared on a tall, many-crested peak, as if made of air.

It was the radiant blind man with his blue eyes open.

He stood with outstretched arms on the sandy, many-crested hill.

His back was bent. His gray hair hanging low.

It was strange to see this silent vision with outstretched arms in the golden air.

He prayed, "Oh, if only they had vision, oh, if only they could see the light. This world is passing."

The field was turbulent.

It was as if the intoxicated wheat was swaying, bending, turning first black then gold.

And spots of a shadow ran along the field, creating turbulence.

As if a spotted golden mantle had been thrown onto the field and now it rushed toward the horizon.

The sunset became palely sad and golden satin.

The golden, spilled wine went dim, as if diluted.

Eternal Rest

It was cold and clear.

Winds from many directions washed over their faces.

They walked wearing novices' clothes, and their packs bounced on their shoulders.

They walked along the plain. Nothing touched them, and nobody stopped them.

It was autumn. The azure sky wept in the distance.

A radiant old man lamented, "She has passed. She has ceased to be."

He rested his hand under his chin and fixed his gaze at the earth.

They came to a lonely cross over the sandy ravine.

It was her grave.

A tree waved its big, dull yellow leaves.

And leaf after leaf snapped off above the grave.

He began to weep, "Will she really not be resurrected?"

A gust of wind tore at the tree, and a new cloud of blowing leaves rustled and flew by their feet.

He wrapped his arms around her grave and pleaded, "Rise up, my love!"

But the mysterious pilgrim put his arm on his shoulder and said, "Why do you weep?

The grave is empty."

He brought his hand to his eyes and saw that the azure sky was laughing in the distance.

The tree, flying around, joyfully shook its bare branches, and a golden spider web stretched out in the clear air. The pilgrim, standing on the sandy slope, laughed kindly with his glowing visage.

He woke up. He opened his eyes.

A brightly shining stream broke through a glowing crack in the shutters and rested on the wall in an oddly pale patterned spot.

That was the noise of the trees.

It was a very windy day.

And the lilac bushes, rustled by the wind, mutely shook and brushed off embraces and kisses.

He thought over his letter to her coldly and clearly.

"Everything has changed. You've changed. I am writing to you.

The cold has overtaken me. You mocked me deliberately while willingly embracing the colonel.

I see that you are dead, dead as death.

I was ill. Now I will leave you. I will leave for the north, for the pine trees.

You, like death, are a mystery. But I will delve deeper with books.

From this day my mouth is frozen in a mournful curl."

That's what he wrote.

And he rustled the dry paper.

"I have seen the future in you. And with outstretched arms I told you that my sun is rising, rising.

But it has set.

And just the uneasy dying of the light remains, and that light is the light of my soul.

A web of evil stretches around you, and you, ensnared by charms, no longer burn as before in the evening sunset.

And my sunset is going out: my golden wine goes dim, as if diluted."

He wrote.

And he rustled the dry pages.

"As I sat and thought about you, you sat and thought about the colonel.

You love one another.

My dreams have passed. And now I sit here again: sit not wanting to think about you.

I have long been tormented by your mystery and I lifted my face to the sunset, but—foggy time has separated us. And first I sadly left you and then came back, losing my serenity.

Thread after thread between us has been broken."

"The world is not unchanging. It rushes forward. It tosses the future into the past.

It has wings to fly away from the present.

That means there is no past: it shrinks.

The stream of time flows from a broken chalice.

When the chalice dries up, the stream of time will cease to stream.

Oblivion will visit me."

"With sadness I sort the events spilled out by time: we didn't know each other.

It seemed to me that we both loved. And now I'm alone: all alone in the world.

May you be in love—in love with old death, but your duty is to shine for life.

I write this clearly and simply.

Farewell. Time will decimate my black sadness."

Above him was a clear sky and a cloud, blown by sadness, gazed with azure streaks.

It looked, it exhaled a sigh, "Nothing has died.

All will return.

Yes, all will return."

It looked: it exhaled a sigh.

He didn't look at the cloud. Two tears had frozen on his cheeks. He stretched his arms. They shattered the blue reflection like clear, mournful lilies.

He had had just one path to the ephemeral, and it had now vanished.

Eternity was extinguished for him.

Golden Autumn

She walked with the famous gray mystic.

He had come to say farewell. He was leaving them for a monastery.

He said to her, "A little longer.

And then I will leave for the pine trees. I will leave you.

But you will come see me."

It was cold and clear.

Nothing had changed. She had changed.

She had received a letter.

Her gray friend adjusted his hat, bent over sadly, and stared at the ground.

He whispered, his pearly teeth flashing,

"This world is a dead world.

Everything here dies."

And Svetlova smiled, "I'm ill. I'd like to go to the north with you, to the monastery.

I will leave this place for the pine trees."

She was pale as death.

Her old friend pulled his cap down further.

They walked.

And the dry leaves rustled.

The vast distance spread out before them.

And stretching out her arms, she said, "The sun is setting—setting."

And it set.

There, where there had been a gold-plated shield, was now just the uneasy dying of the light.

A golden web stretched out in the air.

Her hair, tinged with black, glowed slightly in the evening sunset.

The sunset became palely sad and golden satin: the golden, shining wine, spilled on the horizon, went dim.

As if diluted.

She sat on a bench, "So I would sit here.

Sit and think about him.

We both loved.

That time has passed. And again I sit here.

Sit and recall the past."

The wind blew their clothes.

The old man sat, leaning on a walking stick.

He raised his old, old face to the expanse.

The distant wooded peaks first drooped toward one another and then jumped back, still green, quenched with eternity, but with their pale gold showing through the green.

And leaf after leaf was torn off, glowing.

The world is not unchanging. It rushes forward—always forward, always forward.

It tosses the future into the past: it flies—yes, forward—yes, forward.

It has wings to fly away from the present, always forward—ah, forward.

But that does not mean there is no past.

It grows: the stream of time pounds against the chalice that is offered.

When the chalice is full, the stream of time will cease to flow into it.

And the past will return.

With sadness we sort the events spilled out by time:

"We both loved—and I am white: as pale as death."

"Be white—as pale as death—your eyes, my child, shine like the heavens."

She looked at her friend simply and clearly.

She stood up—the wind tore at her black dress.

On the horizon was a clear wine gold, and, wreathed in it, she looked into the distance.

She looked into the distance and said, "He left. He will not return."

"No, he'll return."

The old man took off his cap and gazed at her face with blue knowing eyes.

On her cheeks he saw two tears.

Clouds stretched out.

They cut up the golden mirror into distinct blue clumps.

Only one bit of wine gold remained, and it too was extinguished.

And eternity was extinguished on the horizon.

They walked and talked about the past.

The past grew.

All that had been was preserved in an ancient chalice—it was lifted.

All that was did not die: all that was splashed on the surface.

A little longer.

Time will stop: the world will cease to rush forward.

And the past will return.

In the Monastery

She opened her eyes.

In front of her she saw a pale turquoise ocean of autumn air.

The aromatic ether wafted in her face.

The silhouette of a pilgrim with an enlightened pearly face grew.

Sunny curls and a golden, slightly parted, beard glowed in the evening sunset.

It was him, her vague dream.

Suddenly he raised his hand in blessing, in the shadow of a banner, but the cowl of a bowed nun blocked her view of both the pilgrim and the pale turquoise ocean.

She got up.

She was lying in a small cell with a bright open window.

The cold wind made splashes in the sapphire chalice through the window.

The pilgrim wasn't there.

A woman elder, leaning on a walking stick, was bent low over her, watching inquisitively, "I saw, you know—our secret joy."

The whistle of the wind echoed in the window, and there was the sadly familiar rustle of autumn leaves.

Noisy red birches shook uneasily in the pale heavenly turquoise.

Black clothing glowed among them.

The face of a young nun, white as death, gazed out from the red leaves, curiously looking at her.

Another silhouette appeared, the decrepit woman elder holding a rosary, and the woman elder, shaking off leaves and wrapped in a veil, walked to the beckoning call.

Her velvet cowl flickered in the leaves.

Soon after one nun there were others, and a whole row of nuns, novices, adolescents stretched toward the beckoning call.

And the birches were sadly noisy and shimmered with an eternally pale autumn turquoise.

When they had all gone into the cathedral and nuns, and novices, and youths, and adolescents no longer flickered among the birches, he appeared as if made of air.

She said, "Madness, spirit—again, now again."

He stood with his arms in the air under the gossamer gold of the falling leaves.

He closed and opened his eyes.

He stood reconciled—motionless.

His agitated chest heaved heavily.

The sunny silk of his hair, ruffled by the wind, stormed in shining locks around his gossamer pearly face.

So he stood still, showered in leaves—in golden time, flying by.

Two leaves got caught in his beard when he lifted the palms of his raised arms and, in a voice like a sigh, called enticingly from time,

"Enough!

Soon everything will fly around—fly by.

Time has dried up. It rustles, like a scroll: time, like a scroll, rolls up.

It's time!

Because everything will fly by and golden time will grow dim.

Hello, hello!

It is I who have returned to speak of resurrection because we shall be resurrected and we shall see one another there."

An ashen cloud floated in the sky.

With horror she saw the edge of the cloud through the palms of his raised arms.

He walked slowly beside the birches.

Bright red leaves were spread out in front of him. And spread out behind him as well.

As if he were draped in a blue, eternally fluttering mantle speckled with the red gold of swirling leaves.

That was the eternal waterfall of time.

She whispered, "Hello, hello—you have returned, as before: the world is not unchanging."

She left the cell and followed the pilgrim.

They walked.

Nothing touched them. And nobody stopped them.

He led her to an unknown grave on a many-crested sandy peak and, smiling, spoke to her as if inquiring about something, "Look: the grave is empty."

Worshippers gathered on the high, red, sandy hills.

There they erected a crucifix.

An unknown priest, seemingly made of air, stood in a golden robe streaked with turquoise.

Dissolving, the robe merged with the sky.

He stretched out his arm into the pale turquoise distant world.

The pale turquoise distant world was streaked with amber and gold.

Everything was doused in gossamer viscous amber and imbued with it.

The viscous amber was enveloped with fiery gold.

It became thicker, shimmered more.

The worshippers, in white shirts and bareheaded, stood with beeswax candles, slightly dripping.

The unknown priest placed a wooden bowl with holy water on the table; he dipped a bunch of ripe rye into the water.

He sprinkled the piney expanse with the rye.

He stretched out his arms into the pale turquoise world: the pale turquoise world was streaked with amber and gold.

"Oh Lord, the world has ripened like this rye: come to it, oh Lord.

Lord!

I erected my chapel among the trees: on the sandy hills I planted a crucifix.

Come to it, oh Lord!"

Everything was doused in gossamer viscous amber and imbued with it.

The viscous amber was enveloped with red gold: it became thicker, shimmered more.

The unknown priest took a sickle and made the sign of the cross in all directions with the sickle,

"Adorn, adorn the great church of the world with flowers, you—laypeople, and you—clergy.

Raise up your vestments—your hearts, deacons of the world.

Let us lift up our hearts."

He stood on the high, sandy, red hills deep in prayer.

He made the sign of the cross to the wind.

In a voice like a sigh, he called the field hands to the harvest.

"The abbot of the earth is coming, made of the shining of sickles.

The bridegroom of the earth is coming, born from the holy rites in the fields.

You, bridegroom, come to our chapel, knock on our tombstone.

From the distant world beyond the grave, envelop us in life and sun.

We shall meet you, our abbot, with wheat, with wheat, with wheat.

Take root in our souls.

For we are your fields: fields, fields, ripe fields.

Come to it, field hands."

His turquoise robe dissolved. It melted into the sky, streaked with pearls.

His white face, awash in silky gold, gazed with surprised blue eyes at the worshippers, like a sunny cloud with two streaks of azure.

His two arms stretched over them—his two snow-white patches.

And it seemed to the worshippers that he wasn't a pilgrim but a distant cloud; this wasn't a robe, but a peak.

They all prostrated themselves.

The pilgrim's voice still echoed over them from the distant expanse like beckoning bells,

"My robe is air, gold.

The horizon is so amber."

But that was the wind whistling, and the worshippers were alone.

The sky was above them.

There a sunny cloud with two streaks of azure had frozen in place.

Munich.[20] *1906.*

PART THREE: EXCITED PASSION

Dewy Tears

It was warm and bright.

Someone blew a stormy lily from the roofs: casting flickering crosses off of it, stars.

He danced on a lonely pipe over the street.

It was the snowy jester.

He jangled his icy bell and entreated,

"Rise up, little blizzard."

The wind blew the jester into the air like a shining cloud of snowflakes.

The jester grabbed his cap. He shook his beads and spewed a snowy stream into the street.

He screamed—the spring wind burned him, "I am already a dying jester.

I am already melting."

There was singing, "My snow flows. I can't snow with my hissing storm—it hurts.

Let you be told, boiling snow, melted, how much I desire to believe and love."

The transparent yellow lace of the slush lay on the road.

The road grimaced with the iron laughter of shovels.

Shovels shuffled along the slippery sidewalk, slipped.

They were bogged down with water.

The damp wind sang passionately, "Mad sunsets, golden sunsets, sunsets covered in the snow of the final storm."

The city was laid bare in wet desolation.

That was the old time going by, spring.

And the wind swooped by, running its wet hands along the silver strings of droplets,

"Sunnnsets whiiiite

Wiiiith the finaaaal stoooorm."

The wind ripped the jester from the roof and dragged him in the wind by the scruff of the neck.

The jester turned silver.

Everything that had been in his pockets was covered in snow—it turned to stars on the street.

He whispered to the wind, "Shall I not scatter too? Lie on the stones and sprawl out on the road like diamonds?"

Nothing changed. The season changed.

Spring approached.

They smiled to one another, "It will be spring, it will be summer: ice flows down the river in the springtime, flies by in streams."

"The ice floe rushes by, rushes by, like a swan."

"Between the ice floes is water."

"It babbles and lifts the ice. And the ice floats: floats and melts."

"And in the summer we'll head to the north, we'll rest among the pine trees."

"There are pine trees in the north."

They smiled.

And the wet snow rustled.

The roofs rusted. And a wheat-colored stream burst through a rusty crack and made a strangely pale pattern on the snow. The evening light of the setting sun poured down but couldn't disperse.

But the sun set. And the streams were extinguished.

An icy crust, delicate and white, like a limestone shell, crunched under foot and sank into a yellow puddle like a brown layer.

Circles of light could be seen; flitting around under foot in fright, they could not calm down.

These were bubbles of air.

They were leaking water.

The custodian banged the ice with a heavy iron crowbar.

Bit of ice after bit of ice flew off to the side.

Pustules on the edges broke off in multifaceted lightly flying fragments, shooting at passersby.

A vast hole opened up before the jester. And, stretching his hands towards the pipe, the jester said, "They are falling into the pipes.

Falling."

And he fell.

There, where the snowy jester was spinning, white flies flitted around uneasily.

And in the pipe he remembered, "It was here that the blizzard bride kissed me.

She sat and thought about me.

We both loved.

That time has passed. And now she has melted."[21]

Adam Petrovich's shadow, growing steadily, dashed ahead of him, lengthening and melting on the sidewalk.

Adam Petrovich's galoshes, crunching along, broke up the ice, spilling and sloshing water.

And another shadow grew on the wall, and behind it yet another rose up.

And all of the doubles grew and melted, floating off ahead.

So he walked surrounded by a mass of ghostly doubles.

So he stomped his galoshes, falling into puddles.

When he went back, all of the doubles that had melted reappeared and floated back: grew and melted.

The jester remembered the streets infected with melting,

"We jesters are horsing around—and now everything is melting: melting and spilling out."

He glanced at himself simply and clearly and saw that he was streaming.

And he streamed by.

The thaw laid him down, deathly, like a hill of many tears.

The puddles spread out. They dissected the hill with bluish spots, and the hill softened.

And the streams chatted by the sidewalk.

They would meet one another where the starry lamp sprinkled the slush with purple, shining a light on the image of the Virgin Mary.

Tall and with golden hair, she walked toward him with light and obsequious steps.

Her eyes were evasive flowers; they still shone at him from afar.

He questioned her with his gaze, but she didn't answer and just said,

"I have a sweet summer secret about the Lord."

He asked again; she didn't answer.

She just said,

"You can come to me now."

They lifted their blue eyes at each another and froze, as if not seeing each other.

He smiled, but she passed by without a smile, covering her shameful pink face with her muff.

And there where they had stood, the glow of the lamp flowed, ancient and eternally sad.

All the same.

Everything in the courtyard was falling apart, and a snowy woman, wrapped in warmth, gazed into the distance.

She gazed into the distance and said, "He flew by over there.

He will return.

Yes, he will return."

And when everything had melted a bit, there, where the snowy woman had been, there remained only a broom sticking out.

Drips fell in the courtyard: they descended into the chalice of timelessness.

A pearly moisture gathered.

And the little stream flowed by.

From the right they sang, "Myyy snoooow flooows." "In a cart caaa . . ." And from the left, humming like a silver stream of droplets, the wind added, "Oooo niiiight of the finaaaal stooorm . . ." ". . . aan't leeet you, accccord of my harrrmony" cut in from the right.

And the winds merged,

"And maaaaad niiights, niiights—oooozes for me to believe and love."

And the blizzard roiled again.

The triumphant chaos tossed up a cloud of snow.

Diamonds

A deep sigh could be heard—it had begun long ago and had no end. This was the noise of the snow in an early spring day, stormy.

Through the clear glass, the blue comb of the whirlwind day groomed the snow mounds; and the curls of the snow mounds smoked with silver and gold.

Svetlova returned from the monastery, calm and insightful.

An omen arose in the lacy fabric of her stormy heart like the sun from storm clouds.

She stood frozen by the window for a long time, strewn with memories.

With a whistle, sparkle, and early spring aroma, the gossamer bishop's robe, like a snowy brocade, scratched at the frosty window.

Like a white train of fabric, like a snowstorm, she flew around the room; she bent her white face to the snowy lace, like the sun; she tore her white soul from the bonds of earthly life, ascending toward immortality.

The storm sprayed smoke of white snow—it bloomed like a handful of blossoming flowers, white lilies—a bridal veil of lace made from stars, stars.

The smoke fell on the ground: it settled in a single lacy net.

She sprayed the snow of her silks on the sofa, the diamonds from the fingers of her white lily hand scattered, the necklace on her breast scattered like a fountain of stars, stars; she tapped her slipper, tore at the leopard skin with her slipper.

Enough.

Soon she will sink into monastery life, grow weary.

She told her friend, "It's time.

Because all shall pass.

And all shall be resurrected."

It's rough—

her eyes flashed in the storm, glowed,

because in the window, from beneath the window, a flock of silver threads flapped their wings; with a screech, they bustled their crests and flew away quickly, noisily, joyfully.

And she spoke wearing a stormy, satin, roiling dress, and in the storm of folds the swan—a compact mirror—looked like a shard of ice when, playing with the chain, she waved it.

And her gossamer buttons, like a gossamer icy crust, crunched under foot and shimmered like crystal.

The storm leaped: it began to unwind webs—snow mounds: and brocaded threads curled silver in the windows.

Lilies tossed in the wind, snowy horns, full horns, and dashed off in loud tatters.

The storm leaped toward her: it began to embrace her satin knees, and the airy flower dusted her head with snow.

This was the beauty's silver shawl flying above her on arms of airily drooping lace and settling on her alarmed head.

Unconsciously

her friend rustled her head in her knees as if in a stormy hill made of silver.

And whispered, "It's time—

the storm is raging, he is coming."

So they whispered; Svetlova's puffy fan first flew like almond petals and then, scattering like a branch of flowers, loftily grew above her friend. Her obsequious gold head leaned toward the pale explosive fan, lowering her powerlessly blue, blue eyes.

The snow mound, blown around on the ground, first grew and then, unraveling like a thread of flies, expanded into the sky.

The obsequious gold thread scattered like a pale, explosive fan, like a loud fountain in the blue air, and banged with a hiss, laugh, and shimmer.

Svetlova accompanied her friend.

The snowy train of fabric swayed. Silver stalks, falling from her collar like crystal icicles, first broke and then straightened up.

And shadowy spots ran along her dress, creating ripples.

As if a mantle of snow had been thrown over her, speckled with melting, and now she rustled on the stairs, accompanying a lady into the snowstorm as if to their sweet motherland.

She flew and rustled.

She crashed into her friend's breast like the foamy rustle of silver wheat.

The door opened for the lady.

A white almond bush fell toward the lady's face; snowflakes fell towards her face; gossamer lilies bloomed on her fur coat.

Everything bloomed on the other side of the wall: it began to sprinkle the buildings with cold and tender flowers.

From cracks in the doors a bunch of almond petals sprayed out, gently adorning the lackey's feet.

She flew up the stairs like a blizzard of satin skirts—she floated into the labyrinth of rooms.

On the other side of the wall, they were flying into the clouds and sighing into the sky.

With a screech, they flapped puffy feathers in the cloudy smoke; from beneath the lacy ships, oars rowed in the blue openness screechingly, joyfully, noisily.

With a screech, she lowered her hands in exhaustion; from beneath the lace, they slipped into the depths of the mirror enticingly, sadly, despondently.

A blossoming song could be heard that began and had no end and now twirled up, now descended, like unscattered almonds.

When the lady ran off, she stopped in front of a large mirror.

When the lady ran off, a palely glowing lace shawl wrapped around her.

When the lady ran off, diamond shafts of wheat splashed around her, and the oblique rays of the sunset, fractured with silver, danced on her like a happy swarm of reflections on broken icicles.

Cold fireflies settled on the windows and crawled along the glass.

But her husband appeared, flabby and stout.

The doors shut. Her husband stood in front of the locked door.

The lackey carried a tablecloth past her, setting the table.

The snow splashed upward and, like lilies, rocked over the buildings.

They snapped like glassy fireflies; the fireflies settled on the windows, frozen with snow.

They turned glassy, like dead lilies.

Chaos Astir

He went to her for the first time.

She unconsciously sighed: the rustle of her dress, the sigh of her red silk, was a stream of sunset fire.

He unconsciously sighed: the voice of the past, the rage of her months-long nighttime dreams had been resurrected, like a carnation from under a snowy veil cast by the storm.

She unconsciously sighed: the voice of the wind, whispering to him, hummed in the pipe, shining again like a swan singing about the resurrection.

They unconsciously shuddered: wings flapped, swishing in the window, shining again like the wings of a resurrected swan.

She reached her whole body toward him. She gazed with surprise, she gazed right at him with desire.

He reached his whole body toward her. He gazed inquisitively, right at her with surprise.

Like the velvet paw of a soft cat, her hand stroked his. Like the snowy paw of a white cat, the blizzard scratched at the window.

She burst out with the song of an unforgotten dream and shamelessly nodded, laughing at something.

Was he not the unforgotten dream, since she was shamefully silent in front of him and was searching for something in him?

The blizzard burst out with the song of an old dream that had not gone silent, and it shamelessly tossed brocade, wraps, white silks at the windows—stars and pearls.

It dug through mounds of snow, searching for something.

Adam Petrovich laughed with barely noticeable laughter, with lighthearted and tender reproach from under his flowing hair, from under his beard, silk like a clump of linen.

In his eyes the dark blue velvet of her eyes floated shamefully, quiet and enticing. In her eyes, the furious blue lightning of his eyes flashed powerfully, passionately, insistently.

From under a stormy curtain, from under the necessities of mundane life, she recognized in him the barely perceptible image of the pilgrim with lighthearted and quiet ecstasy.

With a menacing, insistent hiss, the storm called them to the monastery of the fields, woods, and open spaces.

The rooms merged into one mysterious labyrinth, and the moaning colonel, in a deep voice like the rising rumble of time, first made a mute threat and then jangled his spurs on the soft rug—

and if his fingers, scratching at the air, wandered along his aiguillette, the snowy moth, scratching at the air, flew from his aiguillette to Adam Petrovich's face;

and if with his mute threat he uneasily touched the conjurer— rumbling, like the rumble of the blizzard, with thunder—if the moth rumpled the satin, rustling, and shaking a kerchief at the old man,

like the peacemaking lily of her hand,

shaking,

first stretching between them and then pathetically covering her sighing face;

like a snowy bird,

shaking,

the blizzard first looked through the window and then flew off into space.

She shooed the moth with a lacy handkerchief; lacy swarms swarmed by the streetlamps.

The white velvet of the snow first softly crunched in the windows, then bloomed in a handful of buzzing moths, and if she were his soul, the uneasy dawn in the white velvet of a chair, if she leaned toward the hearth like the dawn, like the dawn,

like the sun the burning coals of the hearth, tossed her, like a ray, onto the white velvet of the snow.

The colonel laughed, rearing his gray hair over them—in his aiguillette,

growing dim and blooming.

Now he passionately, menacingly cracked his icy knuckles,

and jangled his spurs with vengeance: he discreetly suppressed the smile on his dim face and went farther into the suite of rooms like a mysterious avenger, an old avenger, an avenger peering through the winter windows: there was the stormy abbot, the stormy abbot rearing his stallion over the buildings—

in diamonds,

growing dim . . . and blooming;

there were his icy hands, his hands shaking a spear menacingly.

Diamonds scattered in the windows like weeping, like weeping they bubbled up and then scattered again.

A forest of spears menaced in the windows, their points flying by, a forest of spears banging at the glass like hail—

shining in the glass.

The swan in the window spilled out its white charm, flew off, and now a screeching flock of swans flew by in the window—flocks flying far away, slicing with their now stormy feathers, slicing with feathers.

Adam Petrovich smiled to her with ancient charm, and feasts burned down in her uneasy soul—like feasts that had burned out long ago,

her breast heaved, alone, always alone.

The more insistently, the more gently he moved toward his dear one, the more tenderly he touched her hands with his, the more plushly his happiness flowed to his heart,

the more ashamedly, coquettishly, impossibly, alarmedly she backed away from his outstretched arms.

The hotter the golden embers burned, the more the twilight flowed over them, the more distinctly the white lawn chairs could be seen in the darkness like swans with wings spread out, the faster they flew, those in love flew on swans' wings.

He said,

"I left you to go to wide-open spaces and expanses, but even there they visited me at sunset, they visited me.

A spotted cat crawled there, obsequious and soft.

The cat beckoned me to a new life, the cat sighed to me about the impossible, the cat sighed to me about those same things."

The blizzard beckoned them to life, sighed to them with a snowy sigh; the winds of the blizzard swirled.

He said,

"The more stormily the streams of wind from the fields pound, the more insistently, the more powerfully I return to you." (The white swan shot up in the air again.)

"I have returned to you, to you, for you, because of you." (The white swan sprinkled diamonds.)

"Holy delights are spread out before us, eternal delights, bright, because all love carries us to Christ as if on wings." (On the swan's back they sat and watched the swan carry them off.)

"I am in love: the good news makes my chest clench: let's go to the woods, go to the fields, and no one will stop us.

In the fields and the woods we will erect a chamber of general happiness." (The swan sang, "We fly to the woods, we fly to the fields—that's where I'm taking you." The swan flew and sang—

the swan of the Ascension.)

He grabbed her waist and asked, "You can do it: oh, be bold, my desired one." (The swan's song, strange, still flew through the stormy fog.)

He whispered.

(The swan flapped its wing.)

"Oh, Christ is in everything, oh, in everything, Unchanging One, the Same. He is between us in the ancient azure, in the whiteness of the eternally sad, wearing the same purple." (The swan's storm is in the snowy whiteness.)

She put her hand on his shoulder, "Well, what, my dear, what are you talking about, my dear?"

"This is all just a dream, all a dream, you are dreaming. Or are you real, are you real, are you real?"

"No, a dream, it's a dream, a dream."

Like a sea of yellowish buttercups above his brow—like a white cloud—locks of hair flew up like rays.

(They sang a swan song in the swan pillar.

The blizzard carried the swans past.)

She said,

"Familiar faces would come here unnoticed and speak about the same things, but I hid from you in a monastery where they wait for the pilgrim with enlightened faces." (The night bloomed with the snowy cries of swans.)

"He rose before me calm and beautiful."

"You are trembling. Why is your breast heaving? Why is the sunny silk of your locks around your gossamer, pearly face?" (The gossamer pearly swans flew again in silver—without end, without end.)

"You are calling, calling."

"The pilgrim rose up with a call, like a swan." (The swan knocked again with its pearly wing.)

"The pilgrim shines to me like a ray of light, like the blizzard shines with snowy foam."

"Is that you, call of the blizzard? No, not you."

"No."

(The swans flew by—there are no swans.)

The sound of her voice sang as if it were the flight of snowy foam; she turned around and gazed with surprise, with fright; a green uniform and a gossamer, clean-shaven face, transparent, in a halo of silver leaves shook, rocking slightly, with soundless laughter—

no, no:

a lamp in a gossamer white shade rocked on a tall green table.

From beneath the grate of the hearth, a yellow and gray cheetah with black rings froze like velvet of coal.

Her hand helplessly fell by her knees: she mournfully directed her gaze at the yellow coals of the hearth, crackling with heat, speckled with flying embers as if with gray spots.

She heard the wailing of a piano. She wanted to say something. She forgot.

She didn't say anything.

From the open doors, as if from the gaping maw of the labyrinth, as if from an enchanted distant land, a net of chords covered them, and they were caught in the net.

There with a whirlwind of gray hair, like some kind of priest—

in aiguillettes,

first blossoming and then dimming—

Svetozarov menacingly reared his hands over the piano; snowy smoke curled fiercely in the windows: there a certain abbot—

wearing diamonds,

glimmering in the windowpanes, glimmering in the windowpanes—

reared an airy stallion above the buildings; snowy smoke curled fiercely in the windows, and the colonel's hands raised and fell.

First he squeezed the piano, then he shook the piano, and it was as if an icy spear pounded the keys.

And the icy spear pounded at the window: someone bubbled up like a blizzard and tossed diamond hail at the windowpanes.

Swarms of buzzing spears flicked the windows.

From the open doors, as if from the gaping maw of the labyrinth, the dull moan of the piano rose up, and there was an insipid, insipid voice,

"Myyyy liiiips are seeeaaaled . . . In siiilent sooorrooow buuuurning, I caaannooot . . . it huuu it

huuu

uuu

uuurts to speeeaaak."

A secret floated by in Adam Petrovich's soul—it was bitter and oppressive.

A secret floated by in her soul, oppressive.

The menacing storm howled in the window; the snowy storm spoke.

His cracking knuckles crunched loudly when he lowered his hands.

Again. And again.

When she approached him, she brightly splashed him with a fiery flower from her cracked knuckles.

She bent over with an enticing twist. His mouth froze in a mournful twist.

From the open doors, as if from the gaping maw of the labyrinth, the dull moan of the piano rose up, and there was a voice,

"Leee
eet the accooord of my haaarmoooony
teeeell youuuu
Hooow I wiiish to loooove and belieeeeve."

A heap of gold burned there, streaked with gray spots like a golden sleepy leopard.

They lowered their eyes so quietly, burned with the fierce flame of passion so gently—

as if the mystery of the cross had crucified them, as if they had been taken down from the cypress tree, as if their larynx had dried up with thirst, as if the cover had been torn from the temple, as if the dead had risen from the grave, as if they watched them, watched their souls

the leaden, dull pupils of their eyes—

they lowered their eyes so quietly, they burned so fiercely in the passionate velvet.

"Grant me happiness, grant it."

Her lips languidly curled into a terrible smile, painfully fiery,

"My dear, eternally desired, my dear—
grant me happiness, grant it."

The keys of the piano laughed in the distance, like stones flying into the abyss, like a dying person screaming with passion, like the mewing, like the mewing of a cat in heat.

"My dear, eternally desired, my dear—
grant me happiness, grant it."

Quickly, powerfully, insistently she grabbed his head in agony with hands wearing tinkling bracelets that bloomed with gold in his eyes, and her cheeks glowed like pink velvet.

She pressed her lips, powdered with gold like a narcissus, shone white in the moiré lapel of his coat—

and she grabbed him in agony with hands wearing tinkling bracelets, quickly, powerfully, insistently, so that only his cheeks glowed like passionate velvet.

And the purple squeal of crimson silk, like the squeal of a mantle tormented with an embrace, and in his hands her hot melting waist, her closed eyes, her fluttering eyelashes all merged into a single inexplicable sadness.

And the cold squeal of the laughing piano keys, like the squeal of the dancing blizzard, and the cold thunder poured into the dying whisper, and the bitingly dancing forte descant sounded from the depths of the labyrinth like a wonderful, enchanting sadness.

He whispered to her,

"The more holily, the more unspeakably the mystery sighs, the more subtly the contours of the mystery of Sodom are distinguished.

The purples—the purples of Sodom and Gomorrah flow by with the blasphemous whirlwind in the brightness and azure of Christ. Like angels, like angels—

they look into the soul alone—

forever alone."

She lured him to the sofa.

When she closed her eyes, their crimson lips, slices of peach, greedily tormented one another, agonizingly . . . painfully; her burning hands sprawled out helplessly, and her dress cascaded onto the floor like a fiery, crumpled petal.

When she closed her eyes, the cries of the piano—the cries of a slaughtered bird—painfully pierced their ears, agonizingly.

When, tearing himself from her, he covered his face with his hands in shame, her leg dropped to the rug and the fabric flew by with a swish, uncovering her leg above the knee, black, silk, outstretched like a serpent on the yellow plush sofa.

When she realized what she had done, she jumped from the sofa; she fixed her dress and hair and said to him,

"Although you speak of mysteries, you yourself have been ensnared by temptation. Leave and let me get a hold of myself."

From the terrible jaws, from the old piano, from the music, the colonel appeared before her with his gray hair.

Predatorily, inquisitively, madly, threatening one and the same thing, the same, the same.

Bending his drooped paws over the piano like a puffy gray cheetah, he pressed his big, grinning head to the music stand in dark circles of smoke with his velvet body, as if preparing to leap,

as if flying in the blizzard.

And in the blizzard, the horseman flew like a whirlwind in a snowy cape of sound.

The colonel glanced at the window:

there the abbot was rearing above the buildings—the stormy abbot, screeching.

He proclaimed, "It draws near."

He waved the wind, whining above the buildings, like a sword,

"Here I am . . . at you . . . here I am . . .

My fury is with me . . ."

The avenging warriors rushed behind him, armored in silver ice.

Fiercely, they flashed their spears fiercely, scattering mounds of snow with their swords, with their swords.

And from the terrible depths of the rooms, from the music, Svetozarov floated off into the blizzard, and when Svetlova caught his gaze in the mirror—waving away a response, the colonel's hands fell onto the piano, his diamonds clinking the keys.

And from the terrible darkness of the snowstorm, from the pipes on the roofs, the stormy horseman flew, and when people looked at the roofs—waving away their gazes, the horseman's hands fell onto his icy sword, flashing on his hip.

His snowy hands slid along the windows, his fingers clinking the glass like piano keys.

The ancient piano roared madly, like the voice of the blizzard, like the avenging wail of the avenger.

And the colonel's mouth opened with a dark cry,
"Hooow
I wiiish to beeeliiieve aaaand
loooove."

The Airy Abbess

Trembling, her husband sneaked up on her, fell on her breast with rings of soft hair, standing up like a rooster's comb, rustling the black moiré lapels of his unbuttoned coat on her dress, the rings of his tinkling watch chain in the red flame of silk, his dry claws tenderly tickling her satin cheek: an agonized cry was wrested from her heart when, modestly pushing away his bothersome feet with her springy foot, she covered her face with her hands.

Her heart was flooded with a worried, stormy voice that beckoned with agitation; a wailing cry about lascivious nights, about dead embraces, about a body that surrendered itself over and over again—a wailing cry filled her soul with sorrow.

So she walked away, but he, squeezing red clumps of her silk, tried to push her down, and his lustful eyes, cruelly shining in their puffy lids, and his frantic hands, twisted in her dress, inflamed him with stormy madness.

The beautiful young woman coldly bent over with trembling nostrils and obediently forced herself to smile: the gold of her hair, her arms stretched out entreatingly, the deep-seated weeping of her reedy voice all provoked in the lecher one and the same, one and the same, "When a young woman lives under my roof, I will take her by force."

When the blizzard blew under the window, its cry was scattered over the thundering roofs; there, in the window, it shook the snowy silk and with a call, a call thrown to the sky, insistently, oppressively beckoned.

In the mismatched fight, she scratched his flabby cheek with her pink fingernail.

He cruelly pushed her down, and the beautiful woman twisted her red satin waist, and her chiseled fingers and her tinkling, dancing bracelets covered her head from the blows of his hands whizzing through the air: so she froze, wincing from the beating; golden embers roasted hotly in the hearth.

She slipped off the white velvet sofa like a red dawn coated with snow, and a glowing clump of embers flashed at her from the hearth like a sliver of the sun as it floated off.

Now her eyes were moist like gossamer pearls, and she screamed like a frightened wild swallow, with fatigue brushed aside a golden cloud of hair, and her call was drowned out by the wild call of the blizzard, by the snowy silk, by a call thrown to the sky, mortally oppressive.

When her offender lad left for his club, she got up off the leopardskin rug: so she stood, covered by her hair with her blue eyes tossed up high and a pearl, not trembling on her marble cheek, and the

sweet aroma of perfume and fingers tearing at a lace handkerchief—
for her it all merged into a single, vague, inexplicable sadness.

The blizzard sang about how the olden days, called to us by
anguish with an airy flight of melodious love, like an airy swarm of
snowflakes—that the olden days sing incessantly, and call and weep,
tenderly rock the light cradle, like children of an orphaned soul:

the blizzard sang, and the snow, the shroud, the brocade flew at
the windows when its greedy mouth kissed the window as it would
kiss in times of old.

The blizzard sang, "Caaaapture the exciiiteemeeent of
passiooooon . . ."

"Sleeeeep, hoooopeleeess heaaaaart . . ."

From behind the ancient piano, from behind the raised music
stand, the colonel stood up with fatigue, his face pale with sadness,
and his gray hair, standing up as if in horror over the top of his head
quietly, so quietly, outlined itself from the semidarkness and floated
away behind the music stand:

"I weeeeep . . . I suuuuuffer . . ."

He appeared before himself from the distance of many years,
from behind black, black deeds—he, still a child—with eyes wide
in horror, pleading for mercy, "Why, I wanted only the truth, oh,
why?"—he stood up and floated off into old times.

She came to him with unintentional desire, wearing a cascading
white peignoir, as if made of air, and with mournful waves of her
dusky, falling hair, wiped the sweat of mortal oppression from her
brow; and her face, still wet, wet from tears, sipped the sadness of
his voice, weeping like velvet, her mouth repeating his words back
to him, tearing at her wet handkerchief on her breast; like a sleepy,
roaring lion, he dropped his pained, pained head with closed eyelids
and a dimming gaze into his hands.

They sang, "My soooul is weeeaaary with sepaaaratiiion."

A nervous, stormy voice spoke about separation, about that which was gone, about where everything flies off to, languished behind a wild handkerchief swishing in the window.

The more helplessly the beautiful woman leaned toward the old man, the more intoxicated was his sadness, the more unconsciously his eyes and hands and lips approached her eyes and hands and lips.

And he pressed his clean-shaven face to her sweet fingers, and with a deep sigh she put her mouth on his tormented forehead, like a sister comforting an older brother in pain, "Together we love: you love me, and I love him; together, exhausted, we are dragged to the grave . . ."

Now the blizzard rose up like an airy white abbess, bending its satin waist under the window, and its cold fingers, with the tinkling of an icy rosary, splashed a silver wave in the moiré mantle like wings swishing in the window: so she reached for the window; the empty heavens gazed tenderly from beneath her eyelashes, tenderly; with her hands she tore at the diamonds of her silk robe, ripped to pale shreds, and a call flew from her lips, beckoning, moaning:

"I suuuffffer . . . I loooong . . . My soooul is weeeaaary with sepaaaratiiion."

She thought about the ancient, ancient anguish beckoning her with sadness with a fire in her breast, the love that croaked, singing to her heart like the blizzard, as if one and the same blizzard, and the very same moon bent over her and its horribly familiar face, as in childhood dreams, when it kissed her hotly somewhere with its kissing lips and, as in the distant past, comforted her somewhere from old times with its gaze lifted to her.

Her pale exhausted head with a silky fire of burning hair on her marble body, her fleeting gaze, as if all of her left in despair, as if she kept summoning death—everything spoke of the riddle of death, everything: both she and the moon, when it steadily raised its silver disk, its long gazes at her, as in the distant past.

The Whisper of Springtime

A trembling spot in the halo of gray hair stretched out a note to the rooster.

He read it and flared up like a flame, as if waves of red Bordeaux flowed in his cheeks.

And the colonel nodded at him, grunting and coughing like a beast scowling at the sunset.

Suppressing a cough, he dryly noted, "This isn't my business. You can get used to any situation. And it's time for me to be on my way."

But the rooster, with a beast's concentration, waved at the old man with his cigar.

A lackey with a tray ran ahead.

In the window, the snow streamed tears. A rickety mound of snow collapsed.

There was a flood of mud shining with spots—dark spots.

They carted the snow off.

Again and again.

And the carts stretched everywhere.

The rooster pleaded, "Colonel, colonel."

Groaning and coughing, the colonel turned his clean-shaved face to him, and the colonel laughed with a twisted mouth: it was unclear what the colonel was laughing at.

His aiguillette was scattered on his green uniform, and his deep bass voice broke the silence, "Yes, hehe, my fellow—hehe."

He embraced the old one and led him to the foyer, and nobody saw the old man's lonely threats with his outstretched arms, with his tired eyes.

The rickety thing came apart with a rustle beneath the window.
Heavy wet feet tramped through it.
A stream babbled. It pleaded.
It fell asleep.

It seemed to the rooster that the lackeys were laughing at him.
One had no beard: he had mowed everything. The other, an old man, with his lips sticking out, neighed into his sideburns. He dragged himself behind his coat and walking stick with an outstretched arm.

They obediently carted off the yellow snow.
Shovels rustled with a rustle like the old woman's whisper of springtime.
The lazy lunar night, babbling with melted spots, poured down in pouring puddles.
Carriages thundered, "Tra-ra-ra-ta . . . the old . . .
The same."
A crow from the melting heap wheezed with surprise at the dampness.

A cabby drove them, rumbling over the stones, splashing the melted slush.
Someone's alarmed cry echoed in the mute darkness: someone was calling someone somewhere.

Everything seemed warm and damp—springlike; everything collapsed with dampness—rain and snow.

The old cabby pulled up the carriage dejectedly, grumpily, and it smelled like home.

They stepped onto the sidewalk: a poor, noseless, gray old woman flew at them from the corner:

"Alms for a blind woman, for Christ's sake."

Svetozarov brought the stout one to a house and, from beneath the fur of his coat, raised his finger to the curtained windows, "She's giving herself to him there: that's where they're fooling around. Embracing and kissing."

"Alms for a blind woman, for Christ's sake."

The poor woman turned her ash-gray face, opened her eyes and the whites of her eyes spun.

And didn't see anything.

Oh, if only she saw, oh if only she weren't blind.

Icicles flew from the gutter like shattered glass, ringing out on the sidewalk with a mute cry, and burst apart like resoundingly sharp silver.

A black shadow fluttered in the window.

She stretched out her dark, dark hands and lowered her shadowy, dark face, dark and black as coal.

Another shadowy outline fluttered—dark, dark: murky, it extinguished the light.

Two old men stood beneath the windows. They embraced and wept.

"Tra-ra-ra-ta . . . the old . . .

The same."

A carriage thundered.

The old men sat in the horsecar: the horsecar was reflected by the glass in the glass; in the reflected glass was the reflection of the dim streetlamps.

They chased after the horsecar in the distance, caught it, and disappeared in the reflection of the glass: there the unreflected lamp blinded the eyes.

The streetlamp was left behind, and the reflection of the horsecar grew again.

Again the reflected streetlamp caught the reflected horsecar.

Svetozarov said, "We all fly behind ghostly life like a ghostly reflection.

We catch it and die."

He cocked his eyes and muttered into the fur of his coat, while Svetlov was still silent and frowning. They were both dully pale in the dull dusk.

Their backs were hunched. Their heads down low.

That's how they stood in front of Svetlov's house, parting with one another.

Someone's alarmed cry echoed from the black courtyard: someone was calling someone somewhere.

The caretaker came from an out-of-the-way spot and pointed his lantern at a wet heap: the heap wasn't a heap: some hooligan was embracing the maid.

The light fell: their heels flashed. And the caretaker cursed: but it seemed that someone was calling someone somewhere.

The colonel saw: the dead light in the doorway lit up; groaning and sighing, Svetlov trembled, shoving his fur coat in the lackey's arms. The lackey shut the door and smiled for no reason with his crooked mouth.

Someone was calling him somewhere, as in childhood, sometime.

He turned.

A blue-eyed girl with a snub nose looked him in the face.

"Hey, old man. I'm fourteen. Let's spend the night."

And his old face, forgotten by everybody, abandoned by everybody, quickly grunted and retreated into the faded fur of his coat, shaking with a tremor of horror, with his eyes wide open at the horror of the night.

He wept tearlessly, not quite laughing, not quite rocking.

The blue-eyed girl splashed him with blue sparks, laughing temptingly with her innocent face, loudly singing an off-color chanson, "Tra-ra-ra-ta . . . Tra-ra-ra-ta . . ."

"The same old," he cut her off.

"Old-old-old," rumbled the carriage. He sat in the carriage. He wrapped himself in his fur.

The carriage set off.

The mounds of snow collapsed like frozen corpses, lit by the pale glow of the streetlamps.

With its tin head higher and higher, the tinkling glass streetlamp cast its gaze into the window.

It lit the room with its radiant arms.

The naked old man bowed his gray head into his hands and staggered onto a chair, weeping.

In front of him, someone's body fell onto a pillow.

He closed the shutters, and it seemed that black waves of oblivion flooded the room.

You could hear rustling and sighs and someone's old plea about a love that was no more.

It was a black night.

Someone was calling someone from the darkness, "Again— again: it hurts, hurts."

Again. And again.

And the rooster crowed.

The dirty lecher—the city—undressed.

A pile of rags cascaded from it like a whispering waterfall, baring its old woman's body.

The more shamelessly the wind kissed it, the more shamelessly she mewed like a smitten kitten,

"Meeeeow-meeew-meeeaoow-meeee-oooow-iiikkhr . . ."

In the Old Days

The familiar outlines of buildings loomed unchanged.

They spoke of one and the same thing, always the same thing.

Everything will leave. Everything will pass. Leaving, it will bump into that which is coming in the opposite direction.

And it will remain unchanged.

The same.

Everything was flooded with darkness, and the tired colonel, with smoky gray rings, collapsed into the black shadows.

From under a mane of fallen hair, his eyes bored into the yellow flame of the hearth like ashy velvet.

A heap of stones blazed there like crackling gold coins, like a sighing leopard.

The leopard sighed for the same reason, the same reason: and the colonel's sleepy body, with its soul buried by gray spots, collapsed into oblivion.

From under the window, it was as if the familiar buildings collapsed into the blue darkness in pale, pale heaps.

The yellow and red sunset floated away behind the buildings like an extinguished cheetah streaked with black rings.

The stream under the window was cut off. Pleaded. Fell asleep.

The cawing of crows could be heard vaguely in the empty silence.

Again. And again.

And the bird flapped its black wings in the window.

The lonely, empty maw took in the hanged man, and he had nowhere to fall.

Under his feet the diamonds of constellations flickered from trillions of miles and days in the old days.

And the one hanging there fearlessly recognized the celestial from which the same voice sang as it did long before,

"Sleeeeplesssss niiightsss . . . Maaaad niiightsss . . .

Fiiiinaaal niii-

ghtsss liiittt

by a flaaaame . . ."

From beneath the wheels of the chair, the colonel jumped up and saw his gaze pricked with stars.

The yellow lace of the fire dragged itself along the ceiling of the scowling room, with peals of laughter thundering above the ceiling,

"Fiiiinaaal niii-

ghtsss flaaaame

aa . . ."

A leopard crawled on the horizon. It rested its heavy head in its red paws.

It lay down.

Its plaintive meow carried strangely from the shredded clouds.

Again. And again.

It was the wind moaning.

The flabby rooster tumbled into the colonel, singing about one and the same thing, one and the same thing, and burning with red spots of coal.

He cracked his knuckles and dropped a brown comb into his hands, "How will I survive this infidelity?"

The colonel looked at him, tired, from beneath his gray hair with a velvety soft laugh . . .

"Tra-ra-ra-ta . . . The old . . .

The same old.

There's always a duel. We're all joking, we're all laughing: laughing and collapsing.

The old . . . The same old . . ."

A heap of cinder was cooling in the hearth like the ashy corpse of a beast.

The stream under the window was cut off. Pleaded. Fell asleep.

Again. And again.

Having taken off the soaked cap, his body was twisted in the vast fur of his coat on the street, always the same, always the same.

It kept whispering with a faded face, whispered with its face, "All will come.

You'll feel like yourself again."

It ran from the shops. It ran to the shop.

At the chemist's counter it whispered steadily, it spoke of one and the same thing, and the flabby chemist stretched his arm and handed over a bottle of bromide, "All will come. You'll feel like yourself again. Bromide is a proven medicine, reliable."

But the weak body listened to him poorly, and his sick face fell into the fur of his overcoat.

So the overcoat spun around the street, returning home at a hurried jog.

But it didn't make it back.

A paper boat flew by on a puddle.

It took on water. It disintegrated.

The old overcoat stood strangely over the wet paper.

Again. And again.

And the caretaker with a broom shouted, "Watch out, your excellency."

Someone showed someone, "Look, look—

it's that soldier again: how old he is, dead."

And the overcoat ran away.

A fence bent over. The branch stretched out.

A slushy smack hit his cap.

Again. Now again.

His face, buried in the fur, poked out from the fur.

People walked by, not understanding what this doomed soul was asking of them in the distance.

Now. Now again.

"Ah, I don't have an ol . . ."

The carriage rumbled, "ld-ld-ld . . . ol-ld . . . the same old . . ."

It pleaded in the wind, "No, I don't have an old bo-dy—
the glooooowing . . . floooower of laaaate autuuumn,"
the weeping song poured from the building.

A dead gray coatrack crawled from under the fur, which had been
dropped on a lackey, and went to a restaurant.

The lackey hung the coat, streaked with velvety fur, like the skin
of a dead beast.

The colonel's body hunched over a chicken's body with a scowling mouth, circled with suede skin, like a big ashen beast.

A woman in the restaurant stared and whispered, fixing the velvet of her eyes at Svetozarov . . . "The colonel, who was spry not very
long ago, now sits there like a dead lump."

From beneath the silver-white crown of gray hair, the spot of a
corpse-like face was pathetically fixed on her, still chewing.

With Your Charm

And the lacy blizzards of the days loomed over Svetlova.

Blizzards loomed over her.

She cunningly trampled them with her silver slipper, like the air,
when she rose up and laughed charmingly, falling higher and higher—

she passed by:

behind her, above her, around her, her white mantle became
snowy with moiré, whistling to the sky, to the sky with its stormy
wings flapping.

Covered in the past, now she slyly, stormily flew backward from
the clouds of her days,

now she gazed into the azure of deep languor, stared into those wells,
and her head in a shining hat was reflected in them, and her breast

jingling with a necklace of cold, frozen swan's tears,

and her hand
with a burning icicle, like a stinging sword—with a loving rod.

Ah, but no:
but she was not wearing a snowy hat—
but the satin cowl of an airy mother abbess with the veil of days,
blown into the past;
and there definitely was no loving rod, but rather a powerful icy
staff to prevent her from wandering off into the rapids,
and not tears,
but an icy rosary, jingling into the past like cold, cold hail.

As if from the clouds of days,
so from the clouds of the blizzards she floated on a silver slipper,
like the moon from the clouds, like a child from a cradle,
like a soul from time.
So her silks were covered in the snow of millions of moments,
and flew up;
and her soul, the child, pleaded to be free of them.

"It's time for her to get sleepy. It's time to bring her down from
the heights.
The shadow will slip under her feet quickly when the black
abbess's shadow flies behind my poor wife.
It's time to open her eyes to the fact that she stands on the edge,
crosses a border that does not obey time."
"Take her over the border."
So said the colonel and her husband.

Her silks, brocades, wraps, snow, and snowy eddies, bubbling
with smoke, smoked them with lace and perfume when she stepped
out of the rooms toward them.

The lackey's sideburns rested on his white vest, like a distinguished mannequin, and he brought her a letter on a tray.

And in the storm of silks, she blushed; and first answered the men graciously, then read the lines of love as if disinterestedly—

but upwards, upwards—

to the moon's rapids, to its depths, shining like the moon, from beneath this satin, from beneath the seething snow of days twirling above her—

she floated up and away.

From beneath the Lyon lace raised to her face, like lace of snow on her fingers, she cast her gaze at the darkness of the lower depths—

at the vigilant colonel: he sat with his aiguillette swaying like a pendulum, marking the time.

As if time was keeping a watch on her—not time: a visage crowned with the laurels of lethal old age. But she, not heeding old man time, quickly stashed the note in her pocket.

And time won:

and the note slid, unnoticed, under the table; the Saint Bernard's drooling snout was fixed on the colonel,

and he pointed the dog toward the note;

and the dog, shuffling its paws, gave him the note with its mouth.

The old man read it on the sly and said,

"Ahem . . . they're planning another tryst."

He took a bitter puff of his cigar:

the smoky serpent, forming airy circles, floated from his mouth and encircled her.

But she walked through it, breaking the serpent with her silky knees.

Getting to her room, she thought about him, him, calling her to the silver temple with love, the abbot, took off her purple robe;

as if arriving like that storm and rising like that moon,

and her crystal hands—horribly transparent—threw open the window for him when the storm seethed there, when she was wreathed in its charm and pressed her biting lips, already kissed somewhere before, to its lips.

So she, the white abbess, stood with a slipper, clear as the moon, that she carried to the windowsill, her icy rosary jangling and frosting the glass; her robes turned her breast silver with the cold of the dancing storm and fluttered in the air over her shoulders.

No, she wasn't standing:

no, she was running through muslin stretched upward, and from there, where it is always empty, the sickle struck her slipper—making her leg shine like diamonds.

Now the sharp end cut her palm

when she

grabbed it, her sad child,

in the empty monastic commune and was burnt, but still squeezed to her breast—

squeezed the moon,

like a furious mother, like a sister drained of her tears, like a shameless lover.

The Fiery Wine Glass

The pink-lipped woman with trembling nostrils stirred and lowered her eyes under a gossamer veil speckled with black spots: and her hat, blowing a cloud of feathers on her neck, and her black moiré train, lifted slightly in her gloved hand, and the silver slippers on her feet, melting in a stormy cream of satin and lace—it all aroused in him vague, unquenchable desire.

He brought her hand to his lips, desiring her shamefully, quietly.

She put her hat by the mirror and fixed her hair.

He questioned her with his gaze, and she replied fervently, lowered her eyes, and her lips—slices of peach—impatiently trembled under her cheeks, under her black eyelashes; that's how she stood, breathing furiously as if she didn't see him.

Pale and squinting slightly, he grabbed her, his hands like the paws of a tiger, tore the black lace moiré on her heaving breast, searched for her mouth with his, pressed into it, and from beneath her mouth, half-open in his, she burned quickly, shamelessly, sweetly.

"My dear, let me be happy . . . let me."

And she let him take off her brassiere.

Her arms, bare and warm, covered her chest.

The soft cups gently swayed under the tight black corset.

When he grabbed her waist, her falling skirt has already ceased to rustle and she was left wearing only gossamer red silk, as if made of air.

Her hot waist softly melted in his hands.

So she froze, one hand covering her fluttering hips and her head dropped to the other hand which was clenching her corset, sunny curls scattered on her head and falling on her round, clearly outlined hips, "My body is tight and supple.

My night is hot and velvet."

Bending over, she swished between the arms of his shirt and he squeezed the emptiness.

She wasn't with him.

She beckoned him from the bed with her lily arm, enticingly sprawled on the white sheet like a red flower.

When he became intoxicated and quietly walked toward the bed, she covered herself with the crimson blanket, following his movements with fright, curiosity, and cruelty.

When he tore the blanket off her, she jumped up on the bed, bringing her knees to her chest, but he pushed her over and fell onto the pillows, and she covered her face with her hands.

When he lay next to her with his arms around her, she tore herself free, scratched him, turned away with rage, pushed him away with one leg and lowered the other leg to the floor, where she stood, naked, with her head down, covering her face with her hands, crying, and not wanted to taste love.

The door opened. Her husband entered, devouring his wife with a hungry gaze.

His laughter strangely echoed among the bright silence.

Again. And again.

And he left.

Reddish curls of hair covered her back and fell to her breast under her shirt, slipping from her shoulders, and she was hunched over pulling her satin stocking on her white leg.

And her red lips and her angry eyes flashed at her dear one when she shook her head, shooing away her thoughts, "It was shameless of me to call for you. It was shameless of you to heed my call. No, you aren't the one I dreamed of.

I am shameless. I will leave and go there. Everything returns there."

Soon she was standing haughtily, wearing a black dress, strapping her hat, lowering her veil, rustling with moiré, and leaving.

The rooster stood alone. He knew that now a duel was unavoidable.

His laughter flickered strangely in the slushy street.

Again. And again.

Carriages rumbled around him, "ld-ld-ld . . .

The same old."

The Little Child

She fell from the heavens, empty but satin.

Her crafty silver slipper got caught in the snow as the moon gets caught in a cloud—she fell with the same charming old days.

Under her was chaos, it streamed around her, and she, pushed away by someone's leg, slid along the hissing waves, a slightly rocking outline, making the shadowy outline of a shadowy flying abbess in a shadowy cowl, in blowing, airy silk, like the wind on a black night, and with a gush of air cutting sharply from her cold hands like a shepherd's staff.

> The moon, a sickle—
> a diamond slipper.
> Ah,
> the heavenly bride is gone—
> gone: many years will pass without the bride! . . .
> Ah,
> without the springtime, the white light will die.
> Ah, moon, a sickle—
> frozen: ah, diamond slipper!

In the shining, the abbess—a Shadow hopelessly threw back its head to admire the path of the desolate fatigue—Snow in a glimmering cowl burning below like white dust—a veil—her audacious diamond rosary jangling like hailstones, glaring with the steely shine of the icy staff, she twirled her snowy moiré toward the sky like a hissing wing.

That one darkened the expanse—the brilliance cut through this, and that one rejoiced—and this one wept: they both became snowy, shadowy, airborne with hissing tenderness—the white one and the black one, the holy one and the sinful one, in the same old place, Eternity.

Poor inhabitant of the earth: where will you find a holy place?
Go into the distance,
golden,
listen to her, to her.

But the mysterious passerby put his hand on her shoulder, "Why do you weep? This is a cold grave."
She awoke from her thoughts by a hole in the ice on a river.
Streams splashed like clear muslin steam.
Here is where she wanted to throw herself into the water; but here is where she began to wonder, "Is everything really lost?"
The streaming old man embraced her, and his white face bent over lovingly, "Remember, my dear, remember!"
She lifted her hand to her eyes and saw that it was her old friend, the one who had left her.

The circle closed.
Dear friend, save me from the torments of my conscience—
from the long road of the grave.
And she listened for an ancient tale. And covered her visage.
At that moment her miraculous and old friend appeared.
He said,
"Wake up"—
and pointed up, at the heavenly ray—
at its golden flames.

The locks of his hair fluttered in the wind, and, weeping, she stretched her hand to him.

He said, "A little longer: all that has gone will return.

You see, the grave is empty.

But run from your house, run to the place where I once ran—to the woods and pines."

He led her along the river. He spoke of the past, that it will return.

It is, it was, it will be.

That which was will be, that which will be is—always, always.

That is the message for the world.

So, yes.

She slid her trusting gaze up along the gossamer muslin, and from there, where everything was empty, a crescent protruded from a cloud—it made a brilliant earring.

He shamelessly slashed her soul with brilliance, a confused little child, and she—the child—she trustingly gave herself to the now empty monastery: herself, body and soul, and her sadness, like a sister drained of tears, like a desired wife, and like a beloved child.

The moon, a sickle—

the diamond slipper—

fell from the sky.

She walked on the snow in her diamond slipper.

Droplets

You, snow—a swarm of flakes; the ray fell—it began to get soaked.

It showered the pavement in tears.

Glowing dust—a yellow-bearing flower—sprayed from the gutter and dusted the passersby.

Snow slid by in the windows—dandelions, moist with the water of the spring day.

A sparking stream landed on the ice and floated on the frozen surface like a cold azure spot.

You could hear the rumble of carriages that started long ago and had no end, "Tra-ra-ra: this is my thundering rumble, my generous, old, spring thunder."

And the snow trickled. And the slush grew.
The springlike, the smiling approached.
It pleaded, "It's time for me to go to the old world.
Time to chase away the snow, spray streams of sparks.
To draw golden scales in the puddles.

Our life is gold brocade flying past on streams—
gold, brocaded reflections.
It's time—
because, if they don't wipe away the shimmer with metal, there will be no spring.
Because you throw yourself into the shimmering and splash the puddle."
The icicles of dripping lilies flashed in the flashing rays of the sun.
And gold droplets, hanging in nets, jangled like rays of sunlight.

The blue stream babbled under foot, first dark then gold.
Combs of white foam churned in it.
As if children had cast a little swan on the stream—a white paper boat—and now it jumped and took on water.
The frosted icicles, like dragonfly wings, glowed like crystals.
The sun struggled in the light-catching nets of water, like a caught fish.

It laughed in the wet glimmer of the wheat.

In the dewy windowpanes, in the jangling streams,
flower-chasing gold crescents danced and the outline of the spring bridegroom, made of sickles, trembled.

You, puddle—mirror of the bride: the sun will gaze, and you shine.

It sets: and you are covered in round icy pearls.

And the amber ice under the passerby's foot shatters like crunching rubies.

More Droplets

The worried duelist bowed.

The wind carried his squeaky voice, and a tuft of hair fluttered under his cocked hat.

His flabby, proper face frowned over what was to come.

Everything seemed sad and wet—springlike.

The muzzle of a revolver was pointed at Adam Petrovich. The moment dragged on.

His life flashed before his eyes.

His surroundings seemed eternally familiar, something tender and velvet began to fall, and he was shocked that he was lying in the snow: someone beckoned him somewhere, as in childhood.

A rooster-like, worried voice echoed in the distance, something in the sunny air felt like home, and his consciousness was extinguished.

The sun shone dully, and the snow streamed silver and tin.

As if everything was covered in tin foil.

Svetlov cried, "Colonel, colonel: our life is a fleeting spirit."

But the colonel was dousing the wounded man's face, strewn with blood, from a pitcher and coldly said, "I don't know and I don't want to know!"

He gagged, and his face wrinkled up not quite from laughter, not quite from coughing, not quite from weeping.

A cheerful rain dripped from the rooftops.

"Tap-tap," they counted the melting slush; "din-din," the pieces fell to the sidewalk and shattered. "Krshshsh," they scraped snow from the asphalt.

"Tak-tak," a red balloon, tied to a boy's coat, jumped cheerfully.

In every glass cover of the streetlamp, blinding balloons ceaselessly and noiselessly burst and flew off in all directions.

Everything melted, everything flew.

The gold sunny scales fell into the slush and crawled with the passersby.

And the rumbling of the carriages echoed, "Tap-tap-ld-ld-din -din-ld-ld-krshsh . . ."

"Tur-lur-lu," this was the water of springtime swirling at the feet of the passersby in foamy bubbles, eternally bursting like beads torn by the water.

The Enchanter

Adam Petrovich's body was weak and limp, he drooped his bloody head as he was carried, and it turned red with spots seeping through the bandage, dark spots.

They laid him down.

"A pillow. Another pillow."

And he drowned in the mild warmth of the pillows.

The blind, cruel walls squeezed him in their stony embrace, and the smoky yellow flame of the candle in a radiant halo, like the cap of a burning dandelion, danced in silent mockery,

"You're free . . . No: you're in prison."

He lifted his fiery yellow face—burning up—off the pillow, and, enchanted by his cell, he moaned when the enchanter floated in on shuffling shoes from the black pit of the door.

His gray, dead face floated from the abyss into the yellow light, and the enchanter's red velvet robe, streaked with dark rings, whispered, whispered about the same things . . . no, not about that, because this was the colonel.

In flowing velvet, his avenging face was fixed on the yellow flame in the hearth.

From beneath the hearth's iron grate, a glowing beast rested its snout on a soft paw, grabbing it with its claws like a maddening golden heap.

The colonel buried the pincers into the glowing crevice and the mad beast gnawed on them, roasting them like a crackling fang.

The colonel said that the darkness will pour over the patient and the patient, running to his beloved, has fallen into the shadow of death;

that he is a faithful friend to him, his old friend; and that his friend had come to the patient to change his bandages.

In stark raving, the patient flailed his wax arms under the pillow; he began to understand that the treacherous enchanter had shackled it, his soul, with these gray walls and that it, his soul, under the enchanter's spell, now languished over his head in a sorcerer's trap.

"With my hand, stormy like the whirlwind, I will smash the walls myself and rescue it from this prison," he moaned when, scrawny, gossamer, white, like a dying swan flapping its wings, he waved his arms and his burst of energy left him: a soft, snow-white swan splashed, piercing the walls with its cold feathers.

A soft velvet robe streaked with gray rings lifted its yellow hand.

A smoky, pale beaded swan, fluttering its splashing feather, on the attack, rocked above the old one.

The yellow and red sleeve tore apart the swan and traced a fiery circle, like lightning, with a cigarette.

Little beads of smoke splintered and dug into the darkness like foam flowing from water.

Sinister currents streamed toward the patient's brow from under the leaden hand that had fallen in the velvet flame.

"Water is dripping from under your wet bandages, Adam Petrovich, so I'll cool you with some ice."

Despairing, she languished above the roof under the enchanter's power over time, and her childish voice asked for mercy when the scarlet enchanter made a circle of time on the table.

The patient moaned, "That's enough, time, she's in his power, she's in agony."

And in the enchanter's chambers the prisoner was in agony, she languished without him, "I dee

sssire . . .

I suu

ffffer.

My soo

uuul laaaanguishes withoooout him . . .

I deesssire, I suuu

uuuu-"

"A conservatory student is singing over your head," said the colonel, "but I'll have her move. This idiotic, idiotic singing isn't good for you now."

From behind the iron hearth the enchanter shuffled and disappeared with his slippers and velvet into the black hole of the door.

She panted from behind the enchanted walls over the patient's head.

He grabbed a candle that had been left behind with his yellow, yellow hand from under the pale sheet.

Red, red stingers, like a downpour of fire, now tore from the flying sword.

It sprayed the black hole of the door with the flame of its burning blade, blocking the enchanter's way.

And the sword falling on the colonel in the darkness elicited swarms of golden sparks from his eyes.

With his pale, waxy brow, flying onto his back, poured sparks from his eyes into the darkness.

The prisoner was killing the enchanter with his wild strength, but the enchanter appeared again and coldly tore the radiant sword from the prisoner and twirled its yellow velvet blade over him.

With his other fiery hand, he took the pincers from the hearth, from the jaws of the beast.

And the patient cried out and stood up and beat the enchanter with his fist and tossed him into the jaws of the beast, and the golden beast stepped out of the iron grate and consumed the enchanter, clasped him with his red paw; and the cursed enchanter gave off puffs of burning filth and stretched his yellow arms from the velvety soft embrace of the fire.

People came running. They screamed.

Again. And again.

And the patient screamed with them, raving over the burning old man,

"I have defeated time."

And there, over the ceiling, the soul was calling, in agony,
I dee
sssire . . .
I suu
ffffer.
My soo
uuul laaaanguishes withooooout him . . .
I deessssire, I suuu
uuuu-"
It called in agony.

The Blue of the Lord

The patient came to; a head lowered toward him, whispered, and disappeared.

"You were sick, bedridden, babbling a lot of nonsense, and burned the old man.

It's not good to burn your friends."

Someone added, "At such times, oh Lord. With a broom, with a broom—

with a broom-oh-lord, Lord have mercy."

A censer flew by, its chain jangling, belched smoke, and disappeared.

He realized that they were burying him.

His puffy body covered in yellow bubbles was lifted on shoulders in a plank coffin and carried to a desolate place.

So they carried him, but under the coffin they whispered, "So you burned me, but still didn't get her.

We will bury you in the desolate past where the Judge of All Things will not see you."

But the dead man said, "Carry me to the Judge: I want only the truth: let the truth of judgment be enacted on me."

And the body prayed, "I am a sick body suffering from shortness of breath and am covered in bubbles."

Then the dead man got up and tipped over his coffin; he walked his bitter path alone.

He turned around—the old days cruelly bit their nails on a cloud, but its long trail circled in the distance.

A white cupola floated closer in the distance. The elder came from there.

He stretched out his arms and approached him penitently.

And a ridge grew and grew in the blue of the smoking clouds.

The miracle-working old man's sparking halo, his foot resting on the snowy hill, the lightning trident in his hands, and his thunderous right hand flying low like a cloud—he had long carried in his soul the image of a saint, a quick-footed helpmate secretly sent to him.

Everything thundered under the saint. The cloud flew into an abyss of shadow.

And from his halo the old man spoke with a streaming beard, pointing with his trident at the same thing, the same thing,

"The serpent crawls under the cloud. His tail, made from time, is winding. It approaches in trillions of moments. It pleads: it's time for me to go to the sky.

It's time to shackle the heavenly heights with an endless serpentine ring.

The serpent shackled the earth. There, the woman escapes from him: she is imprisoned by the serpent's strength.

His tail wraps around her, strangles her.

And the woman pleads: I am on the earth, but I am faithful to the sky.

It's time, my son, to intoxicate her with the sky, to carry her off to the sunny monastery.

Come down to her like a pilgrim.

Not before will the serpent leave the woman, because she is still obedient to time."

He looked beneath the cupola of the cloud. Smoke rose from the earth.

The scaly rings of a dragon crawled into space.

It noiselessly soared into the sky, unchanged.

The lightning trident that the elder had put down glimmered on the edge of the cupola. The elder walked into a cloudy cave; his halo glimmered; thunder rumbled in the cave with a mysterious call.

Clouds covered the firmament. The firmament was blue with reflections.

The hour approached.

The white thundering clouds, bubbling with smoke like a lake with ripples, seized the turquoise flight; it first froze and then scattered like sandy smoke.

Bursting with anger, he stood on the white heights, gazing at the horror of the airy rapids, first flying up with the puffy cloud, then falling.

And the serpent crawled out of invincible life, flashing its scales.

As if a fish head had been placed on it and crowned with a pointy comb of feathers—and now it exuded a stream of red filth into the turquoise sky.

As if a fiery stinger burned the air, dim with soot—and now he thought that down below he was battling the serpent.

Time—a serpent whose rings would draw you to the sky—was floating in blue timelessness.
He stood, rising over time, drinking in the azure.

But it drew you into space, first empty then obscured by clouds.
It crawled upward through space, a watery snake, crawling out of a blue well, first diving under the cloud, then floating above it.
White thundering walls stood over the past, and it perforated them with its gaze.
As if a well had opened up in airy granite—and now serpentine time was floating from the blue well to the cloudy shore—a serpent with tempting rings.

The sun, clothed in brilliance, quietly bent over the well from behind a cloud and its rays—tridents—stung time and the serpent crawling from time with three stingers.
That wasn't the sun—the abbot clothed in might, pouring out brilliance, fiercely tossed his lightning trident down over the serpent.
And his trident stung the past: the past froze, turning glassy like a dry empty web, burnt out like an empty streetlamp, fluttering like clouds and sunny might, falling from heights above the clouds.

When the trident descended on the serpent, time clenched its serpentine rings.
When it spilled out its trillions of moments on the ground, old men ran with cloudy steps, emitting thunder and shouts.

When the dying serpent drowned in the depths and from there radiated a scaly glow like a webbed beetle,
a voice then echoed from the mightiest cloudy tower,
"The Blue of the Lord has defeated time."

Then the gold body of the sun set in the tatters of the clouds.
No one could say that this wasn't a monastery's cupola among snow-covered hills and fields.
A white cloudy road stretched forth from the earth.
It looked like a snow-covered path.
Blue floods of space washed over it like floods of water in the springtime.
The dying serpent lay down here.

And then bees, bathed in light, flowed from the earth to meet the serpent-slayer, carrying candles; the shining abbot victoriously glowed at them.
The radiant woman, its azure, stretched her hands to the abbot, tore the dying serpent apart when she emerged from her ancient dungeon.
The weak serpent, like a beetle, fluttered its dry membrane.
But the abbot shifted the ray of light, and darkness drowned the past.

And he stood with his fire-bearing visage in the pale, pale turquoise.
And the women from the sun's monastery flowed on him in the pale, pale turquoise.
And the old sun, like a warrior shackled in gold distinctly plunging into snow and clouds, stood in the pale, pale turquoise.

Paris.[22] *1907.*

PART FOUR: FUNEREAL AZURE

The White Lily

The storm whipped up a pale whirlwind.

It tossed the snow upward, and white lilies rocked above the fields.

Buzzing, everything flew by, everything flew away.

The storm scattered the smoke of the pale snow—it bloomed like a handful of blossoming white lilies—like a lace bridal veil made of stars, stars.

Ribbons of melodious silver flew up and flew by—enveloping.

They collided, smashing the snow.

The gossamer snowy vestment stretched out over the fields with a hiss, with a glimmer, with the aroma of early spring.

The snow, dancing with a glimmer and fluttering, like lace, with blue, grew familiar.

The abbess lowered her head. Her cheeks began to sparkle.

The silver velvet one crunched toward her; she cast blue, blue flowers at the passing nun from under the saucers of her eyelashes.

With a slightly raised visage, the nun first pressed herself close to her kerchief, then folded her mittens on her breast, "Mother Abbess, you are adorned. You have been pressing lilac branches in your cell.

Who has made our monastery bright?"

But the abbess pointed out the snowstorm to her, "There they are, the lilac branches . . ."

But she walked away helplessly: the sequins of her black silk cast a humble gaze, like a languidly sighing rustle.

The black stream already flowed in the distance: a line of nuns with buckets on their shoulders stretched out to the well and sprinkled clumps of tracks with their feet—clumps of snowy flowers.

The snowstorm breathed with a languid chant, not for the first time.

The snowstorm stretched out its flowering white branches and shook its branches.

And the branches scattered white flowers of the field.

With a squeal, with a squeal the fields bloomed with scattered silver, like the soul with psalms.

In the fields the snowy brother sprinkled pearls of snow with his shimmering miter.

Threads of silver shook on his sleeve, the holy man of the fields.

His cold image descended from the azure on the monastery with a whistle and glimmer.

Covered in white flowers, the abbess silently laughed: you could see how there, past the monastery, the monk fell upon the young woman.

He sprayed silver snow in the young woman's face.

He grabbed her black waist and whispered, "Don't leave, my dear."

She twisted, jumped back, put her hand in the basket, and, waving a rose, resoundingly scratched his face with a thorn.

The young abbess saw it all and laughed at it all, "Fall in love, be affectionate, play with snow and a flower."

The nun scattered flower petals in the snow on the border between the monastery and the decrepit world.

In the distance the snowy brother was turning the vinegar of memory into joy and snow.

Covered in a white robe, he held his diamond arms, like lilies, in the fire of the evening light.

He scattered ecstasy and silver from lilies of the field, loved one, distant one.

And the lilies scattered like handfuls of diamonds. Hundreds of buzzing gnats lay at his feet.

And the gnats went dim.

This was the early spring blizzard.

In the turquoise of the dusk you could see the black silhouette of the hunched-over abbess on the border between the monastery and the decrepit world, where a wooden pillar held up the tender image of the Virgin Mary. A light, dry beetle fluttered above the abbess.

That was the light on the pillar, pealing in the wind: its rays hit the snow like the dry membrane of wings, harsh and yellow.

The lamp, tinkling in the wind, was pestered, pestered by the past.

The hive glowed white in the distance. Yellow wasps crawled along the wall.

Wasp after wasp crawled along the wall and into a hole.

Nuns with lanterns walked along this evening wall, walked around the monastery, and plunged through the gates.

Suddenly a flock of silver birds flapped their wings from under the white wall of a snowdrift: with a screech, their glowing crests rushed about, and they flew off quickly, noisily, rejoicingly.

Everything rushed by like snowy birds—like clear screeches.

They rushed by, flew off, and froze in the distance, screeching.

She lifted her pink, kind face from under her black kerchief.

She smiled.

It was cold and clear. Nothing had changed. The monastery's round cupolas shimmered.

The snowdrift, swirling like a string of flies, grew airily into the sky. The white string spread out obsequiously like an explosive fan;

it pounded with a whistle, a laugh, a glimmer, like a noisy fountain in the blue air.

Funereal Azure

White thunderclouds, boiling with anger like a lake, seized the turquoise expanse with their rings, and from there, a gazing old man was holding a coffin lid; he first grew like a puffy cloud and then put his foot on the snowy hill,

"Rise: for the grave is empty because the blue of the Lord has defeated time."

The softly streaming snow, boiling with smoke, like wings of swishing satin, grabbed the old man, and the one who had died, returned from beyond the grave, rose up and put his foot on the diamond snowdrift, crisscrossed with ice.

He said, "Am I alive? There is blue above me. Have I not died from my wounds?"

A smoky snake descended from the invincible heights, twisting its snowy rings.

Like a fish head, wafting blue and crowned with a silver comb of unkempt snow, it stood on them both—and like a stream of cold snow, it obediently lay at their feet.

And the elder said, "Exactly: the sting of death has pierced you, and you have been sick for two years now. Your mind has gone soft. It's been two years since I brought you to my peaceful cell. I took care of you. I prayed. God has been merciful: it's time, rise up, pilgrim, once again tread on the old earth."

The shroud, roiling with smoke, fluttering with snow in the snow, merged with him, stormed like a streaming blizzard, and the pilgrim recognized his old forgotten friend.

The gossamer white roiling serpent flew up from their feet, and handfuls of sparks adorned his snowy scales with a glimmer.

A vast expanse stretched out before the pilgrim. And, reaching out his gossamer arms, he said, "The sun is setting—setting."

And it set.

A plain covered in ice stretched out around him, and the blizzard danced above it.

But his mysterious friend placed a hand on his shoulder and led him to the grave: in the deep pit, clearly delineated by the boards of the coffin, there was no bottom but rather a stretch of funereal azure reaching for the rapids under the clouds.

When he looked at the funereal azure, he saw a sky and earth beyond the grave; when he looked there, he also saw time: it twisted in serpentine rings—as if they were empty, his scaly panes, drafty with light, lifelessly rattled like dying death.

When he stared into the grave with the sunken dead serpent, the old man's voice echoed above him, "The blue of the Lord has defeated time."

He turned around. The elder sighed, "We both were once alive—and both died: but death has died."

We did not expect it: songs sounded out in the snow, weeping—we did not expect it.

Now sickness, sadness, lamentation have melted in the snow.

The pilgrim understood that the plain covered in ice was just clouds, pouring over the firmament. Above the plain—there in the distance—the serpentine rings of the dragon turned red, and the pilgrim, overcome with fear, hid his face in the old man's robes.

"The serpent is still in the heavens—it rises again."

The elder said, "Now it won't sting. It is not unchanging. It's melting. Judgment is being passed on it."

But this does not mean that there was no serpent.

Everything was covered in snow. His old friend was also covered in snow, "Joyful snow, bright snow—snow."

He squinted at a hut with his face, ruby-red from the frost—a kind face, radiant from prayer.

He went into the hut.

The crimson speck in the lamp gently flickered.

He folded his lilies (not lilies—arms) and bent over slightly.

He whispered, and his eyes were shrouded not with gossamer tears—but with pearls, "Joy, joy—

you are with us."

And the words flowed like the extract of flowers—like a lily (it was a lily, the extract of flowers).

The elder was radiant, like a child.

He approached the book even more radiantly.

He muttered.

And he rustled the amber pages.

You could hear a song blossoming—it began and had no end.

This was the snow falling.

An almond branch stretched through the crevice in the door, and white flakes fell from it onto the old man, coldly adorning his feet.

The world is vast, it is close by, we are on the earth.

On the earth—

so be it, oh, so be it:

old man, why the fit?

Old man, swiftly spill the lily.

The world is vast: it is close by, we are on the earth.

The pilgrim was alone.

The lightly hissing walls soared above him, but someone had knocked them down.

He stared into the well of the grave—nothing was there.

The cross rustled, covered in snowy brilliance and the enamel of a smashed crown on the outline of someone's unknown grave,

"Remember me in Your kingdom.

I have not risen—I am ill, befuddled by reason."

He raised his hand.

His stormy fingers streamed with hissing silver, and it seemed to him that he was not alive—that he was transparent.

Be at peace with the saints: he was both here and far away.

Remember me in Your kingdom, remember: my Savior, in Your palace—

of gold—

remember me in Your palace of gold!

We shall sing, brothers, arms open wide, "Bright palace!"

They sang: no one replied.

The young abbess went to the elder—she was clear as the light of the dawn. And, stretching out her arms, she said, "The sun has set—it's gone down."

Yes, it had set.

There she stood, bowing her black cowl, and the elder's right hand was stretched over her in blessing.

Groaning, he gave her some golden wine, gave her—some wine poured in a cup.

Then he mixed it with water, "Drink, my dear—drink the sweetness."

And the nun drank and sat there, black with a white face. And her eyes—azure—rested on the one praying, like the sky from the clouds, "I sat here yesterday.

And thought about something.

That I too was part of this world.

But that time has passed. And now I sit here.

Sit and think about something."

The old man lifted his old face, bright as the dawn, at her.

And the black rosary first dropped, rustling, into her lowered hands and then flew over her cowl in her gossamer fingers.

The pilgrim's eyes gazed lovingly from under the icy stalks in the window when he was drawn to the song in the stormy pillar.

The nun's eyes flashed like the sun when she looked over from the window at the elder.

But the elder was mournful, "My worker is walking there under the windows. He's lost his mind.

He walks and thinks that he's snowing.

But our time has come. Go, mother abbess: it's time for you to go to the monastery."

He stretched out his hand. White bunches of his robe shattered the golden mirror of the sunset.

He brought her icon to his lips—a piece of gold.

In parting, he said, "A little longer: time will stop; the world will stop marching forward.

And the past will return."

Snowy trumpeters stood in the windows: they trumpeted at the sky with their puffy trumpets, noisily, ecstatically, joyfully.

They trumpeted with blinding flashes.

The abbess smiled, "I am leaving the elder and going back home to the monastery."

Her tracks, black spots, stretched behind her in the snow.

Sorrowful tribe, bitterly imprisoned, ceaseless racing ahead—for how long?
But then:
the pain is soothed with soothing oblivion.
The years will pass and, melting away, time will go dim.
But until then—
the river of time calls.
So, then:
forward, always forward—year after year.
Oh, golden sorrow!

Polyeleos

The woman elder had a dream.

The scaly serpent was rocking smoothly on its golden rings.

When it dragged itself into the church, it crawled onto the altar and performed mass from under its hairy snout, weighed down with spite, caustic gray blasphemy spraying from its larynx.

When it dragged itself over the monastery, the stormy serpent crawled through the sky, spewing snow like crystals of white hail from its cold jaws.

In the morning the bishop rode up to the monastery, and he first stuck his head out of the carriage and then cunningly hunched into his sable coat, "So, what will greet me in this heretical monastery?"

A gossamer stormy bee descended on the carriage.

It stung the bishop with its icy stinger.

The young abbess was already hunched over on the porch with bread and salt.

The rippling snow caressed her, spilling handfuls of flowery stones at her feet, and she burned her gaze into the wailing women, meekly falling before the bishop ("Who doesn't bite their tongue?"), and then inhaled the snowy myrrh of prophecy.

The bishop's carriage drove away from her porch, making a delicate white flower with its golden serpent.

The parquet floor glimmered with wax. The abbess's cross on a chain dangled above it in the black silk on her porcelain neck.

Her mantle rustled behind her in the darkness, "My lord, make yourself at home: we are the same as everybody."

The dead cheekbones of the novice trembled fiercely under her kerchief, and her lips were sealed shut.

Like a thundering serpent, the bishop's face hissed, but the cunning heretic bowed without answering, "I don't know . . . don't know . . ."

The intoxication of meeting the blizzard was mirrored in the threatening noise of fate.

Icy fingers knocked at the windows.

The thundering serpent crawled out of the abbess's cell, rustling his robes.

The bishop led services in the church.

The cuckoo's cry of the clergy cried from the choir when, with a slightly raised old man's face, the golden bishop walked down holding a chalice,

"Most pious, most sovereign . . ."

The cuckoo's cry of the cuckooing stormy cleric cried plaintively in the windows.

The bishop wrapped himself in his fur coat without answering and hissed a hiss in parting, as if flying off on the wings of the blizzard, "Everything here is as it was. They reported you for no reason."

The black abbess cried out behind him, stinging the porch with her sharp stick, "Things are different, you snake, everything here, you little snake, is different."

Through a crack in the carriage, the stormy warrior stormily screeched at the bishop with a stormy sickle.

The abbess grew like silk, unnoticed, among the nuns and penitent and attacked like a black panther, shook her heavy, sharp cross, praised the approaching pilgrim, and ran off.

The stormy pillar buzzed and grew, rushed at her like a white beast, covered her with flowers, and slid away.

The nuns were worried.

The penitent, moved by the spirit, followed the clear-eyed prophetess,

first bending over and then jumping back.

And in the distance the stormy pillar passed through the fields, like a pilgrim, as if it were weeping,

first bending over and then straightening up.

That's how the call to those asleep sounded, but in the distance everything came to a stop in a sweeping whirlwind of rumors.

That's how the call to those asleep sounded, but far away everything merged with the resounding laughter of the dancing blizzard.

The abbess entered the church. Someone familiar dressed a black owl in shining robes of color and lit them with a candle.

A ray penetrated the blizzard. Someone familiar tore up the lace of the blizzard and covered the snow with color: they glowed with the gossamer colored feathers.

The abbess stood wearing gossamer colored feathers; and tears—pearls—filled her glassy eyes.

She ran from the church. Someone familiar, wearing a clerical cap, walked off into the stormy pillar.

He stood there past the monastery in the gossamer feathers of the blizzard, and snowflakes poured from his glassy eyes.

The blizzard sang out, "The years, flowing by unnoticed, have passed, filled up the cup of time, poured out into the past, and returned."

The abbess's eyes, in the shadow of her eyelashes, lowered, glowed with happiness, and went dim.

The pillar of the blizzard rose up unnoticed, rushed at the monastery, covered it in snow, wept enticingly, and flew on.

The sun clothed the woman in a golden mantle of rays streaked with spots, and now the mantle flew from her shoulders.

The abbot, clothed in the sun, gently raised a chalice filled with wine, and now the nuns partook of the blood.

The nuns were clothed in white garments, like linen, streaked with purple flowers, and now they stood holding small candles.

The sun was clothed in stormy foam, like silver, burning with a luster, and now the stormy foam floated above the monastery.

The pilgrim's eyes seemed to gaze lovingly from behind icy glass stalks when he pressed up to the window in the stormy pillar.

Her eyes flashed lovingly at the storm from the altar pulpit when she cast her sharp, sharp gaze at the window.

From its ceaseless prayers to Christ, the monastery was moved by the spirit and assembled the crowds passionately, powerfully, and prophetically with bells ringing into the blue air from behind the monastery walls.

A laughing stream of snow pounded from the ceaseless winds with a cold lacy roar, a hiss, the glimmer of early spring from behind the monastery walls into the blue air.

Drunk on the Spirit

The young abbess made her way through the snow, gathering her black mantle, blowing like a sail, in her hand while fixing her cowl with the other hand and bending her sweet pink face toward her breast.

When the snow blew from under her and seized her waist, she planted her feet on the portico: so she stood with swirling robes, her blue eyes looking up high, making sweeping signs of the cross on herself.

The black, black women elders were bowing, with horns glowing with flame dancing over their cowls, with tails rustling by the altar pulpit and shredded swarms of sparks crawling like red bees into the incense, their brows marked with carnation blood and the flames of wax spears—it all resounded in them about something, the same thing, when they sedately flowed with their aging faces, velvet cowls, and flames.

So they flowed, one after the other, and the beautiful woman, clutching a rosary, drooped her head with its golden lock of hair not hidden by her veil, since she had lowered her veil, which now washed over her shoulders.

This pink-lipped young abbess with trembling nostrils rustled her rosary and bowed, and the dark smoke swirling to the floor from her cowl, the large cross on a chain, and the silver knob of the staff the icon painter was gripping—all froze in her with an appeal, a plea.

Do I, frozen in snowy satin, not seek You, Radiant Savior, kissing—
my Savior?
Do I, with my feet on the ground, not rise up, lighting the blizzard, Radiant Savior—
my Savior?

When the deacon's right hand flew up unexpectedly from the blue space behind the iconostasis, swinging the censer, the nuns bowed, sighed, and stood still.

When the wind enveloped the abbess's red house in silver lace, the house was blown through with pink spots in the blizzard.

When the wind swirled its white cloth, the abbess's exposed house turned red among the snowdrifts; but the wind enveloped it again in its lace.

When the service was finished, the brocaded abbot ran from the altar with a bunch of red flowers.

When the service was finished, the nun braided her velvet cowl with warm, fresh roses.

When the service was finished, the clear-eyed youths in a fire of flowers laughed with one another with crystal laughter.

Gossamer vestments scratched at the church's grated windows with their snowy brocade.

The spirit illuminated the mother abbess, and she bent her satin waist while her dexterous fingers, with a tinkling rosary, flapped the black folds of her moiré mantle like wings swishing in the sky: that was how she stood there, drinking in the joy; her eyes burned hungrily under her silky lashes; her hands tore at the bright sprigs of roses and the cross on a chain on her heaving bosom, and a cry flew from her half-opened lips, tender and crimson and sweet.

Now the sisters, captivated by her cry like big wild swallows whose wings were tired of flapping before a flight, sister with sister came dancing by in their dead robes and bright roses; and from under their pointed cowls, from under their dark and long dresses, they pressed dewy sprigs of flowers to their lips, and the mother abbess laughed in the flowers and kissed them passionately, countlessly.

The pure young girls, the sweet young women,
ah,
raise your dewy, juicy chalices,
flowered!
—"We suuffffer . . . We deesssire . . .
Our soouuul laaaanguishes withoooout him . . ."
Ah, flowers, silk, bows—and you:
you are the ringing of the bells! It pains them—
it pains them with joy, pains!
—"We suuffffer . . .
We deesss . . ."

In the open doors of the church, a shining cloud bowed down toward the porch from the blue, blue expanse. It tenderly sprinkled the dancing sisters with the cold of the snow and a diamond flower.

Its arms, white and drooping like flowers, covered the porch in cold, delicate snow, as if in soft velvet.

One of the sisters was gray-haired: her eyes dashed to the ceiling. The pale whites of her eyes, like eggshells, were fixed on the cupola.

Another sister, a young woman, twirled, frowning.

It was terrible to see the jumping cowls, the sails of puffed-out robes in the bright church.

This was the dance of the spirit.

Have you now guessed that it is I, it is I?

I will open the door.

Dear sisters, do I not sigh in the distance?

In the open doors of the iconostasis, a clear-eyed face was fixed on everybody from the dully shining glass. He meekly came into view among the penitent outbursts, with the blue of his eyes and the ripe stalks of his beard.

His pearly hands spread the red cloth over the sisters like tongues of flame.

It was an icon.

The storm bent over the little windows, pressed up against them, "I am air, velvet.

I am cold, fleeting."

It flew away, and a blue emptiness shone in the little windows.

Take one another by the hand, love each other today: begone with pain and suffering, begone with worry—passion of the Lord.

The more helplessly, madly the sisters, drunk on the spirit, flew in dance, the more hungrily they hovered over the food—the descendent of the abbot and the hunched women elders and the beautiful women, the young women, the young girls, the widows in black, the women with pale faces, pink lips; they handed the chalice to one another, the chalice of light, spread the petals of their lips and swallowed the wine.

And the yellow wine, a roiling flower, hissed in the cups and spread foam on their edges.

The abbess bowed her gossamer face, made of air, above each of them, and the pockmarked woman elder crouching at her feet dipped her bitter roses in the wine, sprinkled her hands with moist purple, kissed her fingers with her withered lips, tore at the cunning black silk on her breast, gave her a glass of wine, and wept; and when the beautiful woman laughed and put her lips to the glass, a diamond bouquet of scattered roses hung in the air for a moment and then flew down in a shower of rays of light.

The storm raged. A pearly face flashed from the altar in a majestic flame of robes: a piece of the frosted glass cracked, flew from the window, tinkled, and shattered.

This was the window breaking into shards in the storm.

And then, extinguishing the fires, he passed through the window with the soft, soft storm showering stars and grabbed her waist; she dropped her head in the wildly flying snow.

—"We suuffffer . . . We deesssire . . ."
"Of your
servant . . .
for there is no
sickness, sadness . . . lamenta- . . ."
—"And it laaaanguishes
withooooout him . . ."

The Dead Man

The pilgrim's clothes fell from him as a lacy blizzard falls from the day; and he shook them cunningly, rising up over death when, doing carpentry for the elder, he laughed madly at his mundane work—he planed the board even more madly:

the bonds of the grave came from him, were above him, around him, washing into the past with hissing shovels, washing; he turned to the past with his cap shining with snow and his awl swishing with shaving on the log—ah, but no:

it wasn't his cap, covered in snow: it was the diamond headdress of the holy man of the fields in flame,

flaring up and going dim;

his icy hands dropped into the days, sliced the days—and the days tumbled away.

And it wasn't a shroud over his shoulder like an oar: timelessness was washing off his shoulders in hazy spots of time and moments.

And his awl wasn't cutting shavings—no, and no: the storm was cutting snowdrifts, and the snowdrift rose loftily to the sky like a string of golden flies—flew over the abbess's window like a lacy fountain, white with foam, hissing, glimmering, laughing.

Yellow shavings fell in the loose snow.

The cap bobbed in the clear light of dawn.

The laughing face of one of the nuns gazed at from behind the bushes, enamored of the one in the cap, and quickly hid when he turned his face, full of reproach, toward her.

Then the nun left for the monastery, where the pilgrim was basking like a gently storming pillar in the blizzard.

Everything in his soul that was covered in snow was hidden for a time.

She saw—he was doing carpentry in the cold, wearing a white robe and yellow birch sandals—gossamer and clear-eyed.

He saw the nun. With an easy motion, he swung his melodious ax at a log.

The icy path of a stream burst through a snowy crevice like a frozen, azure string.

Snow fell like almond blossoms and didn't stop falling.

A path of golden, trodden tracks wound in the snow.

The blind walked along it.

Sighing sadly, he touched their gazes. He silently ran his soft mittens along their faces.

He flared up. Their blind faces flared up.

Their eyes were opened. They saw the light.

As from a cloud of days, as from a cloud of the blizzard, he now floated clear-eyed and transparent, like the moon from the clouds, like a soul from time, like an angel from the tempest of its feathers.

The clear-eyed nun ran toward him, waving her hands, jutting out her peach-shaped lips to drink a snowflake from his yellow sandal.

The pilgrim laughed strangely and shook his finger at her, "You would distract me, but I don't have time: I have to work."

"Ahhhh . . ."

And the nun flowed back to the monastery, ashamed, to cluck out a psalm.

The snowy stream twirled. It sprayed the nun in the face with cold. She fell to her knees.

Again. And again.

The pilgrim stretched his hand out behind her.

His hand flew like a snowy lily. His other hand sprayed snow in the field.

Again. And again.

A large airy tablecloth flew past the nun. He flew by her like a large airy tablecloth.

The elder caught up to the nun, "Don't come here in the evening. My servant isn't right in the head.

He thinks he's snowing."

He ran away from the nun, his black back hunched. A man in a white cap was bent low over a log, planing it.

Walking back to his cell, he kept thinking about how he, he who had risen from the dead, would pull back the stormy robes from the world and the world would turn into the very same storm that seethed sonorously under the blue, palely glowing crescent;

and his crystal hands, horribly transparent, threw open the door when the elder was seething at him there, "What are you, dreaming? You and I are alive: nothing of the sort did or will happen."

But he smiled with the serpentine wisdom of his old friend.

So he—a gossamer dead man—stood with a bright beard, like the crescent moon covered in the blue of the evening, and his fingers frosted the door with ice, as if frozen to it.

The nun ran from cell to cell, flustered by the pilgrim.

You could hear the buzzing of the surprised women elders, the buzzing of many spindles that had begun and had no end: a majestic old woman was running around the courtyard, trailing the wind of resurrection, the wind of a psalm behind her.

You could hear the clear-eyed nuns' majestic clucking of psalms, of bells ringing in the cells and in the snow: and the young women of the choir spread the sweet smell of the prayer candles.

Night came, and the old man forgot the sternness of the day and said, "It's time for dead men to go home."

Silver and gossamer, they flowed back to the grave cunningly, opened the coffin, and, with earthly steps, descended into the glorious past because the snowy field was the field of a big cloud flying along the firmament.

Arches streamed around them and along some kind of cloudy ledge, and they made their way to a hole that looked into a hissing land of ether.

They ran under the moon, down gossamer muslin bridges, and their shadows, running on the cloud beneath their feet like flying black monks, flew along with them like swallows.

With a shameless glimmer, the crystal wings of the heavenly flyers blew in the distance, in the distance like rushing swarm of fireflies, humming under the starry monastery—to them all, to them all: with the mournfulness of the world, and the flying horror, and sadness, and the tears a sister sheds in the world, and the call of the women; and they just barely were able to remember, "Ohhhh. . . . Ohhhh. . . ." And a new word was spoken.

Now two shining monks, crisscrossing the sky with their flight, horrified with ecstasy, were shouting "Ohhhh . . . Ohhhh . . ." but it came out "Holy, Holy, Holy."

In the morning, the elder prayed and the pilgrim did carpentry, not recalling the night.

Riding the Moon

"My dear, make me happy . . . make me."

At dawn the abbess pressed her marvelous face to the unknown grave.

Her warm hands fell on the exposed breast of the gravestone, and her slightly raised chest quivered under her ruffled silk with a swish where her silver cross coldly jangled on the bare gravestone.

When she grabbed the heavy, icy figure of the coffin, her spirits lowered into the distant past, into the porcelain whisper of graveside flowers, and the gnawing of the snow exposed the stone grave, shackled with ice; her marvelous, marvelous face was reflected in the crystallized gravestones with its trembling nostrils, covered with a black wave of her silk kerchief escaping from under her cowl.

The cemetery with many crosses, tormented by gusts of wind, moaned in a passionate voice, widening its fiery lantern eyes—now amber, now crimson—in loving torture, like the blade of a storm swirling in the morning, like the veil of a coquettish bride torn from her by the bridegroom at the very hour of the wedding—it shook and stretched out its crowned arms—dozens of crosses—to it, to the wind: porcelain petals, clinking, fell onto the gravestones.

The wind questioned cunningly, the beautiful woman responded with a tremble, and the ancient cemetery flickered powerfully and turned its amber gaze to the wind; and the porcelain crowns tinkled.

And an unknown gray woman, trampling on the grave from time immemorial, helplessly rushed into the blizzard with a stony gust; the wind seized her chiseled waist with its breezy blizzard, tore at her marble waist and heavy breast with its streams, touched her granite mouth with its cold mouth, and pounded at the unfurled folds of her clothes stormily, shamelessly, powerfully.

With one hand
the mad abbess tore at the gravestone;
with her other hand she
grabbed the cross, pressed her head to it, crimson from the glow of the lamp—
fell down, fell down—
with the silk of her mantle licking the cross like black flames, as if it were washed by the wind from her well-defined legs and thighs.

A snowy shroud wrapped around a blue and kind face in the grave—blue, tender, with eyelashes velvet as the night.

Her white leg, raised above the funereal azure, bent and swished with silk from under her mantle.

The kind one wasn't there: the white crescent shone so deeply, so deeply in the blue languorous well, and the stars just barely twinkled.

The funereal azure beckoned with its delights, showed its vastness, showed that which isn't shown to anyone, and the beautiful woman in black lifted her robe—sprinted there with her white legs:

she raced from above, her clothes fluttering—there, there: there she sunk like a black rose in the blue of a well.

When she bowed down with effort, like a taut black javelin thrown into the rapids, like a screeching swallow flapping its taut wings—past the cloud, past it—to the stars, to the horns of the cracked moon melting with azure; when she mounted the crescent with her warm, white legs and silks flying upward with the long whispering black tail of her mantle, like a serpent, her long robe twisting right and left;

when the moon cut the cool of the bluish-blue air right and left with its extended blade and, whisking it away, set, set;

when she bent her breast to its soft, pale horn, mockingly rattling, and it ripped open her breast with acrid, wild ecstasy, spent long ago:

then everything in her shouted in the funereal azure, everything—she and the stars, gazing at her with long gazes as in old days and kissing her blue with their precious, lofty mouths, already kissed somewhere before:

then her dead white head with scarlet lips, bit by sharp teeth and the red flame of her unwound braids from under a kerchief, and the rosary, jangling in the air like a melodious lash rewarding a strange mocking stallion with its blows, her heart clenched with wondrous delight; then the curves of her satin waist and her black stockings with red laces and over the stockings the milky color of her enchantress's legs and her velvet cowl pointing forward like a dark horn and her evil depraved gaze from beneath the arc of her lowered eyebrows—everything burned with old magic, ancient magic.

But the cold horns of the moon wrapped around her legs—not horns: someone's strong arms dragged her into the past; and it wasn't she who flew, but her saddled back, which drew her on: now from behind her back it rose—big and scowling for her love like a glass head wearing a crown of silver and white hair, and it looked at her with its long gaze. Then time stopped for her—a naked old man galloping through the sky, "It came down to us looking for its dear one and met me instead: I fly, fly, we fly—fly from the fount of forgetfulness."

The desolate heavens gazed tenderly, tenderly. And a cry flew from her lips, enticing, moaning,

"I suu

ffffer.

My soo

uuul laaaanguishes withoooout

him . . ."

There were white puffs of flying, forgetful clouds under the galloping pair of horses. And time dragged her through them, and she was grabbed by cold puffy felt, her fingers: and the bottoms of the clouds tossed thunder and lightning at the silver and white old man, and with his black and purple face aflame, he rode downward.

And so the enchantress remained on the cloud like a black airy shadow, and she was already sliding upward as if she were drawn to the streak of azure of the cloud hanging over everything, and from there she bowed, mad from her memories—and the shadow slid by.

And she was the shadow of the snow-cloud husband.

Now the snow-cloud husband rose up like an airy abbot in a diamond miter bent over at his blinding waist, and his cold fingers calmly and steadily carried the vestige of the moon into the tinkling of shining rays, like the remains of a diamond chalice filled with light.

He drank an ancient drink of days gone past, which called forth anguish, and in the blue streak of the cloud hanging over everything he still gazed with a deep anguish that, like love, calls more and more incessantly—it calls, it weeps, it caresses, and it rocks the child's cradle of the orphan's soul abducted by time.

With his other hand he lowered his pearly trident downward, a radiant, sharp current of lightning into the depths.

His shadow followed him, like the tumbling abbess's cowl.

Now he stood over the streak of clouds—now, look, he stood: taking a drink, he let go of the vestige of the crystal chalice and flew off into the tall heights like the morning moon.

Now he stood above the funereal azure: now he stood, but his shadow lay in the outline of flight as if in a bluish-blue grave, covered in smoke, like snow.

"Caaaapture
the exciiiteeemeeent of
passiooooon-
ahhh."

The abbess awoke on someone's unknown grave, frosted with ice.

The morning crescent hung in the sky like the petal of a bent lily, barely noticeable, white.

The man in the cap stood over the fallen abbess with clear eyes.

He bowed and said to her, "Remember, my dear: the grave is empty."

The wind twisted his clothing like a muslin petal.

He lifted her up, smiled at her, and fixed the flame of the graveside lamp.

The red lamps creaked, blown by the wind.

The cemetery with many crosses, tormented by gusts of wind, moaned in a passionate voice, widening its fiery amber eyes in loving torture; it shook and stretched out its crowned arms—dozens of crosses—to it, to the wind: porcelain petals, clinking, fell onto the gravestones.

She Remembered!

The storm sighed without reply, and she remembered the rustle of violins in the theater where she had once spread out a train of forget-me-nots, where they reveled in her, were in awe of her, breathed her in; where her dear one smiled at her and called her somewhere, as in childhood.

But the stern one in the cap, standing over her, touched her, and they moved away from her memories.

There the snowy lilies of the valley waved their branches: there they took in the expanse with ease.

There was the flight of the snowy foam, buzzing in the expanse and melding with the dusk.

They wandered through the fields all day.

She walked alongside the pilgrim numbly, and her black veil twirled behind her cowl.

She lowered her eyes modestly, as if she were confessing, "I left the world: I loved, but it was a dream I loved, not him."

And the pilgrim bowed his golden beard: the wind began to tear at his curls; his dull face smiled with a velvet smile, just slightly frightening, "No, you loved him!"

He stood there pale, squinting slightly, and the storm sang in his soul, as it did before.

The blizzard's paw first stroked them and then wildly scratched them with its needles, stars, and snowy pearls.

They lifted their blue eyes at one another, blue, and closed them, squinting with the black silk of their eyelashes, sad, not recognizing one another.

The gray uniform rose up, and a gossamer glossy face in a halo of leafy gray hair was fixed on the mother abbess and began singing, as it had sung to her many times before,

"Hooow I wiiiish to beliiiieeeve and looooove!"

But the pilgrim covered the glossy face with his bright palm—and she saw that a lantern with a tin silver top was creaking in the wind at the top of a tall gray pillar.

The pilgrim said, "It's guarding the past at the border of the decrepit world."

They walked by, and the glass lantern spun behind her on its wooden post, "I loved and now I am dead."

The sun swayed toward the earth and plunged down.

And it plunged down.

And there where the earth had eaten its golden fruit, red juice flowed into the sky.

They stood on a gray stone from where the water fell.

The water current had now frozen, and cold pieces of ice, like a crown of delicate strings, rose up from the granite brow into the velvet of the snowdrifts.

She stomped the stone with her fur boot like the skull of a giant that had been thrown back.

The giant's face meagerly gnawed with dead laughter: the wind whimpered in the icy crevice of its mouth, "Friend of my days, I have returned in a dream."

She turned away from the past with a heavy heart.

The blizzard cast snowy embraces.

The fiery yellow sunset went dim over the fields.

She clutched her rosary and said, "Why did my dear one have a bright, bright face? In life he was like a pilgrim."

And he bent toward her: his lips opened like pieces of a crimson peach sliced with a knife, "I too am a pilgrim."

She looked into the pilgrim's unearthly pearly face and recognized the features she had never forgotten.

"It was I who whispered about the resurrection, but you killed me: I died and was resurrected. It was I who fought for you and descended into hell, where you left me."

Like a black swallow, she leaned on the one in the cap, but the breezy abbot wearing a pearly miter screeched the slashing sickle of the storm over her,

"Scree ... scree ... I ... I ...

My fury is with me . . ."

The robed wailing one fell on the stone, and the fleeting face of the blizzard attacked, shattered against the stone: white bees floated under her collar to buzz about the irretrievable.

And in the distance, in the distance the one in the cap left her, dropped his face, outlined with tears, into his mittens, shedding a salty pearl for her and pleading with her for death.

She opened the crimson crown of her mouth behind him, shaking the little crystals of glassy tears off into the snow.

The stormy clouds spread out. The snowy whirlwind called, and the cold cast a perfect snowstorm into the sky.

Song from the Abyss

When the one in the cap left, she remained by the lantern at the border between the monastery and the decrepit world.

The lantern, like a rearing beast, scowled with its glass jaws at her love, spewing out first the snowy whirlwind and then its glass (the storm had shattered it).

Its stormy hands flew over her like the claws of a beast,
flew after her.

"Who runs from me? No, no one . . ."

In fear, she ran from it, fell into a snowdrift, and got up again.

And the beastly, ancient roar chased after her.

All the same.

The monastery was astir.

In those days the pilgrim had left for the many-hilled crest as if he had plunged into a stormy ocean.

Aromatic smoke streamed, and the oblique rays of the sun, splintered by the smoke, splashed frighteningly in the church over the nuns' cowls like distant rays of a call to prayer over the orphaned wailing women.

The abbess walked to her cell and cried out, surprised by a dog's shadow cutting across the snow.

Roaring, it stuck its beastly face at her through the window
and bared its teeth at her.

She said, "Our past is the shadow of a beast running by.

The beast drags itself along with us in the blizzard, leading us home.

Home."

This barking dog, whose bloody jaws were scowling at the woman clothed in silk, had previously been wandering in the fields and was now running just outside the monastery.

Its shaggy snout would appear here and there.

Sometimes it wagged its tail, "Who will feed me? No, no one . . ."

The abbess was afraid and walked around it, but the nuns gave it bread.

And the shaggy dog prowled around the monastery, old, having run from the expanse.

The blizzard swirled, and the dog bellowed, covered with snow.
It plunged into the snow.
The blizzard sang, "I am the blizzard—life flying away.
Now, like a white bird, I will soar like a sea of cold feathers.
I float above you, unchanging—to our motherland . . .
To our unknown motherland."

In the Land of Diamonds

The deceased dead were hunched over in an open grave. Bits of blizzard streamed from the elder's and the pilgrim's robes.

The frosted cover of a coffin lay at their feet, and constellations flared up and dimmed in the funereal azure. Their frosted faces bowed down into the funereal azure where clouds flew by and then flew back.

The pilgrim's eyes were first sad and then rejoiced in nonexistence, and with a reedy voice he said, "Here my spouse is sad and in anguish; and the Lord will permit her to be taken."

A man with many wings peeped out of the coffin, "Who asks of the Lord God?" A white angel peeped out of a streak of azure sky, "Who has not seen the clouds of Glory?" The elder ran to the entrance to the tomb, "But of course tonight He will float by here." The pilgrim ran to the cloudy white entrance, "But of course the Lord will permit her to be taken up."

The blue ether kissed them tenderly and tossed a handful of diamond streaks of lightning at them.

A white church floated by noisily, and the thunderous ranks of elders flashed their swords from the clouds. And swarms of buzzing spears spun in the dark of night from a mysterious cloud. And the thunder of thundering hordes deafeningly thundered with their copper horns from the floating monastery.

Radiant, they prayed on the cloudy ledge.

Diamond insects circled above them, coming out of the jangling censer.

Sprinkled with a buzzing glow of sparks, they first praised the Lord and then pleaded for the death of the suffering abbess.

A pearly, thunderous face showed its crown from behind the smoky altar, and its right hand flew up from the smoke with a censer.

Diamond beetles, a serpentine stream of sparks, flew up and, twisting, were sprinkled in their hair.

The pearly old man stood up and asked, "Who calls me?" The young dead man fell down and asked, "Who am I, to see You?"

The pearly old man pronounced in a whisper, "Let it be as you wish!"

A thunderous roar announced, "Let Thy will be done!"

The cloud floated by and cast handfuls of lightning into the shadows.

The pale day floated in and extinguished the constellations.

And swarms of buzzing dragonflies flew in the sky like a blinding cloud in the pale blue of night: then swarms of distant angels flew down from the ledge of a cloud in a frightened detachment in the burning of the clear dawn.

Third Blizzard Litany

The dead man arrived at the monastery.

His face shone fiercely with thunderous white light.

A snowflake hissed fiercely under his feet like an almond blossom. His cry resounded fiercely,

"The blue of the Lord has defeated time!"

The beautiful woman pressed up against the window frame, praying for her beloved. The beautiful woman met her springtime praying for her beloved.

Her hands tore at a rosary on her breast in anguish. He rested his hands on his breast in anguish, beloved and meek.

"The blue of the Lord has defeated time!"

Suddenly she pounded the little window passionately; she pounded the golden air with a red stream of flowers over the one in the cap.

The storm passionately raised it up under the sun, raised a white stream of flowers into the snowy air over the clear-eyed abbess.

The red flowers fell at his feet. White petals spun past her face.

"The blue of the Lord has defeated time!"

You arrived—unfading color, you are clothed in the lace of snowy robes: your eyes are the blizzard blowing through the sky.

The blizzard gave birth to you: give us a blizzard, give, give, give us white blizzard, a roaring blizzard, a blizzard—a flying blizzard, a hissing blizzard, for you have come from the storm.

Let us pray to the storm!

Hello, hello, white bee flying to us from the hive of the blizzard to buzz about happiness, to collect sweet honey from the honeycomb, from hearts.

You, happiness, are white, honey, wax!

Buzz out the liturgy for us in your bee's voice!

Have mercy on us!

The robed beautiful woman held a rosary, and her pale marble face was everywhere, growing behind the one in the cap. The loud, joyful cry of the blizzard dancers in the snowy fields grew with a fierce voice over the spruce grove.

The blizzard extended its white embrace toward everyone in the monastery, pelting their eyes with white salt, eliciting sadness; it crumbled like birds lying at his feet.

The abbess extended her embrace to him and with a burning pain fixed her eyes on him from under her veil, dark, like the darkness of night. But he shut his eyelashes over his eyes, desired and stern.

When he walked past her, she leaped out at him like an enchantress in black, holding a carnation. When the serpent of the sun lit up the sky, the blizzard leaped and carried away its darkness wildly, wildly like a robed flyer in distant fields.

The pilgrim's lips were mute with barely visible pleasure, but he hid his face with his palms, turned toward her, protecting himself from the carnations.

The blizzard's trumpets thundered with thunderous joy, and the sun's ring concealed its ardor.

Oh bee of bees, oh soul of souls, oh dawn of dawns—they buzz, they bake, they shine bright.

Bees, bees:

now you are bees.

You are leading the king of the bees to the hive.

Swarm, swarm: soon the white king will fly from the hive on golden wings, buzzing.

Fly after him, brother bees, fly to battle with the wasps, flash your stinging tongues in their dark souls.

Yours are with you—dawn with dawn, soul with soul, bee with bee.

Come to us, our bee!

The abbess undressed in her cell. The blizzard whispered under her window.

The white snowy ship swished, sailing to the sunny city on snowy waves; it sailed to the burning circle.

The swish of the black silk waves—the waterfall of the cascading robes, came from the dance of her naked arms.

The abbess undressed in her cell. The blizzard whispered under her window.

A small red lamp lit her cowl, entwined with flowers, and the gossamer batiste wrapped around her breast. The stormy dance covered the monastery in its silk.

The abbess undid the silky fabric on her hair, put on her silver cowl, and wound lily-colored satin around herself as she prepared to meet him.

The storm whipped the purple fabric; a radiant circle rose in the silver of her weeping. It called in a breezy voice, "I love you. Why do you not answer?"

In you, snow, is a kiss, in you is the laughter of the wind—loving words.

Like a glimmer, like a whistle, like a dance, like a lacy robe—like a robe you descend on us.

Like snowy communion, like a cold white fire—blow; hit.

And they sing snowy psalms in the stormy liturgy.

Let us pray to the storm.

Hearts' purple boils like snowy wine, come.

Take the snowy foam for communion, taste the white foam.

Clothe yourself in white foam, in lace: your faces are snow, your lips are purple, your eyes are the sky.

Snow unto snow, sky unto sky, dawn unto dawn!

This silvery crown of the blizzard above you—this bridal crown above you.

Let us pray to the storm.

The Meeting

The whistle of the wind and the sadly familiar rustle of the storm echoed over the monastery.

And snowy robes left for the pale, pale turquoise. The abbess's silhouette was seen with a golden candle, and now she, the white bride, went to the icy fields following the enticing call of the storm.

A pointy crown of fire crackled over her head.

Holding the candle up, she fell under the gossamer gold of the sunny leaves,

"Enough—

for us it's rough: for us the joy is rough.

Ah, you rush to us, to us, and in rays of sun you melt.

And in the snowy fields, pearly, a golden calm is felt."

And he walked into the pale, pale turquoise with a fire-bearing eye. And the blizzard tore into the pale, pale turquoise with a whirl-wind-bearing cry. And he walked into the pale, pale turquoise with a fire-bearing eye.

He . . . No, not him.

The sun beat on the icy pillar of the lamp, and he turned his glassy gaze toward the monastery. The blizzard twirled the windy pillar, as in days of old, and he twisted his dust, glowing.

And a wave of stormy flowers breathed flakes of puff into the pale, pale turquoise.

The blizzard rose up like a large dandelion plucked in the early spring day.

The abbess traced a flame-bearing serpent in the fields with the sparking tooth of the candle.

The serpent crawled along: the light-bearing forerunners had crawled to the monastery on this path of stinging bees.

The brothers of the light flowed like shining stingers.

In the distance they carried the dead man's golden coffin.

The white satin beautiful woman, wearing purple from head to toe, stood holding an icon.

She stretched the icon and flowers toward the coffin.

And he was resurrected from the grave: the sun flowed from his face.

They touched one another with their velvet eyes as if they we going to a familiar, bluish-blue well.

The censer sprinkled snow, red serpents.

They carried the golden holy chalice to the fields; and bright coals glowed in them from behind the clouds. But the coals grew like flowers.

The acerbic copper, the color of the chalice, coated their faces with a dull, waxy languor, and the choir sang,

"He is not without change: he leaves for timelessness—into the pale, pale turquoise.

He has wings to hide from us.

But this does not mean that he is not with us.

He stands up among us: he pounds the azure goblet with metal strings.

When the goblet of blizzards overflows, he spills the snow on us.

He returns . . . he returns."

The abbess led the pilgrim to the altar while she stood by the door.

"Come, abbot made of brilliance, bridegroom born of the candles of childhood in the fields.

Come, bridegroom from distant lands beyond the grave to clothe me in love and the sun.

Your robes are made of foamy brilliance and are awash in luster.

In yours, abbot, your luster!

We will take a bright stalk and wind the stalk around our waist, the stalk, the sunny stalk!

It will grow in our souls!

For we are yours—we are your fields: fields, fields, fields ready for harvest!

Your fields, field hand."

The Serpent Is Defeated

A sea of cowls stirred under the altar pulpit.

She stood with fragrant myrrh.

The abbot's silhouette grew, his face bright and pearly.

His sunny locks of hair and slightly forked smile glowed in the evening light.

"My dear man, you again, again!"

It was he—her vague dream.

He stood as if made of air.

His uneasy breast heaved.

The incense scattered at his feet, the holy bees, cooled like coals.

Two bees were caught in the sunny woman's hair when he lifted his arms above her and called enticingly from time with a voice like a sigh,

"Enough:

Soon everything will fly by—fly past.

Time has dried up and rattles like a scroll.

Time, like a scroll, rolls up.

It's time

because everything has flown by and we will be together.

Because now the one who has been resurrected has come to shout about resurrection!"

She

You, abbot, are a brocaded flower made of snow!

He

You, woman, bride, are my swan.

She

We are under the cupola that has been dropped over us.

Her waist was entwined by a white vestment, and the choir roared, calling them to the liturgy,
"Let us pray to the storm!"

The church doors burst open. The bishop floated in wearing his fiery robes, like a large red dragon.
Flames of candles stretched out on the pale, pale turquoise of the church frescoes behind him like the scaly crest of a golden crawling serpent.
Black crowds of sullen monks thronged behind him, longtime enemies of the monastery.

A group of faithful nuns, praying by the altar pulpit, blocked the dragon's way with burning candles, made signs of the cross over him with candles, and the candles, like swords, fiercely licked the air.
Red clumps of bees, a bright swarm of holy incantations, plunged their stingers into the dark crowd.

Jangling the gold cases of the censers like white rings, they surrounded the bishop, and made his miter glow in a streak of turquoise.

Moved by the spirit, the woman went up to the pulpit and looked at the awful airy rapids, first covered in smoke, then shining as if a fish head with a crown of gold were staring at her—and now the serpent flashed its staff at her.

As if a flash of lightning had cut through the cloud of incense—and she recognized the one whom she had killed with the spirit.

Time—the bishop, robes drawn into the church—went up to the altar pulpit where she had arisen over him.

She stood over the bishop with a cross and a purple flower.

The abbess called from the altar, casting clouds of incense at the crown-bearing serpent.

The clouds were prayers born of the spirit, white stones that flew into the past.

And they were shattered by the glowing miter.

She squeezed the flashing cross in her hand and emitted splendor with the cross.

The old bishop bent over.

The church disappeared, rumbling with the crowd, when white clouds of incense blocked the way to the altar pulpit.

The old man floated up on the stairs as if between smoky cupolas, first dipping his miter, then floating back up.

A cloud of incense hung above him, and he broke it up with his staff like lightning.

And when the golden serpent crawled up to the altar pulpit, the abbot appeared from behind the iconostasis doors, as if he were made of air.

He stood with arms open in the gossamer gold of clouds of incense.

His head, leaning forward from behind the woman's shoulders, was a circle of light above his face; the light of the candlestick that he was holding was terrible as his right hand threatened the serpent—spots of stormy light poured over the woman.

Everything thundered under the clouds, rising up like a black regiment.

And the miracle-working pilgrim spoke to the woman, pointing with the candlestick at the same thing, the same thing,

"The serpent crawls toward us. It will rise up at us and plead: it is time to shackle your purity, woman, with the serpentine ring of return.

You were shackled by the earth. Now you are faithful to the sky.

It is time for us to drink in our love, to smite the serpent, and to leave for the sunny monastery."

And the dragon's mouth opened with a dark wail.

It spewed iron and shredded the woman's robe.

He saw—the sun clothed in brilliance quietly toppling over him from behind a cloud and the light-bearing eight-pointed ray of the cross cutting through space.

It was not the sun, but the woman pouring forth light and clouds fiercely waving a cross over him.

From the dusky turquoise, the past stood before her like a golden insect.

His robes hung from him like dry wings.

When the cross fell on his miter, his crunched skull was bloodied.

When his body collapsed without a sound, writhing in serpentine rings, his miter spun like a golden wheel.

When the dragon was defeated, a cluster of nuns shouted in a great voice, "The woman has smashed the serpent's head."

Only Snow, Only Wind!

The storm raged.

A pearly face flashed from the altar in a majestic flame of robes: a piece of the dull glass cracked, flew from the window, tinkled, and shattered.

The sweet, sweet sky glowed—sweet, sweet funereal azure.

In the blue oceans of languor, the white crescent called deeply and the stars barely, barely twinkled there.

And their robes streamed like the blizzard when they were going there.

Their silver cowls cunningly floated up from the stormy white waves, like children; like children, they laughed madly, madly, rising up—

higher, higher—

they passed by: behind them, under them, around them, their swishing mantles were covered in snowy moiré, like petals of lilies rocking in the air, with white smoke, a whistle, a glimmer, the aroma of early spring.

Higher, higher—

they passed by: from beneath a cloud of robes, as from a cloud of days, they tumbled into the past—now he showed her the azure of blue languor in the air, bent over her by these wells,

bent down with his flashing cap and his whole gossamer body, glittering in her face like trillions of diamonds, frozen diamonds, oceans of tears blown by the snowstorm.

He touched her dying mouth with his mouth, hot like tears.

Ah, but no:

it was not the mother abbess: it was his sister, his sad child, streaming snowflakes into the earthly past.

Tears, tears—her tears: tears of a child falling into a snowy cradle, tears of joy—

filling her cradle: pouring pure crystals over the sonorously roaring monastery.

She bent her blinding waist in the bubbling foam of the sea, and her cold fingers—the edges of feathery clouds—tore the crystal vestige of the moon from the sky in shining rays.

And from this chalice he drank in her love.

They drank in the ancient, ancient drink that induces anguish in our breast with a storm of dying love, singing about the same things—

as in times of old—

they drank in seemingly the same blizzard and the same moon—

and their horribly familiar faces, dreams from childhood, as if tossed about by the same storm, the same bubbling foam—these faces bowed toward the mortal end lifting up the blizzard and the moon and the airy monastery, now and forever.

The red church and red walls of the monastery, clothed in glimmering, in the distance, in the distance, flashed under the clouds,

flashed and floated away.

Not the monastery: the old, red sun, doomed to death, floated into the clouds,

flashed and floated away.

And not it—the image of the world—slid away under their feet—not it: no, it was they who floated away like stormy, spraying foam.

Something sang to her, "I will rush you off into the heavenly heights: you are now awake and you know.

Remember, ah, remember: it is I, it is I.

I am the wind!"

And the wind carried her like an image once dreamed, like the pilgrim who loved her, like ancient, ancient anguish flying away to boundless heights.

And she was—only snow, only snow.

The wind flew by; she rose up like snow, and they soared like a snowstorm.

A Miracle

A white sleeve rose up along the wall. And behind it grew another.

A white sleeve, oozing over the grave, steadily grew. It licked the gravestone.

And slid away.

White sails bellowed over the coffins.

Aerial ships flew over the coffins.

The white-winged flyers rushed off through time . . . to their motherland.

To their unknown motherland.

Puffs of incense dissipated helplessly. The bishop who had stumbled got up with embarrassment.

And the stooped women elders, and the beautiful women, and the novices, and the adolescents, and the widows, black with pale faces and pink mouths, were moving toward the iconostasis doors behind the abbess, behind the pilgrim.

The more excitedly the sisters, drunk on the spirit, searched for the runaways—the bishop and the stooped women elders, and the beautiful women, and the novices, and the adolescents, and the widows, black with pale faces and pink mouths—the more powerfully the elder stood at the altar pulpit, pointing to the iconostasis doors,

"About that which was from the beginning, which we heard, which we saw with our own eyes, which we touched—about the word of life.

I will proclaim that to you.

Do not seek the dead: those who have been resurrected and ascended.

As they have ascended now, so we will ascend—for we too are children."

A clear-eyed visage was fixed on everybody from dull light glass in the open iconostasis doors.

It shone meekly with the blue of its eyes and a beard like ripe wheat among the reverent cries.

Its pearly hands spread its red cloths over the sisters, like tongues of flame.

From there the silver visage of the bowing woman melded into the glass; bowing, the woman poured holy oil at his pearly feet and wiped them with the amber gold of her hair.

In the window, the gossamer swan floated above the crystal ice.

And another flew behind it.

The white swan, dripping snow, flew upward in order to pound at the glass with its stormy wing.

It rushed up high.

Clouds of swans rushed to the sky. The white-winged flyers flew off through time.

The black, black women elders were bowing before the miracle, with horns glowing with flame dancing over their cowls, with tails rustling by the altar pulpit, and shredded swarms of sparks crawling like red bees into the incense, their brows marked with carnation blood and the flames of wax spears—it all resounded in them about something, forever the same thing, when they sedately flowed by with their aging faces, velvet cowls, and flames.

Now the blizzard rose up like an airy white abbess, bending its satin waist under the window, and its cold fingers, with the tinkling of an icy rosary, splashed a silver wave in the moiré mantle like wings swishing in the sky: so she reached for the window; the empty heavens gazed tenderly from beneath her eyelashes, tenderly; with her hands she tore at the diamonds of her silk robe, ripped to pale shreds, and a call flew from her lips with an ecstatic moan.

The cemetery with many crosses, tormented by gusts of wind, moaned in a passionate voice, spreading out its lantern in loving torture—fiery, amber eyes—stormy blades swirling like a veil torn to pieces by the bride at the very hour of the wedding; it shook its arms—dozens of crosses—and stretched them out to Him in ancient anguish.

Petrovskoe.[23] *1907.*

NOTES

INTRODUCTION

1. From the cycle "Sunsets" (*Zakaty*). Andrei Bely, *Zoloto v lazuri* (Moscow: Skorpion, 1904), 13–14.
2. Andrei Bely, *Nachalo veka* (Moscow: Khudozhestvennaia literatura, 1990), 20.
3. On Russian Symbolism and modernism, see Leonid Livak, *In Search of Russian Modernism* (Baltimore: Johns Hopkins University Press, 2018); Jonathan Stone, *The Institutions of Russian Modernism* (Evanston, Ill.: Northwestern University Press, 2017); Avril Pyman, *A History of Russian Symbolism* (Cambridge: Cambridge University Press, 1994); Ronald Peterson, *A History of Russian Symbolism* (Philadelphia: John Benjamins, 1993).
4. See David Bethea, *The Shape of the Apocalypse in Modern Russian Fiction* (Princeton, N.J.: Princeton University Press, 1989); and Irene Masing-Delic, *Abolishing Death: A Salvation Myth of Russian Twentieth-Century Literature* (Stanford, Calif.: Stanford University Press, 1992).
5. See Jonathan Stone, "The Literal Symbolist: Solov'ev, Briusov, and the Reader of Early Russian Symbolism," *Russian Review* 67, no. 3 (2008): 373–86; and Stone, *The Institutions of Russian Modernism*, 35–98.
6. This mantra became familiar to Russian readers from Vyacheslav Ivanov's 1908 essay "Two Elements in Contemporary Symbolism." Viacheslav Ivanov, *Selected Essays*, trans. Robert Bird (Evanston, Ill.: Northwestern University Press, 2001), 28.
7. Solovyov is featured prominently in the *Dramatic Symphony* and *The Goblet of Blizzards*. His brother Mikhail, brother's wife Olga, and nephew Sergei were the Bugaevs' neighbors at Arbat 5 and played an extremely significant role in steering Bely toward a literary career (Mikhail Solovyov even suggested the pseudonym "Andrei Bely").
8. See Stone, *The Institutions of Russian Modernism*.
9. A. V. Lavrov, "Andrei Bely and the Argonauts' Mythmaking," in *Creating Life: The Aesthetic Utopia of Russian Modernism*, ed. Irina Paperno and Joan Delaney Grossman (Stanford, Calif.: Stanford University Press, 1994), 87.

10. In this volume, the *Symphonies* are presented in the order in which they were written, not published. The *Dramatic Symphony* was completed in 1901 and published in 1902, while the *Northern Symphony* was completed in 1900 but not published until 1904. However, even in their first appearances in print Bely labeled them "2nd Symphony" and "1st Symphony," respectively, making the order of composition clear to the readers.

11. Vladimir E. Alexandrov, *Andrei Bely: The Major Symbolist Fiction* (Cambridge, Mass.: Harvard University Press, 1985), 5.

12. Roger Keys, *The Reluctant Modernist: Andrei Belyi and the Development of Russian Fiction 1902–1914* (Oxford: Clarendon Press, 1996), 126.

13. A. V. Lavrov, *Andrei Belyi v 1900-e gody* (Moscow: Novoe literaturnoe obozrenie, 1995), 42.

14. Keys, *The Reluctant Modernist*, 130.

15. Alexandrov, *Andrei Bely: The Major Symbolist Fiction*, 9–10.

16. Andrei Bely, *Simfonii*, ed. A. V. Lavrov (Leningrad: Khudozhestvennaia literatura, 1991), 421–41.

17. E. K. Metner, "Simfonii Andreia Belogo," reprinted in *Andrei Belyi: Pro et contra*, ed. D. K. Burlaka (St. Petersburg: RKhGI, 2004), 44–45.

18. See Keys, *The Reluctant Modernist*, 146.

19. Alexandrov and Keys both emphasize the importance of these thinkers in the development of Bely's literary works. Alexandrov, *Andrei Bely: The Major Symbolist Fiction*, 27–28, 30–38; Keys, *The Reluctant Modernist*, 111–17. There is a wealth of scholarship on Nietzsche's role in Russian culture. His influence on the Symbolists is directly addressed by Bernice Rosenthal and Edith Clowes. See Bernice Glatzer Rosenthal, ed., *Nietzsche in Russia* (Princeton, N.J.: Princeton University Press, 1986); Edith Clowes, *The Revolution of Moral Consciousness: Nietzsche in Russian Literature, 1890–1914* (DeKalb: Northern Illinois University Press, 1988).

20. A. V. Lavrov and John Malmstad, "Andrei Bely's 'Most Beautiful Lady,' " in "Vash rytsar'," *Andrei Bely: Pis'ma k M. K. Morozovoi, 1901–1928* (Moscow: Progress-Pleiada, 2006), 9.

21. Charles Baudelaire, *Oeuvres completes*, vol. 1 (Paris: Gallimard, 1975), 11.

22. Andrey Bely, *Selected Essays of Andrey Bely*, ed. and trans. Steven Cassedy (Berkeley: University of California Press, 1985), 81.

23. Particularly in key works such as "The Emblematics of Meaning" (1909), *Glossolalia* (1922), and *Gogol's Artistry* (1934). See *Selected Essays of Andrey Bely*, 111–97; *Glossolalia: A Poem About Sound*, trans. Thomas Beyers (Hudson, N.Y.: Steiner Books, 2004); *Gogol's Artistry*, trans. Christopher Colbath (Evanston, Ill.: Northwestern University Press, 2009).

24. Bely, *Selected Essays of Andrey Bely*, 110.

25. Valerii Briusov, "Otvet [1894]," in *Sredi stikhov, 1894–1924: manifesty, stat'i, retsenzii*, ed. N. A. Bogomolov and N. V. Kotrelev (Moscow: Sovetskii pisatel', 1990).

THE NORTHERN SYMPHONY (FIRST, HEROIC)

1. Norwegian composer (1843–1907) whose music Bely's mother (a pianist) frequently played in their apartment at the time Bely was writing the *Northern Symphony*. Bely ascribed the *Symphony's* musical influences and emotional tones to Grieg.
2. Valery Bryusov received visiting cards from Bely in the name of Vindalai Levulovich Belorog, a "edinorog" [unicorn]. In a diary entry from 1903, Bryusov reports conversations with Bely about the younger poet's sightings of unicorns and centaurs in Moscow. To the amazement of Bryusov's sister-in-law, these conversations were completely serious. Valerii Iakovlevich Briusov, *Dnevniki, avtobiograficheskaia proza, pis'ma* (Moscow: OLMA-Press, 2002), 153. Similar cards which Bely sent to Blok are reproduced in M. L. Spivak et al., eds., *Andrei Belyi. Aleksandr Blok. Moskva.* (Moscow: Moskovskie uchebniki i Kartolitografiia, 2005), 105.
3. Bely uses the word *korol* for king, a term applied to rulers in the west or in fairy tales and not the standard way of describing a Russian monarch (*tsar* or *imperator*), thus further defamiliarizing the *Northern Symphony's* characters and setting.
4. For Bely, one of the most mystically infused places in Moscow was the park and lake adjacent to the Novodevichy monastery. The swans there purportedly served as the inspiration for Tchaikovsky's ballet *Swan Lake* (1876).
5. August 9–10.
6. The Bear—a common figure in both Germanic and Russian fairy tales.
7. A term for a gangrenous illness that had spread in Russia in the mid-nineteenth century.
8. A star in the constellation Lyra.
9. A hybrid name derived from the word for "roar" (*rev*) and the pre-Christian Slavic god of thunder, Perun.
10. The Aramaic word for "Father."

DRAMATIC SYMPHONY (SECOND)

1. A nineteenth-century term for Russians who were neither of the aristocracy nor of the peasantry and typically formed the ranks of intellectuals and journalists.
2. Mikhail Nesterov (1863–1942), whose painting "The Miracle" (1897) was exhibited in Moscow in the late 1890s and in Paris in 1900.
3. Friedrich Nietzsche's concept of eternal return was immensely important to Russian modernists.
4. A major Moscow street in the Arbat neighborhood, close to Bely's apartment. Now Gogolevsky Boulevard.
5. An inexact quotation from Ruggero Leoncavallo's opera *Pagliacci* (1892).

6. Popular neo-realist writer whose revolutionary subject matter would win him prominence among Bolsheviks and make him one of the most influential figures in early Soviet literature.

7. Immanuel Kant's seminal 1781 work on metaphysics. The tragic hero of Bely's novel *Petersburg* (1916), Nikolai Ableukhov, would also have an unhealthy obsession with Kant.

8. Streets in central Moscow close the Polivanov Gymnasium where Bely studied from 1891 to 1899.

9. His name is, not coincidentally, related to *pop*, a colloquial Russian term for a priest.

10. An allusion to the Swiss Symbolist painter Arnold Böcklin (1827–1901).

11. A daily newspaper with notably conservative leanings.

12. Ryazan is a city two hundred kilometers southeast of Moscow. Cherkasy is a city now in central Ukraine.

13. The Russian psychiatrist Viktor Kandinsky published *On Pseudo-Hallucinations* in 1890.

14. Another Moscow street in the vicinity of the Polivanov Gymnasium.

15. Nickname of the Church of St. Nikolai the Miracle Worker near the Arbat.

16. A traditional dish for Orthodox Christmas.

17. An allusion to Lev Tolstoy (1828–1910) who famously retired to his estate, wore peasant dress, and at times worked in the fields.

18. Which occurred in 1861 (forty years before this scene takes place).

19. "Who is that odd one?" (French)

20. An allusion to the title of Nietzsche's 1885 book.

21. German journalist and doctor whose extremely influential 1892 study *Degeneration* was a detailed criticism of fin-de-siècle European culture that harshly attacked modernist art and literature.

22. The Wanderers (*Peredvizhniki*) were a group of painters from the second half of the nineteenth century whose works contained elements of both realism and impressionism while also often displaying and critiquing Russian social inequality.

23. An allusion to the Hungarian conductor Artúr Nikisch (1855–1922) with whom Bely became fascinated in 1901.

24. "Old Moscow!" (German)

25. A place charged with meaning for Bely and his relationship with Vladimir Solovyov and Margarita Morozova.

26. Prominent Symbolist poets and allies of Bely. See "Introduction."

27. Sirius, or the Dog Star, is among the brightest in the sky.

28. An allusion to the Russian philosopher and religious thinker Vasily Rozanov (1856–1919).

29. First ruler of medieval Rus. The dynasty he founded in the ninth century would last until the early seventeenth century.

30. Headline from the *Moscow News* on May 25, 1901.

31. One of the most influential Russian philosophers and poets for the Russian Symbolists, and Bely in particular. See "Introduction."

32. A regular topic of Nietzsche's, particularly in *Thus Spoke Zarathustra* (1885).

33. Allusion to the four horsemen of the Apocalypse from the biblical Book of Revelation (along with the one "destined to rule all the nations with an iron rod" and the "woman clothed in the sun").

34. Common character in Russian fairy tales.

35. A stanza from Solovyov's poem "Again the White Bells" (1900).

36. Title of Nietzsche's 1878 book.

37. Door on the iconostasis in an Orthodox church.

38. An allusion to the annual Symbolist almanac, *Northern Flowers*, issued by the publishing house Skorpion, which would publish the *Dramatic Symphony*. An article by Rozanov appeared in the inaugural issue in 1901.

39. Fashionable shopping area in Moscow.

40. An echo of the opening line of Solovyov's poem "The Sign" (1898).

41. The first lines of Solovyov's poem "The Nile Delta" (1898).

42. Aleksandr Lavrov cites Ivanov-Razumnik in deciphering the participants in this procession as follows: Norwegian lion—the playwright Henrik Ibsen (1828–1906); Emelian Singlethought—Lev Tolstoy; Zarathustra—Nietzsche; Belgian hermit—the poet and playwright Maurice Maeterlinck (1862–1949); French monk—the Decadent novelist J. K. Huysmans (1848–1907); singer of lies—Oscar Wilde (1854–1900); Parisian magus—the occult writer Joséphin Péladan (1858–1918); Milanese—the criminologist Cesare Lombroso (1835–1909); Max—Nordau. See Andrei Bely, *Simfonii*, ed. A. V. Lavrov (Leningrad: Khudozhestvennaia literatura, 1991), 511.

43. On the Solovetsky Islands in the White Sea (which would become a notorious prison in Soviet times).

44. Medieval Russian version of a knight.

45. An allusion to Dmitri Merezhkovsky's article "L. Tolstoy and Dostoevsky," published serially in *The World of Art* in 1900–1901. Bely's programmatic essay "The Forms of Art" would appear in *The World of Art* in late 1902.

46. An inexact quotation from Afanasii Fet's 1884 poem "I am a priest, with my beard of gray . . ."

47. Lida's surname is derived from the Russian word for "camel" (*verbliud*).

48. A traditional mildly alcoholic Russian drink made from fermented bread.

49. A Sanskrit phrase from the Vedas meaning "You are that."

50. In the summer of 1901, Tolstoy was seriously ill with malaria.

51. Rozanov's name is derived from the Russian word for "rose" (*roza*); a *shipovnik* is a wild rose.

52. An inexact quotation from Solovyov's poem "Waking Dream" (1895).

53. An allusion to Lev Ivanovich Polivanov (1839–1899), the director of the Polivanov Gymnasium, where Bely was a student from 1890 to 1899. Polivanov and Solovyov were buried at Novodevichy Monastery (where Bely himself

would be buried in 1934), and Bely would visit their graves with his friend and neighbor Sergei Solovyov (the philosopher's nephew and a fellow student of Polivanov's).

54. Theosophy was an occult religion founded by Helena Blavatsky in 1875 that became increasingly popular in the late nineteenth century.

55. A pre-Lenten holiday (akin to Mardi Gras) during which bliny (thin pancakes) are baked.

56. An allusion to Ibsen's play *When We the Dead Awaken*, which was performed at the Moscow Artistic Theater in 1900.

57. A very transparent allusion to Fedor Chaliapin (1873–1938), at the time the most famous opera singer in Russia and among the most famous in the world.

58. Aria from Tchaikovsky's opera *The Queen of Spades* (1890).

59. Herbert Spencer (1820–1903), the English philosopher.

THE RETURN (THIRD SYMPHONY)

1. His surname is derived from the word *khandra* meaning "melancholy" or "spleen" (in the poetic sense). His title in Russian is *magistrant*, which indicates that he has completed a master's degree but has not yet written a master's thesis.

2. Khandrikov's wife's patronymic means that her father's name is Chizhik— "little siskin." This is one of numerous names in the story that allude to birds and other animals.

3. Derived from *orel*, meaning "eagle."

4. Another bird allusion—*grach* is the Russian word for "rook."

5. This name, not uncommon, literally translates as "mushroom eater."

6. Minor realist writer Evgenii Chirikov (1864–1932) whose avian-derived surname could be translated as "Chirpov."

7. A work by the German psychologist Wilhelm Wundt (1832–1920) that Bely read in 1900.

8. Gustav Kirchhoff (1824–1887) was a German physicist.

9. Lines from an 1841 poem by Mikhail Lermontov (1814–1841) that were frequently set to music.

10. Lyrics from a popular song.

A GOBLET OF BLIZZARDS

1. A composer and pianist who was the brother of Bely's close friend Emilii Metner (who wrote on German philosophy and music for Symbolist venues).

2. Well-known Symbolist poet and ally of Bely's in the polemics around Symbolism that erupted in the mid-1900s. See "Introduction."

3. From "The windows are covered with curtains . . ." (1907) by the prominent Symbolist poet, novelist, and composer Mikhail Kuzmin (1872–1936).

4. An offshoot of Symbolism, the mystical anarchists sought to infuse the movement with elements of moral philosophy tinged with notions of spiritual unity. Georgy Chulkov (1879–1939) and Vyacheslav Ivanov (1866–1949) were the most prominent representatives of the group, which Bely opposed. Chulkov's 1906 essay *On Mystical Anarchism* (which included an important introduction by Ivanov) was the movement's manifesto. The golden-haired mystical anarchist is Ivanov.

5. The Italian Renaissance painter Antonio da Correggio (1489–1534).

6. The German composer Richard Wagner's (1813–1883) operas and theories of the unity of the arts (*Gesamtkunstwerk*) were extremely influential on the Symbolists.

7. Siegfried and Brunhilde are characters in Wagner's operatic cycle *The Ring of the Nibelung* (1876).

8. Bely's parodic name for Chulkov, derived from the Russian word *nul*, meaning "zero" or "nothing."

9. This stanza and the next contain a litany of references to contemporary Symbolist writers, all of whom were close to Bely but often involved in artistic and theoretical polemics: Fedor Sologub (1863–1927), Alexei Remizov (1877–1957), Alexander Blok (1880–1921), Maksimilian Voloshin (1877–1932), Sergei Gorodetsky (1884–1967), and Lev Shestov (1866–1938).

10. A line from Sologub's story "The One Who Summons the Beast" (1906).

11. An allusion to Blok's collection of poetry *The Snow Mask* (1907).

12. Nevsky Prospect is the main street of central St. Petersburg.

13. Her name is derived from the word *svet*, meaning "light."

14. This is possibly a representation of Vladimir Solovyov.

15. A line from Solovyov's 1898 poem "Signs" (which was also quoted in the *Dramatic Symphony*).

16. Vladimir Dal (1801–1872) first published the most widely used dictionary of the Russian language in 1863–1866. A famously unexpurgated edition was published between 1903 and 1909.

17. Serebriany Kolodez (literally "Silver Well") was an estate near Tula (320 kilometers south of Moscow) purchased in 1898 by Nikolai Bugaev, Bely's father.

18. His name translates as "bright dawn."

19. The word for sickle (*serp*) can also mean a crescent moon. Bely often uses it with both connotations in mind.

20. Bely left Russia for Munich in late September 1906 and would remain there until late November, when he traveled to Paris. This trip was prompted by his unsuccessful courtship of Lyubov Blok, the wife of Bely's close friend the poet Alexander Blok. Bely had challenged Blok to a duel (which did not take place) that summer.

21. The jester scene resonates with Blok's play *The Puppet Show* (1906), which was perceived as an attack on Symbolism's tendency to treat mystical themes seriously.

22. Bely lived in Paris from late November 1906 until he returned to Moscow in early March 1907. There he met frequently with Dmitri Merezhkovsky and Zinaida Gippius, one of the dedicatees of *The Goblet of Blizzards*.

23. Village outside of Moscow where Bely and Sergei Solovyov rented a house in the summer of 1907.

R

RUSSIAN LIBRARY